The Governor's Lady

Also by Robert Inman

Captain Saturday
Dairy Queen Days
Old Dogs and Children
Home Fires Burning
The Christmas Bus
Coming Home

THE GOVERNOR'S LADY

a novel

by

ROBERT INMAN

 JOHN F. BLAIR, PUBLISHER *Winston-Salem, North Carolina*

JOHN F. BLAIR,
PUBLISHER
1406 Plaza Drive
Winston-Salem, North Carolina 27103
www.blairpub.com

Library of Congress Cataloging-in-Publication Data

Inman, Robert, 1943-
  The Governor's lady / By Robert Inman.
      pages   cm
  ISBN 978-0-89587-608-9 (alk. paper) — ISBN 978-0-89587-609-6 (ebook) 1. Women governors—Fiction. 2. Women in politics—Fiction. I. Title.
  PS3559.N449G68 2013
  813'.54—dc23
                      2013009621

10 9 8 7 6 5 4 3 2 1

"There is in every true woman's heart a spark of heavenly fire, which lies dormant in the broad daylight of prosperity, but which kindles up, and beams and blazes in the dark hour of adversity."

Washington Irving

PART ONE

ONE

"For my funeral," Mickey said, "I want a good band and an open bar."

She was teetering on the edge of the hospital bed, feet dangling, struggling against a tangle of wires and tubes that tethered her to monitors and a rack of intravenous solutions.

"Mother, what in the hell are you doing?" Cooper threaded her way toward the bed through a forest of potted plants and cut-flower arrangements. She reached for Mickey, who jerked away.

"I gotta pee," she said.

"No, you don't gotta pee. You've got a catheter."

Mickey looked down at the tube running from underneath her hospital gown to a bag hooked to the side of the bed. "Oh."

Cooper took hold of her legs and lifted, swinging her back onto the bed, pulling sheet and blanket up to her chin. Mickey shivered and then collapsed against the pillow, eyes closed, mouth open, breath rattling.

"I'll get the nurse," Cooper said, reaching for the call button.

Mickey gripped her arm. "No. I'm all right." She motioned weakly toward a bedside chair. "Sit. Just let me . . ."

Cooper moved an arrangement of flowers from the chair, set it on the floor, and pulled the chair closer to the bed. "How did you sleep?"

"I didn't."

"You should ask for something to help. Do you want me to talk to the nurses?"

"No." She turned to Cooper, fixed her with a stare. "Well?"

"Well what?"

"The band and the bar."

"Will you stop it about funerals?"

"It's my funeral. I can have anything I want." Mickey turned away again and lay there for a moment. Pale, shrunken face, gray flesh not much darker than the sheets and pillow. Machines clicked and whirred and beeped. Green spikes paraded across the heart monitor—every so often, a blip, something not right.

"Aren't you going to thank me for coming all this way to see you?" Mickey asked. Her voice was a fraction of what it used to be, in the not-too-distant days when she could speak a word and all manner of folk would leap to do her bidding. Mickey had a big, horsey laugh and a way of saying things that defied contradiction. Cigarettes and scotch had turned the rowdy voice into a rasp. Little of the starch and gristle was left. Pickett had brought home the joke making the rounds in political circles: "Mickey Spainhour has a heart? For what?" As it turned out, she did. And it was failing.

"Big doings today," Mickey croaked. "My dear daughter about to become governor of the goddamn state. Pomp and circumstance, people jumping through their butts and kissing yours." Despite the much-diminished voice, the sarcasm remained. Mickey pursed her lips and scrunched her nose. "Why didn't you invite me, Cooper?"

"You came anyway."

"You didn't answer the question."

"Because I didn't want to."

Mickey had come by ambulance from the upstate the evening before—early enough to make sure the television and newspaper people would cover her arrival. Video on the local newscasts, photo on the front page of the *Capital Dispatch* this morning, Mickey on a stretcher being wheeled into the hospital, waving daintily at the press crowd.

"Damn right I came," Mickey said. "I'm dying, and I wasn't going to let the day pass without being close to the action. Now that I'm here, do you think you could make a place for me on the reviewing stand?"

Cooper shook her head and gave way for a moment to the old, wearying futility that was such a constant in her relationship with her mother. Mickey seemed to always know exactly what she wanted, and if she couldn't get it by simply demanding, she just wore you down. The best defense, Cooper had learned, was to stay off her radar, stay away. For a long time now, Cooper had done that. She had intended to have it that way today—*her* day, inauguration day.

"I wouldn't want you keeling over during my swearing-in," she said after a moment.

"Or grabbing the microphone and making a speech of my own."

"That especially. Tell me, Mother, how the hell did you manage it?"

"I called the Governor's Office. They handled everything. It was the least they could do. Now, since I can't go to your ceremony, let's talk about mine. The funeral arrangements."

"I am not going to talk about funerals."

"The band . . . Southern rock, maybe."

"What do you know about Southern rock?"

"I've got a Charlie Daniels CD. Pickett gave it to me for my birthday awhile ago."

"Did he, now?"

"Yes, a good while ago. He doesn't come to see me. Is that your doing?"

"Pickett's a big boy," Cooper said. "He does what he wants." She knew it was a sore spot with Mickey, who had launched Pickett into statewide politics years ago and helped him climb—legislator, treasurer, lieutenant governor. But then Pickett had become his own man—two terms as governor and now a run for the presidency. Pickett Lanier didn't need Mickey Spainhour anymore.

"He could have come to see the old lady in the hospital, instead of sending his wife."

"Pickett's not here," Cooper said. "He's flying in from somewhere. I've stopped trying to keep up. Iowa one minute, New Hampshire the next."

"They've screwed up everything with all these damn primaries," Mickey said. "The stupid things start in January and last eons. So here they are, a year until the first one, already out kissing ass. I liked it better when me and the boys got together in a hotel room and drank whiskey and smoked cigars and decided who to nominate."

"Did you smoke cigars with the boys? Really?"

"I hope I make it to March," Mickey said after a while. Cooper was staring at the window beyond the bed. The glass reflected the room's dim lights, white bedding, machines, plants, and flowers. "I would hate to die in February. It's a miserable goddamn month."

Cooper got up, went to the window, pulled the curtains back. It was still dark—just the orange glow of the lights in the doctors' parking lot below. And bitterly cold—the coldest day of the winter, the fellow on the radio had said while she was on the way to the hospital.

"Snow in the forecast," she said. "Maybe by the end of the day."

"If Pickett gets to be president, I want him to outlaw February."

"I doubt he'll waste a minute on February."

"Huh!" Mickey snorted.

What this particular snort meant, Cooper didn't know. Mickey used it often, and it generally suggested she was disgusted, frustrated, or just being plain mean. Cooper had heard many of Mickey's snorts in her lifetime.

"Have you seen the paper?"

"They won't bring me a newspaper or anything else to read. They won't let me have a telephone. They won't let me watch television. All they bring are these damn flowers. They keep toting 'em in by the truckload. The place smells like a goddamn funeral parlor—which I suppose makes sense."

The room held a riot of them, a cloying profusion, sickly sweet smell, explosion of color and greenery. Cooper plucked an envelope from the arrangement she had moved to the floor beside her chair. A typed greeting: "'Best wishes for a speedy recovery,'" she read aloud. "'Woodrow.'"

"Of course," Mickey said. "I get a card every few days from Woodrow."

Cooper remembered the first time Woodrow Bannister had come to the house, thirty years ago. She was home for spring break during her junior year in college. He was finishing a term as president of the student body. Someone had told Woodrow that if he wanted to get a start in state politics, he needed to be scrutinized and vetted by Mickey Spainhour. Cooper had answered the door and chatted with him in the front hall before Mickey came downstairs. She found Woodrow's earnestness both amusing and attractive. The attraction seemed to be mutual. He called later, and one thing led to another. In other circumstances, she might have been Woodrow's wife, following him up the political food chain.

"If you won't attend to the details of my funeral, Woodrow will," Mickey said. "He'll see to it that the legislature, a great number of whose sonsabitches owe their political careers to me, will meet in special session and pass a resolution authorizing my lying in state in the rotunda of the Capitol." She paused, laboring for breath. "Then a mile-long procession, lots of limos, a church ceremony, and a eulogy by the governor."

"Which one?"

"You."

"Then I don't think you want a eulogy by the governor."

"Because you might tell the truth?"

"All right, Mother, you win. We're talking about funerals."

"I'm not trying to win anything."

"It's one of your favorite things. Winning."

"I've done my share."

"Not lately."

Mickey pursed her lips. "I still matter, you know."

"Do you?"

"Damn right. I still get a constant parade of fawning assholes at the house, especially since word got out I'm about to kick the bucket. They hold my hand and kiss the hem of my garment and hang on every word of my political wisdom. And they hope that when I'm gone, I won't leave a black book lying around with their dirty little secrets in it."

Cooper doubted Mickey drew anything resembling a constant parade, assholes or otherwise. The word she got, mostly from Pickett, was that Mickey spent a good deal of time alone in her upstairs bedroom, the air thick with the smell of her cigarettes, listening to the ragged sound of her fading heart. She had once been powerfully influential, a woman who pulled strings and maneuvered and strategized, for which people who held public office in the state were quick to give her credit. But over the past several years, she had backed a string of candidates who crashed and burned, some spectacularly. Pickett was her last big success. She had lost the golden touch and was old news. This business now, this descending on the capital, crashing the party—well, Cooper imagined, there might be a good deal of desperation in it. *For God's sake, somebody take notice before it's too late.*

Mickey pushed back the covers. "I have damn well got to go to the bathroom."

"Catheter, remember?"

"Number two."

Cooper reached for the call button. "I'll get help."

"I don't need help."

"Yes, you do, and I'm not it."

"Afraid you'll dump me on my ass?"

The door swung open, and a nurse marched in, a young black woman: broad face, close-cropped hair peeking from under her cap, trim in a white uniform that drooped from the night shift. Nameplate: ESTELLE DUBOSE, R.N. Her quick eyes took in the room as she closed the door behind her. "Good morning."

"My mother seems determined to go to the bathroom."

"Number two," Mickey said. "Or maybe it's just a ruse to help me escape. Either way, my daughter the governor-to-be is just useless."

Nurse Dubose cut a quick glance at Cooper, looking for some sign of how things were in here. Cooper rolled her eyes. Dubose nodded.

"Honey," she said to Mickey, "let's get your rear end to the potty."

It took awhile, what with all the wires and tubes, but Dubose worked sure-handedly. She soon had Mickey slippered and headed toward the bathroom, an arm around her waist, the other guiding the IV rack.

"Take your time," she told Mickey. "Let me do the work. Don't get rowdy. You're not exactly jet-propelled this morning."

Mickey looked at Dubose. "Let me guess. You don't take crap off of anybody."

"Not here," Dubose said. "Here, I'm the boss." She kept Mickey moving, inches at a time, while Cooper stood back, seeing how small and frail her mother was, a shadow of the old Mickey, someone who might drift away if not held firmly.

"Do you take any crap at home?" Mickey asked.

"Not lately. Had a husband, but he was a silly man and not much for work. I ran him off."

"Good for you."

Dubose got Mickey settled in the bathroom and left her there, the door open a few inches.

"Is she okay?" Cooper asked.

"As long as she doesn't do anything but her business, she'll be fine."

"She said she didn't sleep last night," Cooper said.

"Every time I checked on her, she was fine. Must have slept more than she thought."

"Has she been giving you a hard time?" Cooper wondered how much she should tell Nurse Estelle Dubose: *My mother will charm your pants off one minute, take your head off the next. Give her a couple of days and she'll be running the place, making everybody jump. Just wait.*

"Nothing I can't handle," Dubose said, hands on hips. "How about you, Miz Lanier? You'll be governor in a few hours. How are you doing with that?"

Cooper smiled. "Nothing I can't handle."

⁓

"Do you need anything?" Cooper asked when Mickey was settled again in the bed, tubes and wires reconnected, Dubose off down the hallway with a cart full of flowers and plants Cooper had told her to share with other patients.

"Cigarettes," Mickey said.

"Don't start with the cigarettes."

"All right, if you're not going to humor a dying old lady, I'll bribe somebody to bring me some."

"No you won't. The hospital people wouldn't dare, and I'm going to make sure you don't have visitors sneaking in contraband. If I have to, I'll put a state trooper at the door."

Cooper gathered up coat and purse.

"When will you be back?" Mickey asked, sounding petulant.

"I don't know. I'm busy, you'll recall. This new job and all."

And then something changed in Mickey's face, just a hint of softness, lines and angles easing. It surprised Cooper, because she could not remember many times in her life when Mickey was in the least bit soft. She had been mostly hard as nails, the woman everyone called "the Dragon Lady." There was once—when Cleve, her father, died. Mickey had imploded then, had stunned Cooper with her sudden raw, helpless vulnerability. But that was with Cleve. With Cooper, it had been mostly hardness. In the last few years, as Mickey slowly declined, Cooper wondered at times if she ever regretted the way it had been between them—the lifetime of conflict, hurts, disappointments, estrangements. Did she ever feel a sense of loss the way Cooper did? Was she ever sorry it had been that way? Cooper saw no evidence of it. In the recent past, she had kept Mickey at arm's length, avoiding any chance of reconciling. But now, here, this strange glimmer of softness. Was she simply afraid of death? Or was there something else?

"Are you ready?" Mickey asked after a moment.

"For what, the job?"

"For all the shit that goes with it, Cooper. Are you ready for people lying to you, manipulating you, pushing you into corners? Because I'll guarantee they'll do it. When you least expect it."

Cooper took a deep breath. "I did this on my own, Mother. Pickett and his people made it possible, but *I* made it happen. And if I could do that, I can do the rest."

"Be careful who you trust." Then Mickey broke the gaze, looked down at her hands. "But you don't need my advice."

"No," Cooper said, but with no bitterness in it. She told herself she was beyond bitterness, had been for a good while.

"You froze me out."

"Mother," she said with a sigh, "I've spent a lifetime doing what other people wanted—you, then Pickett. But not this time." She turned to go. "I'll tell the hospital to turn on the TV."

She was almost at the door when Mickey said, "You're not ever going to forgive me, are you." It was a statement, not a question.

Cooper turned back and took a long look at Mickey—shrunken, frail, failing, swallowed by sheet and blanket, tethered to technology. For an instant, she wanted to go to her mother, touch her hand or cheek. But she hesitated just long enough to think, *Forgive? There is so much.*

So instead she said, "I wouldn't have any idea where to start."

⁓

The Executive Mansion was an aging beast of a place—two stories of white-painted brick, columns sheltering the front portico, sweeping curve of driveway passing under a porte-cochere on one side, all of it hunkered behind a tall wrought-iron fence, an imposing gate, and a guardhouse manned by at least two state troopers. Part public building, part home, part fortress, the house was more than a hundred years old, a victim of long neglect, presentable enough on the outside, sagging within. Over the years, it had received just enough maintenance to keep it from falling in on itself. A fair number of first ladies had argued with their husbands over the need for renovations, but no governor had shown enough backbone to spend a good chunk of the state's money on his own dwelling. The mansion had been Cooper's home for a good part of her life, beginning with the eight years of her youth when her father, Cleve Spainhour, was governor. Mickey had never bothered Cleve with anything as mundane as renovations. Mickey had her mind on other things. And then there had been the eight years of Pickett's two terms, during which he shrank from the notion of fixing more than was desperately needed. Now, four more years, and things might be different. The issue was hers to decide.

This morning brought barely controlled chaos outside the front fence. The street was clogged with TV satellite trucks, parked end to end out in the middle to keep their sky-probing metal dishes from tangling with the oaks on either side. Street and sidewalk were crowded with people—reporters, technicians, photographers—stumbling about among a sea of equipment and cables, hopping from foot to foot and flapping arms in an attempt to keep the cold at bay, dodging the army of local police and state troopers who wandered about, watching everything. Floodlights, harsh in the predawn, bathed the front of the mansion. Having nothing better to do at the moment, the encamped herd was repeating the story from the early television shows: the state's first woman governor was taking office; the outgoing governor, her husband, was making waves as a contender for his party's presidential nomination. Pickett Lanier had a long way to go, but today was a boost to his profile.

Say what you want about Pickett, Cooper thought with satisfaction, *this is my day.*

Somebody spotted them—Cooper's dark blue Ford, an identical car following with two men from the security detail inside—and started a stampede toward the gate as it swung open. The small army of state troopers there stepped aside to let the car through and then formed a barrier to keep the press people out. Cooper heard the shouted questions as the car moved through the frenzy of noise. A television cameraman, jostled from behind, went down hard on the pavement, twisting his body to protect the camera as the gate slid toward him. The troopers stopped it and helped him up. Cooper's driver pulled under the porte-cochere, jumped out, and opened the door for her. The crowd outside the gate started moving away. Then came more shouts and another rush as a white van with STATE DEPARTMENT OF CORRECTIONS on the side pulled up to the gate. The house staff peered horrified out the windows as the reporters flung questions at them.

Cooper wondered what on earth they thought the house staff could add to the story: *What are you fixing for breakfast? Are the sheets clean?*

She waited inside while the staff piled out of the van—the house manager, Mrs. Dinkins; two cooks; three maids; and two men whose duties seemed to be lifting and toting for the others. When the weather warmed, they would be joined by three groundskeepers. All were state prison inmates, most of them murderers serving life sentences. Many murderers, she had learned, having done their one foul deed and settled into incarceration, were a good deal safer to be around than thieves, who never got out of the habit and would steal you blind.

"Mrs. Dinkins, make coffee," Cooper said, "lots of it. And some food, whatever you can rustle up. That mob out there looks wretched. Maybe if we feed them, they'll calm down."

"Mrs. Dinkins believes they *are* wretched, ma'am." Mrs. Dinkins always spoke of herself in the third person. In her early sixties, she was orderly and organized, brisk and energetic and plain-spoken. She had years ago carved up an abusive husband and stored his body parts in Saran Wrap in her freezer until relatives, beginning to suspect he wasn't really on an extended fishing trip, called the sheriff. She had begun at the mansion the first day of Pickett's term eight years ago, and she and Cooper had straight off learned to accommodate each other. Each had her own turf and stuck to it.

"We'll probably have a houseful before long," Cooper said. "Governor Pickett and his people."

"Pastries, sandwiches, tea, and coffee." Mrs. Dinkins lingered a moment. "Mrs. Dinkins wants you to know," she said formally, "that we are pleased by your accomplishment and hope that we will be able to continue—"

"Mrs. Dinkins," Cooper interrupted with a smile, "this building is in mortal danger of falling in on itself. If you and your staff were not here, a vacuum would bring it crashing down around our heads. So yes, indeed, you shall continue. You are the one indispensable person here, and that includes my husband."

Mrs. Dinkins gave a quick nod and trotted off.

Cooper went to a front window and looked out. She saw a flurry of movement on the street—trucks firing up, antennas folding, crews dashing about. And then they pulled away in a rush of diesel, leaving the premises littered with Styrofoam cups and Krispy Kreme boxes.

Pickett was coming.

TWO

Cooper watched the airport news conference from the upstairs den. A mass of cameras and people were crammed into a terminal conference room because of the cold. It had the look of a spontaneous affair. But with Pickett, nothing was hastily arranged, including his person. He stood cool and elegant behind a podium—dark suit, light blue shirt, maroon tie—gazing over the mass of reporters and photographers elbowing each other for floor space. To one side of Pickett was Plato Underwood, a fussy little man, bald and bow-tied, pinch-faced and humorless—Pickett's political alter ego, chief of staff during his two terms as governor, now national campaign manager. She caught a glimpse of Carter, their son, squeezed between two newspaper photographers along a side wall, looking on raptly.

Pickett was jousting with Wheeler Kincaid, who covered state government for the capital newspaper, the *Dispatch.*

"When, Governor?" Kincaid asked. "You've had people in the Governor's Office working on your presidential campaign for months." Kincaid had a dog-gnawing-a-bone expression on his face. He was in his early seventies—tall, big-boned, intense, a great shock of unruly white hair matched by riotous eyebrows, a shower of dandruff on the shoulders of his sagging corduroy jacket. He had been covering the Capitol for decades. Politicians tried to curry favor with him, learned quickly they couldn't, and settled for being anything from wary to terrified.

"That's right, Wheeler," Pickett said, "and every time you've asked me about it, I've said the state is being reimbursed for their time."

"And every time I've asked you about it, you've promised to release the records. Are there any, Governor?"

"Of course. We keep meticulous records." He turned to Plato. "Don't we?"

Plato nodded.

Kincaid ignored him. "So here we are on the last half-day of your administration, and those records people have had a right to see for months are still nowhere in sight." His eyebrows shot up. "Isn't it time, Governor, to fish or cut bait?"

Pickett stared at Kincaid for just a moment. As the camera bore in close, Pickett was smiling, but Cooper saw the almost imperceptible twitch of his ear. He was annoyed, maybe worse, but he wasn't about to let anybody see it. He might blister the paint off the mansion walls, especially about Wheeler Kincaid, but in public he was the most obsessively self-controlled of men.

He turned again to Plato. "Plato, let's get those records in Mr. Kincaid's hands by noon today."

Plato nodded again. Plato was a man of few words.

The press contingent was by this time buzzing with impatience over what it no doubt saw as a pedestrian local matter. Kincaid, apparently satisfied, sat down.

A dozen reporters began shouting questions all at once.

A young woman Cooper recognized from the *Today* show broke

through the babble. "Governor Lanier, we're hearing that you're strapped for cash and having to cut back on staff."

Pickett turned his most radiant smile on her. "Sara, I can't imagine where you heard that, or from whom. Fundraising is always a challenge, especially this early, but we feel good about where we are. We're raising money, being careful how we spend it. We're solvent, and we're going to stay that way."

The woman tried to follow up, but this time the roar of the pack overwhelmed her. She gave up with a shrug and sat down.

Pickett, of course, had not answered the question. He was a master at that. The artful dodger, the alchemist turning obfuscation into the appearance of forthrightness. Carter, watching his father bob and weave, had not long ago said with a grin, "Dad can make cow shit smell like honeysuckle." Cooper understood he meant it as a compliment.

"When do we get to talk to your wife?" one of the reporters shouted.

"You're speaking of the governor-elect, Cooper Lanier," Pickett said with a touch of solemnity. "When she decides to meet the news media will be up to her."

"Have you been coaching her?"

"Look," Pickett said with a grin, "you know my wife better than that. I'll be lucky if she lets me wind the clock and put out the cat." It produced a round of laughter.

"When will she announce her cabinet?"

Pickett, serious now: "Most of the cabinet in place has agreed to stay on, at least temporarily, to make the transition as smooth as possible. Governor Lanier will make some appointments, I suspect, within the next little while. Whenever she's ready."

Wheeler Kincaid again: "What about Plato?"

Plato gave him a disdainful look.

"Will he stay with your campaign?"

"Absolutely," Pickett said. "Roger Tankersley has agreed to be my wife's chief of staff."

"What?" Cooper burst out. She grabbed the remote, punched its off button, and tossed it in the general direction of the TV, where it landed with a clatter.

For God's sake, Roger Tankersley. Well, we'll see about that.

She ate breakfast alone at one end of the mahogany dining-room table that seemed to stretch forever beneath a blazing chandelier. The table would seat twenty-six—and often did when she and Pickett entertained legislators, lobbyists, delegations of pleaders, staff, hangers-on, business people from corporations the state was trying to recruit. But a great many times, it had been just Cooper and the children. And lately, as they drifted away—Allison to art school in Atlanta, Carter to college and now to his semester off to help Pickett—only Cooper. She could have dined in the small breakfast room just off the back patio, but something about the big table held her—perhaps something that had begun during her childhood in this house. She had often eaten alone at this table back then, too, when her parents were busy and distracted— Cooper the child didn't know why and really didn't care. What she did care about was their absence, her aloneness, which became the most familiar part of her life. In the moments of aloneness at this table as a teenager, she had begun to reconcile herself to their absence, had begun to consider who *she* might be.

She ate in silence now, picking absent-mindedly at the omelet and fresh fruit, listening to the house, alive now with the discreet bustle of Mrs. Dinkins and the cooks in the kitchen, a vacuum cleaner going upstairs.

She thought about this day, and about who she had become in arriving at it. As a child, she had come to despise politics, the way it took people from her, the ones she cared about the most, the ones she should have been able to depend on. Plenty of people were around to take care of her daily needs, but she never felt she had Cleve and Mickey's undivided attention, especially during adolescence. Cleve had tried hard to protect her from the most harshly public aspects of politics, and had mostly succeeded. He never allowed her to be exploited. But still, the world outside owned much of him. And Mickey . . . well, Mickey just didn't seem to know what to do with her. They clashed, often and bitterly. At some point, they both stopped trying.

Along the way, Cooper had reconciled herself to things she couldn't change and had become fierce about being her own self, about having a life beyond the grasping, all-consuming world of politics. She had rejected Woodrow Bannister, who desperately wanted to marry her, simply because he was a politician to his core.

But then she had spent a lifetime at it after all. She had been Pickett Lanier's lady as he went from the easygoing professor she married to the man who now single-mindedly sought the presidency. And now here she was, the long-ago refugee from politics, a politician herself.

She gave a tiny, mirthless laugh and then pushed her plate aside and went upstairs to wait for the next round of chaos.

⁓

It wasn't long in coming. She heard them—Pickett and the bunch Cooper called "the Posse." A buzz of voices downstairs.

Carter reached her first. She heard him bounding up the stairs, taking them two and three at a time, the way he had since his first day in the house. He burst through the open doorway of her office, where she was going over her speech. "Hi, Mom!" As she turned to him, he pulled her out of the chair and enveloped her in a hug, then held her at arm's length, his face a huge, radiant smile. "What a day! Excited?"

She held him for a few moments, felt the familiar hum of energy that was so much his essence. "Yes, I am," she said. "I'm excited."

She released him, and he flopped into a chair next to the desk. "This is history, Mom. Awesome. How's the speech?"

She picked up the two handwritten pages.

"Can I see?"

"No," she said, smiling, keeping them beyond his reach. "It'll be a surprise."

His eyes widened. "Are you gonna drop a bombshell or something?"

"Would I do something like that?"

He grinned. "You have before."

"Well, not today. It's nothing special—pretty tame stuff, no flaming rhetoric. It's all just me."

"You wrote it?"

"Of course. I know how to write. Remember, I used to be a newswoman. You and the rest of the world can hear it when I say it."

"Cool," he said.

"So, how about you, out there on the campaign trail? You know, I hate that phrase, *campaign trail*. Makes it sound like a cowboy roundup."

"Well, it is. Rope 'em and haul 'em in. Get 'em to market. Get more of 'em than the other guys."

"Are you having fun?"

"I've got a real job now."

"What's that?"

"Dad put me in charge of organizing Young Voters for Lanier in New Hampshire. They gave me a car and expense money, and I've been all over the state—colleges, bars, shopping malls, church youth groups. They don't even have to be voting age, just kids who'll get out and work. We're gonna do a big door-to-door thing in Nashua, see how it goes, and then cover every town in the state. It's all up to me."

She touched his cheek. "You're one of the boys now."

"I guess," he laughed. "Yeah, I am."

"It sounds like hard work."

"Not so hard if you know what you're doing."

"And you do."

"Sure. Just about anybody my age does. You don't have to track down every single kid. You pick out a few, get 'em a couple of minutes with Dad, get 'em psyched, and then they start working cell phones and social media. It's crazy how fast it spreads. A friend tells a friend tells a friend, and all of a sudden you've got this mass of people."

"The Posse, they must be impressed."

"A lot of 'em don't get it, Mom. Plato and those guys, they're trying to run a campaign for president like they did the ones back home. A nineties thing. Rallies, civic clubs, handshaking at plant gates, TV and radio, media events, pre-Internet stuff. They think if you've got a website, you're rad. But it's nowhere near enough anymore, not if you want young people involved."

"Have you talked to Dad about it?"

"A couple of times, but he's so busy he hasn't been able to focus on it. He never even checks his Facebook page."

"Neither do I. So . . ."

"I'm doing my thing. When Dad wins New Hampshire, they'll think it was all their doing. I'll be a silent hero."

She smiled. "Maybe not so silent. Maybe you've got enough of me in you that you don't know how to keep your mouth shut."

He stood, went to the window, looked out at the front lawn, the scattered litter beyond the fence. "Must have been a big media crowd."

"They went a little crazy every time the gate opened. They even rushed the prison van. Mrs. Dinkins called them wretched."

He turned back, eyes dancing. "I'll bet. I wish I'd been here."

Carter had loved the Executive Mansion from the moment he first set foot in it, back when Pickett was lieutenant governor. He had dashed away, scouting the place, oblivious to the notion that other people, the then-governor's family, lived there. They had moved in when Carter was twelve. The next year, they had caught him selling autographed photos of Pickett to a busload of Baptists as they finished their tour. And now he was organizing Young Voters for Lanier.

"Guess I better get dressed," he said.

She looked him up and down—faded jeans, plaid flannel shirt, quilted vest, threadbare jogging shoes. "Yes, you'd better get dressed."

"It plays well in New Hampshire."

"It's a casual world these days."

He was almost out the door when he turned back to her. "When I'm governor, maybe you can write my inaugural speech. We'll let it be a surprise."

"I'll tell you a surprise you can start on when you get back to New Hampshire tomorrow."

"What's that?"

"Call me every once in a while."

He blanched. "I'm sorry, Mom. I get so busy."

She made a face.

"Okay, I'll do better." He smiled. "You'll have your own posse. Be sure you tell 'em to let me through." He started to go, hesitated. "I didn't see Allison's car out there."

"She's not here yet. Any minute now."

Carter's face clouded. "Did she give you a hard time about today?"

"I think there are a million places she'd rather be."

"I'll talk to her."

"It's okay. I know how she feels. I've been there. But she's coming, that's the thing. We'll work on the rest."

He shrugged. "Okay." Then he was gone.

Cooper heard his voice and Pickett's in the hallway, and then Pickett was in the doorway. When he was out wooing people in Iowa and New Hampshire and Texas these days, he usually appeared in jeans, open-collar shirt, sleeves rolled up when he was indoors, parka added for outdoors. But now he was all business. In Pickett's first run for office years ago, a seat on the county commission, he had powdered his temples, trying to pass himself off as more mature than his twenty-eight years. People nevertheless referred to him as "that nice young fellow." He won anyway. He still had a sizable capacity for artifice when he thought it might do him some good.

"Good morning, Governor," he said. "How are you?"

She rose from the desk, and he crossed the room and took her in his arms and kissed her. No artifice here.

"Good," she said. "If fact, I'm just damn fine."

He stood back and looked her over—maroon suit, navy scarf, cameo brooch that had come down from a great-grandmother.

"You could have changed the uniform," Pickett said. "It's your show."

"I could have."

"But I'm glad you didn't."

"It doesn't matter. When I change, it'll be something that matters."

He glanced at the desk. "Your speech?"

"Yes."

He reached for it, but she was quicker. "Uh-uh."

His eyebrows went up. "We need to get advance copies to the media people." He glanced at his watch. "We don't have much time."

She held the papers behind her back. "Uh-uh."

"Aren't you gonna let me read it?"

"Nope."

He shrugged, eyebrows knitted. He started to say something, but she cut him off.

"Pickett, I'm not going to make you squirm today."

"You have, often enough."

"Tomorrow, maybe, but not today." She picked up a manila folder from the desk and tucked the pages into it.

"Okay, just . . ." He hung fire for a moment, then turned on the smile. "Like I said, it's your show."

"So if it's my show, why did I have to learn from your news conference just now that Roger Tankersley is going to be my chief of staff?"

He sat beside the desk, wearing a look of surprise. "Didn't Plato call you?"

In fact, Plato had called a couple days ago, but she didn't take the call and didn't return it.

"Hearing it from Plato would have been a lot worse than hearing it from you at a news conference."

He rubbed his face with his hands, then peered at her through parted fingers. "I'm sorry. I thought he had run it by you. I should have made sure."

"Yes, you should have. There's a lot you should have done, like taking time to talk to me about this new job I've got."

He glanced at his watch. "Can we get into this later? I need to make some phone calls. Money stuff. I spend ninety percent of my time raising money."

"All right, but we're going to talk. I mean it."

"Of course." He rose and reached for her hand. "Now, come downstairs and take a minute to speak to the folks."

She held back. "Carter told me about the job you gave him. Is he all right? All that running around on his own?"

Pickett's face softened. "He's just fine. You should see him. And you should see the way the rest of the bunch looks at him. They're a pretty tough crew, but I've seen some genuine admiration there. He's made himself—"

"One of the guys. He's twenty years old, Pickett."

Pickett turned back to her with a smile. "Oh, he's much older than that. He'll go back to school, like he promised. Meantime, he's having the time of his life."

"The bonny prince."

"Yes," he said, "the bonny prince."

They were clustered around the dining-room table, the old gang, the core of the Posse going back so far with Pickett that it was hard to remember who had come on board when. Plato, the first, his college roommate, still the man who held the rest in harness and on task; Conner Wilkinson, the longtime press secretary; several others plucked from state government and set to work on Pickett's latest quest. They stopped whatever they were doing, put down their smartphones, and crowded around her, congratulating, encouraging.

She felt they really meant it, even Plato, who managed a rare smile. "It's a great day, Cooper," he said. "I'm pleased for you—pleased for all of us, but especially you."

Tension had always stood between them. Plato's agenda (which was Pickett's) and hers often clashed. When Cooper said or did something that got Pickett's bowels in an uproar, he often sent Plato to try to talk some sense into her. Plato had won his share, but the effort had made him impatient and frustrated. She tried to overlook most of it, understanding it was never easy walking a tightrope between your boss and his wife. And this morning, he sounded genuine. Whatever devices Plato used, artifice was rarely one of them. He would look you straight in the eye and say exactly what he thought. In that, he was head and shoulders above Pickett Lanier.

She cocked her head to one side and gave him a wry look. "Do you think I'm up to this, Plato?"

"Of course," he said. "Don't you?"

"You bet your ass," she said without smiling.

"Good for you."

She spotted Roger Tankersley hanging back at the edge of the crowd, brow furrowed. She went straight to him with her hand outstretched. "I hear we're going to be working together, Roger."

He blushed. "Well . . ."

She released his hand. "We'll see how it goes, okay? I'll be a work in progress for a while."

"Anything I can do . . ."

"There'll be plenty. Let me get my legs under me, and then everybody can run to keep up." She said it lightly, and Roger's face relaxed. She patted him on the shoulder and moved on.

Next was Rick Jankowski—intensely mid-twenties, deputy in the Press Office for the past couple of years, now her press secretary. She had been consulted on Jankowski, and approved of him. She liked his youth, his energy. In many ways, he reminded her of Carter.

"Busy man today," she said.

"Yes, ma'am."

"Can I ask you to do something for me?"

"Yes, ma'am."

"Don't call me ma'am. Call me Cooper, at least when we're not in public. You're my press secretary, Rick. I'm going to depend on you for advice as well as communication. Let's do it together."

"Yes, m—." He blushed. "I mean, Cooper. That'll take some getting used to. But thanks."

"I'm throwing you a curve ball right out of the gate. Don't release copies of my speech until after I've delivered it."

"The media people are on me about it. It's, ah, precedent."

"Then I'm breaking precedent. Tell 'em it's my decision. Don't take any guff off anybody. You're the man, and you work with me."

He smiled. "You bet."

Finally, Jake Harbin. He leaned nonchalantly in the broad doorway of the dining room, cool gaze sweeping the premises, watching her, watching the others. He straightened as she approached and gave her a hug. He was wearing a tweed jacket and casual slacks, no tie.

"I see you're not in the uniform of the day."

He laughed easily. Jake did everything with the appearance of ease. He was the wealthiest man in the state—real estate, manufacturing, investments, his fingers in a great number of pies. And now he was finance chairman for Pickett's campaign. Pickett flew about the country in Jake's plane, depended on Jake's contacts—and they were everywhere.

"I'll watch it on TV," Jake said, "while you and the rest of the suits freeze your buns off."

"Are you taking care of Pickett?"

"Aw, I'm not much use," he drawled. His hand swept the crowd. "These are the experts. I'm just hanging around, toting the suitcases, listening when the candidate needs to vent, trying not to get in the way." He paused. "We're all doing what we can to help Pickett." He crossed his arms and gave her an arch look.

He means me, she thought. *Everybody serving Pickett.*

"Well," she said, "you keep doing whatever you can to help Pickett, and I'll do what I can to help the state."

He tried a smile, but it didn't quite register. "Of course, Cooper. Have fun today."

"Believe me, Jake, I will."

THREE

Eleven o'clock. Pickett and his bunch were still at it downstairs, no doubt would be until late afternoon when they flew off on Jake's plane. Cooper glanced over her speech, put it away, got it out again, put it away. *It'll be all right,* she told herself. *Not brilliant, but all right. Just enough, not too much.*

She remembered her father's first swearing-in, all the men in swallow-tailed coats, women wearing hats. Nobody wore hats anymore, and Pickett had banished the swallow-tailed coats. Everybody in dark blue, just like ordinary folks, only cuter. Pickett Lanier, man of the people. He had asked her to wear dark blue today. They argued, compromised. The maroon suit, yes, but a dark blue topcoat.

She wondered what had been going through Cleve Spainhour's mind as he stood there years ago with one hand on the massive old state Bible and recited the oath. Triumph, satisfaction, sure. But was there, back where it didn't show, a hint of doubt, trepidation? Probably.

The state was in bad shape then—potholes in the roads, schools ranked near the bottom, money changing hands among politicians and people who needed something from them. Not that she had been aware of it at the time. She was thirteen, and she remembered her trepidation in moving from the familiar, the upstate, the only home she had known, a measure of anonymity, to this. Could she fit in, make new friends, protect herself? She had, but it wasn't easy. Not easy for Cleve either. She knew how he struggled to make things better, lost many fights, won a few. But what she remembered most about her father, all these years later, was his sense of himself. He liked being Cleve Spainhour, and the rest didn't much bother him. She had seen and felt that, and decided she would be as much like him as possible. He was a gentleman, but he didn't back down. She determined to be a lady cut from the same fabric, with the same backbone. Sure, she felt some trepidation of her own today, but she had sought this and won this, and whatever else happened, she liked being Cooper Lanier. All the rest, she would deal with. After all, she had the bloodline.

When she looked at her watch, it read eleven-fifteen. Where in the hell was . . . ?

Carter stuck his head in the door. "Allison's here." He made a face. "She's in her room. I told her I didn't think blue jeans would do. Just kidding, but she got pissed. She's changing."

Allison's door was closed. Cooper rapped, opened it, peered in.

Allison sat, shoulders slumped, on the side of the bed, looking at the unopened duffel bag at her feet. She turned to Cooper. "I hate this place."

Cooper sat beside her on the bed, gently tucked a strand of hair behind her ear, then reached for Allison's hand. She flinched but let Cooper take it.

"I know that, honey. It's okay. You don't ever have to live here again if you don't want to."

"I don't."

Allison was quiet, shy, inward, intensely private. From the time they moved in eight years ago, when Allison was fifteen, she had recoiled from the noise and bustle of living in the state's most public home. She was suspicious to the point of paranoia. Was the house staff poking in her closet? Why was the door of the medicine cabinet in her bathroom ajar? What were all the strange noises? Cooper did what she could to shield her but knew she often failed. Allison had a perpetually wounded look and hunkered inside it, trying to keep the world at bay, just as she hunkered over whatever sketch pad or easel she was working on, hunkered over her food at the table. "Sit up, Allison," Pickett would say at the rare meals when he was home. "I *am* sitting up," Allison would reply, and slump her shoulders even more.

"I'm glad you came," Cooper said after a moment. Pickett had wanted to send a state plane to pick her up in Atlanta, but Allison insisted on driving. Cooper glanced again at her watch. They would have to leave for the Capitol in fifteen minutes.

Allison looked up, saw the glance. "Don't worry, I won't make you late. And don't worry about me misbehaving and screwing things up."

Cooper stood, went to the closet, opened it. It was full—dresses, coats, shoes. Allison had left the nice stuff at home when she went off to Atlanta. "People at school who dress like freaks usually don't have much talent," she had said. "They think if you look like an artist, that'll get you by. People who have talent don't bother." And Allison had talent. She was stunningly good with a brush or pencil—quick, keenly observant, creative, eager to try anything. Honors in college. Now at one of the best art schools in the country.

"Do you want to get dressed now?"

"I'm not wearing a dress. I know Dad'll be pissed, but I'm wearing slacks." She had a shy inwardness but also a stiff backbone. She could be maddeningly stubborn.

"Slacks will be fine," Cooper said. "Don't worry about Dad. It's my day, not his."

Allison didn't move. There was something wistful in her face. "I'm sorry, Mom. I know it's your big day. But it's the same old thing all over again—being on display, people watching everything you do, pulling and tugging."

"That's hard on you."

"Yes, it is."

"And you thought it was behind us."

Allison rose finally, went to the closet, began rummaging. She pulled out a white blouse and a pair of gray slacks. She might be an artist, but she wasn't much for color in her clothes. *Maybe*, Cooper had often thought, *she's trying not to draw attention to herself.*

She held the two garments up. "Okay?"

"Sure."

Allison shucked off jeans and hoodie, tossed them on the bed. "Yeah, Mom, I thought it was behind us. You kept saying, 'When it's over, when Dad's term is up, we'll get out of this place. We'll do this, we'll do that, we'll be normal people. We'll have our own house, we'll be able to go to a movie without the security spooks following us.' I thought you really meant it."

Cooper felt a rush of despair. "You know, honey, it's a little late for that. Before I agreed to run, we talked, or at least I tried to. You just gave me this pained look and walked off."

"But what if I had said, 'No, Mom, you can't do it'? Would that have made a difference?"

"I don't know. I honestly don't. But you didn't say that. Why didn't you?"

"I never thought you had a chance. I thought you'd lose and maybe it would be a little humiliating, but that would be okay because finally it *would* be over. But it's not, and I'm beginning to think it never will be."

"So it didn't turn out the way you thought—or hoped. I understand you're hurt and disappointed, and I'm sorry. But Allison, today is today. Regardless of what accident or fate or black magic or whatever else got me here, I'm here."

Allison sighed. "Okay, Mom. Whatever. I won't embarrass you or Dad. I'll smile and wave, just like I've been taught. And then I'll get in my car and go back to Atlanta and try to be invisible."

"That's fine, honey. I'm just glad you came. Thank you."

"Carter said Grandmother's here. In the hospital."

"Yes."

"You didn't invite her, did you?"

"No."

"You know she loves that stuff."

Cooper made a wry face. "Maybe that's why I didn't invite her." She reached for the doorknob, then turned back. "Allison, I hope you can be invisible in Atlanta, and I'll do everything in my power to help keep it that way. But I'm going to be anything *but* invisible. And do you know the God's truth? I like it."

Pickett had wanted a convertible. "It looks better," he said. "It says you're open, accessible. It looks good for the cameras."

"No," she replied, "it makes you look like an idiot. People will see it and say, 'What are those idiots doing up there, going blue in the face and getting frostbite? Don't they have any sense?' No, Pickett, I'm not riding in a convertible. I'm not going to look like an idiot, and I'm not going to arrive at the Capitol with my mouth not working because it's frozen."

So here they were in a plain blue Ford, easing along the parade route behind a high-school band that did look close to frostbite. Plain blue Fords were all Pickett had allowed in the small fleet of automobiles that bore him and his entourage about. The two governors before him had used black Lincolns, big boats with darkly tinted windows, which Pickett banished along with the swallow-tailed coats. *Pickett Lanier, motorist of the common man,* Cooper thought.

"I may get me a limousine," she said. "Does Jaguar make one?"

Pickett glanced at her and rolled his eyes. He lowered his window and leaned out, beaming and waving. On her side of the backseat, Cooper waved from behind glass. Ahead and behind were National Guard units, Boy Scouts and Girl Scouts, a frenzied troupe of Shriners on tiny motorcycles, decorated flatbed trailers carrying everything from business and labor groups to a delegation from the Knights of Columbus—groups that had backed Pickett in years past and had, however reluctantly, let him convince them to work for Cooper.

She was surprised at the size of the crowd on the sidewalks as the parade inched along the wide avenue toward the Capitol at the far end. Young, old, parents holding children on their shoulders, everybody bundled like mummies. A steady barrage of flashes from cameras and cell phones. A sea of placards: COOPER FOR GOVERNOR. And a few touting a different goal: LANIER FOR PRESIDENT.

Cooper said, "I didn't expect so many people, not on a day like this."

"We bused 'em in from all over the state."

She understood again how much all of this was about Pickett, at least in his own mind. Over time, he had become the most self-obsessed person she had ever known, and that included Mickey. Maybe she had asked to run for governor, but Pickett had absolute veto power over the idea, had in fact vetoed it at first before he changed his mind. Pickett made things possible. As much as Cooper spoke her own mind, sometimes to the point of infuriating him, she never got over the feeling of being an appendage. *Well, maybe now . . .*

She glanced back at the other plain blue Ford following them. Carter had his window down, waving, a big grin on his face. Allison was barely visible beside him in the backseat, window up. They had been close as small children, Allison three years older, protective of her brother. But through the years, as Allison realized their great differences—Carter's enthusiasm for a public kind of life, her shrinking from it—she pulled back. He seemed to understand and accept it. It was what it was.

They were at the Capitol now, the dome glistening in the weak sun, the broad marble steps cascading in tiers from the portico to the street. The reviewing stand, set up at street level, was already packed with dignitaries. Security men descended on the car, indistinguishable from each other in their dark suits and sunglasses, cords from their radio earbuds disappearing behind their jacket collars. Carter and Allison's car pulled up behind. Carter bounded out, shaking hands. He knew all the security people. Cooper remembered his sheer delight, eight years ago during Pickett's first inauguration, at discovering that the trunk of the security detail's car contained automatic weapons. Carter talked incessantly about it, imagining battles with terrorists, until she made him shut up and told the security detail to keep their guns to themselves.

They were almost at the wooden steps at the side of the platform when Plato stopped them to whisper in Pickett's ear, glancing at her.

Pickett made a face, spoke quietly to Plato, and then turned to her. "Mickey's causing a ruckus at the hospital, trying to get 'em to bring her down here."

She had a brief flash—ambulance pulling up in front of the inaugural stand, Mickey being lifted out and brought on a stretcher up to the platform to recline regally beside her daughter, basking in a moment she had little to do with but was perfectly willing to take credit for.

"I took care of it," Pickett said. "Come on, we're backing up traffic."

The security detail crowded at their backs, moving them up the steps. On the platform, she and Pickett made quick work of shaking outstretched hands as they moved to the front of the four rows of chairs. Cooper paused for a moment with the ancient chief justice of the State

Supreme Court—defiantly clad in swallow-tailed coat, striped pants, and cravat, as he had always been for inaugurations. Old enough and ornery enough to stand dodderingly for tradition. She shook his hand, leaned close, and spoke into his good ear: "I like your suit." He pulled back slightly in surprise, and she winked at him and moved on.

And then came Woodrow. They regarded each other for a moment, and then he stuck out his hand and turned on a smile that seemed genuine enough. "Congratulations, Governor."

She held his hand for a moment, then released it. "And you, Lieutenant Governor. I look forward to working with you."

"We'll see what we can do," he said.

It sounded formal, as it should—not just because of who they were here today, but what they had been to each other eons ago, in those days when she might have been Woodrow Bannister's first lady. Woodrow was alone today. His wife hadn't been seen in public since back in February, when he announced he was backing out of the race for governor because of her unspecified illness, leaving the field open.

Cooper moved on, knowing Pickett and Woodrow would be exchanging polite banalities now. She didn't want to see or hear that.

They greeted the other elected officials and their families—the incoming attorney general, secretary of state, treasurer, auditor, secretaries of agriculture and education, all to be sworn in and given brief moments to speak. They all looked distressed—pinched cheeks, red noses, watery eyes. She hoped the cold would keep their speeches short. She had already warned Pickett when he asked if she minded his saying a few words: "All right, but if you try to make a campaign speech, I'll start groaning. Loudly. Mine is two pages. See if you can do half that."

And he did. When the other swearing-ins were over, he rose to the applause swelling from the crowd. They were packed together for warmth—people from the sidewalks, the band members, others from the parade. Cooper glanced at the television camera mounted on its own platform to the side, part of the live broadcast, saw that it was sweeping the crowd. It must look impressive, as Pickett wanted. Keeping his remarks short and familiar, he trod well-worn, comfortable territory. More than sixteen years ago, running for lieutenant governor, he had appeared in a TV ad, standing in front of the Capitol and wearing a look of righteous indignation: "This is *ours*, not *theirs!*" That had become his mantra, and still was. Pickett Lanier, champion of the little guy. She listened and in her mind silently spoke the words with him. Had he collapsed, she could have given the speech herself.

"You have given my wife the great honor of leading and serving." He was finishing up. "I am incredibly proud of her, and confident that she will lead and serve with grace, dignity, and commitment. She will do so with my love and support and gratitude."

He stepped back from the podium and motioned to her.

She reached first for her children, taking each one's hand, holding it tightly for a moment.

Carter's eyes glistened, his face wreathed in something far deeper than a smile. "Go get 'em, Mom," he whispered.

Allison took a deep breath. "It's okay," she said.

Cooper released their hands, and they stood together and started toward the podium.

The chief justice joined them. Pickett held the Bible that had been handed down from the first days of statehood. Her left hand rested on it while she raised her right and repeated the words, "I, Cooper Lanier, do solemnly swear . . ."

When it was finished, Pickett kissed her cheek and then leaned to the microphone: "Ladies and gentlemen, friends and citizens . . . Governor Cooper Lanier."

Warm applause swept over her, a mixture, she thought, of many things: a sense of the significance of this moment in the state's history, a bit of wonder and even puzzlement that it had come to pass, an expression of hopeful goodwill leavened with a healthy dose of skeptical expectation. She and Pickett and Carter and Allison stood together, arms linked, while the applause went on. Then she released them, they went back to their seats, and she took the pages of her speech from the folder and placed them in front of her, smoothing them at the edges where they had become wrinkled from much handling. She looked out across the throng and thought for a moment of the inaugurations she had witnessed from this platform. Always, she had felt a sense of being on the cusp of things possible.

"Now," she said, "we begin."

FOUR

Swallow-tailed coats and limousines weren't the only traditions Pickett
Lanier had turned on their ears when he took office as governor. There
had always been, and everyone assumed always would be, an Inaugural
Ball—a glitzy evening of sumptuous food, twenty-piece orchestra, and
the state's glitterati dressed to the nines—eagerly financed by lobbyists, who arm-wrestled to have their names in the largest type on the
engraved invitations. The crowds, the social dazzle, had grown over the
years to epic proportions.

Until Pickett.

Oh, a ball was still held. The glitterati and the lobbyists wouldn't
be denied that. But Pickett had shocked them by decreeing that the
evening's festivities would not be an official part of the inaugural activi-
ties. They argued. Cooper had been going to Inaugural Balls since she
was an adolescent; they were rare times when her father didn't shelter
her from public view. She was dazzled. Everybody was in high spirits. She still enjoyed them when Pickett was lieutenant governor. They

were good dancers. People put off pulling and tugging on her until the ball was over. But no, *Governor* Pickett and his lady would not appear. Pickett let it be understood he had nothing against it; he was just trying to make political hay with the masses.

Instead, Pickett's official celebrations served up tons of pork barbecue, baked beans, coleslaw, sweet tea, and bluegrass music. They were sprawling, rowdy affairs in the Agricultural Exhibit Hall at the State Fairgrounds, every living soul in the state invited. Many came, the mighty and the lowly and all between, to enjoy the food and music, to see and be seen, some simply out of curiosity. The lobbyists willingly financed it, too.

Cooper and Pickett headed for the fairgrounds after the Capitol ceremony and stood patiently for more than four hours, shaking every offered hand. Allison left early, before Cooper had a chance to talk to her, and was already on her way back to Atlanta. Carter stuck around for a while, then dashed away with friends before going by the mansion to cram fresh clothes into a bag for the trip back to New Hampshire.

It was nearly dark when the last of the mighty and lowly departed and they headed to the mansion.

"All right," she said before they had gone a block. "Talk." He cut a glance at the driver. She ignored it. "When Plato called about Roger, was he going to ask or tell?"

He took a moment. "Ask, of course."

"Well, on TV this morning, you told."

He kept his voice low. "What can I say? I messed up."

"So I'm stuck with Roger Tankersley. For now."

"Roger's okay, hon."

"Roger is a weasel. And I'll bet his butt is puckered shut at the thought of being left here to tend to me while the rest of you gallop around the country making merry."

"Roger knows the ropes." He paused, waiting for a reaction. She kept her silence. "Look, it's just for starters, okay? Give you time to set-tle in, get familiar with things, the day-to-day stuff. You tell Roger what you're comfortable with, what you aren't. Feel each other out, give it a chance to work."

She made no attempt to hide her irritation. "Pickett, there's a hellu-va lot we should have talked about. I kept asking, and you kept put-ting me off while you dashed away to far-flung places. Too busy to care about the inconsequential stuff back home. I've hardly seen you since November. And now I have the whole damn thing in my lap."

"We did the briefing book," he said, "Every cabinet department—"

"You can't govern from a briefing book." She gave a jerk of her head. "So now I've got Roger Tankersley to help me figure it out."

"Cooper," he said evenly, "you asked for this."

"Yes, I did."

"And you knew what the agenda was. We were clear on that."

"Keep hold of the home base while you try to save the world. But dammit, Pickett, things don't grind to a halt here."

He sat silent, studying his hands. Finally, he said, "All right, you're in an awkward spot. But that's why I'm giving you help. You'll have most of the cabinet in place. And Roger. Just let 'em do their jobs while you get your feet on the ground."

"I don't really have any choice, do I?"

Plato was waiting when they reached the mansion, and he and Pickett hustled off to the airport. She sat alone at the dining-room ta-ble, picking at a plate of food from Mrs. Dinkins, enjoying the silence, drained of energy but mind still humming. It had been a good day. She gave herself the luxury of a little trepidation; there was so much she didn't know. But then she shoved that aside. It was what it was, at least for now. People were ready to help. Roger Tankersley, for all his nerdy fussiness, knew the nuts and bolts, and that was a start. She knew she was a quick study, and she had good instincts. And then there was her political pedigree—Cleve, who had governed well, and Mickey, who despite the disappointments, hurts, and estrangement was the consummate political operative. She figured she had absorbed a great deal, even as she had tried for so long to keep politics at bay.

I will help Pickett where I can, because that's the deal, but I'm the one who has to govern, and by God, I will put body and soul into it.

⁓

The next morning was cold and overcast, the local TV news lively with the prediction of snow late in the day—just enough to enjoy, not enough to cause problems. It never snowed much, not since the blizzard years ago during Cleve Spainhour's governorship.

The blue Ford was idling at the portico, Ezra Barclay standing at the open rear door.

"Mr. Barclay," she said as she descended the steps, "I thought you were retiring."

"Not just yet," he said.

"Well, then, good morning."

"And to you, Governor."

Barclay was a state trooper lieutenant—close-cropped salt-and-pepper hair, gold-rimmed glasses, mid- to late fifties. He had been Pickett's driver since he took office as lieutenant governor sixteen years ago.

As the car turned out of the driveway onto the street, another plain blue Ford with two plain-clothes security officers leading the way, she leaned toward the front seat, watching Barclay's reflection in the rearview mirror. "So tell me about this."

"I got to thinking about it," he said, glancing at her in the mirror.

"I don't hunt, don't fish, don't golf, can't make things grow. Retirement sounded dull to me, and downright terrifying for Eileen. So I thought I'd put it off awhile longer. That is"—another glance—"if it's okay with you."

"Good Lord, yes. I bet you've never gotten lost in your life."

"Not since I was a teenager, courting Eileen. I could find my way to her house just fine, but at the end of the evening, I'd sometimes have a little difficulty finding home."

She laughed. "Ain't love wonderful."

"Yes, ma'am. Me and Eileen have always agreed on that." He shook his head. "Sorry, I do ramble on sometimes, Governor. Advancing age, I guess, though I've always been a little garrulous. I'll try to watch that."

"Mr. Barclay, I expect to have all sorts of people throwing facts and opinions at me, whether they know what they're talking about or not. So it will be a great comfort to be in the presence of someone who occasionally just rambles. So ramble."

"Thank you."

"So, you'll stick around to see the show?"

A nice, easy smile in the mirror now, and a wink, too. "I wouldn't miss it."

"Well, Mr. Barclay, we'll see what kind of mischief we can scare up."

Eight o'clock now, traffic heavy, cars with their lights on. Everything pale, washed out, under a thick, dull sky.

They stopped at a light. Barclay turned in his seat and thrust a card toward her. "Something you should have, just in case."

She took it: EZRA D. BARCLAY, LIEUTENANT, DEPARTMENT OF PUBLIC SAFETY.

"On the back," he said.

She turned it over. Two handwritten numbers.

"Home phone, cell phone. Anytime, night or day."

"Ezra, isn't this above the call of duty?"

"No, Governor, it's part of the call of duty."

She tucked the card in her purse, grateful for the gesture but determined not to use the numbers unless she faced a catastrophic emergency—terrorists firing bazookas at the Executive Mansion, something like that.

She asked Ezra to turn on the radio. A wisecracking boy-girl disc-jockey team was saying that what was coming might be ice, might be snow, but was looking now as if, whatever it was, it would arrive by late afternoon, sooner than expected. They made jokes about staging a figure-skating championship on the streets. Or bumper cars.

"Do you remember the blizzard?" Cooper asked.

"Seventy-three," Ezra said. "Nine or ten inches, as I recall."

"Where were you?"

"Just out of trooper school, working here in the capital."

"It was a mess."

"First day, it was. Then most folks who weren't already in a ditch figured out they weren't going anywhere and just sat it out."

"Troopers, too?"

"We put chains on our tires and kept going. Us and the National Guard. Picked up folks stranded on the roads, evacuated several nursing homes where the power was out. Went without sleep for a couple of days, but I'd lots rather help folks than arrest 'em."

After a moment, she said, "We built a snowman."

"I remember."

"You do?"

"I escorted the Guard truck that picked up your friends and brought 'em to the mansion. When we came back to take 'em home, y'all were out there on the lawn with that snowman, some camera people taking your picture. Your mama served us hot chocolate."

At the Capitol, a swarm of workmen were busy on the front steps dismantling the inaugural platform, loading scaffolding, plywood, and folding chairs onto a flatbed trailer. The car swung left and around the side of the building and stopped at the gated entrance to the underground garage, the security car behind now. Ezra tapped several numbers into a keypad on the dashboard. The gate opened, and the car eased down into the garage.

Her cell phone rang, and she fished in her purse for it. Pickett. But just as she was about to flip it open, Ezra said, "Uh-oh."

She stuck the phone back in the purse and leaned forward, peering through the windshield. Wheeler Kincaid and Roger Tankersley and three uniformed Capitol police officers were at the entrance to the private elevator that led to the Governor's Office two floors above. The cops had surrounded Kincaid, who was yelling and flapping his arms. Roger watched, arms crossed.

Ezra stopped the car and spoke into his jacket cuff: "Orange."

Noise from the car behind, doors opening and slamming, then two security men sprinting past.

"What's going on?" she demanded.

"Just sit tight, Governor." He shifted the car into reverse and kept his foot on the brake.

She tried the door. Locked, no inside release. "Open it," she said.

Barclay turned to her, frowning.

"Now!"

She heard the click, but before she could pull the handle he was out, dashing around the car, opening the door, keeping himself between her and whatever was going on at the elevator.

She peered over his shoulder. "What in the devil is happening, Ezra?"

He mumbled again into his cuff: "Situation?"

One of the security men gave Ezra a wave.

"Seems to be okay," Ezra said, keeping a step ahead as she strode across the garage, heels clicking sharply on the concrete.

"Good morning, gentlemen. Do we have a problem?"

Everybody looked at Roger.

"This area is off-limits to the press, Governor, except on special occasions," he said. "Mr. Kincaid knows that—"

Kincaid raised a hand. "Guilty."

"—but he insisted on violating the rule, and now we'll have to—"

She cut him off. "What, arrest him?"

"Well . . ."

"Let's all just straighten out our wedgies here," she said. "Mr. Kincaid, what's so important that you'd risk incarceration by breaking Mr. Tankersley's rule?"

"I need to talk to you," Kincaid said, straightening his jacket and shooting his cuffs. "Now."

"We have procedures," Roger said. "Written requests."

Pickett's doing, she knew. Pickett hated surprises, especially being ambushed by press people, most especially Wheeler Kincaid. She put a light hand on Roger's shoulder. "I'm sure you have rules, Roger, for good reason. And I depend on you to enforce the ones that are reasonable."

She looked around the circle. The security men had stepped back a pace, watching everything warily. *At least they didn't pull out their machine guns.*

"I thank you all for doing your jobs. I'm impressed by your professionalism. But I think I'll declare this a special occasion. My first day in office. A historic event. And in the future, I think we'll declare this area open to the press. With, of course"—a nod to the security men—"proper precautions. Mr. Kincaid, tell your fellow members of the press corps not to come armed with anything more dangerous than pads, pencils, and cameras." Her gaze swept the circle again, rested on Roger, whose neck was showing red splotches. "So let's get on with our day. Mr. Kincaid, allow me a few minutes to get settled, then join me in my office."

Coat off, gloves in pocket, coat and gloves in closet. What to do with her purse? She laughed. Roger looked puzzled.

"No governor in the state's history has had to deal with a purse, Roger. My first dilemma." She stowed the purse underneath the desk and sat in the enormous leather chair. "I think I'd like to have a somewhat smaller chair, Roger. This one just swallows me up. I can't have people coming in here thinking I'm not big enough to fit the chair."

"The chair goes with the desk," he said.

"Then maybe we'll rethink the desk, too. For now, we'll do the chair. See if you can rustle up something."

Roger stood his ground. "I really don't think this is a good idea."

"What, a reasonable chair?"

"Wheeler Kincaid."

She studied him for a moment. "Okay, here's how we'll work this out. You'll take care of the chair, and I'll take care of Mr. Kincaid. But don't take this as a put-down, Roger. Let's just say I'm feeling a bit feisty this morning, exercising a prerogative. I depend on you to advise me on the truly important things, and as we go along, feeling our way, we'll figure out what the truly important things are. Can we live with that?"

"I still think—"

"If nothing else, Roger, just humor me. Now, get me a chair I feel comfortable with, then send in Mr. Kincaid."

Once she was alone, she had a few minutes to wonder what had prompted her to talk to Wheeler Kincaid. By reputation, he was arrogant, heartless, fearless, dogged. Pickett had once said of him, "He knows where all the bodies are buried, and he digs 'em up when he needs 'em." People told things to Kincaid they didn't tell anybody else. He had been covering the Capitol for the *Dispatch* for as long as anyone could remember. Beyond that, nobody seemed to know much about his personal life. His wife, said to be a schizophrenic recluse, had died the year before. He had a great deal about him that was unfathomable. He kept his own secrets, and if you were a source for one of his stories, he kept yours.

But Cooper had glimpsed a different side, and it still baffled her. Early in Pickett's first term, Kincaid had stopped her in the lobby of a downtown hotel after her speech to a League of Women Voters luncheon.

"Could I have a minute?" he asked, and his brows shot up, making unruly arcs over intense brown eyes. The security officer who was with her moved to cut him off, but Kincaid said, "You really should."

Something in his voice made her say, "All right."

Just the two of them in the hotel manager's office.

"You've got a new personal secretary," he said.

A young woman, daughter of a wealthy supporter of Pickett's. She was not, Cooper had decided, either bright or interested in the job. She handled first-lady details from a small office on the ground floor of the Executive Mansion. She had wandered once into the kitchen and had beaten a hasty retreat when Mrs. Dinkins asked her icily if she was lost.

"Her family has a weekend place up on the lake," Kincaid said. "Parties, young people running around without any clothes on, a good deal of alcohol and drugs."

Cooper felt her throat constrict. "How do you know?"

"Got a tip, went to see for myself. Took some pictures."

"Why are you telling me this?"

"Because you might want to do something about it. Before—"

"I read about it in the paper," she finished for him. "But you're not—"

"What the girl does in her spare time isn't at the top of my list of crucial matters of state, not right now. But somebody else could get a tip, you know. It would embarrass you." He reached in a coat pocket, pulled out a spool of film, held it up, and put it back in his pocket. "I'll hold on to this for now."

She stood to go. "Thank you."

"By the way," Kincaid said, "that was a helluva speech you gave the ladies just now. It's not the kind of stuff I generally hear coming out of your husband's office. Did he clear it?"

"No," she said. "Why should he?"

Kincaid smiled. "Just asking."

Cooper went straight to the Capitol and pulled Pickett out of a meeting of the Oil and Gas Board.

"My God," Pickett said, ashen-faced. "How do you know?"

"I just know."

"*How* do you know?"

"I know."

Within twenty-four hours, the young woman was gone, dispatched to an obscure job in the Commerce Department. Two days later, a small padded envelope addressed to Cooper arrived at the Executive Mansion. She opened it, pulled the long roll of film from its spool, and dropped it in the trash.

Why had he warned her? To curry favor with Pickett? If so, why not just tell Pickett? If not, then what? Then she had thought, *He said it would embarrass* me, *not Pickett.* And why hadn't she told Pickett where the information came from? Some instinct—she puzzled over it—had led her to keep that part to herself. Afterward, when she was around Kincaid at public functions, neither had spoken of it again.

Roger brought her a chair and then reluctantly ushered Kincaid in.

He asked about Mickey. They went way back, he said, to when he was a young reporter on his first job covering the Capitol and Mickey was a minor clerk for the speaker of the House, just in from the country and secretarial school.

"She's holding her own," Cooper said noncommittally.

"She's one of a kind, was from the beginning."

The door opened, and Roger poked his head in, glancing at his watch. "Meeting of the Arts Commission in fifteen minutes." He held out a manila folder. "I've got your briefing paper."

Cooper ignored the folder. "Thank you, Roger. Check on me in fifteen minutes."

Roger didn't budge. "Did I show you . . . ? A buzzer is right there beside the middle drawer. If you need anything."

"Thank you, Roger. I feel well equipped. I'll let you know if I need you."

She saw the flush starting again around his neckline and spreading up his cheeks, his hand tightening on the folder, wrinkling it. He gave a curt nod and closed the door.

"The eyes follow you," Kincaid said. He was looking at the wall behind the desk.

She swiveled in her chair to the huge oil portrait of Pickett hanging there. Pickett in dark suit and power tie, that incredibly appealing half-smile that made people want to know him, trust him.

"No matter where you move in the room, he seems to be looking at you," Kincaid said. "And now he's looking over your shoulder."

"I suppose I should get my own portrait."

"Or maybe a picture of Roger." He nodded toward the door. "He seems fixated on looking over your shoulder, too."

She hesitated, choosing her words carefully. "It might seem that way, I suppose. Roger and I haven't had a chance to talk about ground rules."

"Who sets those rules?" Kincaid asked with a trace of a smile. And then when she frowned, he added, "This is all off the record."

She hesitated. Off the record or not, this was Wheeler Kincaid. "The person who sits in this chair sets the rules," she said.

"You seem pretty sure about that. Good for you. But don't be surprised if you need to have a come-to-Jesus meeting with Roger."

"I can do that."

"Again, good for you."

"Roger might be a bit upset that he's not out campaigning with Pickett," she said.

"Roger is highly pissed. He's been around a long time, thinks he's earned a shot at the big dance."

"Instead . . ."

"He's here because he's third-rate, and Pickett can't afford to have third-raters on his campaign payroll. Roger's like a well-trained dog—obeys commands to the letter but doesn't have a lick of imagination."

"I don't know that the rest of them do either. Carter told me . . ."

"Off the record."

"Carter says they don't get it—social networking, all of that." She stopped again. "Why am I telling you this? They all think you're toxic."

He smiled. "Only at times and in places where it's warranted."

"And it's not warranted here?"

"I wouldn't be off the record if it were."

"Back to Roger."

"Yes," he said. "He's been vocal about his assignment, vocal around people he shouldn't be vocal around."

"And what is he saying?"

"That he's babysitting."

Cooper held herself, took a moment and a deep breath. "He has nothing to babysit. I'm the governor."

Kincaid glanced up again at Pickett's portrait, then gave Cooper a long look. "Are you?"

"Damn right."

"I really, truly hope so. When somebody tries to rope you and haul you in, I hope you can say exactly that: 'Damn right.' Because there are people who don't think you are." He held out his hand. "Could I take a look at your schedule?"

He scanned the paper Cooper handed him. "Full day. Arts Commission, photo-op with some Girl Scouts, two hours for lunch. Afternoon meeting with a delegation from Banks County." A glance up. "Do you know what that's about?"

She sat stone-faced.

"They want some money for levee work. Lots of flooding in Banks County during the fall. Cows floating downriver, all kinds of misery." Back to the paper. "Then home to the cozy warmth of the Executive Mansion." He shoved the schedule back onto her desk and pulled a sheaf of folded papers from the inner pocket of his jacket. "And then there's all this."

"What?"

"The morning's output from your Press Office." He read, "'Governor Cooper Lanier Approves Funds for Coffee County Road Construction Project. Governor Signs Proclamation Designating Multiple Sclerosis Week. Governor Pledges Support to Congressional Delegation on Waterway Bill.'" He tossed the press releases alongside the schedule. "You've been busy already with the state's business."

She half-rose from her chair. "Mr. Kincaid, you're way out of line."

Kincaid stayed put. "First day of a new administration. No cabinet meeting? And what about a press conference? A restless mob is in the Capitol pressroom, just itching to ask what you're going to make of being the state's chief executive, other than just minding the store." He ticked off items on his fingers. "The legislature convenes in three weeks. Are you working on your State of the State address? The budget?"

She was taken aback. *No, I'm not. Damn Pickett for brushing me off. Damn me for letting him.*

She stood. "I think we can end this." She reached for the buzzer.

His voice stopped her. "Felicia Withers is going after you."

Her hand froze. She sat back down.

Felicia was owner and publisher of the *Dispatch*. Her family had started the paper during the Civil War and held on to it over the years, making it one of the few dailies left in the country that wasn't owned by a chain. It boasted a long line of fierce publishers, one generation after another. And now Felicia, who was the fiercest, acid-tongued in person and in print, arbitrary and ruthless, profoundly independent. Popular wisdom said it was far better to be Felicia's enemy than her friend, because if you were her enemy, you at least *knew* she was out to get you. Felicia had few friends, but she cultivated legions of enemies, and somewhere near the top of her list was Pickett Lanier. She had taken an acute dislike to him when he was lieutenant governor. Maybe he was too smooth, too successful, too seemingly immune to Felicia.

"Felicia called a staff meeting last evening. Everybody on the payroll, down to the kid who sweeps the floor. I've never seen her so worked up. Thought she was going to blow a gasket. She ranted for a half-hour, but the sum of it was, the paper's mission is to expose this"—his hand swept the room, including Cooper and Pickett's portrait—"for what it is."

"And what does Felicia think it is?"

"A farce."

"And what does she think I am?"

"A phony."

"Good God," Cooper said softly.

"You know how she feels about Pickett. Well, she's in a fine rage over what he's pulled off here."

"Mr. Kincaid, Pickett didn't 'pull off' anything, as you put it. I was elected governor of the state, with Pickett's help, of course. But people voted, and they voted for me. Does Felicia Withers have some problem with people voting?"

"It's not just that. It's personal. Felicia can't stand powerful women. She thinks this town doesn't have room for both of you. You're right, you got elected, and she can't get rid of you, but she'll do her best to make you look—"

"Like a phony running a farce."

"Inconsequential. Irrelevant. Powerless."

Cooper stared out the window, feeling Kincaid's eyes on her, feeling the cold, suffocating grayness outside. She turned back. "I intend to *be* the governor. I wouldn't have run otherwise."

"Well, Felicia doesn't believe that. She thinks you'll dance at the end of Pickett's strings, and she thinks having good old Roger here to babysit is proof."

"What's your role in all this, Mr. Kincaid? This campaign of Felicia's."

"I'm a reporter. I'll do my job," he said flatly. "Felicia Withers doesn't tell me what to do or how to do it because I don't let her."

"Do *you* think I'm Pickett's puppet?"

"I'm waiting to see." He stood. "But let's leave it at that. Thanks for your time."

"Why are you telling me this?"

It took him a moment. "I've been hanging around this place for forty-five years, and I've seen every sorry-ass excuse for so-called public servants you can imagine. I'm hoping you'll be different. You have a chance to be. And God knows, this place needs it."

She took a deep breath. "Okay." He turned to go, but she stopped him. "Any advice?"

He gave her a piercing look. "First of all, don't for a moment entertain the idea you're bulletproof. That happens to people who run for office. It's an ego thing. Issues, ideas, all that is secondary. You're saying to voters, 'Choose *me*.' If they don't, it's rejection on the most personal level. If they do, the tendency is to think you're more wonderful than you are, maybe even that you're bulletproof."

"I don't think that, I can assure you."

"And then, for all your plans of being your own boss, there's Pickett. His campaign is getting attention, and that makes the big boys, the national press, start digging. And from there, it's a straight line to here. If you're a phony running a farce, they'll have you for lunch."

"And Pickett, too," she added.

"If he really means for you to *be* the governor, he's taking the risk you'll do something that embarrasses him. If he tries to be a puppet master, that proves you're a phony and he's pulled a fast one." He cocked his head, waiting.

"I'm not a phony, Mr. Kincaid," she said quietly. "And I'll prove it."

He shrugged. And then he was gone.

Roger bustled in, all atwitter. "What did he want?"

Cooper sat lost in thought, ignoring him.

"Kincaid. What—"

"It was an off-the-record conversation. On both sides."

"And . . ."

"Off the record means it's not to be repeated."

"But . . ."

"To anybody."

He came into the room and stood behind a chair, gripping the leather back so tightly his knuckles turned white.

"You don't want to be here, do you, Roger?"

"That's beside the point."

"You'd rather be with Pickett."

He started to say something, stopped himself. "We're all working for the same goal, Cooper. We're all working for Pickett."

"We are?"

"Sure. It does Pickett no good if we get blindsided by something Kincaid's got up his sleeve."

She rose, smoothing her skirt. "Mr. Kincaid doesn't have anything up his sleeve, Roger. We had a private, personal conversation."

She watched Roger make the great effort to gather himself, to swallow for a moment all that made him frustrated and pissed off—the years of accumulated slights and menial jobs and ignominy. That had been his reward for absolute loyalty to Pickett Lanier. And now this. Babysitting. She felt sorry for him.

"It's okay, Roger, believe me," she said, summoning patience, keeping her voice gentle. "I appreciate your concern. You're doing your job. But here's this: I am not working for Pickett, and you are working for me. Now, send Rick in here."

～

She held up the sheaf of press releases. "Rick, where did this stuff come from?"

"Left over from the last crowd."

"Have a seat."

Rick sat at the conference table in front of her desk.

"Look," she said. "From now on, whatever goes out of here to the media, I want to know about it. This is *our* press office, yours and mine."

"I'm sorry."

"Let's not let it happen again."

He hesitated. "There's one other thing. Your mother."

"What about her?"

"I'm getting a lot of questions—her condition—and the hospital isn't authorized to release anything."

"Okay, what do we do?"

"Well," he stammered, "what do you . . . ?"

She leaned toward him and gave him a smile. "Rick, we're both new at this, but you know more about it than I do. So I depend on you to give me your best advice. I may not always follow it, but I damn sure need it. So?"

"Well, Roger said—"

"Roger is my chief of staff, not my press secretary. I want to know what *you* think."

Rick sat up straighter. "It's been almost twenty-four hours, and the press people have had nothing but the barest facts. One reporter tried to sneak in, but the hospital has things buttoned up tight."

"So?"

"We need to give 'em something solid."

"What are the options?"

"We could let the hospital take care of it, put out a release, maybe even send an administrator and your mother's doctor out to answer questions. Or we could put out a statement from our office. Or you could talk to 'em yourself."

"Who *is* her doctor?"

"A cardiologist named Cutter."

"Nolan Cutter?"

"Yes."

"An old friend."

"He'll be helpful?"

"I'm sure of it." She sat back in her chair. "So what's your advice?"

He hunched over the table, fingers drumming on the wood, then looked up. "A statement from us, just some basics—her present condition, resting comfortably, hospital doing a great job, yada, yada. Then later today, the administrator and the doc talk to the press folks, keep it to your mother's medical condition, nothing personal."

"Personal?"

"I've had some questions about why Mickey wasn't at the inauguration. Asking if you and she are . . . estranged."

"I see. Well, I could say that's none of their damn business, but I guess in my present state of affairs, just about everything is their damn business. Or at least they think it is." She rose and reached for her coat. "My mother didn't attend the inauguration because she's sick. But just stick to the statement."

"You want to see a draft?"

"You know what to say. Line up the hospital people. Sooner or later, probably sooner, I'll need to have a press conference myself. This, things in general. But not just yet. Let's see how things shape up."

"Gotcha."

She picked up the sheaf of press releases and gave him a smile. "And no more of these."

When he was gone, she stood at the window, looking out at the Capitol grounds, the sky even darker now, a somber, lowering gray, the crew at the bottom of the marble steps finishing their dismantling of the inaugural stand, traffic moving up and down the boulevard. Everything ordinary now, things moving on, business as usual. The vast machinery of state government grinding along as if nothing unusual had happened yesterday, and wouldn't today or tomorrow. And here she was, in this cavernous room with its massive desk and its flags and portraits. *This must be*, she thought, *the way it was for every person who won this office, no matter how massive of ego, no matter how brimming with confidence. After all the hoopla, sobering reality.*

She felt the aloneness in spades. But something else, too. Unlike the others, she hadn't spent a lifetime clawing her way up the ladder, piling up political debts, dragging baggage that included worn-out ideas and ways of looking at things. All right, she had an understanding with Pickett, but that damn sure didn't mean she was a puppet. And it damn sure didn't leave room for being babysat.

FIVE

She was finishing lunch when the call came from the hospital: Mickey had taken a turn for the worse. She said she was dying.

Cooper was halfway there when Pickett called. "I hear you had a visitor."

"Word travels fast," she said. "Where are you?"

"Keene. Cooper—"

"What's in Keene?"

"A college."

"Is Carter with you?"

"Yes. No, he's here, but not with me at the moment."

"Tell him to call me."

"All right, all right," he said, exasperated. "Why in the hell were you talking to Wheeler Kincaid? Roger said you wouldn't let him sit in, wouldn't tell him what it was about." He rattled off the words, bit off the ends of his sentences—all business, all Pickett with his butt puckered at the prospect of a nasty surprise.

"It was an off-the-record conversation," she said.

"Cooper, for God's sake!"

She laid the cell phone on the car seat and gave him a good thirty seconds of silence.

"Cooper, are you there?" his voice came tinnily.

She picked up the phone. "Is Roger checking in with you by the hour? Is it part of his babysitting duties?"

"Nobody's babysitting," Pickett snapped.

"Well, Pickett, my sources tell me Roger describes it as babysitting."

"I'll speak to Roger about that."

"No, you won't," she said. "I'll handle Roger. You spend your time winning Keene."

"Cooper . . ." He was almost pleading now.

"All right, Pickett, here's what happened. Wheeler Kincaid asked to speak to me alone. I said okay."

"The man's dangerous. If he's up to something—"

"Hush and let me finish. What he came to tell me was that Felicia Withers is on the warpath, and I'm the wagon train."

"Shit!"

"She told the people at the *Dispatch* she intends to expose me as a farce, and you as a snake-oil salesman."

"Shit, shit, *shit!*"

"Come on, Pickett, you aren't surprised, are you? It's Felicia."

"I just thought she might give us a little time."

"Felicia doesn't think there's room in town for both of us."

"I've got to go," he said. "I'll call you later." He rang off abruptly.

She tried to imagine him climbing out of his car, forcing that great smile, thrusting out his hand. *Hi, I'm Pickett Lanier. Running for president.* Was it snowing in Keene or just a miserable, bone-jarring January cold? She wished for a brief moment she could be there with him, tell him, *Hey, it's okay, Pickett. Go win New Hampshire. I can handle this back here, me and Roger. You do that, I do this.*

But she wasn't there with him. Pickett would have to fend for himself.

⌒

When Cooper got to the hospital, Mickey was sitting up in bed, bright-eyed, color good, a bit cocksure. Cooper stared, taken aback.

Before she could speak, Nolan Cutter was there, tousled and white-jacketed, stethoscope dangling, flipping intently through pages on a clipboard. "Hi," he said with a smile.

"Hi yourself."

Mickey glared at Cutter, eyes narrowing. "Who the hell are you?"

"Nolan Cutter, Miz Spainhour. Old friend of the family."

"Where'd you come from?"

"Down the hall."

"Are you a doctor?"

"Last time I checked."

"Are you *my* doctor?"

"Yes. I was here yesterday when they brought you in. I checked you over and got you settled. Been back a couple of times since. Remember?"

"Maybe."

"Well, think about it. Later, I'll give you a pop quiz." Then to Cooper: "Give us a few minutes. A consultation room is down the hall on the right, sign on the door."

Fifteen minutes, and Cutter was there with two Styrofoam cups of coffee. He handed Cooper one, gave her a hug, and plopped into a chair. He looked weary—deep lines around his eyes, stubble of whiskers on pallid skin. He sipped his coffee while she waited.

"False alarm," he said.

"The hospital called and said she was dying."

"Well, she is, but not just yet. Being who she is, the hospital . . ." He shrugged. "When I got here, she seemed okay. She might have had a panic attack."

"Knowing my mother, probably not."

Nolan Cutter had been her first boyfriend, after a fashion, beginning that February day when she was thirteen, the blizzard. Nothing much was moving except the National Guard. Cleve had dispatched one of the Guard's big trucks to the homes of a dozen of her classmates, boys and girls, and brought them to the Executive Mansion, where they built a snowman in the front yard. Nolan was one of the kids—easy grin, nice, open face, shock of blond hair that poked out from under his toboggan. Cleve watched from the window of the upstairs bedroom where he had set up a temporary command post. Later, he came down and put a hat on the snowman's head while a TV cameraman and a photographer from the *Dispatch* took pictures.

When they finished the snowman, they trooped around to the back door for hot chocolate and brownies in the kitchen. The National Guard truck returned to load them up for the trip home, and Nolan was the last to leave. She lingered to tell him goodbye, just the two of them, and when he opened the door to go, he turned suddenly and kissed her. It wasn't just a peck on the cheek either. His lips lingered on hers for a moment, and her hand went on its own accord to his cheek, and she tasted warmth and chocolate and something else indescribable. Then he pulled away, eyes dancing. "I had a really super time," he said, and bounded out the door, leaving her open-mouthed with astonishment, her hand lingering in the air where his cheek had been.

She told no one. This was just hers, something to hold close and savor. For a few weeks after, they held hands shyly at school and talked on the phone at night. And then the whole thing passed in the way of junior-high romances, and they found themselves just friends, which they had now been for years, seeing each other occasionally, mostly at social functions. Every time, Cooper felt the faint taste of chocolate drifting up from some well-protected place.

"You look like you've been up all night," she said.

"Emergency surgery about three this morning. Seventeen-year-old kid on a motorcycle tangled with a stop sign. Ripped his chest open. Tried to patch things back together."

She waited a moment. "Did you?"

He shook his head.

"I'm sorry. Go home and get some sleep."

He smiled through the weariness. "Yes, Mom."

"You know, Nolan, you should have stuck with me."

"I should have stuck with somebody, that's for sure." Nolan had been through two wives and was now enmeshed with a rather infamous local attorney who had been through two husbands. "We could run away, I guess."

"To where?"

"I was in Zambia last year. Medical mission, small villages out in the bush. Sleeping in thatched huts, lions wandering through and roaring in the middle of the night. After a while, I got used to the lions and just slept through the parade. Forgot about the rest of the world. Are you game?"

"Ask me again in a couple of months."

They sipped their coffee.

"Do you remember the big snow, the snowman?" she asked.

It brought a twinkle to his eyes. "Of course. I've still got the clipping from the paper. All of us, and your dad and Mickey, with the snowman."

"Mickey was there? I don't remember that. I don't remember her being there at all."

"Check the clipping."

"So what's her situation now?"

Nolan finished his coffee and tossed the cup into a trash can. "Congestive heart failure isn't something to recover from, but we have ways to keep it at bay. Medicine can help, but there are also things that have absolutely nothing to do with medicine."

"Such as?"

Nolan spread his hands. "Maybe something like force of will. People go on long after you think there's nothing keeping them here."

"How long can she keep it at bay?"

"Anywhere from now to next year. I learned a long time ago to stop guessing. She's a good bit better than yesterday. Things are stable. Her heart is precarious, but it's still ticking."

"Maybe her orneriness is keeping her alive."

Nolan studied her for a moment, then: "Whatever works."

⁓

"If I don't get a cigarette," Mickey growled, "I'm going to hit somebody."

Cooper stood at the foot of the bed. *Yes, orneriness. Sick and dying or not, it's stuck like glue to her.* Mickey looked almost perky, eyes showing a trace of the old dance and flash. She was still hooked to the IV tower and the heart monitor, but the oxygen tube was gone.

"Is that what you called me over here for? A friggin' cigarette?"

"You don't have to be nasty," Mickey said primly. "Such language is inappropriate for someone in your position."

"Mother," Cooper said, "you are absurd."

"They won't even bring me a newspaper."

"But they brought you a telephone, for God's sake. I'd like to know which idiot did that. Whoever brought it can come get it."

"How can I keep up with all the foolishness going on in the world without a telephone or a newspaper? They keep saying I need rest. Well, I'm worn out with resting." She rolled her eyes. "I'm almost dead anyway. What's a cigarette going to hurt?"

"You're in a hospital, Mother," Cooper said, trying to keep her voice even. "They don't let people smoke cigarettes in hospitals. You can blow yourself up with all the oxygen around."

"I'm not on oxygen anymore," she said grandly. "I'm remarkably improved. These people"—she waved her arm, taking in the whole hospital—"can't believe it. I may last another hundred years."

"You just said you're almost dead."

"Well, maybe fifty. But if I can't smoke, and if I can't talk on the telephone or read the newspaper, I'd just as soon go ahead and croak. Then you wouldn't have to interrupt the crucial affairs of state to tend to your poor old mother. Everybody could say, 'What a relief for Cooper. The old bitch finally bought the farm.'"

Cooper threw up her hands and collapsed in the bedside chair.

"Tough day?" Mickey asked sweetly.

"Don't."

Mickey was studying her. "Well, if I can't have a cigarette, how about a little conversation? These people have no conversational talents whatsoever. All they want to do is stick a thermometer down my throat or a needle in my butt. What shall we talk about? The weather? Hog prices?"

"I can't think of a thing we can talk about, Mother. We've never had much to talk about."

"Is it snowing?"

Cooper rose, pulled back the curtains, and stood looking out at the lights on the broad boulevard. It was midafternoon now, but street lamps were already on. In the cones of light beneath the lamps in the parking lot below, she saw the first twinkling specks of white.

"It's starting," she said. She turned back to see Mickey staring at her.

"How is it going at the Capitol? Not quite what you thought it would be?"

"I'm not sure *what* I thought it would be."

"What did Pickett tell you about it?"

"Not much."

"Why not?"

"He was busy."

"Pickett's never too busy to do what he wants."

Cooper's eyes narrowed. "What do you mean by that?"

Mickey pursed her lips. "Just watch yourself."

Cooper picked up her coat and purse.

"You know, you wouldn't be where you are without me," Mickey said.

"You didn't have a damn thing to do with it. I made sure of that."

"I don't mean your campaign."

"Then what?"

Mickey wrinkled her brow. "I mean everybody who came before you, all the women, me included, me especially. I proved that women can be as good at politics as men—just as hard-assed, just as stubborn, just as persistent. I never ran for office, but by God, I helped a lot of women who did get elected. Look at the legislature. I've lost count. Even fifteen years ago, it was almost entirely an old-boy club. They could spit on the floor, tell dirty jokes, without anybody paying much attention. Now, they have to deal with women, and it has cleaned up the place considerably. And look at all the county commissioners and school-board members, even a woman sheriff upstate. People vote for women, and part of the reason is women like me."

The effort took the wind out of her. She slumped back against the pillow. "You wouldn't have stood a chance, even with Pickett's help, without women like me. We paid your dues."

"You're right about all that," Cooper admitted. "It was your obses-sion, as I know better than anybody, and I give you credit for it." She started for the door. "And now, since I've stood on your shoulders and won, I'm going back to work."

"And I'm getting out of here," Mickey said. "I'm going home, where

I can have a telephone and cigarettes and whiskey and a newspaper and watch all the goddamn television I want."

"Going home. Of all the things you've said since you got here, that's the one that makes the most sense."

Snow was coming down steadily, beginning to stick to streets, sidewalks, lawns, a white swirl making it hard to see the Capitol at the far end of the boulevard as Ezra turned onto it and ran into a snarl of traffic. They crept along, pulling even now with the Highway Department building. Workers were pouring out in a rush, heading for the adjacent parking deck, which was disgorging cars and adding to the confusion. Not far from the deck entrance, two cars had tried to occupy the same space and had dented sheet metal to show for it.

Cooper looked at her watch. Just after three. "Ezra, turn on the radio."

". . . Public schools are being dismissed early, and Piedmont Community College has announced that tonight's classes are cancelled. And this just handed to me . . . The Governor's Office says state employees have been sent home. Lots of traffic on the streets, folks, so remember to take it easy. . . ."

"Want me to take you home?" Ezra asked.

"Do I look like a state employee who needs to be sent home?"

"No, ma'am."

"Sorry, I didn't intend to bark."

"Quite all right."

Her outer office was empty except for a harried-looking Roger and Grace Stoudemeyer, who sat behind her desk next to the inner-sanctum door, white-knuckling a handbag. Grace had been Pickett's secretary for sixteen years, and now Cooper had inherited her. She was a sturdy but prim woman in her early sixties, graying hair pulled back tightly from her forehead and anchored at the rear in a ponytail. Half glasses sat perpetually atop her head.

"Grace, what are you still doing here?"

"Mr. Tankersley asked me to stay." Grace pulled the glasses down onto her nose and gave Roger a stern look over them.

"Well, go home. Be careful and take your time."

"Miz Lanier . . . Governor . . . Not much in this world scares me, but I'm frightened half to death of snow and ice."

"Good grief, what do you want, a police escort?" Roger snapped.

Cooper kept her eyes on her secretary. "I think that's a healthy attitude, Grace. Wait a few more minutes and you can ride with me. Mr. Barclay doesn't strike me as the kind of fellow who's scared a bit by snow and ice."

Roger started to protest. "Governor—"

Cooper turned to him and pointed to her office door. "In here," she said.

Roger followed her and stood while she took off her coat and settled behind her bare-topped desk. She turned and looked out the window. Snow was falling ever more thickly now. The avenue was a parking lot. Flashing red and blue lights. More wrecks, people in a panic. The capital had no equipment to handle snow, and obviously no plan.

"Could be several inches," she said. "I heard it on the radio. I also heard on the radio about state employees being sent home." She turned to Roger.

Roger shuffled from one foot to the other. "It was . . . The snow and . . ."

"The snow didn't send them home."

Roger hesitated, then said, "Me. I sent 'em home." A flash of stubborn defiance. "Do you want me to call 'em back?"

Cooper met his eyes. "I think it's an excellent idea, sending them home."

"I thought you would."

"But I heard about it on the radio." She placed her purse on the desk, opened it, and pulled out her cell phone. "Have you seen my new smartphone? Got it yesterday, right after the inauguration. Latest model, all the bells and whistles. Maybe you don't have the number. Yet."

Color rose around his shirt collar. "No, I have the number. I didn't—"

"Did you think it was too minor a detail to bother me with?"

"You were at the hospital. With Mickey."

"That's true, I was. Maybe this new phone doesn't work at the hospital. Thick walls, all those beeping machines. Signal just can't get through."

Roger stood there, his gaze fixed somewhere above her head. She realized he was looking at Pickett's portrait. Looking at Pickett looking over her shoulder.

"How many state employees are there, Roger? Here in the capital?"

"About fifteen thousand."

She pointed out the window at the traffic on the boulevard. "Fifteen thousand. How long have you known the snow was getting here faster than we thought?"

"Couple of hours."

"Well, my goodness," she said. "If I were one of those fifteen thousand state employees, I'd want to be sent home, too. About two hours ago. And it might have been smart to stagger the dismissals so they wouldn't all be clogging the streets at the same time. Now, Roger, if I'd gotten a call on my cell phone two hours ago, I might have dithered. Or I might have sent 'em on home. But"—she dropped the phone back into her purse—"no call." She stared at him, then sighed, weary of it. "What else are we doing, Roger? Besides sending state employees home."

"We've got a command center at Colonel Doster's place." Doster was head of the Public Safety Department, the state trooper boss. "We'll stay on top of the situation."

"And?"

"See what needs to be done. We've got resources on alert."

Roger's cheeks were flushed now. *He's excited,* Cooper thought. *This is real stuff, not busywork. The big guys are off running a presidential campaign, and ever-faithful Roger has a real sure-enough job here.*

"So you'll monitor the situation, stay on top of things, be prepared to dispatch those . . . what did you say, resources?"

"Yes."

"And you'll . . ." She waited.

"Keep you informed, of course." He started inching toward the door. "Make sure you're constantly and completely briefed on the situation."

"Should I be at the command center, Roger?"

"That's not necessary, Governor."

When he was gone, she sat for a few minutes, remembering the snow of her thirteenth year, the command post on the second floor of the mansion where Cleve, in sagging sweater and bedroom slippers, listened to reports coming in from around the state, mobilized the National Guard, dispatched help, explained everything to her as she sat next to a table where the then-head of the highway patrol manned a tangle of phones and radios. Her father a ship's captain with an easy hand on the tiller.

She wished for him now, right here—his smile, his calm self-assurance. His safety. She didn't feel the least bit safe. Twenty-four hours in office, and her hand hadn't come near the tiller.

⁓

Ezra had commandeered a National Guard Humvee—two, in fact, including one for the security detail. They rumbled next to the elevator in the basement garage, hulking things in shades of tan and green camouflage paint.

"Isn't this a little overkill?" she asked as Ezra helped her and Grace into a rear seat and saw that they were buckled in securely. "It looks like we're going to war. In the desert."

"Most folks out driving right now don't have any business on the road. Don't know what the devil they're doing," Ezra said as he climbed behind the wheel. "If they're gonna run into something, I'd rather it be one of these things than a Ford sedan."

As it turned out, a fair number of people were running into things. A couple of inches of snow had already accumulated on the streets, more was falling rapidly, and the cars and trucks that were still moving were slipping, sliding, and colliding. Law-enforcement vehicles weren't doing much better. A police car was slewed up on a sidewalk a block from the Capitol, an officer standing next to it staring glumly at a crumpled fender. At an intersection a bit farther, Ezra eased the Humvee to a stop as a pickup careened through, a wild-eyed man helplessly gripping the steering wheel as his truck spun in a complete circle and shuddered to a stop on the far side.

"I see what you mean," Cooper said.

Ezra waited a moment to make sure the intersection was clear before he eased the Humvee forward again.

She turned to Grace, who was staring out at the snow and clutching her purse tightly, looking spooked. "Grace, are you all right?"

"Just fine," she said thinly. Then: "I feel a little sick. I really do hate snow."

Cooper pried one of Grace's hands from the purse and held it in both of hers. "Let's take Grace home first, make sure she's okay. Then to the mansion. Grace, we're in the best of hands with Mr. Barclay."

"I'll get you where you need to go," he said, smiling into the rearview mirror. "I was a long time in the National Guard. Retired last year. A transportation company. We drove these things all the time. Big eighteen-wheelers and tanker trucks, too."

"Do you think we need the National Guard now?" Cooper asked.

"Yes, ma'am," he said firmly. "And the governor is the only one who can mobilize 'em."

She remembered that now, from Pickett's days in office. Maybe it was somewhere in the briefing book. She hadn't gotten to the part about the National Guard.

"Should the governor do it right now?"

"Well, you could wait and see how much of the stuff we get, but if you guess wrong, the state'll shut down. The upstate will be where they're needed most. Local folks—police, fire, rescue—get overwhelmed. Enough of it and Guard people get stranded at home, too."

"What would the National Guard do?"

"Keep the roads clear, as much as possible. Likely to be lots of folks like that fellow in the pickup truck back there. It doesn't take but a couple of wrecks to tie up a highway. Cars stranded, people spending the night in 'em, small kids, things like that. No way to stay warm but keep the motor running, at least until the gas gives out, and that can be dangerous. Carbon monoxide kills people. So does cold."

Kids, cold, carbon monoxide.

"So, what do we need?"

"Every big vehicle you can get your hands on. If it gets really bad, power's out all over, vehicles to evacuate folks."

"Such as?"

"Nursing homes, that kind of thing."

She thought about that for a moment. "Do you think the people in Colonel Doster's command center are on top of things?"

"Well, I sure hope so."

"Do you?" she insisted.

He hesitated. "None of those folks know much about handling snow, Governor."

They were past the downtown now, into a residential area of old homes. Snow piling up on lawns, cars left haphazardly street-side.

What if things went badly wrong? It wouldn't be the people at the command center who got the blame. She would—that, or look totally irrelevant. Felicia Withers would make sure of it.

"So maybe I need to light a fire." She fished her cell phone out of her purse.

An ambulance was in the mansion driveway, red lights dancing off the house and the snow thickening on the lawn. A gray SUV was parked behind it. Every light in the house was ablaze. It glistened, like something out of Disney.

Ezra reached for the Humvee's radio.

"Don't bother," she said. "I know what it is."

She took the stairs in a rush, brushing past Mrs. Dinkins, who stood at the bottom wearing a look of baffled disapproval.

Voices from one of the spare bedrooms. Laughter. Mickey. The door was blocked by two paramedics, who emerged wheeling a gurney, laughing at something that had been said inside—until they saw the look on Cooper's face. They mumbled an apology as they hurried past.

Mickey had a ribbon in her hair. She was sitting up in bed, hands folded primly in her lap, color high in her cheeks. She gave Cooper a Cheshire cat smile. Estelle Dubose, the nurse from the hospital, bustled about, giggling at something Mickey had just said. Nolan Cutter was leaning over a nightstand, scribbling on a prescription pad. Machines—heart monitor, oxygen, an IV drip of some kind.

"Well," Mickey said brightly, "here's the governor! Good evening, Governor."

Nolan looked up from his pad.

She motioned with her head as she turned from the doorway. After a moment, Nolan followed her into the hall.

She turned on him. "Nolan, what in the hell is going on?"

"What do you mean?"

"My mother. Here. Why?"

He squinted at her. "You didn't know?"

She stared at him.

He waved an arm toward the bedroom. "They said bring her here."

"They? Who?"

"I don't really know. Mickey called somebody at the Capitol, and they told the hospital to send her over here."

"You should have checked with me, Nolan. God*damn*!"

"Whoa, Cooper. When somebody from the Governor's Office issues orders . . ."

"Well, they weren't mine."

"Then you might want to figure out who's issuing orders over there."

"And what am I going to do with her?"

His eyes narrowed. "There's nothing you need to *do*. She's okay. Her condition is stable, so she doesn't need to be in the hospital. She'll have nurses around the clock. All the monitors are tied in to the hospital's system." He paused, took a step toward her, reached out. She flinched, and he drew back, stood studying her a moment, then glanced at his watch. "I've got evening rounds." He pulled a card out of a jacket pocket, jotted a number on the back, handed it to her. "My cell phone. Anything. I'll be here." He poked his head back in the bedroom doorway. "Everything okay in here?"

"Send scotch," Mickey said. "And a carton of Marlboros."

Cooper followed Nolan downstairs.

At the front door, he said, "Look, I'm sorry about this. If you want to move her tomorrow—wherever—I'll make the arrangements."

She shrugged.

"Cooper," he said, "Mickey is hanging on. I don't know how or why. Do you?"

"I don't have any idea, Nolan."

"All I know is, she was determined to be right here. And she is."

She heard a throat-clearing behind her and turned to see Mrs. Dinkins standing at the far end of the entrance hall. "Mr. Lanier is on the phone."

She made Pickett wait while she went to the kitchen, poured a glass of red wine, and stood for a moment at the doors to the patio, watching the snow. She finally answered, holding the cordless in one hand and the wine in the other.

"Cooper, what's going on?"

"It's snowing. Where are you?"

"Manchester."

"What are you doing in Manchester?"

"We're at the airport, waiting for the weather to lift so we can get out of here."

"To where?"

"South Carolina," he said, his voice impatient. "Cooper—"

"Is Carter with you?"

"He already left. Speaking to a youth group in Greenville tonight."

"And you just sent him off on his own."

"Of course. Carter can take care of himself. He's fine. Not to worry."

Behind her, the microwave dinged. She turned to see Mrs. Dinkins taking out a plate, recognized the smell of crabmeat étouffée.

"Hold on a minute, Pickett. Mrs. Dinkins, why on earth are you still here? Is the rest of the staff here?"

Mrs. Dinkins held herself erect, fingers intertwined at her waist. "Mrs. Dinkins and the staff want to be helpful."

Cooper couldn't help smiling. "Mrs. Dinkins, you are a dear person, and I appreciate you immensely. Now, the best way you can be helpful is to go home. Well, I mean . . ."

"Mrs. Dinkins understands."

"So I want you to get on the phone and call the Corrections De-partment and tell them the *governor* wants you and the rest of the staff picked up immediately and delivered safely. Can you do that?"

"Yes, I can."

Cooper turned away, took another sip of wine, then held the phone to her ear. "Okay, Pickett."

"Look, the reason I called . . . I just talked to Colonel Doster."

"And?"

"This business of the National Guard . . ." She could tell he was making a great effort to keep his voice light, even.

"What about it?"

"This isn't a good idea."

"Pickett, do you have any notion of what's going on down here?"

"I've been briefed, yes."

"By whom?"

"Doster, Roger. Look, I think you're getting way ahead of yourself. Calling out the National Guard right now, it's premature. Rousting all those people out of their homes, putting them in the armories and on the roads tonight, all the expense of it . . . It's just not necessary." Ten seconds of silence, and then he added, "I'm just trying to be helpful."

She could feel anger rising. "You're meddling."

"No, Cooper, I'm trying to keep you from making a big mistake." An edge was in his voice now. "I'm trying to keep you from looking like you don't know what you're doing. Playing right into Felicia Withers's hands."

"And if I don't know what I'm doing, that makes you look like an idiot, too," she shot back.

"Yes," he snapped. And then he got himself under control again. "Look, hon, we're on top of the situation. Doster tells me there's no need for the Guard. He's got everything under control. No harm done, good intentions and all that. Doster's the only one who knows, and he knows how to keep his mouth shut. We'll alert a few Guard units, then see what we need in the morning. It may not snow much. You know how unreliable the forecasts can be. Just let folks do their jobs."

"It's *my* job."

"Cooper," he said firmly, "the National Guard isn't going anywhere."

"Pickett, you are a gold-plated asshole!" But then she realized he had already hung up.

Her face burned. She was still holding the wineglass, holding it so tightly the stem might snap. She poured it full again. It was dark now across the back lawn, snow swirling through the glow of the security lights. She drank, seething. As the wine began to take the edge off, she calmed a bit and asked herself, *Is he right? Did I go off half-cocked?* But then the other: *Being called to heel like a disobedient dog . . .*

From upstairs, the distant sound of laughter. Mickey, Nurse Dubose.

And then the sudden bark of the intercom above the kitchen counter, startling her: "Governor Lanier, this is Sergeant Veazey at the guardhouse."

She set the wineglass down, crossed to the intercom, and keyed it. "Yes?"

"The newspaper guy, Kincaid, is here. He says he needs to talk to you. I tried to get him to leave, but he's still out there on the sidewalk. Nothing on but a sports coat."

Good Lord. All this, and now Wheeler Kincaid.

"Did he say what he needs to talk to me about?"

"No, ma'am. Just said it's urgent. And Governor . . . he seems a little . . . tipsy. Should I arrest him?"

"My God," she said softly. She stood there for a moment, feeling utterly drained, wanting nothing more than to go to bed. A deep, dark, blessed Ambien hole of sleep. But Wheeler . . . He had told her this morning about Felicia. She was still puzzling over that, wondering why he had done something so plainly out of character. Why her? And what now?

~

Sergeant Veazey had a firm hand on Kincaid's arm.

Kincaid clutched himself, shivering, face a pallid gray in the porch light, snow flecking his jacket and hair. She ushered them in and left Veazey nervously reluctant in the front hall while she took Wheeler to the den and motioned him into a chair. He bent at the waist, elbows on knees, wobbly but trying hard to keep himself together. In the small, closed room, the liquor smell was overpowering. His eyes were feverish.

"Do you want some coffee, Mr. Kincaid?"

He considered that for a moment. "I quit."

"You quit drinking coffee?"

"I quit the paper."

"What?"

"Felicia. A big row." He stared at his hands, then looked up at her. "I don't do dirty work. *For* anybody, *on* anybody." He sat back in the chair. "I want to go to work for you."

She blinked, stared. It took her a good while to recover enough to say, "Do you have any idea what I'm dealing with at the moment, Mr. Kincaid?"

"It's snowing like a sonofabitch, I know that."

"My God, this is just incredible. It's too much. Go home and sober up. Do you have your car?"

"I walked. It's not far."

She called to the front hall, "Sergeant Veazey, come get Mr. Kincaid and find him a ride home so he doesn't freeze to death."

When she saw Kincaid to the door, he stopped and gave her an arch look. "You didn't say no."

She went back to the kitchen and her wine, sat for a long time staring out at the gloom, snow drifting thickly in the harsh glare of the security lights. Her mind was a jumble—the snow, the National Guard, Mickey, Pickett, Kincaid. Mostly Pickett.

Out of the howl, one thought kept repeating: *Pickett lied. How can I possibly be surprised?*

PART TWO

SIX

Cooper had experienced, throughout her life, an abiding sense of loss she associated with politics, with the people it took from her. Beginning with Jesse, son of Cleve Spainhour's first marriage, already eleven when his father, a widower state senator, met and wed Mickey.

By the time Cooper was born, Cleve was a rising force in state politics and Mickey was busy learning what it would take to help him make the next step. They didn't seem to have a great deal of time for Cooper, so Jesse became as much parent as stepbrother.

He was a wispy, beautiful boy with wavy brown hair like his father and nice lines and angles to his face and a slow, almost sleepy smile that seemed oddly to complement his sad eyes. When Cooper thought of her early childhood, it was always of Jesse. Sweet, sad Jesse, often in trouble, usually with Mickey. Even at that age, Cooper could feel the stubborn battle of wills between them. When Mickey yelled at Jesse, he seemed to go off someplace inside himself where she couldn't reach him. He didn't complain, he just went into that someplace and stayed awhile until things smoothed over. When he came back, it was always first to Cooper. She worshiped him and thought of herself as his ally. In return, he filled a great many of her empty hours.

She was six or thereabouts, her loneliness stretching into days as Cleve and Mickey were consumed with his campaign for lieutenant governor.

Jesse found her playing with dolls at the base of the enormous oak tree that filled most of the side yard of the Big House. Huge, gnarled roots made a hollow where she had set up house.

He eased down beside her, back nestled in the crook of the tree, hair tousled, shirttail out, shirt unbuttoned with a sliver of torso peeking out, that slow, sad smile spreading across his face. "How's Ginger's cold today?" He knew all her dolls' names. Ginger had the sniffles, and sniffles in July heat were the worst. Cooper had suffered from a cold last week, and now Ginger had caught it.

"She's some better, but she still has the dripples."

Jesse laughed. It was a word they had made up together. Drips and sniffles. Jesse was always coming up with funny words. Like mucous membrane. It was part of your nose, Jesse said, but it didn't sound like anything nosey.

"Maybe she ought to see the doctor," Jesse said. Cooper thought he sounded funny, his words sort of running together like thick syrup pouring slowly from a pitcher.

"Yes, she might," Cooper said. "She's got a rash, too." She showed him where she had painted red dots on Ginger's face with some of Mickey's nail polish.

"Yeah, that could be serious. It looks like it might degenerate"—

another one of those big, delicious words—"into galloping consumption." Jesse was full of big, delicious words. He read a lot of books, and sometimes he would read aloud to her. Jesse was seventeen and could read everything, pronounce all the words, and even knew what most of them meant.

Cooper's eyes widened. "Is galloping . . . whatever . . . is that pretty bad?"

"Well, *I* wouldn't want to have it."

"Me, too."

"Then maybe she really ought to see the doctor."

"Could you call him for me?"

"Oh, I wouldn't wait for him to get all the way out here. I'd take her to town right now."

It was awkward at first, Cooper perched on top of a stack of thick, leather-bound law books from Cleve's library. The books kept slipping and sliding every time she tried to turn the steering wheel as they headed down the long gravel driveway toward the two-lane. Ginger sat on the seat between them, looking dripply.

"I don't like this," she said, irritated at the awkwardness of it. "I want you to drive."

"I can't. I told you, I don't have a license. And Mickey said she'd skin me alive if I drive without a license."

Yes, she did remember somebody had taken Jesse's driver's license away from him because he was doing something he wasn't supposed to do. Mickey had been upset about that and said she ought to skin him alive. Cleve had been upset, too, but not as much as Mickey.

"We're gonna stop on the way to the doctor's office and pick up my license," Jesse said. "They said I could have it back after thirty days, and that's today. So I can't drive until I get it back."

"But you're doing the brakes and the gas. Iddn't that driving?"

"Aw, no. If you ain't got your hands on the wheel, you ain't driving."

"Well, I'm gonna fall on the floor any minute now, and then you'll have to drive."

So Jesse stopped the car just before they turned onto the two-lane, tossed the books in the grass, and got a sack of sunflower seed from the toolshed. That was better. She was up high enough that she could see through the steering wheel, and Jesse was right beside her with his feet working the brake and gas pedals. When the car would start to ease too far one way or the other, wheels bumping on the shoulder to the right or across the yellow line to the left, Jesse would help her with a light nudge of his hand on the wheel.

"You got your hand on the wheel," she said the first time he did it.

"Well, not much," he said. "It's a matter of degree."

They took it real slow, and after a little nervousness at the start from all that slipping and sliding on top of the books, she began to enjoy herself.

"I guess Mama and Papa won't mind," she said.

"Oh, no. It's just a short trip. We'll be back home before you know it. Before they know it. And remember, this is just between us, okay?"

"Okay. This iddn't hard."

"Automatic and power steering. Anybody can drive one of these things."

"I think I'm getting pretty good."

"You're doing fine."

He looked down at Ginger and put a hand on her forehead. "I think Ginger's okay. A little fever, but not too much. Has she ever been in a car before?"

"With Mama."

"Riding with your mama, that doesn't count. But now she's riding with you. That counts."

Jesse reached in his shirt pocket and took out a cigarette and lit it with the push-in lighter on the dashboard. She had never seen him smoke a cigarette before. It wasn't one of those neat, round white sticks like Cleve smoked, it was kind of mushed up and crooked, like somebody had sat on it. And it didn't smell like Cleve's cigarettes either.

"Mama's gonna get you for that."

"Um-hmm." He took a long drag, held it awhile, then let it go.

The smoke made her eyes water. "Can we roll down the windows?"

"Buttons are right there on the door."

Jesse held the wheel for a moment while she played with the controls, zipping the windows up and down, front and back, one at a time and then all at once. She finally just left them down to allow July in and the smoke out. It was a nice day to be out for a drive. Jesse pulled on the cigarette and worked the pedals and sang softly to himself—something about walking to New Orleans, over and over, as if he had gotten lost in the song and couldn't find his way out.

A car passed going in the other direction. A man was behind the wheel, and he waved with a little flip of the hand, and Cooper took one of her hands off the steering wheel and stuck it out the window and waved back. Then she saw the man's eyes go wide as the car went by. He stared at her and said something to himself.

"Uh-oh," Jesse said.

"What?"

Jesse was looking in the rearview mirror. "He turned around."

After a moment, they heard a honk behind them.

"What's the matter?"

"Just keep going. Nice and easy."

Several more cars passed, and some of them turned around, too. After a while, Jesse said, "We've got a little procession going here." She liked that word, *procession*. It sounded like the Easter pageant at church. Jesse waved his arm out the window, motioning them to stay back, and she supposed they did, but she couldn't see the rearview mirror, and she didn't want to turn and look back for fear she might fall off the sack of sunflower seed, which jiggled and rattled under her every time she shifted her weight.

They were in town now. "We're gonna make a right-hand turn here," Jesse said.

They were at the courthouse, where Cleve sometimes brought her when he came to walk the halls and shake hands and talk to the fellows about the weather and crops and voting and so forth. Next to the courthouse was the squat yellow Sheriff's Office, where Cleve sometimes got into a pinochle game with Joe Banks, the sheriff, while Cooper sat in a big chair in Joe's office and drank an RC Cola from a tall bottle and listened to Joe's deputies talking to each other on the radio.

Two deputies were there now, leaning against the side of a patrol car in the parking lot and talking. One of them glanced at Cooper's car as it pulled into the lot, followed by all the others. Then he raised himself up and pointed and started shouting something. And then all of a sudden they were stopped and the deputies and the people from the cars behind them were running, surrounding the car, all yelling at once.

"What's the matter?" Cooper asked Jesse.

"They're just amazed, that's all," he said calmly.

She sat in Sheriff Banks's big chair, cradling Ginger in her lap, while someone sent for Mickey. Jesse sat in a chair across the room with his hands folded across his chest and his legs splayed in front, staring at his feet. Every once in a while, Sheriff Banks came in and said something like, "Boy, that was the dumbest damn-fool thing I've ever seen a person do. What on earth were you *thinking?*" Jesse would look up at him without changing a muscle in his face, and Sheriff Banks would throw up his hands and walk out.

They heard Mickey before they saw her, raging down the hallway, voice rattling the air. She burst into the room with Sheriff Banks right behind her, raising her pocketbook as she headed toward Jesse and belting him right on the side of the head. He fell out of the chair onto the floor and stayed there a few moments, crumpled in a heap with his knees drawn up to his chest and his hands covering his head.

"Get up!"

He flinched, but that was all. Mickey raised her pocketbook again.

"Leave him alone!" Cooper screamed. "It wadn't him driving the car, it was me!"

"Shut up!" Mickey commanded.

Cooper started sobbing.

"You want me to take her down the hall?" Sheriff Banks asked.

"No. I want her to stay right here. Give her your handkerchief." To Jesse again, her voice a little lower now but flat and deadly: "Get up."

He pulled himself up from the floor and into the chair, bent at the waist while Mickey towered over him, glaring down at the back of his head.

"Do you realize . . . ?" Then a disgusted shake of her head. "Of course you don't. You don't realize a goddamn thing. Your father trying to run a campaign, everybody picking apart every little thing he does and says, scrambling around trying to find some dirt . . . And *you*." She whirled on Sheriff Banks. "What are you going to do?"

"Miz Mickey, we can't ignore something like this. We've cut Jesse a lot of slack in the past—helped out where we could, you know, at least until the thing with the alcohol and all. Had to take his license for that. But this time . . ." He spread his hands in a helpless gesture.

"What are you going to do?" she demanded again.

Sheriff Banks straightened and hooked his thumbs in his gun belt. "I'm gonna have to charge Jesse with reckless endangerment. There's too many people knows about this. It's all over town now."

"What about the marijuana?"

"Nobody knows but me. I found it in his shirt pocket after we got him inside."

"Good God," Mickey said. "Can you imagine what the papers would do with that?"

"No reason for 'em to know," Sheriff Banks said.

"Make sure they don't."

Cooper snuffled into the handkerchief Sheriff Banks had handed her.

"Hush, Cooper," Mickey commanded. "You ought to have better sense. Him"—she jabbed a finger at Jesse—"he doesn't."

A long silence rode on top of the hum of the air-conditioning unit at the window. Cooper buried her face in the sheriff's handkerchief, which smelled of old boogers and tobacco juice. Her stomach lurched, and then she threw up all over Ginger and started sobbing again.

When they got back from cleaning up her and Ginger in the bathroom, a jail trusty with a mop and bucket was working on the mess. Jesse didn't appear to have moved an inch.

"I want you to lock him up for the night," Mickey said to Sheriff Banks. "Let me think about what on earth we're going to do with him."

"The military might could straighten him out, but he's only seventeen."

Mickey stood there for a moment thinking, and then she said, "We can fix that."

⌒

She heard them arguing that night in the upstairs bedroom down the hall—or Mickey arguing and Cleve mostly listening, from the sound of it.

And then Jesse was gone.

She saw him only once before he left for Vietnam. That was during a picture-taking of the four of them on the steps of the Capitol with a lot of reporters and photographers present. Cleve had just won the lieutenant governorship. Jesse was in a dress blue uniform with red piping, Mickey and Cleve on either side of him. Jesse smiled when prompted, the same old sad, sleepy smile, but something else was there now, maybe something the Marine Corps had given him, or done to him, something Cooper couldn't fathom.

Then he was gone again, and what was shipped home from Vietnam was only bits and pieces.

SEVEN

The four years Cleve spent as lieutenant governor were largely consumed with positioning himself for a race for the state's top job, and then with the campaign itself. He lived a good bit of the time in a capital-city apartment and spent nights and weekends campaigning. No civic club was too small, no barbecue cookoff too inconsequential. Mickey orchestrated things from the Big House, keeping his schedule, making and working connections, expanding his base into a sprawling political network that reached into every corner of the state. She had an instinct for when to ask and what to ask for, when to wheedle, when to browbeat. To her instinct she added knowledge, a vast catalog of things both important and trivial. She came to know everybody and everything worth knowing.

Except her own daughter.

It was a time of aching loneliness for Cooper, of growing dread and resentment: Jesse dead and gone, Cleve away constantly, Mickey obsessed with his political life.

She made a few friends through school, but even that was not easy. She was the daughter of the lieutenant governor, living in the white-columned Big House miles from town. She experienced, inevitably, a certain amount of jealousy, and with it the petty but painful cruelties of elementary school. She learned to keep her own counsel, to mostly ignore the slights, to find a precious few, boys and girls, who seemed not to give a rip about her baggage. She rebelled against Mickey in small ways she knew were mostly ineffective, but at least she had a sense of trying. Mickey insisted on having the man who tended the grounds drive her back and forth to school. That led to a terrible row. Cooper stalked out of the house and got on the school bus. Mickey threw up her hands and went back to her Rolodex.

And then Cleve won the governorship, and they moved to the beastly, old Executive Mansion in the capital, and she lost all she had gained. It was that awkward time, the beginning of adolescence, when fitting in, not being different, became everything. But she *was* different. The daughter of the governor, starting all over with baggage infinitely more burdensome, the loneliness and sense of isolation compounded by the mansion with its cavernous rooms, house staff bustling about, strange people coming and going. It was an alien, public place. Cleve made a point of including her in some of the many social events. But after acknowledging her with inane pleasantries, most people lapsed into the same old thing that had come to infuriate her: politics.

She focused her anger and frustration on Mickey. Cleve, she reasoned, was an important and busy man. His job, as in the past, took him away a great deal and left him surrounded with people who waited on him and others who wanted things from him. But Mickey . . . Okay, she had helped Cleve get the job he wanted, and that had consumed a huge amount of her time and energy. Now, could she try being a mother for a change? It seemed she was so absorbed in political life that she had forgotten how—if she ever knew. Their relationship was awkward at best and increasingly in open conflict. They recoiled from each other, Mickey baffled by the mere fact of a child moving beyond childhood, Cooper with her smoldering resentment. Mickey retreated into her political world, which began to expand beyond the borders of the state. She became, in the larger world of Southern politics, a player.

And thus it was that Cooper was taken completely off-guard in 1972.

It was May, the weather warming, the mansion grounds in bloom. School just out, time stretching infinitely before her. Lethargy, sloth, her room a wreck, the house staff forbidden to enter. She fled outside, found a shaded, cool spot in a corner of the backyard that had a fountain and a bench. A refuge where she went with books. Mickey found her there, a book in her own hand. Cooper ignored her, then finally looked up.

"I'd like for you to read this," Mickey said, offering the book.

Cooper looked at the title without taking the book: *The Making of the President 1968*. Then she ducked her head and went back to her own volume, a mystery.

But Mickey didn't go away. "I thought you might find it interesting," she said, keeping her voice light, "since I'd like for you to go to the convention with me."

Despite herself, Cooper looked up again. "What convention?"

"The party convention. July. Miami."

Cooper felt her mouth drop open. Nothing came out for a long time. Finally, she said, "With you?"

"With me."

Cooper was dumbfounded. But she read the book.

They flew to Miami on a Saturday, just the two of them. Cleve, who as governor would head the state's delegation, would arrive on Monday, in time for the convention's first session.

Mickey was a member of the Credentials Committee. She had already attended a contentious committee session ten days before in Washington, and a fight loomed over the seating of several delegations, the big ones being South Carolina and California. She went to great lengths to explain things to Cooper, who didn't understand most of it but listened attentively because she knew Mickey was trying to pull back the curtain of that shadowy, foreign world of politics and politicians that so absorbed her. She was reaching, making an offer, and Cooper did her best to accept it.

They went shopping. They went sightseeing, taking in the sprawling white-sand beaches, absorbing the sights and sounds and smells of a city that seemed mesmerizingly exotic, a roiling stew of cultures, faces, accents, the air crackling with the added mix of several thousand people from all over the country pouring in for the convention. The lobby of their hotel, the Fontainebleau, was a crush of people, all in motion, all talking, talking, talking. Cooper had never imagined such a place. She was intrigued. So this was what it was like out there beyond her twelve-year-old world. Mickey lavished her attention on Cooper, who felt something opening between them after so long a clash of minds and wills.

And then Mickey disappeared.

When Cooper awoke in their suite on Sunday morning, Mickey was already gone, having left a note saying she was off to a committee meeting, telling Cooper to order breakfast from room service. She sat alone—bored, restless, irritable—through the day. It was late in the afternoon before Mickey returned. They went to dinner downstairs. Mickey knew people. She had a good table. But dinner was a nightmare for Cooper. Mickey was fuming, distracted. She spat the name *McGovern*.

He was taking over everything, she said, his people dictating, pushing the "professionals" aside. Making a wreck of the convention, the party. A steady stream of people stopped by the table, all of them pissed off at McGovern, frustrated by their impotence. Cooper felt sick. She picked at her food, tuning them out. She finally gave up and went back to their room, watched a stupid show on television, went to bed. She was only vaguely aware of Mickey coming in sometime in the night. And the next morning, she was gone again.

Cleve bustled in with his chief of staff and two security men. He spent a few minutes with her, promised to take her to the zoo that afternoon, then dashed away to a meeting of the state delegation. He was back after lunch, and they made quick work of the zoo, Cleve gamely feigning interest, glancing often at his watch. Then back to the Fontainebleau, Cleve and Mickey quickly off to the convention center for the evening's opening session.

And so it went for two days. Cleve and Mickey came and went, both of them absorbed in the chaotic business of the convention, McGovern, things turned upside down. They snatched an occasional quick meal with her, but they weren't really there. She watched television, crushingly bored, alone, cut off from anything that held even the slightest interest.

With one exception: Flamingo Park.

One of the local TV stations had a report, pictures of a sprawl of tents, the park turned into a campground for the hundreds of young who had come from all over to celebrate themselves and their candidate, McGovern. "A love feast of the insurgency," the reporter called it. The police let them be, overlooking a lot. The reporter didn't explain what they were overlooking. Cooper was fascinated.

Flipping around the radio dial, trying to find something other than convention coverage, she happened upon a station carrying something called the Pacifica Network. The announcers were young, part of the insurgency (whatever that meant), trying gamely to play the convention straight. And then one of the announcers said, "And now we go to our correspondent at Flamingo Park, Mad Dog Bashinsky."

Mad Dog was in the middle of it, interviewing the insurgents. They were against the war, for civil rights, for abortion, against the establishment. They were, it seemed, in jubilant rebellion, convinced that their man, McGovern, could change everything. Peace and justice.

And then it struck her: *Jesse!* He would have been their age. She knew beyond doubt that he would have been there, with his sweet, sad smile and his quiet but insistent way of pushing against whatever the establishment was, certainly against whatever Mickey stood for. These young people Mad Dog Bashinsky was interviewing, they were Jesse's kind. He was everywhere.

She went.

Down Collins Avenue, past the hotels of the old party regulars and their entourages and hangers-on—the Doral (McGovern's hotel), the Ivanhoe—the sidewalks crowded with people, everything in motion.

And then Flamingo Park—a sea of youth, the air electric and thick with July heat and the same smell she remembered from Jesse's cigarette in the car. The sounds boiled around her—music, guitars, bongo drums, the steady drone of urgent, giddy talk. In the heat, a lot of clothing had been shed. A young woman ran past, laughing, stark naked. Nobody seemed to pay her much attention. Cooper realized she was overdressed. She took off her shoes, stashed them under a bush. Somebody was passing out McGovern buttons. She took one and pinned it to her blouse.

Then, suddenly, a flurry of movement, people running—a few, then a gathering crowd, headed toward something across the park, she never knew what. She was swept along, jostled. She went down hard, cowered, covered her head with her arms as the crowd surged around her.

Then somebody was kneeling over her. "Are you all right, kid?" She recognized the voice instantly. Mad Dog Bashinsky.

The crowd moved on. Mad Dog stayed, helped her up. "Are you hurt?" he asked.

"I'm okay."

He had some sort of radio contraption slung across his shoulder, a microphone stuck into a shirt pocket. He looked her over, frowned. "You staying here, kid?"

"No."

"Where?"

"A hotel that way." She pointed up Collins. "The Fontainebleau."

Mad Dog's eyebrows went up. "What's your name?"

"Cooper."

"Cooper what?"

"Spainhour."

"Where are you from?"

She told him.

Mad Dog's lips formed an O. "The governor?"

"He's my daddy."

He eyed her McGovern button, thought for a moment. "Wanna be on the radio?"

"What do you want me to say?"

"Just answer a few questions."

"Okay, I guess it's all right."

"Sure it is." He pulled the microphone out of his pocket, flipped a switch on his radio thing, spoke into the microphone: "Hey, guys. Bashinsky here. I got something. Kick it to me."

It took a couple of minutes, but then they were on. He introduced her. And then: "I see you're wearing a McGovern button."

"Yes, sir, I am."

"Are you for McGovern?"

"Sure, I guess so."

"What do you like about Senator McGovern?" She pondered that. "I don't know, I guess maybe he'll do a good job. All these people here think so, don't they?"

"Yep. And what does your dad, Governor Spainhour, think about it, you being a McGovern supporter?"

"I don't know. I haven't told him yet."

"What do you think he's gonna say, seeing how he's not for McGovern?"

"I think he'll be all right with it. He's pretty easy to get along with."

Mad Dog's gaze swept Flamingo Park. "What do you think about all this?"

She smiled. "I think it's neat. I'd rather be here than at the hotel. It's boring. I wish my brother was here."

A few more questions, and then it was over. She wandered around awhile longer, wide-eyed, then retrieved her shoes and went back to the Fontainebleau.

⁓

Mickey burst into her room, bellowing, jolting her out of sleep. "What in the goddamn name of hell is wrong with you, Cooper? Wake up!"

Cooper looked at the clock radio. It was just after five o'clock in the morning. The convention must have gone on all night. She looked up at her mother, towering over the bed just the way she had over Jesse in Sheriff Banks's office.

"What in God's name are you trying to do to us?"

Cooper pulled the covers tight around her, cowering from Mickey's rage.

"On the goddamn radio? McGovern? Damn you!"

And then Cleve filled the doorway. "Mickey," he said, his voice carrying command. "Leave it alone." Mickey turned to him with a jerk, started to speak, but he stopped her. "Come away, Mickey. I'll handle this."

She threw up her arms and stormed past him, out of the room. He came in, closed the door, sat on the edge of her bed. He looked incredibly tired, the muscles of his face sagging, eyes red and watery. He sat for a long time without speaking.

They had heard about it in the convention hall. A young member of the Illinois delegation, seated across the aisle, had been listening to the Pacifica Network, heard the interview, reported it in gleeful detail to Cleve and Mickey. The news spread. Wheeler Kincaid, the reporter from the *Dispatch*, learned about it. He had a floor pass, was roaming the delegation, asking questions, writing a story.

Another long silence, and then she asked, "Is it okay?"

"No," he said, his voice low and even, "I'm afraid it's not. First of all, you should never have left the hotel. The street and the park are no place for a child."

"I'm twelve years old!"

"And then there's the interview. I'm sure you've gathered by now that your mother and I aren't for McGovern. We've been trying since we got here to keep him from getting the nomination."

"Why?"

"Because we think he'll lose, lose badly, and take a lot of other people down with him."

"Don't a lot of people think he's okay? All those people in the park . . ."

"A lot do, yes. But out there in the country, a lot don't. In our state, most don't. Senator McGovern scares them." He took her hand. "So, honey, when you get on the radio and say you're for McGovern . . ."

She heard and saw the weary disappointment and began to cry. He took her in his arms, held her close while she sobbed against him.

Finally, she mumbled into his ear, "I'm sorry, Daddy."

"It's all right," he said. "It's no disaster. It'll be forgotten in a couple of days." He paused. "Do you know what I told Mr. Kincaid?"

"What?"

"I told him I will support the ticket like the good party man I am, and that my daughter has a right to speak her own mind."

"Do you still love me?" she asked.

"Nothing," he said, "could ever change that."

They flew home the next day on the state plane, the two of them, leaving Mickey—still fuming, punishing Cooper with icy silence—to attend mop-up committee meetings.

When they got off the plane at the capital airport, Cooper said to her father, "I hate politics."

He gave her a long look, his face gentle, and said, "I don't blame you."

EIGHT

College, she was determined, would be different. But it wasn't easy.

They arrived on campus as she insisted, Cleve, Mickey, and Cooper in a plain brown Chevrolet, the trunk packed with her things. Cleve, now in his second term as governor, drove, his first time behind the wheel in a good while. No security detail tagged along. She wanted no fuss. But then she saw the TV news crew and a newspaper photographer waiting on the steps of the administration building when they pulled up in front, Cleve insisting they pay a courtesy call on the university president. Cooper was furious. Who had tipped them off? Why? She refused at first to get out of the car. They all sat there for a moment.

"Cooper," Mickey said from the backseat, "would you just once stop being bull-headed? You're the governor's daughter. Live with it."

"Not here," she snapped. "If it's gonna be this way, just turn around and take me back home. I'll go to college in Oregon if I have to."

Cleve stared out through the windshield, then finally turned to her.

"Honey, I'm sorry. I think somebody in my office is responsible. Just put on your best smile and get it over with. Do it for me?"

"All right," she said with a sigh. "But this is it, Daddy. After this, I want the rest of the damn prying world to leave me alone."

"I'll do my best to make sure that happens," he said.

By late afternoon, Cleve and Mickey were gone and she was settling into the dormitory room she would share with a girl from downstate who had a big, breezy laugh and a great collection of Rolling Stones music and cussed like a field hand. "I don't give a fuck who you are," she said with a smile, flipping her cigarette out the open window.

"Then," Cooper said, returning the smile, "we'll get along just fucking fine."

She was a curiosity, she knew that. She picked her way carefully, sensing who cared about her status and who took her just for who she was. She made a few friends, gravitating toward the slightly off-beat. She avoided sorority rush her freshman year but then found a group— not among the upper tier—who suited her when she was a sophomore. They were boisterous, irreverent, slightly bohemian. Mickey was appalled, and that cemented the deal for Cooper.

She arrived with no settled idea of what she wanted to study, plodding through a menu of introductory courses the first semester. And then she found the campus newspaper. She knew she liked to write, and when, at the urging of a friend, she applied for a staff job and began to get assignments, she discovered she had that combination of persistence and curiosity that made a journalist. Her first byline produced an adrenaline rush unlike anything she had ever known. She was hooked.

By her junior year, she was the assistant editor, and when the editor came down with mononucleosis early in the second semester, she took the top job. And she began to make waves. She took on the university administration, assigning reporters to dig into the use of student fees to support the athletic program, the cozy relationship with the company that had the food service contract, the bungling management of the student health center. She wrote pithy editorials. She was getting a reputation for feistiness. She knew that, and she liked it. She locked horns with the paper's faculty advisor, one of her journalism professors. He was catching flak from the President's Office. The football coach was pissed; the vice president for business affairs had his back bowed over the food service contract story. Could she walk a bit more softly, carry a slightly smaller stick? "You're going to make a fine journalist," the advisor said, "but Cooper, you've got to curb your inclination to take on everybody. Criticize too much and you'll just be a whiner. Pick your fights."

But no, she would speak her mind. And she could. Student sit-ins in the mid-seventies had won some concessions from the administration, including a hands-off policy toward the student newspaper.

Then came the condom controversy. The paper's advertising manager walked into her office one evening with a request for ad space from a prophylactic manufacturer. Cooper looked over the copy. It was tastefully done. She handed it back. "Okay."

The ad manager's eyebrows shot up. "Really?"

"Can you think of a good reason we should turn it down?"

"Well . . ."

"Do you think there is any condom usage on our campus?"

He grinned.

"So they're an item of interest to our fellow students."

"Yeah."

"Are condoms illegal?"

"No."

"Do we need ad revenue?"

"Sure."

"Okay, back to my first question: Any reason we should turn down the ad?"

"Because if we run it, all hell's gonna break loose."

"I'll deal with it. Run the ad."

Instead, he took the ad to the faculty advisor, who took it to the President's Office, to which Cooper was quickly summoned.

When she was ushered into the inner sanctum, the president wasn't there. Mickey was. She was standing at a window behind the massive desk, her back to the door, looking out across the campus. Neither spoke for a long time.

Finally, Mickey turned to her. "Drop it," she said.

"No," Cooper replied.

"Yes, and I'll tell you why: because you are causing a shitstorm of embarrassment to your father. It's easy for you to sit up here in your comfortable little academic playhouse"—she bit off the words—"and make your pious pronouncements about this issue or that."

"I'm—"

"Listen to me! You have no earthly idea how things really work, Cooper. You don't *want* to know, because you're pissed at me, pissed at the world, pissed at politics."

"Goddamn right!"

"Well," Mickey said, lowering her voice until it was flat and hard, "here's how things work. Your father is trying to get something done he's always wanted: free textbooks for every runny-nosed school child in this state. Can you imagine what that would mean? Every child, no matter if his daddy is a tycoon or a sharecropper, has his own book, instead of having to look over somebody's shoulder, or worse, do without. He learns. He has a chance to do something with himself. Little kids, Cooper. Little kids who, unlike you, don't have a pot to pee in. But you know, textbooks aren't really free. They cost money. So to make sure those little kids get textbooks, somebody's gotta pay. And that means a *tax hike*. A nickel on cigarettes, a nickel on alcohol, one percent on utility bills. Do you think Cleve Spainhour just waves a magic wand and the legislature passes something like that? It's almost impossible, but he's getting it done, or was. Until you started playing Miss High-and-Mighty with your little rag of a newspaper. Every asshole who gives money to the Athletic Department is on his neck. People who do business with the university are up in arms. And now, fucking rubbers! My God! Are you out of your mind?"

Cooper felt the floor dropping out from under her. She sat heavily in one of the leather armchairs in front of the president's desk.

Mickey moved toward her, leaning over the desk, bracing herself on her hands, staring Cooper in the face. "Your father," she said, "has enemies. Powerful enemies. They will do whatever they can to keep him from accomplishing anything, especially if it might take a few precious dollars out of their wallets. And they will use any excuse, any issue, to undercut and distract and derail. He is exhausted and despondent. What you are doing here is cutting the legs out from under him." Mickey straightened, arms folded across her chest. "So think about it, Cooper. You're hurting your father. And think about those little school kids."

Without another word, she walked out.

Cooper was devastated. Everything was crashing down about her— the life she had staked out that she thought was her very own. She felt trapped between herself and the world Cleve and Mickey inhabited, all of it pressing in on her, taking from her, as it had from the beginning.

She stumbled in a daze back to the newspaper office and killed the condom ad.

But what about all the rest—the editorship, her voice in the paper? No, she wouldn't quit. She had worked too hard at being her own person to give it up. But she decided—what choice did she have?—that she would lower the volume, at least for a while. She loved her father, even if he had sent Mickey to do his pleading. She would not hurt him.

She finished her editorship at the end of the semester and walked away from the newspaper. She stayed on campus for summer school, then moved from her sorority house into an apartment for her senior year. She felt herself withdrawing, pulling protective covers around her. She ached with disappointment.

And then there was Woodrow Bannister, just at the moment when she felt most wounded and vulnerable. Woodrow cared, truly cared, and that meant a great deal.

They dated throughout her senior year, from just after the summer day he showed up on Mickey's doorstep, hat figuratively in hand, to be examined and vetted. Cooper knew him, of course. He had gotten himself elected president of the student body during the year of her editorship, and their paths crossed occasionally. He was in graduate school now, in psychology, when he called just after his visit with Mickey to ask Cooper for a date. Mickey had said, "You might like him. He's a nice young man. He has PP."

"What?"

"Political potential. He has the touch."

"I would have to overlook that," Cooper said.

"He's still a nice young man."

At some point, it became a relationship. Woodrow courted as ardently and as single-mindedly as he pursued his political ambitions. When they first made love, he was so exquisitely careful that she felt like a finely tuned glass instrument. *Am I being politicked?* she asked herself. *Or is politics itself a sort of love affair?*

That marked an interlude in Cooper's life when she and Mickey arrived at a sort of standoff. Cleve was finishing his second term as

governor, celebrating the successful passage of his free textbook program. Mickey was resting on her laurels, sizing up the next crop. She
and Cooper eased sideways around their differences. Cooper tried not
to think much about Jesse and made an honest, if halting, effort in dealing with Mickey. She tried to separate Mickey the person from Mickey
the political manipulator.

But there came a time when she was assaulted by doubt so fierce
it ripped open the wound, gave rise to the old poisons, and made her
question everything anew.

It began at home, at the breakfast table. It was March, two months
after Cleve had left the governorship. A warming spell, the promise of
spring. Through the dining-room window, she could see the broad dent
in the earth that ran the length of the far pasture, the line of trees along
the shaded creek that trickled through it. For years, Cleve had talked
about damming the creek and forming a pond. "After all this is over," he
said. Cooper had understood him to mean all the running and serving
and being at other people's beck and call. And now it was time.

A month earlier, she and Cleve, bundled in heavy coats and stocking
caps, had walked the land. He had shown her where the earthen dam
would go, the five acres or more that would be flooded. It would become
a still, quiet place, the pond's raw edges healed with grass and shrubs
and trees—redbud, willow, mimosa, dogwood, birch, his favorites. He
would stock it with bream and bass, and they would fish from the bank
or a rowboat. Even in the starkness of February, she could see it.

"When?" she asked.

"As soon as I can get the work started. Fellow's coming to see what
needs to be done."

"It's been a long time."

"I wish I'd done it sooner."

She wondered what he meant by that—built the pond sooner, or
stepped aside from politics sooner? Maybe both. She saw the gentleness

in his face, the comforting stubble of whiskers of a man who no longer was compelled to shave every day. She felt a great rush of joy for him, and also for herself. She took his hand and gave it a squeeze.

Cooper had arrived late in the night from school this March weekend and expected to awake this morning to the sound of heavy equipment in the pasture, but it was quiet and empty. At breakfast in the dining room, she heard only the clink of silverware and china, desultory small talk.

And then Mickey said, "We're thinking about the Senate."

Cooper froze. She stared at Mickey, then at Cleve.

"Fincham's sick," he said after a moment. "They've kept it hushed up, but word's beginning to leak out." Clifford Fincham was a venerable fixture in the United States Senate—seven terms. Even in his early eighties, he was unbeatable. "The election's not until next year, of course, but we have to think ahead."

Cooper turned away, unable to look at either of them. She felt herself give way to a great, frustrated sadness. *It's her doing. He would build his fishpond, be a farmer.*

"It's an opportunity," Cleve said.

She glanced at Mickey, who remained silent. "For another office," Cooper said.

"To do some good, I hope," Cleve said. "Fincham hasn't sponsored a piece of legislation for years, just keeps the folks back home happy by hanging on, taking up space. The state needs somebody—"

"Like you," Cooper said.

"Maybe. We'll see."

She rose, pushing her chair back, folded her napkin, placed it carefully under the edge of her plate. "I've got to get back to school. Midterms are coming up."

She went upstairs, packed the few items she had brought, and took her duffel to her car. Mickey was standing next to it. She watched without speaking as Cooper opened the passenger door, tossed the duffel onto the seat, and walked around to the other side. Mickey's hand was on the door handle.

"You just couldn't stand it, could you?" Cooper said.

"You think I've dragged him kicking and screaming into everything we've done?"

"Something like that."

Mickey shrugged and backed away from the car. Cooper opened the door and slipped behind the wheel.

"Grow up, Cooper," Mickey said. "Stop deceiving yourself. Live in the real world."

Cooper pulled the door shut, started the engine, and drove away without another look.

She wrestled with it through the long drive downstate to the university—the disappointment, and then the puzzle of how Cleve and Mickey fit together. Cleve ran for office and won and served well, and Mickey helped him get there. Cooper thought it was like poker to Mickey—knowing when to get into the game, how much to risk, playing her hand adroitly, understanding when to raise, when to bluff, when to fold, when to call. She almost always won and walked away with the pot. But who needed what from the game? They were joined hip and soul, but exactly how, she could not fathom.

She was miles down the road when it came to her that she could never really know. She knew only that she had felt very much outside their world for as long as she could remember. She had always felt, and always would, a lingering hurt and disappointment, a sense of loss, a sense of things and people being taken from her, kept from her, a sense of defeat from being unable to understand why.

But she also understood that she had for a long time been beating herself up with her losses. And she had to somehow move on from that, accept what she couldn't know and especially couldn't change. She would be graduating from college, moving into the wider world. Not their world, but hers. *I can't forget it, but I can get over it.*

As much as it pained her to admit it, Mickey was right about one thing: It was time to grow up.

~

She slept in on Monday, missing two classes. The phone rang several times, but she ignored it. Woodrow, no doubt. She didn't want to talk to him just now.

When she finally awoke around one, she made coffee, showered, ate a bagel, opened books, and started boning up for a media law exam.

Woodrow came around five with beer and sandwiches from the deli down the street. They sat at the kitchen table.

"I heard about the Senate," he said.

"What did you hear? Where?"

"The jungle telegraph. Fincham's dying, your dad's running."

"He told me this weekend, but it didn't sound quite that final."

"Sounds like it's pretty well set in stone. Somebody's putting the word out about Cleve, and that will scare off some people who might be thinking about it."

"I honestly thought he might retire."

He laughed. "You're kidding."

She shrugged. "Maybe he can't. Or at least Mother can't."

"Both, I imagine. They're like two firehouse dogs. When the bell rings, they're up on the seat of the truck."

"She's the one who rings the bell."

Woodrow gave her a close look. "You've seen him campaign, Cooper."

She thought back through the jumble of years. "Not a lot. He didn't take me along."

"Any idea why?"

"I think he was trying to protect me from all that—the bright lights, the people trying to use him, the bullshit."

"About ninety percent of politicking is bullshit," he said. "And about seventy-five percent after you win and take office."

"So ninety percent of what *you* do is bullshit."

"Sure."

"And is that what my father does?"

"Better than anyone I've ever seen. He's a helluva campaigner, Cooper. It's an art form with him."

"What do you mean?"

"He's like . . ." He thought for a moment. "A golfer, a really good golfer. He makes this long, easy, flowing swing—you think it's got nothing on it—and when the club meets the ball, it takes off like it was launched from Canaveral. And you think, *Jeez, the guy barely swung the club, and look what happened! How did he do that?* That's the way Cleve Spainhour is. It looks absolutely natural, effortless, whether he's doing the bullshit part or the stuff that matters."

"He's not a phony," she said.

"Anything but. He's that rarest of all things political—he's genuine. He understands the game and all the rules and what the stakes are and what the prize can be. Not winning, but doing what really matters."

"But still, there's the bullshit. And it gets all over people," she said. "Me."

He sat there a long time, not saying anything, taking an occasional sip from his beer, looking out the window. Finally, he turned back to her. "I know you wrestle with all that. And I think it has a great deal to do with you and me, with what we might be." He looked away again.

"Yes, it does," she said.

He finished his beer, crumpled the paper wrapping from his sandwich, took the beer bottle to the sink, and tossed the paper into the trash. She watched him, saw the troubled look on his face.

He sat down again across from her, reached for her hand. "There's just this," he said. "I love you. Desperately. But I am who I am."

⁓

The weather warmed, the earth greened. Welcome heat radiated from the sidewalks. Convertibles had their tops down. Shirtless boys tossed Frisbees on the campus quadrangle while groundskeepers tended beds of shrubs and flowers. Dogwood trees showed their first blooms.

She didn't see Woodrow for days. She understood he was giving her time, that they had come to a place in their relationship where all its dimensions had to be considered—who they were, where each was going, whether it might be possible that they belonged together.

Then Cleve called: "Let's go fishing."

They went to their familiar place, as was part of the ritual—the small pond on Fate Wilmer's neighboring farm. Wilmer had for years been Cleve's doctor, but also much more: friend and confidant, a man who valued Cleve for his private, not his public, self.

Wilmer drove them in his rusting pickup along a rutted path to the pond on the secluded backside of the property, where a small aluminum boat was tethered to a tree on the bank. He hooked up the electric trolling motor and left with a promise to be back in a couple of hours.

They had brought the usual simple gear—two cane poles, a cardboard container of crickets, a plastic tackle box with hooks, weights, floats, and spare monofilament line, a bucket for the fish, a small cooler. Cooper at the bow, Cleve steering as they slipped easily through the water to the far side of the pond. They anchored several yards from where low-hanging bushes shaded the shallows.

Dawn mist had lifted from the pond, and a slight breeze nibbled at the surface. But mostly quiet and stillness, the feeling of a place in waiting to see what the day might reveal. Cooper got the poles ready—small weights a few inches above the hooks, red and white plastic floats adjusted to the depth they wanted to fish, depending on water, weather, time of day. He had taught her when she was six years old how to bait a hook with a worm or cricket, had observed without comment that she wasn't a bit squeamish about it. In those early days, Cooper had been full of chatter, eager to share her small life with her father in the rare moments when she had him all to herself. But in time, she had also learned to treasure silence.

The fish weren't much interested today. An hour produced two bream for Cooper, a smallmouth bass for Cleve, strung on a line and left in the water at the side of the boat. She heard Cleve stir behind her, fumbling in the cooler, the sucking pop of a can being opened. She turned to see him holding out a beer to her, gave him an arched-eyebrow look.

"Come on," he said. "Don't tell me you don't drink beer."

She smiled and took the beer. It was exquisitely cold.

"By the time I was a senior in college," Cleve said, "I had drunk enough to float the *Queen Mary*."

"Did you ever do anything stupid?"

He snorted. "Still do. It doesn't take liquor to make you do stupid things."

"Like?"

His gaze never left her. "Not being honest with you."

So now here it was. She had tried in the days since Cleve's phone call not to anticipate too much, to leave her heart and mind open to possibility. He looked away, opened his own beer, took a long slug, set the can beside him on the narrow seat, went back to his fishing. Several minutes went by.

"You really love it, don't you?" she said.

"Yes, I do love it—the laying on of hands, the give and take, the winning, the serving. But I wish . . ." He paused, searching for words. "I realized the morning at breakfast when I brought up the Senate that I haven't talked to you about what I am and what I do, not enough. When you left, I felt something was unfinished. You're grown up now, and I have to think of you that way. And be honest."

They were quiet for a long time. A few nibbles at their bait, not even much of that. It was midmorning, heat beginning to settle over the pond.

"The Senate," he said.

"I hoped you were through."

"I might have been, except for this thing with Fincham. It's an opportunity."

"For you . . . and Mother."

His eyes left her. He stared for a long time at his float bobbing in the water before he turned back. "Cooper, make no mistake: It's my doing. I'm the one you should blame."

"I don't *blame* anybody."

"Of course you do."

"She seems so . . . *obsessed* with all of it."

He shrugged. "She loves it, too, but it's different for her. I'm the fellow out front, she's busy in the back room, doing all the gritty stuff—raising money, twisting arms, making connections. That's the part she loves. But when the running and winning are done, I'm the guy who gets to stand gloriously in the spotlight. She's stuck in the back room. People look at her as slightly grubby, hard edges, hands soiled. The Dragon Lady."

"And isn't she?" Cooper insisted.

Cleve shook his head impatiently. "Ask *her*. Talk to her, Cooper. Talk it out. She wants that. She wants to be understood. You want to be understood."

"Daddy, I've wanted to be understood for a long time. But what I've been, what I've felt, is just . . . left out."

Cleve laid his pole aside. Another minute, then: "That's the other thing I regret. I didn't listen enough. I didn't take *time* to listen. If I had, I'd have known how you felt—about me, especially about your mother. And maybe I could have helped, or at least known I had to do things differently. But I didn't listen." He paused, and his voice broke. "I am profoundly sorry for that, partly because I didn't listen, but mainly because it may be too late. You're a grown woman, and there's so much that can't be undone." He turned away, put his head in his hands.

Cooper felt herself close to tears. "Daddy," she said softly, "I love you. Nothing could ever change that."

It took him awhile to compose himself before he turned back. "For your sake, Cooper, for your and Mickey's sake, give it a chance. Give *her* a chance. For me."

He waited, but she couldn't answer. Finally, he said, "It's getting hot. Let's pack it in."

They wrapped the lines around the poles, retrieved the fish they had caught, and put them in the bucket. Cleve engaged the electric motor and guided the boat back to its spot on the bank. Cooper rose and turned toward the stern to see that Cleve was still sitting there, looking at her.

"I'm still gonna build that pond," he said. "Senators like to fish, too."

Give it a chance. But she couldn't make the overture, didn't know how. Instead, Mickey did.

It was two weeks after the fishing trip. She was gathering her things for an eight o'clock class when she heard a knock at the apartment door. She opened it to find Mickey in the hallway looking rumpled and nervous, hair not quite so perfectly in place, dress slightly askew, mouth set in a thin line, almost a grimace. Cooper squinted, looked Mickey up and down. All she could think to say was, "You've got on one brown shoe and one blue one."

Mickey looked at her feet. "It was dark." She made a slight move toward the open doorway.

"I've got a class," Cooper said, but then she stepped aside and Mickey entered, crossed to the middle of the room, and stood there with her back to the door while Cooper closed it. She didn't turn around until Cooper said, "When did you get here?"

"I left home about four." She hesitated, then said, "I'm on the way to the capital."

"This isn't on the way to the capital."

"Yes, it is," Mickey insisted.

"Well, okay." Cooper picked up her books and bag. "You want to wait here?"

"Skip your class," Mickey said.

"I've got an exam."

"Skip it." Her voice had that imperious ring to it that Cooper hated. But then Mickey said, "Please."

Cooper couldn't recall ever hearing Mickey use that word. So she put down the books and bag and gestured to the sofa. Mickey sat and Cooper took the chair, so they could look directly at one another. *Okay, whatever this is, give it a chance.*

"I wanted to ask you," Mickey started, then hung back for a moment. "How would you feel about Woodrow working in the campaign?"

Whatever Cooper might have expected, it wasn't this. Or was it? An oblique approach to an issue both different and the same. That seemed typically Mickey. She took her time. "Woodrow can do what he wants. He's a big boy."

She could see Mickey's wheels turning—brow furrowing, mouth making little side-to-side gestures. This was wholly new, Mickey asking. Mickey didn't ask, she told.

"Mother," Cooper said after a moment, "I don't want to talk about my relationship with Woodrow, but he doesn't need my permission to work in anybody's political campaign."

"He wants it."

"You've discussed this with Woodrow?"

Mickey spread her hands. "I talked to Woodrow about the campaign. We didn't discuss your relationship, so don't get your back up."

"So why are you here asking me if Woodrow can do it?"

"That's not what I said. I asked how you feel about it."

"What's the difference, Mother? Sorry, but I'm missing the subtleties here. What is this?"

Mickey gave an angry toss of her head. "I told him it wouldn't work."

Cooper understood instantly that she meant Cleve, not Woodrow. *Give it a chance. For me.* He had no doubt said the same thing to Mickey. And it was Mickey who was making the effort, not Cooper.

She took a deep breath. "Okay, let's start over."

Mickey looked at her lap, where her hands were intertwined so tightly it was hard to tell where one left off and the other began. She loosened them, picked a piece of lint from her dress, dropped it on the floor, then looked up. "We'd better try while we can," she said.

"Woodrow loves politics, and he's good at it," Cooper said. "I can either deal with that or not. I'm wrestling with it. What I can't do is stand in his way."

Mickey nodded. "He wants you to be part of it." She held up her hands quickly. "I'm not meddling, Cooper. I'm not going behind your back, not trying to be an intermediary. But I know Woodrow Bannister loves you, maybe even enough to give up all the rest."

Cooper sighed. "He couldn't. You know what Daddy always says about finding your passion. Daddy found his, and it's the same as yours. I understand that better now."

"And you've always been odd man out," Mickey said quietly.

"I always thought you stole people from me. Daddy . . ." And then she stopped. She couldn't bring herself to say the other name, the one she hadn't spoken aloud in years because it gave her such pain. Cooper shook her head. "I'm trying to figure out a lot of things. I'm trying to figure out you and Daddy and Woodrow, but mainly myself. I need some time." And then it was her turn: "Please."

Mickey tried but couldn't quite manage a smile. She rose, then reached for Cooper, pulled her to her feet, and hugged her. It took Cooper completely by surprise. It was a brief hug, not enough to span all those years. But Cooper accepted, gave back, felt something in herself ease a bit.

At the door, Mickey asked, "Where did the time go?" There was a wistfulness to it, as if Cooper had gone missing and then turned up unexpectedly, grown in the meantime into her own person and something of a stranger.

"You've been busy," Cooper said.

"I'll try not to be so busy."

"You've got a campaign to run."

"As I said, I'll try not to be so busy."

And thus a truce flag was raised. Cooper decided to accept it for what it was, accept Cleve and Mickey for who they were, and set the baggage aside. It was part of the moving on, the growing up.

About Cleve, she had a clearer perspective. She could separate the father from the politician, could understand he could be both without having to be judged on a scale of perfection.

And now she would consider Woodrow in the same light, but with a good deal more at stake, because it was her future, not what had gone before. Woodrow was the most thorough of political animals. He would go far, and a price would be paid for that—by him and everyone around him. How might the two of them, if they chose to do it together, handle the conflict? She was convinced Woodrow was as genuine a man as he was a politician. He loved her, she knew beyond doubt. She loved that *about* him. But did she love *him*, enough to take the risk?

It was something she couldn't figure out from a distance.

She was waiting for him in front of the psychology building when he emerged from class, bounding down the steps with an armload of books, neat in khakis and knit shirt, everything in place, a look of earnest concentration on his face, a purposeful young man on his way. Then he saw her and stopped in his tracks and stared, and everything about him seemed to ease and soften. They stood there several yards apart, searching each other, and then he crossed quickly to her.

He started to speak, but nothing came out. Finally, he said, "You're too thin."

"Probably."

He reached for her hand, enveloped it in his. "Can you deal with me?"

"I don't know. Let's see."

NINE

The Psychology Department picnic was a staid affair at a tree-shaded park alongside the river that ran near the campus—beer keg and hot dogs, faculty members' kids clambering over playground equipment while their parents held court among clusters of graduate students pretending to pay rapt attention. Most of the grad students, Cooper suspected, wished they were someplace where they could get truly drunk without having to worry that they might say something stupid and jeopardize their theses and dissertations.

The exception was Woodrow, who moved confidently from cluster to cluster, staying with each long enough to make sure the faculty member noticed and acknowledged his presence. A knowing smile here, a respectful question there. Woodrow, of a mind that a graduate degree in psychology would be helpful to his political career, was politicking the department and learning the secrets to parsing voters' minds.

Cooper followed Woodrow for a while and then, bored, wandered to a bench near the playground equipment. She sat finishing her beer and watching kids dangling from monkey bars and doing belly flops on the sliding board. And she watched Woodrow.

"He could politick a convention of the deaf, dumb, and blind," she had once said to Mickey. Mickey had both agreed and approved. She and Woodrow were quite at home with the use of *politick* as a verb. It helped define who they were and what they did, a combination of instincts and skills that included the ability to size up a crowd, figure out who was worth courting and who wasn't, and then give both worthy and unworthy a moment of look-'em-in-the-eye connection that made them remember.

In Woodrow's case, it was deep in his marrow. He was compelled to politick. He couldn't *not* do it. He had nothing phony or plastic about him. Sure, when he politicked you, there was no escaping the raw heat of his ambition. He made no attempt to hide it. But he also made you feel, with his firm handshake and knowing smile, that you were, for at least that moment, truly important to him.

Woodrow knew who he was, and he was honest about it. For example, he told Cooper early in their courtship that it was pretty much impossible for him to pass up a funeral. If he was driving past a church and saw a gathering of cars and a hearse out front, he would stop, go in, and quietly take a seat. He would follow the procession to graveside and, when the departed was finally lowered, work the crowd. Woodrow's family went way back in state history, and he was legitimately kin, at least distantly, to a great number of people. But legitimacy didn't matter. He would labor tirelessly until he found some way to make a personal connection with every soul he could lay hands on—kinship, school ties, a long-ago acquaintance at some summer camp. If all else failed, he would make something up. He never left empty-handed.

"Make something up?" she asked.

"Stretch a connection," he said. "Maybe that's a better way of putting it."

"But that's not honest."

"A white lie," he admitted. "But look at it this way. Can't a white lie serve a good purpose? You meet somebody, look 'em in the eye, and work hard at finding common ground. Make 'em feel good. And what's wrong with making somebody feel good?"

"Do you ever get caught?"

He smiled. "I'm nimble."

Cooper at first thought of Woodrow's funeral-going as a game, a particularly Southern game that might be called "Who Are Your People?" But it was much more; it was part and parcel of Woodrow.

The more she understood him, the less she knew with any conviction about the big questions of their relationship. They were often apart for days at a time. He was up to his eyeballs in Cleve's campaign for the Senate. She didn't know exactly what he was doing, didn't really want to know. When they were together, he made only vague references to his work. He was juggling all that with the demands of graduate school, doggedly staying with the seminars and papers and all the rest. At times, he looked near exhaustion. Meanwhile, she waited on her heart, took stock of her life, and watched Woodrow, hoping that if she looked closely enough she might find some clues to help answer her questions.

Just now, he had cut a fellow graduate student loose from a herd and was working him—one hand shaking, the other elbow-cupping, head slightly cocked to one side, brow furrowed, listening intently. Connecting. Woodrow could startle with his come-on, and his present prey looked taken aback. But Woodrow was boring in with his big, agreeable I-know-just-what-you-mean smile. He might be startling, but he was also careful not to overdo it. He was habitually careful, his radar always finely tuned.

For example, his cup of beer, which he had set aside on a picnic table while he worked the grad student. He had a half-beer rule. He would drink enough to appear sociable, one of the gang, but not enough that the cup would appear to be nearly empty and someone might thrust a fresh one on him.

A final shake and smile, and Woodrow turned his prey loose and cast about for another. It would go on this way a bit longer, and then he would sense the party was winding down and come looking for her. He would give her a quick kiss and put his arm around her, then turn his beam on her for a while.

"He's good at that," she heard, and turned to see that someone was taking a seat beside her on the bench, holding two cups of beer. He offered one, and reflexively she took it. Then his hand. "Pickett Lanier."

"I know," she said. "I'm in your Intro to Marketing class."

"I know," he said.

He was tall, trim, angular, with features that stopped just short of being too sharp—lively, deep hazel eyes, high forehead, brown hair a bit longish at the sides and back, drifting over his ears and curling at his collar. He had a resonant voice and an earnestness in front of her class. It was his first year on the faculty, and he had told his students he was nearly finished with his dissertation.

"What are you doing here?" she asked.

"Date with a faculty member. That's her over there in that group your date just latched onto."

Cooper picked her out. She was mildly attractive, brunette hair pulled back in a ponytail, wire-rim glasses propped on top of her head. "Does she need those? The glasses?"

"Interesting you should ask. No, not really. She's junior faculty, like me, hasn't been around long enough to pontificate to graduate students. I think the glasses are part of the image."

"What image is that?"

"Somebody to contend with, at least eventually. Like Mr. Bannister."

"Do you know Mr. Bannister?"

"Only by reputation."

"And what's that?"

"Someone to contend with."

"In what way?"

He laughed. "As someone potentially formidable. Do you think he's formidable?"

She shifted on the bench and looked down at the beer cup in her hand. "Is this proper? Plying students with beer?"

"Of course. You're twenty-one, we're not in class, I have no hidden agenda."

"How do you know I'm twenty-one?"

"I looked it up."

A slight flush. "Who gave you permission to go poking around in my records?"

His eyebrows shot up. "Hey, nice."

"What do you mean?"

"You just told me off. Good for you. Some of my female students, totally without my intending them to, stammer and simper when I speak to them."

"I don't see anything to stammer or simper about."

He smiled. "Sorry if I offended you in any way."

"Apology accepted."

"Your beer's getting warm."

She handed it back to him. "Thanks, but I'll pass."

He took the cup, set it on the bench beside him, sipped from his own, and gave her a long look. "What are you doing in an introductory marketing class? Most of the others are freshmen."

"I'm a journalism major. A journalist ought to know at least a little something about supply and demand. And as you've explained, marketing is creating demand so somebody can supply it and make money. Crass, but that's the way things are."

"The great capitalist experiment. Do you like the class?"

"The material is as boring as dishwater."

"You've got a solid A so far."

"Useful things can be boring, Mr. Lanier. I have a pretty good grasp of the law of supply and demand, so now I'm ready to get it over with and get on with things that aren't so boring."

"Fair enough. How about the lectures? Give me an unbiased student evaluation."

She looked away for a moment, searched for Woodrow, spotted him at a swing set giving one of the faculty kids a push while chatting away with the kid's mother. She turned back. "If you're fishing for a compliment, I'll oblige. The class is okay. You explain things so I can understand. The freshman girls think you're a hunk. They're the ones who stammer and simper, right? Should I go on?"

His smile turned to a grin. "I *wasn't* fishing for a compliment, but I'll take it."

She stood. "You're welcome. Thanks for the offer of the beer."

"If not beer, how about coffee?"

"It's too hot for coffee."

"I don't mean now."

"No," she said firmly.

He peered up at her. "I'm a faculty member, you're a student."

"That's right."

"You wouldn't want to get me in trouble."

"I wouldn't think of it."

And then Woodrow was at her elbow, and Pickett Lanier was standing, offering his hand, beating Woodrow to the punch.

"Pickett Lanier," he said.

"My marketing professor," Cooper said.

"Right. Woodrow Bannister. Pleased to meet you." Woodrow reached for Lanier's elbow with his free hand, ready to home in on a fresh target.

Lanier dropped the handshake, crossed his arms nonchalantly over his chest, and leaned back ever so slightly. "Miss Spainhour and I were just talking about the law of supply and demand." He turned to Cooper, winked. "It's pretty boring stuff." He offered his hand, and she took it. "Well, see you in class."

She nodded. He turned and headed toward his date. She glanced at Woodrow, saw the odd look on his face, and realized what it was. He had failed to politick Pickett Lanier.

⌒

She was cleaning out her apartment, the accumulated junk from four years of school, several layers of dust. *The place ought to look like a working girl lived here*, she thought, *not a student slob*. The window air conditioner was on the fritz, all the windows open. Sweat dripped into her eyes and down the collar of the old shirt of Woodrow's she was wearing over shorts. The phone. She ignored it for several rings. She didn't want to talk to Woodrow right now, and for sure didn't want him seeing her like this. She finally picked it up.

"Okay, finals are over, you're no longer a student, no problem with having a cup of coffee with a faculty member."

"No thank you."

"Or dinner."

"Again, no thanks."

"I know this great little place upriver. It doesn't look like much, but it has the best barbecue you ever tasted. Hush puppies, coleslaw, baked beans, bottomless iced tea. And it has a pretty good band some nights."

"Mr. Lanier—"

"Pickett."

"Mr. Lanier, it's nice of you to call, but . . ."

"Mr. Bannister?"

"That's right."

"Word around campus is you're practically engaged."

She didn't try to hide the irritation. "Don't you have enough to do with your faculty responsibilities without having time to gossip?"

"I said practically, not completely. Is that right?"

"Look—"

"It's not like I'm an older man. You're twenty-one, I'm twenty-five. We're both adults, both gainfully employed."

"What do you know about my employment?"

"The editor of the paper was a couple years ahead of me in high school."

She had an entry-level job at the local daily. The chair of the Journalism Department had heard about the opening and urged her to apply. Unless, of course, she wanted something in one of the larger cities, maybe even at the capital *Dispatch*. With her political connections and all . . . She had told him—and the editor—she wasn't the least bit interested in using her connections.

"So you and my new boss have been passing my personal information back and forth?"

"Of course not. He just mentioned he'd hired you. He thinks you've got talent, even if you're too feisty."

"Feisty?"

"I read the student newspaper. You seem to enjoy picking fights."

"I say what I think."

"Obviously."

"Anyway, I haven't written my first word for your editor friend yet."

"Don't sell yourself short."

"I don't. Mr. Lanier—"

"Pickett."

"I'm busy." She didn't need to offer an explanation but found herself doing it. "I'm cleaning my apartment. I'm hot, tired, dirty, and real short on patience."

"I should be cleaning my place, too. If you saw it, you'd think I'm a bohemian. But I'm not, really."

"Have a good day." She hung up.

The phone rang again within seconds. She picked it up with a jerk. "Look—"

"I didn't get a chance to say goodbye."

"Mr. Lanier, I hope you won't call again."

"But I might. Goodbye for now."

She sat for a moment, annoyed she had wasted time on the phone when she had so much to do. She looked over the wreck she had made of the apartment. Books, magazines, class notes strewn about, a stack of clothes for Goodwill, an antique typewriter, cracked dishes. It was oppressively hot. She went to the bathroom, washed her face, put a cool washcloth on the back of her neck. She got a beer from the refrigerator, drank half of it, called Woodrow.

"What are you doing?"

"Writing notes," he said. "Folks I met at the picnic."

It must have taken laborious research in the campus directory—addresses, titles to go with the names he had set to memory. Woodrow was good with names, and to help his memory he kept a small notepad in a rear pants pocket.

"What are you doing?" he asked.

"Cleaning."

"Should I come over?"

"No, Woodrow. Do your notes."

She finished her beer and thought about Woodrow at his desk, choosing his words carefully, just enough to let his new contacts know they had made an impression, and to make sure he had. The personal touch, the attention to detail—all part of Woodrow's plan.

Tonight, they would have a quiet dinner at his apartment—which would be neat, clean, everything in order, unlike the chaos that was hers—talk, make love. He would bring her back to her place, go home to his. He was leaving early in the morning to join Cleve's campaign full-time, running a regional office downstate. Some of the older heads in the campaign thought he was far too young, at twenty-three, for that kind of responsibility, but Mickey had anointed him, and nobody was crossing Mickey. The campaign was in high gear—primary in August, general election in November. Both parties had stout candidates, but the smart money was on Cleve Spainhour. There seemed almost an inevitability about it.

She thought, suddenly and unwillingly, of Pickett Lanier. His calls were certainly irksome, but she recalled something he said: "Word around campus is you're practically engaged." The notion of people talking about her rankled, an oblique invasion of sorts. But gossip aside, was he right? *Were* she and Woodrow practically engaged, at least in other people's eyes? Perhaps, but not in hers. She was trying to focus on the next moment in her own life. The moment after that might include Woodrow, but for now she was trying to keep the thought of it at bay. She was not practically engaged in anything so much as the notion of *not* being practically engaged.

And then, before she rose and resumed her cleaning, one other thought: *Pickett Lanier might believe the gossip—that we're practically engaged—but he called anyway. Cheeky bastard.*

TEN

Friday, end of her first week on the job, covering a meeting of the Water and Electric Board, a droning debate over whether to install a rebuilt carburetor on a city truck or spring for a new one. Work had been a series of stories ranging from the inane to the mundane. An overturned truckload of chickens, a rambling speech by the mayor to the Rotary Club, interminable meetings of various governmental bodies, a feature story on a woman who made art objects out of gourds. Rookie stuff, the assignments experienced reporters tried to avoid.

"When are you gonna let me do something worth a damn?" she asked the editor.

He gave her a slow smile. "Cooper, I may one day turn you loose on the School Board, or maybe the police beat. But not yet. Pay your dues, bide your time. Besides, the police chief is a horse's ass, and knowing you, a fistfight might ensue."

So she watched and listened and tried to absorb as much as she could about newspapering in the real world. She was busy. Woodrow was away. He hadn't called, and thankfully neither had Pickett Lanier. She had given neither of them anything but fleeting thought.

A tap on her shoulder, a woman from the Town Clerk's Office. "Miss Spainhour? The paper said you should call right away."

Mickey, voice strained, sounding like someone a continent away: "Cooper, Cleve's in the hospital."

"What? Why?"

"He collapsed while he was getting dressed. Fate Wilmer's with him. I'm waiting to hear something."

It took three hours to drive home to the upstate. At first, her mind was roiling with questions, uncertainties, fears. She had seen Cleve a week ago at graduation, when he had given the commencement address and been awarded an honorary degree that caused public controversy, criticism from a primary opponent who accused the university of providing Cleve an unfair pulpit. Cleve had considered declining but agreed to go through with it when Cooper insisted. After he accepted his degree, he presented hers with a hug and kiss, and they posed briefly for the news cameras. His voice was strong, his color good, his smile brilliant. He was tired at the end of the busy day, but not unusually so. He had lost a little weight, which he attributed to the grind of the campaign. And then she had talked with him by phone yesterday. He sounded fine, the campaign going well. And he had been in touch again with a contractor about building the fishpond. A surveyor would be on site next week. Cooper drove on, letting her mind go blank except for what kept echoing in her head: *It will be all right. It has to be all right.*

Cleve's chief of staff and campaign manager, Willis Tuttle, was waiting for her in the hospital parking lot. Mickey was the mastermind, but Willis was the candidate's keeper, the man in the background—balding, round-faced, droopy-eyed, tireless, unflappable. She climbed out and stood for an instant with the door open, searching his face for a clue. "Willis . . ."

"Nobody knows, Cooper."

"What do you mean?"

"People . . ." He waved his arm. "It hasn't gotten out."

"What hasn't? What's going on?"

"They're doing tests. It's probably just fatigue. He's been working pretty hard."

She took off toward the building, Willis on her heels.

"We're keeping things low-key. No need to raise an alarm."

When she reached the door, she looked back and saw that Willis had stopped and was standing in the lot, looking as if he needed to do something but had no idea what. Cooper felt a pang. Willis was much more than a political addendum to Cleve. He was friend and confidant, a man Cleve trusted above all others. She went back to him, gave him a hug. "I'm mighty glad you're here," she said.

The hospital had put Mickey in a tiny conference room—three metal-and-canvas chairs, a small round table, bare walls, pallid fluorescent light. She looked up slowly as Cooper opened the door. She was wan, drawn, hair a mess, clothes rumpled. She shook her head. "Nothing yet. Fate's been in a couple of times. They're doing some tests . . . I can't remember what."

Cooper closed the door behind her. "What happened?"

Mickey stumbled over the words. "We were up early. Willis was there, they were heading to Ashton for a campaign thing. We had breakfast, Cleve went upstairs for his tie and jacket. Fifteen minutes and he didn't come down, so I went up. He was standing there with the two ends of his tie in his hands, just frozen, looking at himself in the mirror, and he turned and gave me this awful look and then . . . he just fell down."

She took a chair next to Mickey, and they sat in silence. Then Mickey reached for Cooper's hand and clutched it tightly.

"He looked fine last week," Cooper said. "Had you noticed anything?"

"He had a physical last month. Nothing."

A long, awkward silence. A wall clock ticked. Cooper wished the room had a window, wished she could look past the stark, bare walls that pressed in on them. A light rap on the door, and they both looked up with a jerk as it eased open. Willis.

He stood there with just his head poked in. "It's getting out, Mickey."

"For God's sake, Willis, come on in," Mickey said.

Willis closed the door and stood with his back to it. "I just had a call from Wheeler Kincaid," he said. "Somebody tipped him off, probably somebody here at the hospital."

Mickey pursed her lips but didn't say anything.

"He's pretty much got the story, as much as there is at this point. Now, he wants more." He paused, studying Mickey. "What do you want me to tell him?"

Mickey stared at him blankly.

Willis's brow furrowed. He cut his glance to Cooper, back to Mickey. "We should get out ahead of this thing as much as we can," he said. "If rumors start flying . . ."

Still, Mickey said nothing.

"Mickey . . ."

"Tell him the truth," Cooper heard herself saying. "Tell Mr. Kincaid that Daddy's resting comfortably, undergoing tests." A glance at Mickey, who was staring now at some vague point just above the door, "Mother, is that all right? Mother?"

"Yes," Mickey said faintly. "Yes, that will do."

"Okay," Willis said. "I'll be just down the hall. If you need anything." He cut another quick look at Mickey, then left.

Cooper turned back to Mickey and started to speak, only to freeze when she saw in Mickey's upturned face the glazed, feverish cast of her eyes, the look of sheer, mindless terror, the trembling lower lip. She had never seen Mickey cry, nothing remotely close.

Mickey's voice was a bare, ragged thing. "I could never begin to tell you how much I owe Cleve Spainhour," she said. And then she pulled away, withdrawing, huddling into herself while Cooper, unnerved, fought against the panic rising in her own throat.

~

They waited through what remained of the afternoon, though time ceased to mean anything. Willis brought coffee, returned sometime later with food that was still untouched when Fate Wilmer came to them finally. Exhausted, devastated, he slumped into a chair, elbows on knees. "I'm sorry." It was all he could say for a long moment, which was all it took for Cooper to know her father was dying.

Fate gathered himself. "Pancreatic cancer."

Mickey sat mute and still.

"How . . . ?" Cooper breathed.

"It's hard to detect," he said. "There aren't many symptoms—maybe a little weight and energy loss, sometimes abdominal discomfort, often not even that. Nothing to raise a red flag until it spreads to nearby tissues or gets in the bloodstream and moves to other organs."

"And has it?" Cooper asked. "Moved?"

"It's all over his body." He bowed his head. His voice broke. "I wish to God . . ."

Cooper stared at the top of his head, an unruly mass of hair that he kept worrying with the fingers of one hand. He and Cleve had been friends from childhood. Cooper reached for his hand. "If you didn't spot it, it couldn't be spotted."

Fate looked up, tears brimming. "We'll take good care of him. He'll be comfortable."

"At home," Cooper said. "We'll take care of him at home."

"Of course. At home." Fate looked up at the clock. "And let's get him there now, before the vultures start gathering."

As it was, a couple of still photographers and a TV camera were outside the hospital when the ambulance pulled away just before ten. And by the time they were home, others were clustered by the county road, kept at bay by sheriff's deputies. Willis, hollow-eyed with shock, was at the house, answering the constantly ringing phone, parrying the curious as best he could.

Woodrow called. "I'll be there first thing in the morning."

"No," she said firmly. "Don't come, Woodrow. There's nothing you can do here. Stay and work." A dumb thing to say, of course. Word had spread: Cleve Spainhour's campaign was over.

A long pause. "Work?"

"Take some time," Cooper said. "Decide what you want to do." Silence. "One of the other candidates . . ."

"Goddammit, Cooper," he said. "I just want to be with you."

She felt the hard, unyielding denial inside her begin to fracture. She began to sob, and then on the other end of the line she heard Woodrow crying, too.

He was, as he promised, there by morning.

For the next week, the rest of the world was a blur. She was vaguely aware of things going on outside, people coming and going, flowers and cards and telegrams. The state was in a political uproar, the scramble among Cleve's opponents in both parties for the apparatus of his campaign going full bore, some of it discreet, some shamelessly open. Visitors were politely but firmly discouraged, and if they insisted on coming anyway were even more firmly turned away by Willis and Woodrow. They made no exception for the governor, who roared up unannounced in a motorcade and wandered about downstairs, grousing to anybody who would listen, then finally gave up and roared away, stopping up at the road to share with a gaggle of reporters that his good friend Cleve Spainhour was in fine spirits and resting comfortably.

The medical personnel did, as Fate Wilmer promised, make Cleve comfortable. The massive rice-carved bed in the upstairs bedroom was taken apart and removed, replaced by a hospital bed. Nurses worked in shifts around the clock. One intravenous tube fed glucose, another a powerful painkiller that kept Cleve in a near-twilight state. His eyes rarely opened, though he occasionally mumbled things Cooper couldn't understand. The room became a cocoon where time had no meaning. She stayed at Cleve's bedside almost constantly until exhaustion drove her away to a few hours of fitful sleep. She had no appetite, no desire or need of any kind except to be there with him. She had missed him so much for such a long time; she would not miss this time with him now.

Mickey was a wreck, wandering in and out of the bedroom, grieving and lost. Mickey, who had never been anything but in control and in charge—both of herself and everything around her—was now simply adrift. Cooper tried to start conversations, but Mickey seemed incapable of putting words together.

At first, it baffled and unnerved Cooper. And then it came to her on the third day as evening crept at the window beyond Cleve's bed. They hadn't turned on any lamps yet, and the light was soft, just past sunset. Cooper sat next to the bed, reading aloud. Fate had assured them that Cleve was more aware than he appeared, that he could hear and often understand, even if he couldn't respond. He had lucid moments, but they became fewer. So Cooper had talked about everything she could think of—her job, friends, memories. And when she ran out of things to talk about, she read—the newspaper (omitting anything remotely related to politics), a collection of poems, just now a book of Southern folk tales.

She stopped when she heard the door open. Mickey slipped into the room, crossed to the bed, and stood there a long while looking down at Cleve and brushing idly at his hair with her fingertips, her face gaunt, her eyes pleading. Cooper recognized it as pure, unadulterated fear—of what was happening to Cleve, of course, but perhaps even more than that, what might become of her without him. Cooper watched, mesmerized, understanding then that she was intruding here. She laid the book aside and left them, went down the back stairs to the yard, took a seat in an Adirondack chair, from which she could look out across the pasture toward the place where the pond was to have been.

Fate was there at least twice every day, and Cooper saw how he stooped under the burden of his own sense of loss and failure, a physician without the power to heal his dearest of friends.

On the fourth morning, Cooper sat in a chair in the hallway next to Cleve's room while Fate was inside. After several minutes, he came to the door and said quietly, "We need to talk."

They went to a small sitting room down the hall.

"Have you and Mickey discussed arrangements?"

"No."

"I think you'll have to take charge, and there are things only you can decide." He looked at her closely. "Can you do that?"

"Yes. Of course."

She went to Mickey's room, dark except for slivers of morning plucking at the edges of the shades. She turned on the bedside lamp. Mickey was burrowed under the covers, the top of her head barely showing.

Cooper stood over her. "Mother," she said, "we've got to talk."

It took a minute, but Mickey finally rolled over, pushed the covers back to just below her chin, and peered bleary-eyed up at Cooper. Her voice was so small and fragile it seemed like porcelain. "I don't know what to do."

"I know. It's all right."

"I'm sorry."

Cooper took a deep breath. "I'll check everything with you."

"No need," Mickey said. "Willis can help, but you decide. Whatever you decide, it'll be fine."

Willis, hollow-eyed from fatigue and his own private agonies, proved a font of information—history, protocol, necessities, proprieties. He suggested, she decided, and then Willis and Woodrow worked the phones. By the end of the day, the arrangements were virtually complete.

Late in the afternoon, she heard the faint rumble of machinery that became a groan of diesel when she opened the window next to Cleve's bed. She sat next to him and touched his shoulder. "Daddy. You hear that?"

His eyes fluttered open. "Is it . . . ?"

"Of course. I called them yesterday and told them to get busy."

He lay there a long time, eyes open. His hand, frail and thin, found hers. His grip was surprisingly strong. They sat quietly, listening to the distant growl of the bulldozer out in the pasture.

"Cooper . . ."

"Yes, Daddy."

"Sometimes, I think we're the sum of our regrets."

She waited for him to go on.

"I could have stopped it. Not a day goes by that I don't wish I stopped it."

She knew, of course, what he meant. She sat mutely, stung again by the ancient grief.

"We talked about it," he said. "Jesse was a mess, in trouble and headed for more, maybe something serious."

"Daddy, we don't have to talk about this, not now."

"We don't, but I do."

She waited, then finally gave his hand a squeeze.

"Mickey said maybe the military would do him some good. I think she got the idea from the sheriff. We thought about the air force." He paused, brow furrowed, remembering. "I wanted him to say no, he wouldn't go. But he didn't. He just said, 'Okay, but if I'm gonna do it, I want the marines.'"

"Why?" she whispered.

He shook his head. "I don't have any idea where he got the notion. But we said, 'All right, if that's what you want.' He was almost eighteen. We waited until his birthday." His head was almost off the pillow now, straining toward her, his face rigid with the effort. But then he sagged back, closed his eyes, his breath coming in small, ragged gasps. Then a long, agonized sigh. "I am so sorry."

Cooper sat stunned, clutching his hand, trying to get her mind around it. She knew he spoke the absolute truth—he had no time for anything but truth—and it contradicted almost everything she thought she knew about the loss of Jesse. She yearned to reach out, find Jesse somewhere out there, grab him by the collar, cry out, *Why, Jesse? Why?*

She let go of Cleve's hand and moved to the window. She stood there battered by the words, the knowledge. But after a moment, she felt her heart turn away from her own need to that of her dying father. She could not give him absolution—no earthly soul could do that— but she could tell him she understood and shared the pain. Most of all, she could tell him with all the fierceness she could muster that he, they, must never let themselves be the sum of their regrets.

She was at the window for no more than a minute. But when she turned back, he was gone.

ELEVEN

His body lay in state in the Capitol rotunda for twenty-four hours—
noon to noon—draped with an American flag and flanked by an honor
guard of state troopers and National Guard soldiers. Had Cleve had
any say in the matter, he would have agreed to that, but only reluctantly,
as with the honorary degree from the university. He had a deep respect
for the office he had held, if not for all who aspired to it or served in it.

The people came, an endless line stretching out the massive doors
and down the steps to the edge of Capital Avenue.

It was seven o'clock on the morning of the second day. At midday,
the honor guard would bear the casket down the marble steps to the
waiting hearse, and they would begin the long journey home, pausing at
First Presbyterian for a service. Cooper had come early, an hour before
the doors would open and people would start filing in. She sat in a chair

behind the casket, out of view, lost in thought. Hearing the scraping of another chair, she looked up to see Mickey dragging it across the floor of the rotunda, and then a trooper scurrying to help her with it.

Mickey settled next to Cooper. "I couldn't sleep."

"Me neither."

"It'll be a long day. Are you all right?"

"Yes, Mother. I'm fine. Are you?"

"I don't know. I guess I didn't think this part would be so hard. The giving up, that's what I thought would be the hard part, and the rest would be going through the motions."

They sat for a while, not speaking. The troopers and soldiers had discreetly withdrawn, leaving them alone in the hollow stillness.

Cooper spoke up finally: "I think we should bury Daddy by the fishpond."

"Can we do that?"

"I checked with the Health Department. Since a family plot is already on the property, they'll just call it an extension of that."

"You want to finish the pond."

"Of course."

Mickey hesitated. "I've never given any credence to the notion of the dead hanging around, spirits and hauntings and all that. When I'm gone, you can plant what's left just about any place you want. But I understand about the fishpond."

"Maybe it's more for me."

"That's all right. You did love to fish together."

"I don't remember you ever going with us. Why?"

"Once, when you were small, I went along. I even caught a fish. But that was the only time."

Cooper looked away. "I thought you didn't care."

"I thought it was your time, yours and his."

Mickey moved to the head of the casket and stood there, smoothing the flag over and over while Cooper watched. Mickey seemed more at ease now, gathered and braced for the day, if not so much for what lay beyond.

She looked up and pointed at a space across the rotunda next to a statue of Jefferson Davis. "It was right there where we met," she said. "I was a lowly clerk in the House Speaker's Office. Cleve spent most of his time on the Senate side. He'd come over once in a while, and he was pleasant, said hello to everybody, but I was at a desk over in a back corner of the office, and I don't think he ever gave me a moment's notice. Until the Fairfax County bill."

Cooper waited, watching a slow smile spread across Mickey's face.

"Lovey Andrews was the representative from Fairfax. Cleve and the speaker wanted him to support a bill, I don't remember exactly what, except that it was something the governor wanted badly, and they were the governor's people in the legislature. They worked on Lovey for weeks. He was a stubborn, ornery sonofabitch, and he'd been around for something like thirty years. Head of the Finance Committee, and he refused to bring the bill up for a hearing. The speaker was just beside himself. So . . . I fixed him."

"What do you mean, you fixed him?"

"I was working late, typing up the final draft of a budget bill. Page after page of boring crap. And then I got an idea about how I could help the speaker put some heat on Lovey. I wrote up a paragraph and buried it in some stuff about road funding, abolishing Lovey's county."

"Abolishing?"

"Wiping the place off the map. Just leaving this big, blank hole where Fairfax County used to be."

"Good God."

"I didn't tell a soul. The next day, the bill came up for a vote, and it passed unanimously."

"With Lovey's support."

Mickey laughed. "The old fart voted to abolish his own county."

"Did you tell anybody you'd done it?"

"Not for a couple of days. Then I went to see the speaker. 'Look, Mr. Speaker, I just noticed this thing that slipped into the budget bill.' He stared at it, and then at me, and I thought, *Oh, my God, he's going to fire me right here on the spot.* But then he said, absolutely deadpan, 'Thanks for bringing this to my attention.'"

"What happened to Lovey?"

"The speaker collared him and showed him what he'd voted for. He panicked. He fell all over himself saying he'd back the bill Cleve and the speaker wanted. And they sneaked something into another piece of legislation reestablishing Fairfax County. Nobody ever knew a thing about it but Cleve and the speaker and Lovey. And me. And I've never told a single other soul until you."

Cooper hesitated before asking, "Why me?"

Mickey's face went soft. "I was crossing the rotunda a couple of days later when Cleve stopped me. 'Miss, I need a word with you,' he said, and he gave me this long, serious look, and I thought, *I'm about to be chewed out.* But he put a hand on my arm and gave me this sly grin and said, 'Nice work.' And then he walked off. And the next day, he called and asked for a date. And all that led to you."

Cooper gave Mickey's hand a squeeze. "Thank you." And then: "How did it occur to you to do that to Lovey Andrews?"

"I had the instincts. Even back then, I had the instincts."

At midmorning, she felt a light pressure on her sleeve and turned to see Woodrow standing there, slack-jawed and red-eyed with weariness. He had hardly slept for a week. He had been constantly at Willis Tuttle's side, helping with the details, first at the house, then at Cleve's campaign office in the capital. Cooper had seen him only once, briefly, when he met her and Mickey at their hotel.

"You look like hell," she said with a smile.

"I love you, too. Are you okay? Anything I can do?"

"Be here."

"I am."

Woodrow took up a post in a corner of the rotunda for the rest of the morning while the crowd moved through. He kept to himself, speaking only when someone approached him, unobtrusive in his dark suit. She didn't see him again until the church service was over and she and Mickey were moving through the crowd toward the car that would follow the hearse back home.

Woodrow caught up with them at curbside. "My car's here. I'll follow you."

"No, Woodrow. From here on, it's just us."

As the car pulled away, she glanced through the rear window to see Woodrow standing there at the curb, hands loosely at his sides, watching them. And then he turned and stuck out his hand to a woman standing next to him, reaching for her elbow with the other hand. Cooper settled back in the seat, closed her eyes, and gave way to exhaustion.

Two days later, Cooper and Mickey gathered with Cleve's old friends—Fate Wilmer and the like. The casket had been lowered the day before, the grave covered, only a stretch of green artificial turf covering the freshly dug earth. The great mounds of flowered wreaths had been left behind in the capital. What would soon be the pond was now a raw wound in red clay where the bulldozer had been at work. But when it was filled with water from the creek behind the earthen dam, the grave would be a few yards from the bank, sheltered by an ancient, venerable maple that Cleve had insisted years ago be given a chance to recover after a lightning strike.

No minister was present. Mickey had recoiled from the idea of saying a few words, so Cooper spoke.

"Daddy loved the earth. He found beauty in small things like crickets and fish." Her smile drew easy laughter from the gathering. "He relished the warm months, when things came to life and then flourished and finally blazed with color. He knew about nature, about how plants and animals follow the rhythm of seasons. He showed me, and he talked about it, and when he did, he gave me gifts of beauty and imagination."

She paused and looked out over the raw cut of the pond to the trees beyond. "I can imagine this when it's finished. Can't you?" Knowing nods. "I can imagine coming here and being at ease, as Daddy would have done." She looked at Mickey for a moment, then the others. "I don't know how you feel about the separation of body and spirit, whether there's anything here of Daddy besides a casket and remains. But that's not so important. I think Daddy would have loved this quiet place. Maybe he does." Her gaze swept the crowd. "He took the greatest joy in you who are his friends, who asked nothing and offered nothing but your friendship. I hope you'll come here often and enjoy the quiet of this place. If you find anything else here, that's to the good. But I think just marveling is enough."

TWELVE

The phone was ringing when she opened her apartment door, home from work a week later. Woodrow, no doubt. Mickey had found him a job in Arkansas, working in another Senate campaign, and he had left two days after the funeral. She didn't want to talk to Woodrow. She got a beer from the fridge, opened it, propped herself on her bed with a cushion of pillows, and stared at the phone. It kept ringing. She felt a tightening at her temples, first twinge of a headache. *Woodrow, please . . .*

"I just wanted you to know I've been thinking about you," Pickett Lanier said.

She took a deep breath. "Thank you, Mr. Lanier."

"Pickett."

"Pickett."

"Had dinner?" he asked.

"No."

"Can I pick you up in thirty minutes?"

Another breath, and then before she knew it: "Yes."

~

She heard the beep of an odd little horn and looked out her upstairs window to see a motorcycle rumble up to the curb, Pickett Lanier astride it, long black case strapped to his back. She raised the window as he killed the engine, kicked down the kickstand, and unfolded himself from the seat. He was leaner, lankier than she remembered. He pulled off his helmet and shook loose his dark brown hair. It had grown longer since she last saw him. He wore jeans, an untucked Rolling Stones T-shirt, black boots with buckles on the sides. He looked up to see her in the open window—gape-mouthed, she realized. He grinned.

"Where's your car?"

"This is it."

"You don't have a car?"

"Not much of one. It has vapor lock."

"What?"

"The fuel line gets too hot, and the gas turns to vapor, and a car won't run on vapor. So it's in the shop, has been for a couple of weeks. I told 'em I wasn't gonna come get it until they solved the problem." He shrugged, then another grin. "But the bike's more fun. What are you wearing?"

Cooper looked down at her sensible summer dress. "I'll change."

"Jeans," he said. "And a light sweater. Might be a little cool coming back."

She started to close the window, then: "What's that on your back?"

"Guitar."

"What for?"

"I play in a band. Well, something resembling a band."

"You're taking me to work with you?"

He laughed. "Oh, ma'am, it ain't work. It's art."

"I'm not in the mood for a loud evening with a band."

"Maybe we'll play some Mozart." He lifted his arms imploringly. "If you don't go, it'll break my heart, and those of all the other band members I've told you're coming."

"You're pretty damn sure of yourself."

He made a sweeping bow. "Your humble servant."

Cooper closed the window and stood rooted to the floor of the living room. *This is crazy. I'm crazy. Why am I doing this? I can't do this. I'm not going to do this.* She looked down again at him, now sitting side-saddle on the bike, legs stretched across the sidewalk. He was holding the guitar case across his lap, fingers drumming on it, swaying slightly from side to side, head bobbing. He looked so . . . what? *Physical.* He glanced up at her and twirled a finger in the air. And then she thought about the prospects of a long evening alone in her apartment. *All right, all right, I'm going to do this.*

He fiddled with the helmet, tightening straps, then handed it to her. "Where's yours?"

"This is my only one," he said.

"Isn't that—"

"Reckless, irresponsible, foolish. Here, let me help you." He took the helmet, eased it onto her head, smoothing her hair and tucking it in back. His fingers lingered at her temples for an instant. Then he backed away, picked up the guitar case, and held it out to her.

"What do you want me to do with that?"

"Hold it."

"I'll fall off."

"You won't," he said solemnly. "Trust me."

They rode east, the setting sun making long shadows in front of them. Past the university campus, on to the edge of town. He took it slow, clicking smoothly through the gears, the bike making an easy rumble beneath them. One arm around his waist, the other cradling the large end of the guitar case, the small end under his arm and resting on the handlebars. Her hand sensing the hard muscles of his midsection through the T-shirt. She tried to keep her touch light, but when they made a turn or eased off from a stop, she instinctively tightened her hold.

When they stopped at a traffic light, he asked, "Comfortable? Everything okay?"

"Yes. I'm fine."

"It's all right to hold on tight," he said. "I won't break. I work out. Five-thirty in the morning, six days a week."

"You stay fit, but you're not wearing a helmet."

"A two-wheeled dichotomy."

They were past the edge of town now, a scattering of houses and then pine forest crowding the roadsides. Their route ran alongside the river, flashes of late sun on water through the trees. He sped up, the bike leaning into curves, warm wind whistling at the edges of her helmet. She had a sudden urge to close her eyes, lean her head against his broad back. That wouldn't do, of course, but she felt that if she did, it would somehow be okay.

They rode for twenty minutes. The road curved away from the river, and then the cycle slowed and turned onto dirt and gravel heading back in the direction of the water, the way barely wide enough for two vehicles, pines tall and close on either side. She felt the throb of music before she heard it. And then instruments began to surface out of the throb—guitar, mandolin, fiddle, bass, keyboard.

They rounded a curve, and the road gave way to a gravel parking lot jammed with cars, trucks, motorcycles, a dune buggy, a couple of ATVs.

Mouth-watering smell of barbecue smoldering over hickory, the music coming from somewhere beyond. Pickett eased the motorcycle to a stop at the edge of the lot and held it steady while she climbed off.

"Was it okay? The ride?"

"I think so. I've never ridden a motorcycle before."

"You're kidding. You did great. You were leaning with me."

"What?"

"Into the curves. Some people ride on the back of a bike, they get all stiff, and when you turn, it's like they're fighting it. But you were loose, going with it." He unbuckled her helmet and lifted it carefully off.

She shook her hair loose. "What is this place? There isn't a sign."

"Cicero's."

She felt her eyebrows go up. "Oh."

The scene of legendary no-holds-barred brawls, it was notorious, so much so that the university had some years before declared it officially off-limits to students, who ignored the edict in droves. Anybody sporting a black eye or missing tooth on campus was said to have a Cicero, whether it came from the place or not.

"You've never been here?"

"Not the kind of place for a governor's daughter."

"Or the kind of place Mr. Bannister would frequent."

She tried to imagine Woodrow at Cicero's. Not a chance. If it was officially off-limits, then it was off-limits to Woodrow. He'd never risk it. And then, too, he had that one-beer rule. Cicero's didn't look like a one-beer place.

"I'm hungry," she said. "And thirsty."

He grinned. He seemed to have an endless supply of grins. "I can fix that."

⌒

Cicero's, it turned out, was a good deal tamer than its reputation.

It consisted of a small, unpainted cinder-block building where the cooking was done, and beyond it, stretching out toward the riverbank, a broad expanse of deck, some of it sheltered, mostly open, crammed with picnic tables crowded with people, all of it lit by bare light bulbs strung from towering pines.

She sat at a long table with wives, girlfriends, band members' families. They were friendly and welcoming. They mentioned her father's passing, but nobody made a fuss over her. The band had already started, but before joining the rest of the musicians on the small stage, Pickett brought her a plate of barbecue, hush puppies, baked beans, and coleslaw and the sweetest iced tea she had ever tasted. She ate with relish and then pushed her plate away. Pitchers of beer arrived. She sat back and gave herself to the music.

It was the first time she had really seen him, seen the whole of his person wrapped up in something—the music, the intimate business of man and guitar. And in all the years to come, she could never look at him without picturing him in just this way, wrapped around the guitar, caressing it, easy slide of left hand on the fret board, dancing fingers of the other on the strings, a slight smile softening the angles of his face, all of it of a piece, the easy, graceful essence of him.

The band was all over the map musically—the Eagles, Johnny Cash, Dolly Parton, Tom T. Hall, an intriguing instrumental that *did* sound vaguely like Mozart, only much hipper. The band members—five men and a young woman with a clear, strong alto—took turns with the vocal leads, while the rest added harmonies. Pickett sang James Taylor's "Steamroller Blues." He didn't have a great voice, but it seemed honest, muscular, earthy, and he didn't try to do things with it that didn't fit. When he finished, he looked straight at her and flashed an incredible smile that made her blush and grab for her beer cup. She finished the beer in a gulp, poured another from the pitcher, and decided to let it all slide.

The band played for the better part of two hours. During a couple of short breaks, the musicians crowded in at the table, Pickett at her elbow, the talk loose and easy, the night soft and warm. By the time they finished playing, she was pleasantly tipsy and decidedly mellow, the anguish and stress of the past weeks fading beyond the edge of her consciousness. The others packed up and headed off, leaving Cooper and Pickett at the table. Cicero himself came out and sat with them awhile. He was short and round, a middle-aged, bald fireplug with a big laugh. "Stay as long as you like," he told them. The last of the crowd drifted away, leaving just the two of them on the deck, a faint breeze murmuring in the pines overhead, the river nearby. Pickett got the guitar out of its case and played and sang a couple of things he had written himself—one funny song about a pot-bellied pig, the other a soft, sweet ballad about falling in love in a dream and waking up to find the dream come true.

"They're good," she said when he finished. "Why didn't you sing them with the band?"

"I'm still working on the one about the pig." He strummed a few chords from it. "I keep adding verses. I'm playing with one about how the pig enters the Porker Special Olympics." Then he stopped playing and looked up at her. "The other one I wrote this morning, right after I woke up and knew I was gonna bring you out here this evening."

"Before you even called me. Pretty presumptuous."

"Okay, I'll confess. I wrote it a couple of years ago about a girl I was dating. But it suits you better. In fact, it suits you perfectly."

It hung there in the air between them, and she felt herself blushing. Then, for some reason she couldn't explain, she started to cry. Maybe it was the sweetness of it, the way she felt airy and light and enveloped by something both comforting and startling, something she needed very much. Or maybe it was hearing the word *dream*. *What the hell,* she thought, *maybe it's just the beer.*

"I'm sorry," Pickett said. He reached for her hand, wrapping his big, firm one around hers. "Should I take you home?"

"No," she whispered, "I don't want to go home. I'm all right."

He gave her a minute to compose herself, then started singing again about the pig to make her laugh. He ran a few licks, then put the guitar away and went for another pitcher of beer. She watched him—long legs, easy, graceful stride, maybe an athlete. He walked like a man who was sure of himself. Not in the way Woodrow was, not so especially sure of where he was headed, but entirely comfortable in the place he occupied now. In someone else, it might be swagger.

She blushed again, and this time it wasn't from embarrassment. It was, she realized in a dim, beer-drenched corner of her mind, lust. *My God.*

Sometime later, Cicero called out the door, "I'm leaving. You can stay here all night if you want, but I'm going home."

"What time is it?" she asked.

Pickett peered at his watch. "One forty-five."

"Oh, hell," she said. "I've got to be at work at seven."

"I'm sleeping in." He laughed.

"Asshole."

She was wobbly when they crossed the parking lot to the motor-cycle, wobbly and a little loud, leaning against Pickett. After managing to get both of them aboard, he ordered her to hang on to him like barbed wire.

She remembered little of the ride back to town, only the sensations of the rush of cool wind and of clinging fiercely to him. What she did remember when she awoke the next morning with a wretched head was that Pickett Lanier had kissed her good night, and that it was a damn good kiss. She remembered that well.

He reached her at the newspaper. "Beer after work?"

"No," she said.

He laughed. "One rough night and you've sworn off beer?"

"Please," she said, "don't call." She realized right off how abrupt, how final it sounded. She didn't mean it that way. "For a few days."

"Is there anything I can say, should say?"

"No, there's nothing you can say. I've got to . . ."

"Of course."

She hung up, sat staring at the phone, got up finally and went to her editor to ask for some time off.

She called Fate Wilmer. "Can I fish?"

"Of course," he said.

"Just me. Tomorrow. Quietly."

"I'll have the boat and everything ready. No need to stop at the house, just go on to the pond. Nobody'll bother you." A pause. "Are you all right, Cooper?"

"I'll see after I drown a few crickets. Just . . . let this be between us, okay?"

She was up early, in the car before first light, driving upstate, stopping once for gas, coffee, and donuts. She had slept badly, had been aware all night of being just at the edge of rest, had finally given up an hour before the alarm went off. She was on the water by eight, gliding across the mist-covered pond, the hum of the trolling motor and the easy slap of water against the boat an undercurrent to the awakening of the pond itself—birds, the occasional splash as a fish broke the surface, the chatter of squirrels. She drifted to the far end, anchored twenty yards from the shrub-thick bank, got a line in the water, and sat back to let the morning reveal whatever it might have to offer.

She thought, full-hearted but dry-eyed, about her father, about his need for still, quiet places amid the tumult. She thought about William Faulkner, his speech when he accepted the Nobel Prize for Literature, his words about the secrets of the human heart. She felt she didn't need to be a writer to explore those, and that if she were wise enough to want to know what her heart's secrets were, she also had to be wise enough to shut up and listen. And she couldn't do that in the midst of the boiler factory that was life lived by the day. She needed the time and space to shut that out, to hear the undercurrents and subtexts, the deep places where those secrets lived and might, if she were gently patient, reveal themselves. She needed her pond, figuratively and literally. Everybody needed a pond.

In this quiet, still space was the question that had lingered since Cleve's passing, that had brought her here now: Could she carve out and jealously guard these quiet, still places in the midst of the boiler factory that was political life? Cleve had managed it, but at the end he had spoken of being the sum of his regrets. Cooper didn't delude herself about the matter of regrets. A life with any substance to it was bound to accumulate a peddler's sack full of them. Even at twenty-two, she could look back on things that made her cringe with embarrassment and weep with grief. But would she be the sum of her regrets? *No, I will not let that happen.*

And back to the question, which at its core amounted to Woodrow. She couldn't escape the image from the church just after the funeral service, Woodrow reaching, smiling, politicking. He was a good man, honest about who he was and where he was going. She believed he loved her for herself. He would be successful in politics, and if she chose to strike out on that path with him, she would be an asset to his career, might even have some opportunities through his public life to do good things.

But then there was Pickett Lanier—not so much his person, attractive as it was, but the fact of his *otherness.* He was *not* Woodrow. What he seemed to represent to her just now was a life alternative. In the stillness of the morning, her mind swirled with the insistence of it all.

She was snapped from her reverie by a violent jerk that nearly tore her fishing pole from her hands. She caught it at the last moment, gripped it, hauled back on it, setting the hook, giving herself completely to fighting what she realized was the biggest fish she had ever encountered. A largemouth, she suspected, an ancient and daunting fish with all the wiles that had kept it for a great long time out of frying pans.

Cooper flung herself sideways, one leg over the seat, straddling it now. She reared back with a foot braced against one gunwale, her back against the opposite side, mind racing through all her fishing knowledge. Then she could hear Cleve: *Give him some room, but not too much.*

The fish broke the surface with a fabulous shake of its body, flinging head and tail in opposite directions, trying to shake the hook. *My God, it's huge!* Five, six pounds at least, a magnificent specimen. She leaned forward, gave the line a bit of slack so the fish couldn't strain against it, either bending the hook or ripping it loose from its cavernous mouth. And then it fell back into the water and swam directly for the boat, the line going loose in the water. She knew instantly what it was up to—swim under the boat so she lost control of the tension on the line, or tangle it in the propeller and snap it. She stood and almost lost her balance, hauled back hard on the pole, which bent violently as she fought to keep the fish out in front of her, away from the boat.

The fish was powerful and cunning, but Cooper had the advantage of a strong line, a supple pole, and a gathering feeling of exhilaration and abandon. She had no idea where it came from, that absolute conviction she would see this through.

And suddenly, it was over. There was no sense of the fish gradually beginning to tire, but instead a moment when it seemed simply to surrender. She waited, suspecting it might be a trick to lull her, then began to cautiously pull it in, lifting the pole to shorten the line and then reaching for it. The fish seemed almost docile now, breaking the water with its broad, beautiful back, a gentle swish of its fins and tail. When it was next to the boat, she gave it a long, admiring look, noticing for the first time an odd, thin streak of white along one side of the dorsal fin. Then she hooked a hand in one of its gills and took a moment to collect herself. Holding the fish, she reached for the tackle box, opened it, found the pliers with the sharp edges, and bent to snap off the barbed end of the hook and pull the rest of it free from the fish's mouth. She turned it loose. The fish floated near the surface for a moment and then, sensing freedom, gave a flip of its tail and dove away.

She opened the cooler, cracked a beer, drank it in slow, easy sips. Heat was on the morning now, the air close and sodden and alive with the buzz of insects.

She laughed, thinking how easy it would be to read too much into this. If this morning were a piece of fiction, it would be tempting to make the fish a profound, life-altering, Hemingwayesque symbol. But what the hell, it was just a big, old fish that had lived in this quiet place for God only knew how many years and would likely live here many more. If the fish had done anything for her, it was to jerk her out of the wallowing she had done in her mind and soul and remind her to get on with things, to face squarely what she had been looking at obliquely for a long time. At last, she knew.

She drove straight to the capital airport and then flew to Arkansas to find Woodrow, to tell him she could not share his life.

THIRTEEN

The call came before seven, as she was getting ready for work. She let the phone ring several times before she picked up.

"I talked to Woodrow last night." Mickey's voice was calm and even. Cooper waited. "He's heartbroken, I'm sure you know that."

Woodrow had pleaded and cried, begged her not to be so final about it. He asked her to wait, give it time, don't close the door. But for all the pleading, he had never for a moment offered to give up what separated them. He couldn't, she knew that. And neither could she. Their choices were irreconcilable.

"I don't have to tell you that Woodrow's deeply in love with you."

"I know that, Mother."

"Then surely you can work things out."

"We have nothing to work out," Cooper said. "I didn't rush into this. I've thought about it a long time."

"We've both been through a lot lately. Changes in our lives. Losing your father . . . Did that have something to do with it?"

"Maybe it brought things to a head."

Mickey was silent for a moment. "Cleve did things with his eyes wide open. He didn't try to fool himself or anybody else."

"I know. I had a hard time understanding that, coming to some kind of peace with it," Cooper said. "But I did, and it led me to the conclusion about Woodrow and me. My eyes are wide open, Mother."

"Woodrow will go a long way," Mickey said evenly. "Maybe all the way. He has the gift."

"And I can't go with him. I know that's what you'd like."

"What I like doesn't matter."

"Doesn't it? Didn't you and Woodrow have a plan, for him and for me?" Cooper felt an edge creeping into her voice.

"All right," Mickey said. "I hoped you would be with him. He needs you."

"But that's not what I need."

Mickey's voice rose a notch. "And what do you need, Cooper?"

"To be myself. To be what *I* want to be, not part of somebody else's plan, somebody else's appendage. I tried to make Woodrow see that, and maybe in a way he does. And I need you to see it, too."

"Be yourself?" Mickey snapped. "A stupid little newspaper reporter?"

Okay, here it is. She's done with being Mrs. Nice.

"Well, if that's what I am, a stupid little newspaper reporter, it's because it's what I chose. If I make a go of it, or if I totally screw it up, it's still nobody's but mine."

"You're stubborn and willful. Always have been."

"How the hell would you know, Mother? You never paid any attention."

In the long silence, Cooper thought Mickey might hang up. Instead, when she finally spoke, her voice was a hiss. "I know what you're up to, Cooper. It's underhanded and deceitful."

"What are you talking about?"

"Sneaking around behind Woodrow's back with some two-bit college professor."

Cooper was stunned. *How did . . . ?* No sense in asking. Mickey Spainhour had tentacles everywhere.

Feeling herself being shoved, she pushed back. "Mother," she said calmly, "I appreciate your concern, but frankly it's none of your goddamn business. It's my life."

"And you can goddamn well live it without me!" A crash on the other end as Mickey slammed the receiver, missed the cradle, then again, and finally a click as the connection broke.

Cooper set the phone down, put her trembling hands in her lap, breathed deeply, fought back against rage, tried to calm herself. She felt overwhelmed by the old weariness, the ancient disappointment. They had gotten along so well in the days of Cleve's dying. But now it seemed all smoke and mirrors. Mickey either got what she wanted or made people suffer. *But I'm through with that. I have to be, for my own sanity.*

She rose, drank another cup of coffee, ate cereal, finished dressing, put on makeup—shutting away Mickey and Woodrow and Pickett Lanier—and went to work.

It came on her in a rush, the great feeling of freedom. Everything seemed lively and quick and filled with possibility. If it was all a mistake, it was a mistake she had made on purpose, and she was willing to take that chance.

She kept Pickett at arm's length. He called, at first to ask her out and then, when she made it clear she needed time and space, just to chat. "Look," he said, "I understand." He didn't press. He was easy to talk to, seemed genuinely interested in her work, the day-to-dayness of her life. At odd times, often late at night, he would call, and when she answered, he would put the phone down next to him and play his guitar and sing, maybe something he had been working on. And when the song was finished, he would simply hang up.

She found a note thumbtacked to her apartment door one evening: "Off to Washington to finish dissertation research, back in August. Have a good summer. Pickett."

She immersed herself in her work. The editor assigned her to cover the Police Department and Sheriff's Office—a promotion with a bit more money and a lot more responsibility. She had a scanner on her desk, and the editor had another installed in her car. She spent hours chasing their traffic, even the most mundane calls, sometimes late into the night—every incident an opportunity to be around officers, get to know them, watch and listen and learn who they were and how and why and what they did. A few were gruff and dismissive with her, but she passed it off to testosterone and kept working until even the most hard-bitten seemed to grant her grudging acceptance. She welcomed exhaustion, slept soundly, and healed.

And then there he was on an August evening, sitting on the front stoop of her apartment building, legs stretched across the sidewalk, hair even longer, spilling over the collar of his T-shirt, guitar nestled against his torso, fingers drifting idly across the strings, coaxing notes and chords. He looked up, squinted at her, and then his face broke into a dazzling smile. He put the guitar aside, stood, reached out to her. "I'm crazy about you. I'm *going* crazy about you. If you don't let me into your life, I shall surely die."

⌒

She did let him in, fell headlong into him, both frightened and exhilarated by the intensity of it. She was stunned by the way he focused such white heat on her, making her giddy and weak.

They made love—laughing, crying, breathless.

"Marry me?" he asked after a bit.

"No," she said, "not now."

Instead, she went to live with him in the woods.

It had started in the distant past as a two-room log cabin and been expanded over the years with frame additions until it sprawled untidily across a clearing on a low rise, lofty pines and old hardwoods pressing in comfortably on three sides. A sagging, weathered shed in the back, a garden plot, and stretching beyond that an unbroken view across pastures, cultivated fields, groves of trees, a meandering creek, all the way to the university town several miles away. It was close enough to be convenient, distant enough to be refuge.

They lived together in the woods for three unbroken months while summer eased into fall and cooling breezes flowed through the open doors and windows. Then the leaves turned and the grass browned and there was frost. They gathered in the last of the garden. She listened to the sound of Pickett splitting wood behind the shed. They spent long evenings making love before a crackling fire and huddling in a blanket. She felt safe, protected, cherished. It was all she had ever wanted.

They had their work, Pickett with his classes and then in the evening at a clattering electric typewriter with his reams of notes, finishing his dissertation, Cooper at the newspaper, prevailing on the editor to let her give up the police beat and take on city hall, something less intense and time-consuming.

She thought of Woodrow only in rare moments. Gone now, dropped out of graduate school. She heard he had taken a job in a congressman's local office at the other end of the state. Woodrow had loved her, but not in this way, not so completely. Pickett had no other mistress.

⌒

"Guess who showed up at my office today," Pickett said. He was at the table with his typewriter and notes when she came in from town in the late afternoon.

She sensed it immediately, something strangely guarded about him. "Who?"

"Your mother."

She felt a stiff blow to her stomach, a rush of the old poison. She stared at him, then turned away and walked in a daze through the back door. He caught her at the edge of the garden plot, now ugly and weed-clotted. He touched her. She turned away, shivering in the cold.

"Why can't she just leave me alone?"

"Could it be that she cares about you?"

"If she does, she has a history of bizarre ways of showing it."

"Well, listen to what she said. She told me if I hurt you in any way, she will—and I'm quoting verbatim—'cut my nuts out.' She told me to do the decent thing and marry you and make you happy."

Cooper could only stare, speechless.

"We've got to talk about you and her, and us," he said. She let him take her arm and lead her back into the house.

They talked long into the night. She told him everything—the hurt, the anger, the loneliness, Jesse. He listened and then held her. She nestled in his arms, exhausted from unburdening herself but eased by the effort, by his being there and listening and caring. She drifted into profound sleep and awoke at first light, cuddled with him on the floor in front of the fireplace.

He kissed her forehead. "Okay?"

She nodded.

"Marry me," he said.

"Yes."

PART THREE

FOURTEEN

The clock said 4:17. She had dozed fitfully but never got soundly to sleep. She parted the curtains at the bedside window and looked out. The snowfall had eased, random flakes drifting through pools of light. What had been sidewalk and street were now a solid blanket of white, broken only by the tall wrought-iron fence.

All night, and not a peep from the command center. Should she wait? Call? She seethed, let the anger boil up again. *All of them sitting over there at the Public Safety Building feeling smug, Pickett's Posse still running the show, Pickett pushing buttons all the way from New Hampshire.*

She called. A young man answered.

"This is the governor. Let me speak to Roger Tankersley."

"Mr. Tankersley went home just awhile ago, ma'am. Said he'd be back shortly."

"Colonel Doster, then."

"He's, ah, resting."

"Well, wake him up!"

"Yes, ma'am."

After a minute, he came thick-voiced on the line: "Miz Lanier . . ."

"What's going on, Colonel?"

"Well," he drawled, "we don't really know yet. It's still dark."

"All right, Colonel. Go back to sleep."

"I'll call just as soon as we—"

She hung up on him, sat a minute longer, then pulled on a robe and slippers and started down the hall toward the stairs. A sliver of light under the door to Mickey's room. She cracked the door and peeked in. Mickey was sitting up in bed holding a newspaper, reading glasses perched on her nose, cigarette smoldering in an ashtray on the bedside table.

Mickey looked up and rattled the paper. "This damn thing is three days old. Send somebody out for today's." She looked shrunken, engulfed in a sea of pillows and bedclothes, but her voice was strong, some of the old bite there.

The air reeked. "Mother where did you get the cigarettes?"

"I sent a trooper out for 'em," Mickey said, "before the snow got bad." She laid the newspaper on the covers, took off her glasses, reached for the cigarette, fingers trembling as she guided it to her lips, took a long drag, stubbed it out. "What the hell's going on?"

Any other time, Cooper would have turned on her heel and marched out. None of Mickey Spainhour's damn business. But now, she had this acute feeling of impotence, and nobody to tell. "I don't know," she said.

"Snowed like a sonofabitch last night, didn't it?"

"From the look of things, yes."

"And . . ."

"I called out the National Guard, or tried to. Pickett stopped it."

Mickey gave a low grunt and chewed on the information for a moment. "Stopped it?"

"He made it clear that I could issue all the orders I wanted, but it was not going to happen, not last night."

Mickey peered intently over the top of her glasses. "He can't legally do that."

"Maybe not, but he did it anyway."

Mickey pursed her lips, knotted her brow, let out a breath. "I knew this would happen. Pickett's a control freak. No way will he let you run things. There are a thousand ways he and his bunch can undercut you, and you damn well better believe they'll do it. When he agreed to let you run, what was the deal you struck?"

"I said I'd try to hold down the home base and do what I could to help him run for president. He needed me to do that, and I needed him to bring it off."

Mickey shook her head. "Did you have any idea this is what would happen?"

"I should have. But after the campaign was over, he was out barnstorming the country and we never talked much about how I'd actually do the job. I'm surrounded by his people—Roger Tankersley, the cabinet."

Mickey sighed. "You made a deal with the devil, Cooper. It was your idea to run, and he backed you, and now he assumes you'll be a good little girl and let him stay in charge. Do you feel an obligation to go along?"

"I don't know."

"Well, *I* know. You're the one with the job, and you have to decide whether to shit or get off the pot. But you'd better decide right now. Let Pickett get away with this and you'll never have much say. He'll make sure of that. Right now, you've got the snow."

"Pickett made a mistake when he interfered last night," Cooper said.

"But you're the one who'll get the blame for the mess, unless you clean it up."

"But how? They're practically holding me hostage."

"Get help. Wheeler Kincaid."

Cooper's eyebrows shot up. "What do you know about Wheeler Kincaid?"

"I know he quit the paper and wants to go to work for you."

"My God."

"Wheeler and I go way back," Mickey said. "We stay in touch."

"So you know *why* he quit the paper."

"Yes, and I don't want Felicia Withers to win either. The bitch. If you'll let him, Wheeler can help. He's a friggin' pain in the ass, but he knows things. If you take him up on it, it sends a signal, and it will chap Pickett and his Posse's collective asses." She paused. "And then there's me."

Cooper laughed. "Now, after all this time?"

"I can't change the past, Cooper, but right now, I want to help. I've spent a lifetime learning things." She tapped her head. "I have a lot of stuff up here."

Cooper's voice dripped with sarcasm. "You'll ride to the rescue."

"I ain't doing much riding these days, but I can help you. Why the hell do you think I got my dying ass down here to the capital two days ago? And why did I get myself toted over here last evening?"

"So you can guide poor, dumb little me through the woods?"

Mickey spoke slowly. "You'd better get help from somebody, because it appears you're flat on your ass and don't have a clue how to get vertical."

She felt a flush of anger. "Goddammit, Mother . . ."

Mickey dismissed her with a wave of her hand. "Cooper, go get me some coffee. Can you at least do that?"

Cooper stalked out, slammed the door behind her, descended the stairs. She paced from room to room, cursing and flipping on lights until the entire downstairs was ablaze. She ended in the kitchen, got the coffee maker going. She sat on a stool at the center island, fingers drumming on maple, heart pounding. *A deal with the devil? Yes, and I'm trapped.*

She felt utterly isolated here in this ancient, sagging place—isolated by the storm, but even more by what was going on outside, beyond her control. *They have shut me away like a deranged old relative in an attic.*

The coffee maker rattled and hissed. She fetched a mug from a cabinet, poured a cup, sipped it black and bitter, trying to settle herself, feeling the weight of the long-neglected house around her. Then she thought, *She's right, I'm flat on my ass. About that, she's damn right.*

She poured another mug and headed back upstairs.

"All right," she said, "talk to me."

Mickey didn't say anything for a while. She finally set her mug on the bedside table. "Did you mean it when you stood up there two days ago and said, 'Now, we begin'?"

"I meant every word of it."

"Regardless of what Pickett thinks?"

She hesitated. "Yes."

"Then begin. If you don't fight, you'll just let them have it, and they didn't earn it. You did."

"How?"

"First, find out as much as you can about what's going on. Don't fly blind. That's when you crash into something. That guy out there in California, Unruh, said, 'Money is the mother's milk of politics.' Bullshit. It's information. Intelligence."

"This isn't politics, Mother."

"Goddamn right it is. It's all politics. What the hell do you think politics is, running and winning? That's the sideshow. The real deal is getting things done. It's *how* things get done."

"But I *am* flying blind. The Posse—"

"Fly over 'em."

Cooper thought about it, and as she did, she felt something rock-hard stubborn begin to replace her impotent anger. "All right," she said.

Cooper turned to the door. When her hand was on the knob, Mickey said, "One other thing: While you're sorting things out, think about your father."

And she did. She pictured him in the room down the hall in his command post during the big snow all those years ago, moving about in his droopy, threadbare sweater as people came and went. Listening, absorbing, deciding—he had seemed so incredibly calm and sure of himself. Things had been a mess, but he got them all through it.

"You've got the pedigree," Mickey said. "Use it."

She called the number Ezra Barclay had scribbled on the back of his card.

"I'll get there as quick as I can," he said. "It's pretty bad out."

"Pick up a couple of folks on the way. Grace and . . ." She considered for a moment, then said, "Wheeler Kincaid. Do you know where he lives?"

There was the slightest pause on the other end. "I can find it."

By the time she showered and dressed, they were there, Ezra's Humvee rumbling through the gate and up the driveway, parking under the porte-cochere. They bustled in, shaking snow from their hair and coats. Ezra and Grace looked fit and bright-eyed, faces full of questions. Kincaid looked a wreck, bloodhound bags under bloodshot eyes, ancient, shapeless brown sports coat, frayed shirt, food-stained tie, rumpled pants. But he was clean-shaven and held himself erect, ignoring the wary looks from Ezra and Grace.

First, they cleared out a room on the ground floor that had been Pickett's office, grabbing up stacks of papers, files, books, junk, piling everything on the floor outside.

When it was done, she said, hands on hips, "I've got to know what we're up against out there."

"Governor," Ezra said, "would you like to go to the command center at Public Safety? They've got good communications."

"For now," she said, "we'll work from here. Ezra, start calling around—trooper posts, local police, anybody you can think of. Grace, help Ezra and see what you can find out from the media." She glanced at the clock. Five-thirty. "Thirty minutes. Paint me a picture." Grace and Ezra nodded. "Grace, call the prison and get Mrs. Dinkins and her crew over here as soon as it's safe to travel. Tell them not to use the van. Ezra will arrange transportation. Mr. Kincaid, come with me."

He followed her to the kitchen. She poured him a cup of coffee, and he took it with unsteady hands. Beads of sweat glistened on his forehead.

"How old are you, Mr. Kincaid?"

"Seventy."

"Have you thought about quietly retiring? Writing your memoirs? It would make quite a read."

His mouth twisted. "If I, as you say, quietly retired, I'd croak."

"What you said last night, some people would consider it ludicrous."

He nodded. "Some people."

"I've already got a press secretary. I'm comfortable with Rick. What do you think you could do for me?"

"Anything you want. Tell you where the bodies are buried."

"You've got a map?"

He tapped the side of his head. "In here."

"Can you protect me from Felicia Withers?"

"No," he said, "I can't do that."

She turned away to look out the kitchen window at the backyard, bathed in security light. The snow had stopped now. When she turned back, Kincaid was looking at her intently. "For now, help Ezra and Grace. You know a lot of people. Start calling."

Kincaid didn't move. "They've put you on ice, haven't they?"

She didn't respond.

"It doesn't take a genius to see what's going on." He jerked his head in the general direction of the Capitol. "The idiot assholes down there at the *command center*"—he spat the words—"are beginning to figure out they've got a cluster fuck on their hands, and you're sitting here being spoon-fed from a bucket of pure horseshit."

"You sure do have a foul mouth, Mr. Kincaid."

"When I say something, people understand me." A moment, then: "Where's the National Guard? I didn't see a friggin' one of 'em on my way over here."

Moment of truth. She either trusted him or she didn't.

"I was inclined to call out the Guard last night, but I was . . . persuaded otherwise. No, that's not right. I was countermanded."

He started to say something but stopped himself, brow furrowed, mouth twitching. He nodded slowly. "I see." He took a swig of coffee, set the cup on the counter, and thrust his hands deep in the pockets of the shapeless jacket. "You've got a big, nasty crisis. You need every resource you can get your hands on. It's bad, and it's going to get worse."

"How much worse?"

"People could die. May already have."

Her stomach turned, but she kept silent.

"This, right now, it's not about somebody's decision last night. It's about whether you're up to doing the job."

"Mr. Kincaid, I'm going to do my damnedest to do the job. As for whether I'm up to it, we'll find out today. People out there who need help can't afford for me to be irrelevant."

"I have to believe you," he said. "I think you've got a chance to be different from all the others."

"I hope so. Now, advise me."

"Lead," he said without hesitation. "Figure out who the good people are. I can help you do that. Take advantage of what they know, filter their advice through your built-in bullshit detector. Then tell them what you want, what you expect. Let 'em help you. You've got good instincts, so trust them. Don't worry about all the other crap."

"Such as?"

"Pickett," he said flatly. "I don't know what's going on between you two, but I do know this: The snow's an opportunity. Go downtown and take charge and kick some ass. They'll hear the thud all the way to New Hampshire."

"That's pretty much what my mother said to me this morning."

"I know. Listen to Mickey. She knows more than the rest of us put together."

⁓

By six o'clock, as the first glimmerings of daylight reached the edge of the trees across the side yard of the mansion, they knew: The state was a mess. It had snowed hard all night, a storm that had fooled the forecasters with its ferocity. It was an uneven blanketing. The southernmost counties had gotten as little as four inches. A good bit of the upstate was buried under eighteen. Here in the capital, a foot. Everything was paralyzed—roads impassable, power lines down, motorists stranded, law-enforcement agencies at a standstill. Cooper hunched over a legal pad, jotting notes as the others relayed what they were learning. Media outlets, their people just as snowbound as everybody else, weren't much help. As the details added up, she felt a growing sense of the magnitude of things—not just the storm, but the larger business of what it meant to be responsible in a situation like this. Pickett and his bunch might think they were still in charge, but this was bigger than any of them— whispering instructions into their cell phones—imagined. She flipped through the legal pad—five pages of catastrophe.

"What about the National Guard?" she asked.

"A handful of units here and there on standby," Ezra said, "but mostly sitting at home, in the same shape as everybody else."

"Stranded," she said.

"Useless."

One of the telephones rang. Grace answered, then held out the receiver to Cooper. "Colonel Doster."

Ezra rose. "We'll just—"

"No," Cooper said. "Grace, let's all hear this."

Grace put the phone on speaker.

"Mornin', Miz Lanier. Just wanted to bring you up to speed here, let you know how things are going."

She felt the others' eyes on her. "I've been waiting."

"Got reports coming in now. Lots of snow, up to our keisters in places. Problems here and there with roads and power."

"Here and there."

"Yes, ma'am."

"And what are you doing about it?"

"We've got the emergency plan in full operation."

"I'm glad to hear that. Could you give me some details?"

"Mobilizing everything. Mobilizing all our resources."

"The National Guard?"

"Well," he said, "not just yet."

"Why not?"

"We, ah, don't have the authorization for that. Not just yet."

"All right, Colonel Doster. Is Roger there?"

"Should be back anytime now, I'd say. Just went home to clean up and get a change of clothes."

"Well, thank you so much for your report."

"We'll keep you up to speed, Miz Lanier. Not to worry, everything's moving right along. Anything you need there at the mansion, you just let us know."

"I'm most grateful," she said, and nodded to Grace, who jabbed a finger to cut off the call.

Grace's eyes snapped. "*Miz Lanier.* That asshole!" She caught herself, mortified. "Sorry."

Cooper smiled. "That's exactly what I thought."

～

She called Roger's cell phone. Still at home. The SUV that had brought him was slued sideways in his driveway, jammed against a bank of snow. Two state troopers were digging it out.

"All right, Roger," she said. "Get there when you can. But tell me what you know."

"It's, ah, well, I haven't been there for a couple of hours, but I think the situation's all right."

"I just talked to Colonel Doster, and frankly, Roger, it appears to me that the expert staff at the command center doesn't know what's going on, or if they do, they have their thumbs up their butts."

She heard Roger suck in a long breath.

"When you get there," she said, "size things up and call me with the absolute unvarnished truth. Understand?"

He paused, then clipped his words briskly: "Yes, Cooper. I understand."

"It's *Governor*."

～

Atlanta, too, had snow. She called Allison's cell phone. Several rings, then finally voice mail: "This is Allison. Try me again sometime."

Cooper dialed again. Again, voice mail.

"Allison, call me. Let me know you're all right."

She waited. Nothing. She called again. This time, after several rings, Allison answered.

"Are you okay?"

"No, I'm not okay."

"Where are you?"

"In my apartment. I'm snowed in. Thank God, I'm snowed in."

"What's wrong?"

"Don't worry about me."

"Of course I worry about you. Now, what's going on, honey?"

"I'm being quiet, trying to keep my head down, trying to be halfway normal, hoping nobody knows who I am, and now my picture is all over the TV and newspaper."

"What?"

"Your inauguration, remember? Now, everybody knows. I've got"—her voice quavered—"reporters calling me. How they got my cell-phone number, I don't know. But they want to interview me, Mom. They want to ask me questions about Dad, and you, and me. They want to write about me, take pictures, put me on display, and ruin it all."

"Honey, I'm sorry."

"I hate it, Mom. I just hate it."

"I know."

"No, you don't."

"Yes," she insisted, "I do. I've been there. Now listen, don't answer the phone unless it's a caller you recognize and want to talk to. Because of the snow, people are going to be busy with other things. Just stay where you are, take a deep breath, be quiet. I'm going to arrange another phone for you, something with a secure number. And once we get past the next couple of days, we'll talk about what we can do to take the pressure off. I'm sure the school will help. We can't shut out the world entirely, but we'll try to make things easier. I'll do my best."

After a long silence, Allison's small voice: "Okay." Then: "Are you all right, Mom?"

"I've got my ass hanging off a limb, and some folks with chain saws are circling the tree. But some others are bringing a ladder."

"What?"

"I'm okay. Just take care of yourself. I'll call you later. I love you, Allison."

She hesitated, then: "Me, too."

⁓

Six-thirty. Roger called, and this time he didn't sugarcoat anything: The command center was a chaotic mess, fingers pointing, people squabbling over who was in charge, nothing much getting done. General Burgaw, the head of the National Guard, was hamstrung because he had no authority to act and was in a high state of outrage because of it. Colonel Doster was trying to send his troopers galloping off in all directions, without success, because most of their vehicles were useless in the snow. Calls were pouring in from local officials screaming for help and getting excuses.

When he was finished, she said, "You're a good man, Roger, and I'm going to see that you get rewarded for your work."

She called Pickett's cell phone. Plato answered. "Give the phone to Pickett," she said.

In a minute or so, Pickett came on, voice scratchy and full of irritation. "What's the matter?"

"Have you talked to Roger or Colonel Doster?"

"For God's sake, do you know what time it is? I've had about three hours of sleep. And I'm catching a cold."

"So," she said, "you don't know what's going on down here."

"What do you mean?"

"A cluster fuck."

"A *what?*"

"We've got a catastrophe, Pickett, and you screwed up."

His voice rose an octave. "Cooper, what in the hell are you talking about?"

She told him. He listened without interrupting.

When she finished, he didn't say anything for a long time. Then: "God*damn*."

She could imagine what it must be like for him there in the dark cold of a South Carolina morning, on the edge of exhaustion, loathing nasty surprises as he did, feeling the ground shifting under him. She could imagine, but she damn sure didn't sympathize.

"You said last night Doster was the only one who knew about the National Guard business," she said. "In hindsight, it was a big, whopping mistake, not calling out the Guard, getting everybody in place."

"Goddammit," he rasped, "don't fuss at me, Cooper. I don't need that shit at six-thirty—"

"The kind of mistake a brand-new, wet-behind-the-ears governor would make."

It took him a moment. "What?"

"If Pickett Lanier were on the job, he'd never mess up like that. But it's not Pickett, it's his wife, who's going through on-the-job training." She let him absorb that and went on. "So his wife, the trainee, is willing to throw herself on her sword, admit her mistake, take the heat."

"It won't work," he said. "I'll catch shit anyway."

"Maybe, but here's the other part, Pickett. Felicia Withers is saying you pulled off the biggest scam in the state's history and got your wife elected governor, but she's nothing but a stand-in, and you're still pulling the strings. If that's true, you *are* responsible, it *is* your screwup. But if I take the heat, say that I blew this all by myself, that says Felicia got it wrong. It gives you deniability. 'Look, folks, she's on her own. I'm just out here trying to be president.'" She could almost hear his brain humming, digesting and spitting out political ones and zeroes. She bore in on him. "You better damn well hope it works, Pickett. You better hope I can cover for you on this, because if I can't, you might as well come home and take up gardening."

"Can I call you back?"

"I'll give you five minutes."

He was back in four, voice even raspier, but calm now. And hopeful. "I'll get Plato to call Doster and Burgaw."

"But that's not all."

A long, deadly pause. "What else?"

"I'm not just bailing your ass out, Pickett, I'm horse-trading. I take the heat, you get your hands off the steering wheel. Back off and take the Posse with you."

"Goddamn, are you crazy? There's too much at stake. You can't handle it. You have no idea what you're doing. You'll fuck it up, and that'll fuck me up."

"Or," she said, "we can kick it up another notch. If we were to have a public pissing match about whether I'm going to do the job ..."

"You wouldn't do that," he croaked. "You wouldn't."

"Try me, if you want to take the risk."

His voice rose a plaintive octave. "Why are you doing this to me? Why are you being bull-headed and unreasonable? We have a deal, Cooper. You understood from the get-go."

"I understood I would help you run for president. I wouldn't say anything controversial or do anything that would hurt your chances. I didn't say I'd let you and the Posse micromanage by long distance. *You'll* fuck it up. As you did last night. So I'm keeping my end of the bargain. I'm helping you. Look, Pickett, I don't kid myself, you know a lot that I don't. I'm willing to listen and learn and take advice. But I won't let you humiliate me."

In the long, empty space that followed, she knew she had won, at least for the moment. Pickett never, ever played his whole hand. He had an exquisite knack for knowing when to cut his losses, put the best face on things, save something for the next round.

"Yes," he said wearily. "Goddamn. All right."

"Good. Now, you and Plato get the word out, and then tell Plato to call and give me your collective wisdom on what I might do about this mess we're dealing with." She started to hang up but then decided she had something else she needed to say. "Pickett, you lied. You thought you could finesse me just like you do so many other people. But did you give the least thought to what might happen when I finally figured it out?"

A long silence, then: "Goddammit, I told her this wouldn't work."

I told her . . . She knew instantly and exactly what he was talking about.

"Where will you be tomorrow?"

"Des Moines," he said.

"Good airport in Des Moines?"

"Well, yeah."

"Roger will be flying to Des Moines tomorrow to join your campaign."

"Cooper—"

"I have a new chief of staff."

"What? Who?"

"Wheeler Kincaid."

FIFTEEN

She called Purvis Redmond, the Governor's Office legal advisor. He reported that he was huddled in the cold and dark of his home, swaddled in blankets.

"That's okay," she said. "What I need, you can give me by phone—an order mobilizing the National Guard."

In the long silence, she thought she could hear him squirming. "Nervous Purvis," Pickett's Posse called him. That was one reason he had been left behind when they galloped off to save the world.

"I thought . . ."

"Purvis," she said calmly, "you can either help me do my job, or I can find somebody who will. Are we clear on that?"

He hung fire for a moment. "All right."

"As my legal advisor, tell me if I have sole authority to mobilize the National Guard."

"You do."

"Fine. Now, tell me how."

"It's pretty simple. Do you have somebody who can take it down?"

"I have pen and paper," she said.

When she had it, she called the command center and asked for General Burgaw, the adjutant general, head of the National Guard. "General, I have in my hand the authorization for you and your folks to get moving. You are all now officially on duty."

"About goddamn time," he barked.

"I agree."

"This other bunch here has their thumbs up their asses and their vehicles in the ditch. If you hadn't called, I was about to put my people to work and damn the consequences, because we've got to—"

"Shit or get off the pot."

"Yes, ma'am, that's the honest truth."

"So you can tell that other bunch that you and I have had a meeting of the minds, and that you are mobilized."

"Thank you, Governor."

Cooper tapped on the door and eased it open. Mickey's eyes were closed.

"Mother . . ."

"So?"

Cooper told her the basics—the storm, the Guard, Wheeler.

Mickey nodded. "You've talked to Pickett?"

"Yes, I have, and we struck a deal. Pickett really screwed up last night, and right now, his ass is in a sling. I'm going to try to get him out."

"And what did you get?"

"He'll stay out of my way."

Mickey opened her eyes now. "You believe him?"

"For now, he has no choice."

A slow smile spread across Mickey's face. "Well, good for you. So don't stand there scratching your ass, go to work."

Cooper didn't move. "Pickett said something just now. He said, 'I told her this wouldn't work.' Want to tell me what he meant by that?"

Mickey made a face, stared at the ceiling, then looked back. "Go tend to business. Then we'll talk."

~

They piled into Ezra's Humvee—Cooper, Wheeler, and Grace. They picked up Rick at his apartment.

"Here's the deal," she said. "Grace, you are now my executive secretary. You run the office. Mr. Tankersley is joining the presidential campaign, so Mr. Kincaid will be my chief of staff. There's a lot I don't know, so help me. Don't tell me what you think I want to hear, tell me what I need to know. Ezra, that includes you. We'll mess up some, but that's okay as long as we're trying our best. Especially today. Right now, we're going to the command center at Public Safety."

"Do the folks at the command center know that?" Ezra asked.

"No," Cooper said, "we'll make it a surprise."

As the Humvee crept through the capital streets, Cooper got her first look at what the snow had done. It was chillingly quiet, nothing moving, not a soul in sight. Most of the street lamps and traffic lights were dark. Abandoned vehicles clogged the streets. The metal awning of a storefront had collapsed under the weight of snow. Power lines down, broken limbs everywhere, a city trapped in crushing whiteness.

It took almost thirty minutes, easing around obstacles and taking detours, but they finally reached the Public Safety Department, a hulking five-story building, narrow, tinted windows chiseled into granite, looking warily beetle-browed across the Capitol complex. Like the

Capitol, it had an underground garage with an entrance at the rear. As the Humvee approached, Cooper was surprised to see two young officers standing guard. Bundled in camouflage parkas, cradling automatic weapons, they looked pinch-faced and thoroughly miserable.

"What's this about?"

"Trooper cadets," Ezra said. "Two of 'em there twenty-four hours a day."

"Why?"

"Part of their training. After September eleventh, Homeland Security said law-enforcement facilities should tighten things up, so Colonel Doster turned the place into a fortress. Besides the two kids here on the sidewalk, there's a couple more on the roof with a fifty-caliber machine gun and a grenade launcher. Everybody inside packs a sidearm, and there are weapon stashes throughout the building."

Cooper turned to Wheeler. "Did you know that?"

"Not the machine gun and the grenade launcher."

As the Humvee turned into the entryway, one of the cadets stepped in front, blocking the way, while the other approached the driver's side.

Ezra lowered the window. "Governor Lanier," he said.

The cadet pulled a walkie-talkie from a parka pocket.

"Put that away," Ezra said, his voice steely. "I told you, it's the governor. Now, step aside and maintain radio silence. That's an order."

The cadet backpedaled, waving to his partner to get out of the way. Ezra stomped on the gas, and the Humvee roared past into the garage.

⌇

They crowded into an elevator, Ezra punched in a code on the keypad, and they descended with a lurch.

"Down?" Cooper asked.

Ezra arched his eyebrows. "Wait 'til you see this place."

The doors opened to a cavernous room filled with consoles and electronic gear, one wall taken by a huge, blinking map of the state. "Mission control," Ezra said. The only thing missing was people. Troopers clustered around a television set in a far corner, a couple of military types at the big map. Otherwise, the room was empty. Intermittent crackle from radios, the insistent beeping of a telephone, the mutter of a local weathercaster from the television.

One of the troopers looked up, did a double take, and scurried toward the elevator. He wore gold leaves on his lapels and a look on his face that told Cooper she was the last person on earth he expected to see. "How the hell did you people get in here?" he blurted.

"Hey," Ezra barked, "this is the governor, Major Kavanaugh."

Kavanaugh looked thoroughly nonplussed. He was sallow-faced with fatigue, uniform rumpled, one hand rubbing furiously at his stubble of beard, gaze dancing from one member of the group to another. And then he spotted Wheeler. "Well, he can't come in here. Press ain't allowed in the command center."

"Why not?" Cooper said.

Kavanaugh waved an arm, taking in the room and maybe, she thought, even the heavy artillery on the roof. "This is a secure area. Everybody's gotta have clearance. No press people got clearance."

"Lots of high-powered stuff going on here, I can see. A real hotbed of activity, Major," Cooper shot back. "Well, Mr. Kincaid isn't press. He works for me. So do you. All these people here work for me, and since I'm the governor, they have clearance."

Kavanaugh backed away. "I'll have to talk to the colonel."

"Where is he?"

Kavanaugh pointed to a row of glass doors at one side of the room that led to what appeared to be offices and a conference room. Through one door, Cooper saw the squared-off forms of Colonel Doster and Major General Burgaw. Burgaw, at least six inches shorter than Doster, was snarling up into the colonel's face, just inches away. Doster was snarling back.

She started toward the doors, then spun back on Major Kavanaugh. "What are those two young people doing out there on the sidewalk in front of the garage?"

"Guard duty," he said, drawing himself up to full height.

"In a snowstorm?"

"You never can tell when they might—"

"Terrorists?"

"Yes, ma'am," he said with conviction.

"Well, they are, as of this moment, relieved of guard duty. Get 'em in here and get 'em thawed out. We need people. And the bunch on the roof, too."

She strode quickly to one of the glass doors, snatched it open, and stepped inside. Doster stared, speechless. Burgaw sized her up, nodded. Doster's tall form was stuffed into a freshly starched uniform with eagles on the shirt collar. Burgaw—stocky, block-shouldered, square-jawed—was in desert tan fatigues.

"Is this a shooting war?" she asked. "If it is, I've got the big gun."

Burgaw straightened, halfway to attention. Doster gave a disbelieving shake of his head, as if she might be an apparition.

If Pickett and Plato are putting out the word, she thought, *Doster hasn't gotten it yet.*

"Is there a problem here?"

"Yes, ma'am," Burgaw said. "There sure is. The colonel is having a hard time accepting that we're getting our butts in gear."

"I haven't seen anything that gives you authority," Doster growled.

"Well, gentlemen," she said, and handed each a copy of the authorization Grace had typed up.

Doster's face flamed. His eyes danced across the page, then looked up at her. His mouth started to form what might have been the name *Pickett*, but he checked himself.

"Colonel Doster," she said, "do you see whose name and signature are at the bottom of that piece of paper? Do you have any question that, as governor, I have the legal authority to mobilize the National Guard?"

"Well . . ."

"Hear me," she said, biting off the words. "I do have the authority, and since you work for me, you will do what you're supposed to do, and I will decide what that is." Doster's eyes went wide. "We have a mess on our hands. We don't have time for turf battles or pissing matches. We cooperate or we fail. Anybody who can't handle that needs to go home and build a snowman. Is that clear?" She looked from one man to the other.

"Yes, ma'am, Governor," Burgaw said firmly.

Doster shrugged. "I reckon."

She gave them a thin smile. "Good. General, keep doing what you're doing. Colonel, pry your people away from that TV set out yonder, get those cadets off the sidewalk and the roof, put everybody on the phones. Call every law-enforcement agency in the state, find out as much as you can about who needs what." She glanced at a wall clock. "In forty-five minutes, we'll get together and see what we know." Her cell phone rang. She fished it out of her handbag. It was Carter. "Let's get to work," she said.

They left, and she let the phone ring while she slumped into a chair, took a deep breath, tried to still her trembling hands.

"Hi, honey."

Carter's voice was high, strained. "Mom, what the heck's going on?"

"We have some snow, son."

"No, I mean with Dad."

"What about Dad?"

"He's throwing things. He's in this little office, him and Plato, and there's stuff flying around. A telephone, things off his desk. I stuck my head in and asked him what was wrong, and he yelled, 'Ask your mother!'"

A moment while her mind raced.

"Well?" he insisted.

"Honey, it's nothing you need to—"

"Dammit, Mom!"

"We're working out lines of authority."

"What do you mean, lines of authority?"

"Carter . . ."

"Tell me!"

"About who's the governor."

After a long silence, he said, "You are."

She felt a rush of gratitude. "Thank you."

"Goddammit! You mean he never meant to let you—"

"But I'm going to do it anyway, and I've told him that. I imagine that's why he's throwing things."

"I'm coming home," he said. "I can help."

Yes. Let him. An ally, God bless him.

But instead, she said, "No. You are not going to be in the middle of this, and you're not going to take sides. You signed on with Dad. You've got a job to do, and you're going to stick with it."

"Dad's gone ballistic. I can't handle that." He sounded close to tears.

"He'll cool off. We'll work this out, Carter."

After a long moment, his voice came raggedly over the connection. "Is it bad there?"

She forced a laugh, trying to break the tension. "The snow or the people?"

"Both."

"Well, son, I just kicked some uniformed butts. The snow may take a bit more doing."

"I love you, Mom."

"I love you, too. Don't worry."

"Are you kidding?"

She hung up, set the phone on the table beside her, and stared at it for a moment. It rang again. She gave a groan and picked it up.

"Cooper, are you sure you want to do this?"

"Do what, Plato?"

"Change the game plan."

"Plato," she said, "as far as I'm concerned, there was never but one game plan, and that was for me to do the job. If you and Pickett had a different idea, that's your problem. And right now, I don't give a rat's ass about your problem. I've got plenty of my own, and your meddling has made the situation infinitely more complicated."

"Pickett is afraid—"

"I know, that I'll screw it up. Maybe I will, but I'll make it clear to everybody that it's *my* screwup, not Pickett's."

"You're firm on all this?"

"Goddamn right, Plato. Now, are you doing what Pickett and I agreed you'd do?" She looked through the glass door into the command center. General Burgaw was huddled with several of his staff people. Doster was nowhere to be seen. "Have you and Colonel Doster had an enlightening conversation?"

"Not yet."

"What are you waiting for?"

"Look," he said. She could tell he was trying to keep his voice even and reasonable. It was one of Plato's most effective ploys. He could eviscerate you but sound thoroughly reasonable doing it. "If you'll just let the people there—"

"The people here are a big part of the problem. Doster and his folks have been sitting around all night. General Burgaw's hands have been tied because nobody would give him the green light to get the Guard moving. And the two of them are in a pitched battle over who's in charge. Truth of the matter, nobody is. They don't even know who the governor is. I asked my husband an hour ago to make that clear to the people down here, but it appears he's been too busy throwing telephones to talk on one."

"He's a bit upset."

"So here's what I can do. I can call in what's left of the Posse here, anybody besides Roger you've got on babysitting duty, fire 'em on the spot, and get some people who aren't joined at the hip to you and Pickett."

"You wouldn't," Plato said flatly.

"Try me."

"All right, Cooper. But hear this: You're climbing way out on a limb."

She laughed. "Plato, you just don't get it. We have a disaster. The state is paralyzed. People are in danger. And you and Pickett can't manage things from Iowa. If you tried, you'd make more of a mess than you already have. Do you want to take the heat for that?"

"No."

"All right. So now, give me your best advice."

"Mine?"

"Plato, I wish you were here right now. You know this business like nobody in the world, not even Pickett. But you're not here. I am. So help me."

Cooper waited, knowing he was weighing all the options.

"Do you need to talk to Pickett?" she asked after a while.

"No, I don't need to talk to Pickett."

"I'm putting you on the spot."

He grunted. "That's where I hang my hat, Cooper. On the spot."

"I understand."

"All right," he said, drawing a deep breath, "here's what I think."

By the time they finished, she had a few scribbled notes—not much detail, but a framework, a way of getting at the details.

"One other thing, Cooper. Wheeler Kincaid."

"Look, Plato . . ."

"I probably shouldn't say this, but if you're really going to take the bull by the horns . . ."

"And I am."

"It's brilliant. If you ever tell anybody I said that, I'll say you lied."

⌒

She took a few minutes alone to compose herself. She felt overwhelmed, going like a bat out of hell into territory she knew nothing about, playing it all by ear. But then she told herself, *No, I am not alone. I have some good people here, and they just need a bell cow. And then there's the other thing: Cleve Spainhour's hand on my shoulder.*

She took a deep breath and felt calmer—until Wheeler and Burgaw appeared at the door.

"We've got a missing school bus," Wheeler said.

SIXTEEN

They gathered at the big electronic map of the state.

"Up here," General Burgaw said, using a remote to zoom in on the upstate. "Foxhall County. The bus left an elementary school yesterday afternoon when the snow was starting, dropped off several kids, then disappeared."

"All night?" Cooper said. "And we're just now hearing about it?"

"Parents started calling when their kids didn't arrive home, but by the time the word got to the right people, the snow was so heavy nothing could move."

"Eighteen inches up there," Wheeler said.

"How many on the bus?" Cooper asked.

"As far as we know, three kids and the driver."

"And we don't know where?"

"The school people have given us the bus route, so we know the general area. But there's a long stretch beyond where the last of the other kids got off."

"How can we help?"

"Search and rescue," Burgaw said. "I've got an aviation company a hundred miles away. Helicopters, fixed wing. We're rounding up people."

"How long?"

"We should have a couple of choppers airborne in a half-hour. We'll search the area, try to spot the bus."

"What about people on the ground?" Wheeler asked.

"We're stretched damn thin in that part of the state in the best of times. I've got a support company in the county—cooks, supply clerks, people like that. The biggest piece of equipment they have is a mobile kitchen."

"Colonel Doster, what have you got up there that could help?" Cooper asked.

"Some of our trooper posts have four-wheel-drive vehicles."

"Can they travel in eighteen inches of snow?" Burgaw asked.

Doster glared but didn't say anything.

"Sweet Jesus," Cooper breathed.

"We're doing all we can," Burgaw said. "And I'm sure that goes for Colonel Doster's people."

"Nothing to do but wait," Doster said.

"No," she said, "that won't do. Get me the names and phone numbers of those parents."

⁓

They were painful, wrenching calls—the hysterical parents of a boy and two girls, and then Carl, the sobbing young husband of the bus driver.

"She's got a cell phone!" he cried. "I've been trying all night. If Stacy was okay, she'd answer. Wouldn't she? She'd answer and tell me everything's okay."

"Maybe the battery went dead, or the phone can't get a signal," she said. "But that doesn't mean Stacy's not okay. We've got the army going in there. They're going to find that bus and Stacy and those kids. Carl, is anybody there with you?"

"No. Just me."

"Okay. We'll work through this together."

"All right," he said, his voice calming.

She waited while he found pencil and paper, wrote down the number she gave him at the command center.

"Now, Carl, if you hear anything, call me."

She gathered them around the conference table, the numbers swelled now to include the state transportation director, the head of the emergency management office, the commissioner of education, and the state health officer, whose department regulated nursing homes. She glanced over the single page of her notes from Plato, then folded the paper and set it aside.

"We've never been here before, not with an emergency of this sort. Am I right?"

Doster said, "We've got contingency plans—"

"Yeah," the emergency management head interrupted, "plans for dealing with chemical spills, localized flooding, but not something that involves the whole state at the same time."

"This ain't New Hampshire," Burgaw growled.

"So we're flying by the seat of our pants," Cooper said, "making things up as we go along. First thing, I'm declaring an official state of emergency. It gives us room to maneuver, work around restrictions.

We've got to get as many people as possible, as quickly as possible, in places where they're needed. General Burgaw, what's your situation, other than the bus?"

"My people are moving," he said. "We're putting boots on the ground as fast as we can."

"What about wheels?"

"Most units have vehicles that can handle snow—trucks, Humvees. It's a matter of getting folks where the equipment is."

Cooper gave her notes another glance. "All right. I'm putting the National Guard in charge of the effort. Everything."

"Hey!" Doster said.

Cooper cut him off. "The Guard has the people and the ability to move them, and every county has at least one Guard unit. They'll work with the local folks. If we look at this thing statewide, it's chaotic. But if we tackle it town by town, county by county, we can make sense of things. Colonel Doster, your people will coordinate with the Guard units. We'll use General Burgaw's chain of command."

Doster stared at his hands, the color high around his collar. An awkward silence fell over the room.

"Colonel?"

"I have to protest this," Doster said finally.

Cooper's gaze swept the table, then landed again on Doster. "Everyone, work with General Burgaw. Everyone."

Doster sat back in his chair, rubbing his face with both hands.

"I'm incredibly glad you're here," she said, rising. "You're professionals. I can depend on you."

They filed out, all but Kincaid, who sat watching her.

She closed the door, took a deep breath, and turned to him. "All right," she said.

"Yeah, all right."

"Is that all?"

"What do you want me to do, write up a proclamation and award you an attagirl?"

"Look, Mr. Kincaid, I don't have time to waste on sarcasm. Give me something I can use."

"Good move, putting the National Guard in charge. Burgaw will kick ass, take names, and get the job done. Was that something you got from Plato?"

"How do you know I talked to Plato?"

"He called me, too. Read me the riot act. I'm a loose cannon, a dangerous, muckraking sonofabitch, and if I'm behind this craziness of yours, if I'm fueling the fire, he'll have my nuts on a platter."

She picked up her notes. "Plato helped me."

Wheeler gave her a hard look. "Look, you've got 'em over a barrel right now, but later, when the snow's gone, see how helpful Plato is. Remember this: Whatever Plato says or does or thinks, he's inside Pickett's head. So in the end, it's always you and Pickett."

"So what did you say to Plato?"

"I said how much I appreciated his candor, thanked him for giving you the benefit of his wisdom, and told him to go fuck himself." He stood. "One other thing. If you don't start calling me Wheeler, I'm gonna quit." He walked out into the command center, which was filling up with people struggling in from the snow to man the consoles, the phones, the radios.

The door swung open, and a National Guard major stuck his head in. "We've got a guy on the phone out here, about the bus. He insists on talking to you."

~

"I found her! I found her!" Carl screamed.

"What do you mean?"

"I kept calling, and then all of a sudden she answered. I know where she is!"

Cooper waved a hand, summoning Burgaw and Wheeler. "Carl, the National Guard's sending helicopters. Can you give them the location?"

"They're holed up in a barn. The bus ran off the road, but they found this barn and spent the night in there."

They had Carl on speaker now. People from all over the command center crowded around.

"One of the kids hurt his arm, but they're okay. Cold, scared, but okay."

"Carl, this is General Burgaw with the National Guard. Are you on the phone with your wife right now?"

"No, sir."

"Can we reach her?"

"I don't think so. She said she dropped the phone in the snow last night and didn't find it until just now. It was working, but the battery was about gone. She had just enough left to call me. You can try, but I don't think you'll get through."

"Where are they?"

"Gray Mountain Road. About three miles north of Highway 10, it goes steep downhill to a sharp curve. That's where the bus went off the road."

Someone switched the big map to a satellite view and zeroed in on the area.

"We've got it," Cooper said. She turned to Burgaw. "Are you flying?"

"Fifteen minutes."

"The Guard's on the way," Cooper said.

"Tell 'em to hurry!"

"They will, Carl. Everything's going to be okay."

Rick Jankowski was at Cooper's elbow. "We need to get word out to the media."

"Get 'em in here where the action is," Wheeler said. "Let everybody see what's happening."

Colonel Doster's head burrowed through the crowd. "Can't do that. This is a secure area."

Cooper ignored him. "If any press people need transportation, Rick, work with the Guard folks to provide it."

"Governor," Burgaw said, "the choppers may not be able to land when they find the bus, so I've had one of them pick up some folks from the ranger company in Graceville. They can rappel in from the choppers and lift the people out."

"Is it dangerous?"

"They know what they're doing."

"Good. You're way ahead of everybody on this."

Cooper felt a hand on her elbow. She turned, and there was Woodrow.

There had been no avoiding each other over the years, especially after Pickett began his rise in state politics. It had been terribly awkward for a long time. At first, after she broke up with Woodrow, he virtually disappeared from political life, and he disappeared completely from Cooper's.

And then, two years later, they met quite unexpectedly. The paper had sent her to cover the National Honor Society convention in the capital. En route to a speech by one of the state's business leaders, Cooper was working her way through a hallway crowded with noisy high-schoolers when suddenly they were face to face. They both stared. Finally, he spoke her name and offered his hand, and she took it.

"How are you?" he asked.

"Okay," she said. "I'm okay. You?"

He shrugged.

And then she managed, "What are you doing here?"

"Running for Congress."

The congressman he had been working for had decided to retire. Woodrow, barely of legal age to serve, intended to succeed him.

"I hope you win," she said, and knew it was genuine.

He gave her a brief attempt at a smile and disappeared into the crowd.

His campaign was a disaster, though he exhausted himself in the effort. Two wealthy and powerful opponents—a real-estate developer and a veteran legislator—joined the race, and he never had a chance. They referred to him as "the kid"—raw, inexperienced, in over his head. He finished a distant third, well out of a runoff. It took him years to repair the damage, both to his political image and, Cooper was sure, to his psyche.

Woodrow went to law school, established a practice in his home-town, dabbled in other people's campaigns, and resumed the tedious work of rebuilding political contacts. When he emerged from his self-imposed exile, he was in his early thirties. He ran for a seat in the legislature and won. His rise in the statehouse was diligent and patient. By the end of his second term, he was chairman of the Appropriations Committee, a man known for bringing warring factions together, a pragmatic politician. He continued to work the state, building a fresh base, then ran for state treasurer and won. Along the way, he married a high-school classmate. She was nice, quiet, had a pleasant smile, stayed mostly in the background. They had no children. Now, he was in his second term as lieutenant governor. And here he was, looking almost boyish in a white cable-knit sweater, jeans, and boots, a heavy parka over one arm, flakes of snow melting around the collar.

"Plato called," he said when it was just the two of them. He took a seat at the far end of the conference table.

"I'm glad you came," she said, and meant it.

"What can I do to help?"

She studied him. The overeager earnestness was gone now, replaced by something more reflective. His hair was graying at the temples, and his face was more angular. If anything was left of the guile—and surely there must be, in a man who had so successfully revived a political career—he wore it well.

"How much do you know?" she asked.

"Some."

She gave him a quick rundown and told him about putting Burgaw and the National Guard in charge.

"So that's where we are. Ideas?"

Woodrow smiled. "I know just about everybody in the state worth knowing, right down to the lowliest member of the Water and Sewer Board in Dogpatch. So . . ."

The door opened, and Wheeler stuck his head in. He looked the two of them over, eyebrows raised. Cooper motioned him in. He took a seat halfway between them, crossed his arms, glanced back and forth from one to the other, sizing things up.

Cooper nodded toward Woodrow. "The lieutenant governor was just telling me he knows some guy on the Water and Sewer Board in Dogpatch."

"And," Woodrow added, "I was about to say I can get on the phone to all of the mayors and county commission chairs in the state to put a personal touch on the state's efforts."

"But it will be more efficient if we divvy up the list and both start making calls," Cooper said quickly.

Woodrow gave her an odd look she couldn't fathom, then said, "That's even better."

"Good government, good politics," Cooper added.

Wheeler pushed his chair back, gave them a long look, and walked out without a word.

"That man can be insufferable," Woodrow said.

Cooper smiled. "That's why I made him my chief of staff."

Ten seconds, and Wheeler was back. "You need to see this."

~

Somehow, a television station's helicopter had managed to get airborne and was beaming video. It filled the big screen, the image shaky and frequently breaking up. They could make out two larger, olive-drab helicopters moving fast. Everybody—Woodrow, Wheeler, Guardsmen, troopers, civilians—crowded around, riveted.

Rick was at her elbow. "Channel 7," he said. "I don't know how the heck they did it."

The screen went blank, to loud groans from the room. A minute, two, five. The tension was unbearable. "Come on! Come on!" somebody pleaded.

Suddenly, the picture was back—the two National Guard helicopters hovering above an abrupt curve in a narrow, snow-clogged road. Then the camera panned to show, perhaps thirty yards off the road, a broad slash of yellow that was the rear end of the school bus, the rest of it hidden by thick underbrush and snow. And then, a short distance away, a dilapidated barn and a woman standing just outside, wildly waving her arms.

They watched, spellbound, as ropes snaked out the open doors of one of the choppers and two soldiers descended them into the snow and disappeared inside the barn. In a few minutes, they were back, carrying blanket-bundled children. After being strapped into harnesses, the kids were lifted into the chopper, followed by the driver and the two soldiers. The choppers hovered a moment longer, then flew up and away.

The command post erupted in cheering.

Cooper realized she was barely breathing. "Thank you, Lord," she said softly. "And you, General Burgaw."

"Thank the guys who did it," he said, and for the first time all day, she saw him smile.

"I will, when I pin medals on them."

As the room settled back to business, Cooper felt the renewed energy. She took time to walk around, shake hands, pat backs, and chat briefly. She hadn't really done anything except to be there in the middle of it with them. It seemed to be enough.

She put in a call to Carl. "Did you see it?"

"Power's out," he said. "But one of your folks there gave me a play-by-play." He took a deep breath, and his voice broke. "You're all incredible. Thank you." He hesitated, then: "I gotta tell you, I didn't vote for you."

"Maybe next time," she said with a smile.

The pressroom was packed with reporters and photographers in a hot glare of lights.

"So far," she said, "we've put the priority on responding to emergencies, and I believe we've done a fair job of that. Now, we start digging out and getting services restored. We've got a long way to go. We have to help each other and be as patient as possible. I'm confident the state will do that."

She turned the briefing over to Burgaw, who spent fifteen minutes going over details. And then she opened it up for questions.

Wheeler had warned her: Doster had tipped off Felicia Withers, who had given marching orders to a reporter from the *Dispatch*.

"When did you mobilize the National Guard?" the reporter asked.

"This morning," Cooper said, looking the man straight in the eye.

"Not last night?"

"The National Guard was mobilized this morning. I signed the authorization at seven-thirty. Rick, do we have a copy we can hand out?"

"Yes, Governor."

"Does that answer your question?"

"Not really," the reporter said.

"All right, let me say this: I should have put the Guard on duty earlier. We would be in better shape if I had. That was my mistake, and I take full responsibility for it. I am proud of the Guard, state troopers, local folks—everybody who's working to get us through this, the Guard especially. I put them in a hole, but they're climbing out of it magnificently."

The reporter wasn't satisfied. "You didn't try to call out the Guard last night?"

"I repeat," she said, keeping her voice even, "I mobilized the National Guard this morning. I don't know how to say it any more plainly."

Woodrow took a couple of quick steps and joined her at the podium. "Excuse me for interrupting, but I want to say this: I admire the way Governor Lanier is handling this. It's about as difficult a baptism of fire as I can imagine, but she's doing just fine."

"The lieutenant governor has been a huge help," she said. "I value his experience and his advice." The *Dispatch* reporter's hand shot up again, but before he could fire off another question, she said, "Thank you all for coming. I know you're having a difficult time covering this situation. Tell us how we can help. We'll do the best we can." And she walked out.

⁓

Wheeler closed the door to the conference room and stood with his back against it. "So that's the deal."

She gave him an arch look. "Yes, it is."

"It was a royal screwup that put you in one helluva bind."

"Right, Wheeler. Yes, I took the fall."

"Why?"

"Because I got something I wanted. Pickett agreed to back off and let me do my job."

He gave her a long look, then left the doorway and flopped into a chair at the other end of the table. "I don't want to meddle in anything personal here."

"I don't see any way to avoid it. If you're going to help me, I have to be honest with you. So here it is. It's obvious, as you've figured out, that Pickett never intended for me to be anything but a stand-in. He left Roger behind to babysit. He kept his Posse in place. And last night, when I tried to do something on my own, he cut me off."

"And you didn't suspect something before now?"

"I didn't ask enough questions. Pickett was vague. I let him be. Assumed too much."

"You trusted a conniving politician whose only concern is himself."

"Do you hate politicians, Wheeler?"

"I've made my living off 'em since I started scribbling for newspapers. What I hate is dishonesty. Politicians lie, to others and themselves. They rationalize what they do so well it becomes an art form."

"Are we politicians being dishonest when we make deals?"

"Hell no. If you want to get something done, you bargain and compromise. Your father was a master deal-maker. He wasn't a saint, but he rarely made a deal I thought was dishonest or self-serving. And Mickey understands how all that works, better than anybody I've ever known. She's a consummate politician. You've got the bloodline, and I think you've got the instincts."

"So the deal I made with Pickett . . ."

"As you say, you got what you needed to do your job."

"I hate that the state's in such a mess, but it played into my hands."

He nodded. "Will the deal hold? Can you trust him on this?"

She took a deep breath. "I don't know. Any advice?"

He looked out the glass door into the command post, where Doster was bustling about, trying to look importantly useful. Her eyes followed his.

"Yeah. Fire that sonofabitch."

She pondered that for a moment. "Tell me about this place."

He scrunched up his face so his thick eyebrows pinched together. "Public Safety is the worst kind of old-boy club. Doster and his crowd are incompetent. They protect each other's asses and come down hard on anybody who doesn't go along. The people in the ranks are demoralized because they know clowns are running the place."

"Are the clowns corrupt?"

"Some minor scandals, but Doster's bunch is pretty good at keeping the lid on. Everybody over here is afraid to talk."

"Why didn't somebody, Pickett included, clean out the place?"

"It's like J. Edgar Hoover and the FBI. A whole string of presidents wanted to get rid of him, but they were afraid to. Hoover knew too much about too many people."

"Does Doster know too much?"

"Nobody outside this building can say for sure what he knows."

She rose at her end of the table, gathering up notes she had made during the day. "We'll come back to this. Soon."

Wheeler started for the door but stopped before he opened it. "Most politicians go into office with a shitload of baggage—IOUs to people who helped 'em get there. Your only baggage is Pickett, because he engineered things. You've got freedom most don't have. You'll have to bargain, just like every politician. Just be honest about it, especially with yourself."

"I will, Wheeler. I promise you that."

She spent most of the afternoon making calls, Woodrow beside her at another console. She talked to mayors, commissioners, fire and police chiefs, sheriffs, rescue squad members. They each seemed surprised by the call and grateful for the simple act of making contact. The calls gave her a humbling appreciation for the vastness of her job, all those people depending on each other and now on her.

She was exhausted, drained by the mental and emotional toll of the day but satisfied she had done everything she could. Cleve Spainhour, she told herself, would agree.

Woodrow appeared with two paper cups, handed her one. She took a sip, and her eyebrows went up. "Let's go to my office," she said with a smile.

It was just the two of them in the conference room. She took another sip and felt the scotch warm its way down into her stomach. "Glory be," she said quietly.

They drank in silence.

"Thank you for today," she said.

"Part of the job."

"But more than that."

"Well, yes . . ." He paused, studying his cup. "Considering everything."

Considering everything? She started to ask but then thought about the thing that had been nibbling at the back of her mind since this morning.

"Plato called you," she said.

"Yes."

"And?"

"I told you, he said you might be able to use some help."

"That's all?"

He studied his cup again. "He said you were . . . that you wanted to be more hands-on."

"And I might screw things up? Run the bus into a ditch?"

He frowned. "Look, Cooper, this is dicey."

"What's dicey about it?"

"You and me. Not the ancient past—that's long over, and we've both lived a life since all that. But this situation now. Don't you think?" He gave her a long, searching look.

She thought, *He's fishing. Why? For what?*

"Well," she said, "I hope we can work together on a lot of things."

Woodrow polished off his cup, rose. "For now," he said. He tossed the cup into a waste can and moved toward the door.

"Woodrow, what do you mean by that?"

He stopped, stood for a moment with his back to her, then turned. He had the oddest look on his face—something she read as a mixture of wariness and confusion.

"Are you kidding me?"

"Of course not."

He stared awhile longer, then shook his head. "My God. You really don't know, do you?"

"Know what?"

"You owe me, Cooper. You and Pickett, you owe me."

Before she collected herself enough to speak, he was gone.

⁓

She sat there for a long time, numb, unmoving. *What has Pickett done?*

The door opened. Wheeler poked his head in, started to say something, stopped, gave her a searching look. "Are you okay?"

It took a moment. "No," she finally said.

"What?"

She started to blurt it out but thought better of it. She shook her head.

"Ready to call it a day?"

"Yes."

"I'll get Ezra and round up our gang."

She took several minutes to compose herself, then took a deep breath, straightened her shoulders, and walked out into the command center. She found General Burgaw and got a quick update. "Call me," she said. "Anything. Thank God you're here."

As they headed toward the elevator, she felt somebody plucking at her sleeve and turned to see Doster.

"Governor, could I have a word?"

"Of course." She nodded to Wheeler and the others, and they went on to the elevator.

"I just want you to know," Doster said, "no hard feelings. If there's been any, ah, friction of any sort, we'll just write it off to the stress of the situation. It's, ah, a pleasure to work with you, ma'am. Just anything you need now, remember that. Anything at all."

He gave her a saccharine smile and thrust out his hand. She ignored it. Behind her, she heard the ring of the elevator bell.

"I'll be in my office tomorrow," she said. "I'll expect to have your letter of resignation on my desk by nine o'clock."

SEVENTEEN

The strain of the day assaulted her as she reached home. She was bone-tired, drained, a victim of post-adrenaline crash. And all the problems would be there tomorrow.

She was barely in the door when Pickett called. It had taken him thirty minutes.

"You can't do that!"

"Of course I can. I'm the governor. I can fire the whole friggin' bunch if I want to. Get my own Posse."

"You are sabotaging my chance to be president. I've got new poll results, Cooper. I'm gaining. Money's starting to come in. I'm adding staff. I am busting my ass, and so are a lot of people helping me, and it's working. If I keep moving like this, I can win South Carolina and New Hampshire. And if I win there, other things begin to fall into place."

"Pickett, the primaries are a year away, for God's sake."

"But now's the time when I either become a contender or flame out.

People are beginning to think I'm real, and I either capitalize on that or slide back. There's no standing still. One screwup and I'm dead meat." He paused, and the silence hung between them. "You are dumping all your problems on me—Roger and now Doster."

"I'm dumping *your* problems on you."

He ignored that. "What the hell is going on with you? Are you *trying* to screw me?"

"What's the issue with Doster?" she asked. "What does he know about you that you wish he didn't?"

He hesitated. "Nothing worth sweating over. But it's not me."

"Who?"

"A *lot* of people. Plato, for one."

She could guess what. Plato was a lifelong bachelor. There had never been a whiff of public scandal, but something an investigator might find by digging deeply would be another matter.

"So," he went on, turning on his reasonable voice, "you can't get rid of him. Later, but not now."

"Pickett, listen to me. Doster was a pluperfect, eighteen-carat asshole today, fighting a turf war while the whole state was in chaos. Maybe he knows too much where you're concerned, but he didn't know his ass from his elbow today. If I hadn't been able to count on General Burgaw, we'd have a lot bigger mess than we do. I won't let Doster get away with that. You wouldn't if you were here."

"Yes, I would," he came back. "I'm not in the business of stirring up shit."

"You're an expert at *not* stirring up shit. I told him to have his letter on my desk in the morning, and if he doesn't, I'll call a news conference and tell the world what an incompetent and insubordinate sonofabitch he is."

Another long silence, and then he surprised her by saying, "I'm coming home."

"When?"

"Tomorrow."

"Why?"

"Well, what would it look like if the former governor didn't come to see his people?"

"Oh, that. A photo opportunity. Then come on."

"And while I'm there, I'll deal with this colossal fuckup with Colonel Doster."

"I'm firm on this, Pickett. I will not back down on Doster."

A long, weary sigh. "I'll meet you at the airport at ten. Arrange a helicopter. We'll fly over the snow and make clucking noises."

"You have turned into a cynical man," she said, and hung up, feeling again the abiding sense of disappointment and loss that had been at her core for such a great, long while.

Mickey was in the hallway, shuffling along with one hand gripping a rolling IV stand, the other on Estelle Dubose's arm, slippered feet sliding along the carpet, a fierce look on her face.

"That's enough," Estelle said, tugging on the sleeve of Mickey's housecoat.

"No. Down yonder." Mickey jerked her head toward the far end of the hallway.

"You'll get down there and I'll have to carry you back," Estelle said.

"Down yonder," Mickey said, louder.

They kept moving. Cooper watched as they reached the end of the hall at a glacial pace, turned, and headed back.

"Go eat your supper," Mickey called to her. "Then come back and talk to me, if this bossy woman doesn't bludgeon me in the meantime."

"Miz Mickey," Estelle said, "you're not worth bludgeoning. For a worn-out little old lady, you are a royal pain."

When Cooper returned in a half-hour, Mickey was parked in a wheelchair, telephone in one hand, cigarette in the other, while Estelle bustled about the room changing sheets, checking monitors, hooking up a fresh oxygen supply, and then taking the cigarette from Mickey.

"Sit up," Estelle ordered. "You're slumped over like you're on a three-week drunk."

"I wish," Mickey said. "Estelle, you have no respect for your elders."

"If you didn't have me around to get you straightened up, you'd be a puddle."

"I love you, too, Estelle," Mickey said. "If not for you, they would have plowed me under days ago."

"Estelle," Cooper said, "you need to go home and rest, or else my mother will drive you stark, raving nuts."

"I am," Dubose said. "Another nurse is on the way. I'll be back in the morning. Nobody else can put up with her for long."

When Estelle was gone, Cooper unplugged the telephone. "This is going out of here."

"How the hell am I gonna know what's going on without a telephone?"

"Ask *me*," Cooper said. "How do you feel?"

"Like I've been kicked in the nuts."

"You don't have nuts."

"If I did, that's what I'd feel like. But I still have about a quarter-tank of piss and vinegar."

Cooper collapsed into a chair.

"And how are you?" Mickey asked.

"Kicked in the nuts, but I'm all out of piss and vinegar."

"I talked to Wheeler. He said you did okay. He said you fired Doster."

"Yes, I did."

"Good for you."

"Pickett's furious. He says Doster knows too much. He's trying to get me to change my mind."

"Don't," Mickey said.

Cooper smiled. "No chance. Firing that asshole was the highlight of my day."

They fell silent. Cooper took a minute to close her eyes, rub her temples, focus.

"All right," she said, "talk to me. What Pickett said last night. 'I told her this wouldn't work.'"

Mickey made a tent of her hands, cupped them over her mouth and nose, snorted, lowered her hands. "Pickett came to me last year, told me you had come up with this cockeyed idea of running. I told him that if he didn't find a way to get one of his people in office to hold down the home front, he'd be stuck with Woodrow, and Woodrow hates his guts. So he'd better damn well figure out how to sandbag Woodrow. Two weeks later, Pickett came back. Woodrow had decided not to run, he said. But why should he let you? Could you win, and if you did, would you be a good little girl? I put a sales job on him. With Woodrow out of the way, you'd have a good chance—the pedigree, name recognition, all that business. And you'd be safe. He didn't think so. He said you were too goddamn stubborn and independent. But then he went off and thought about it some more, and the next thing I heard was your announcement."

"Why did Woodrow drop out?"

"I don't know, but I didn't buy what he was selling. Yes, his wife was sick, that much was real. But a politician with his ambition would walk over his invalid grandmother to stay in the game."

"Plato called Woodrow this morning, and Woodrow showed up to help."

"Wheeler told me."

"But later, we had this absolutely weird conversation. I said I looked forward to working with him, and he said, 'For now.' When I asked him what he meant, he gave me an incredulous look and said something like, 'You really don't know, do you?' And then he said, 'You and Pickett owe me.'"

Mickey frowned, looked away, lost in thought. Then: "There's some kind of deal."

"What kind?"

"I'm not going to speculate. But I do know you'd damn well better find out."

They sat in silence while Cooper worked it over in her mind.

"Pickett's coming home tomorrow to take a helicopter tour of the state. And deal with Doster."

"And you're going to ask him about Woodrow."

"I'll play it by ear."

Mickey nodded. "Your father was a master at that. He was like Jack, nimble and quick."

"I've thought about Daddy a lot today."

"I think he'd be proud of you." That lingered for a bit. Then she added, "I am."

"Thank you," Cooper said, and meant it. "Now, I'm going to go put my weary fanny to bed, and you're going to do the same, and I'm taking the damn telephone with me." She picked it up, started for the door.

"Do you know why I wanted you to run for governor?"

Cooper turned back. "To help Pickett, of course."

"I couldn't care less about Pickett."

"Is that because he doesn't need you anymore?"

Mickey's eyes narrowed. "I helped Pickett get where he wanted to go. We used each other, because that's what politicians do. But we're even, and neither one of us owes the other anything."

"Then why?"

"Because I wanted something for you."

"After all these years."

"Cooper, hear me: I am old and sick, and I don't have a damn bit of time to fart around with anything less than honesty. I have been a piss-poor mother. I just didn't know how, and once we got to a certain point, I guess I gave up." Her voice cracked, and she bit off the words, eyes flashing. "I am all hard edges and rough spots and don't have much milk of human kindness in me, and not enough patience with people to fill up a thimble. You and I are who we are, and we can't change that. But right now, I'm looking at you and thinking, *By God, she's got the stuff.* You're in a tough spot, and you've caused a helluva ruckus already, and I hope you'll let me help you make sure the bastards don't wear you down."

Cooper took a deep breath. "All right."

Mickey snorted. "But I can't do that without a goddamn telephone."

Cooper plugged the phone back in, set it on the bedside table, and left without another word.

She was back the next morning, ready to head for the airport. She had something else she needed to ask Mickey, something that had come to her in the night.

"Mother, did you sabotage Woodrow?"

Mickey's eyes narrowed. "Did I what?"

"After we broke up."

"After *we* broke up?"

"All right, after I dumped him. He ran for Congress and got clobbered. Was that your idea?"

"I tried my dead level best to talk him out of it. He was too young, too eager. But he wouldn't listen. He got eaten alive, just like I said."

"Then why did he do it?" Cooper asked.

"To prove something, I imagine. To you, mostly. Maybe to you and Pickett."

"I'm sorry he did that."

"It took years for him to recover."

"Did the two of you stay in touch?"

"No," Mickey said. "When he decided to run for the legislature, I sent word offering to help, but I never heard back. Give him credit, he climbed out of the hole and almost all the way to the top. Almost, but not quite. Maybe someday he will, and I think he'll consider that the ultimate vindication. But by God, he has to earn it. Now, about the agenda today."

"A helicopter ride."

Mickey nodded. "Pickett's people will have a crowd lined up somewhere out yonder, far enough from town to give the feel of the boondocks but close enough that the media can get there. He'll be on all the newscasts."

"That's the idea."

"And what will you be doing while he's getting his picture taken?"

"I'll be right there wearing my boots and looking like I know what I'm doing. I make a fairly good picture myself."

Mickey looked at her appraisingly. Then a corner of her mouth turned up in the beginning of a wry smile. "My daughter the governor."

⁓

A crowd was gathered in the blustery cold at the airport's private aviation terminal, where a National Guard helicopter sat throbbing as Jake Harbin's plane taxied in. Wheeler and Rick and the security detail from her office, Burgaw and some of his staff, several state troopers, Plato and some others from Pickett's operation, reporters, cameras. The doorway folded out, and Pickett bounded down the steps, looking full of vim, smiling, making a beeline for her. A hug and kiss, then his arm around her, waving to the crowd as they moved toward the helicopter. Shouted questions from the media people. "When we get back!" he called out with a big smile. "Don't want to keep the governor waiting."

A crewman helped them get strapped in and don headsets. They flew north, toward the deepest snow. It enveloped everything, a vast white sea. Some main roads were being cleared, utility crews were working on downed lines, and vehicles were crawling. Pickett kept up a running intercom chatter with the pilots. "I'd like to set down for a moment in Graceville," he said.

"General Burgaw told us," the pilot came back. "About ten minutes from here."

Pickett glanced at her. She looked away, out the window.

They landed in the parking lot of Graceville's National Guard armory, home of the rangers who had pulled off the bus rescue. They were there, along with a scattering of locals, some press. Pickett's people had been at work.

Pickett climbed out, headed for the gathered throng, caught himself, and waited for her. They worked the crowd—first the rescue team, then the others, handshakes, back pats, encouragement. Lots of pictures. Then Pickett moved toward the press bunch. She stayed a step back while he made the right noises: "Stunning . . . never imagined anything like this . . . good people working together . . . these incredible Guard folks who save lives. I've got a call in to the president to see—"

That's when she interrupted him. "Actually, the president and I spoke this morning. He's declaring the state a federal disaster area, and we're assessing the damage to see exactly what we'll need from him. And about these rangers from the Guard unit. General Burgaw will have them in my office by the end of the week to accept the state's highest decoration." She made a point of not looking at Pickett. "We've made a lot of progress, but we've got a long way to go. The effort from everybody is magnificent and inspiring. The weather folks say we'll get some significant warming over the next few days, and that will help." She took Pickett's elbow. "I appreciate the former governor coming today. I'd say his heart is still here at home."

"How's she doing?" one of the press folks asked Pickett.

He picked it up neatly. "Splendid. I'm so proud." A glance at his watch. "Fundraiser tonight in Washington. Great to see you all."

They flew back to the capital in silence.

～

It was just the two of them in a small terminal room.

"I met with Doster," he said.

"When?"

"Early this morning at Jake's house. This"—he waved in the direction of his waiting plane—"was just for show."

"Of course."

"You have put me in a big bind, Cooper. He's mad as hell, threatening to bring everything crashing down. Do you have any idea how much shit that man could stir up?"

"Tell me."

"Look, this does nobody any good—not you, not me, not the people you and I depend on. You have to reconsider."

"No."

He screwed up his face, and the muscles along his jawline rippled. He threw up his hands. "Then I'll have to—with everything else I've got going—try to keep this contained. I've offered to make him head of the Secret Service when I get elected."

"Can you do that?"

"No, and I wouldn't if I could. Can you imagine being protected by that idiot?"

"Did he go for it?"

"It's not enough."

"Then what?"

"I'll think of something else." His stood and reached for his coat.

"Have you talked to Woodrow in the past twenty-four hours?"

He turned with a jerk, on guard. "No. Why?"

She told him.

"What did he mean, Pickett? What am I supposed to know that I don't?"

He flashed with anger. "Goddammit, I don't have time to fool with this right now. You have piled enough crap on my plate."

She kept her voice steady. "You can tell me what you and Woodrow cooked up, or I can ask him myself."

They glared at each other. Then Pickett gave a dismissive shake of his head and threw his coat back on the table. "All right," he said, his voice steely, face grim. "He stays out, you hand it over."

"Hand what over?"

"After the election. If I win, you become first lady. If I don't, you plead fatigue, incompetence, whatever. You bow out gracefully and pass the gavel to Woodrow. That's the deal. That's why he dropped out. It's a lot easier and cheaper to be anointed than to have to run."

Pickett waited.

Finally, she said, "You actually promised him that?"

He didn't answer.

"And you thought I would go along?"

"You've mostly been reasonable, Cooper. Not always, but mostly."

"God forgive me, too many times. Pickett, this is the second enormous lie I've caught you in. A lie a day. How in the hell can I ever again trust anything you say?"

"I didn't actually *lie* to you."

She looked at him for a moment, then slowly shook her head. "I think you really believe that, Pickett. My God, what's happened to you?"

"Cooper," he said, pleading, "this is the real deal. I can be *president*, for God's sake. How many human beings can say that?"

"So, to get there, it's okay to lie to people, trample on them?"

"It's a brutal game. Sometimes you have to—"

"Compromise," she finished for him. "Compromise your sense of decency and loyalty, or at least the sense of them I thought you had. Pickett, you don't get it. This deal you cut with Woodrow, it isn't some business arrangement, it's about *us*."

His face was impassive, and she realized in that instant just how far he had gone, and how little chance she had of getting him back.

"Whatever happens, I will not quit."

He pondered that, then said with a shrug of his shoulders, "Okay, don't. When the time comes, just don't."

"And Woodrow?"

"It won't be the first time we've screwed Woodrow."

"Don't try to put a guilt trip on me, Pickett. Woodrow may have some notion that you and I owe him—atonement for an old hurt, something like that— but we don't. It's ancient history."

"Maybe *we* don't, but right now, I do."

She reached for her own coat and pulled her cell phone out of a pocket. "Let's clear the air with him."

He grabbed her arm. "Good Lord, no. If he gets wind of it, he'll fuck me over. And he could do it." She pulled her arm away. "Help me, Cooper. Please, help me. Keep quiet about Woodrow. Don't make waves. We'll deal with it later. Okay?"

She didn't answer.

"Plus, think about this: You've got a legislative session coming up. Woodrow could scuttle anything you want to get done." His cell phone rang. He pulled it from his pocket, glanced at it, put it back. "I'm running late."

She waved her hand. "Then go."

"Walk with me to the plane?"

When they were there, just the two of them, buffeted by the wash from the plane's propellers, he gave her a peck on the cheek. "Please," he said. "Don't do anything."

"Keep your hands off my business."

"I will," he said. "I promise. I really mean it."

He climbed the steps, turned at the top to give her a last look, then disappeared inside as the door swung up and closed. She stood unmoving for a moment, then turned and walked away, giving way to hurt, loss, grief, the knowledge of things once cherished and now all but irretrievable. For her, for them. They had passed over some continental divide of the heart and seemed to have no chance of turning back.

PART FOUR

EIGHTEEN

Did politics change Pickett, or just bring something to the surface that had always been there? She thought about it often during the years.

It started innocently enough. A member of the county commission, a university professor, died of a massive heart attack on an anthropology trip to Central America. The remaining commission members approached the university president about having another faculty member fill the unexpired term. The president called in Pickett.

Cooper was hesitant but saw how much he wanted to do it, and with her heart full of him and what they had together, she said, "All right. Do it. Just don't make a habit of it." But when the term was up and he wanted to run for a full four years, she relented again, more reluctant this time but reassured by the way he had so carefully kept it from coming between them.

He won handily. It was a joyous thing for him. He was by nature competitive, and there was a zest to his approach to contests of any kind, a free-flowing looseness that was as much about the game as about the prize. In that one respect, he was perhaps more like Woodrow Bannister than he would have admitted.

He relished the office, the give and take, the jousting and negotiating and accommodating, even the phone calls from constituents grousing about potholes in the roads in front of their homes or the latest property-tax assessment. He was patient and had a self-deprecating sense of humor that deflected criticism and helped him accomplish things. He maneuvered an overhaul in the county Social Services Department to put more emphasis on child protection. He persuaded the commission to approve a modest property-tax increase that went to the school system. He was progressive but cautious. When a citizens' group demanded the commission reprimand the long-serving sheriff, an entrenched vote-getter with a reputation for roughing up suspects, Pickett and the rest politely heard them out and went on to the next item of business.

There was some awkwardness about that. The newspaper backed the citizens' group with editorials and a series of articles on the sheriff's abusiveness. Cooper had seen and heard enough to know the paper had its facts straight.

"He's a nasty sonofabitch," she said to Pickett.

"Uh-huh," he agreed amiably. "I hear he swings a mean piece of rubber hose."

"So?"

"I applaud the newspaper's crusade. Muckraking journalism at its finest."

"*And?*"

"Let the voters take care of him."

"So you're not going to stick your neck out."

"If I'm learning anything, it's when and where to pick a fight, and how to avoid pissing into the wind." He turned on his smile, trying to take the edge off the conversation. "So, no, my darling, I'm not sticking my neck out."

He reached for her, and she pushed his hand away. He gave her a hurt look and walked out. She spent an hour in huffy silence, then went looking for him.

She heard his guitar and found him in a rickety chair tilted back against the side of the weathered toolshed next to the garden, shirt off, feet bare, picking idly at notes and chords, eyes closed, a look of utter serenity, bathed in gold by the late-afternoon sun. He must have heard her coming, feet crunching through the litter of drying weeds they had pulled from the garden, but he didn't open his eyes as she stood over him, her shadow crossing his face. He kept picking, fingers coaxing a rich texture of notes from wood and steel. And then he started singing:

If I was a three-legged dog, two legs front and one leg rear,
I'd rouse myself in the evening time, get my three old legs in gear;
Leave my place in the cool, cool shade, drink my fill of Gatorade,
And hippity-hop to you, my dear.

He kept playing, fingers flying, intricate licks and runs, spinning out the melody and humming along, finishing with a flourish. Then he finally looked up at her. "I love you, and you love me," he said. "Let's don't ever let anything get in the way of that." He put the guitar aside, then reached for her. She went to him, and they made love right then and there with her on his lap, the old chair banging wildly against the shed until pieces began to fly off and they collapsed, rolling and howling with laughter, in the grass.

Two weeks later, she missed her period, and then came Allison. They took an exquisite joy in her. They wrapped themselves around the baby and each other and made a hiding place of their lives, keeping the other things that mattered in their place.

Pickett was adept at separating the parts of his life. He relished teaching, worked hard at it, and was awarded tenure. People at the university had their eyes on him—maybe department chair someday, even a dean. A sharp, attractive young man who got along. He worked, too, at being a commissioner. Cooper saw him as balanced, and saw, too, a fine balance in their life together. It was better than she could have imagined. She even found herself beginning to look at politics in a different light. Pickett's light. *It might be possible*, she thought, *to be* in *it without being* of *it*. Pickett seemed profoundly un-Woodrow.

Then life, she understood later, caught up with them. Allison ("She's such a *good* baby," people said) turned sickly. Nothing really scary, just a series of bouts of colic, rashes, respiratory ailments, strep throat, an intractable ear infection that kept her in a constant fit of angry pain. For Cooper and Pickett, it meant long nights walking the floor with her, trying unsuccessfully to soothe and comfort, an unending struggle that left them harried and exhausted.

And then Cooper was suddenly, stunningly, pregnant again. There was never any question that they would go on with it, but the thought of another baby and the constant worry over Allison, along with the daily pressures of their jobs, cast a pall over them. Her new pregnancy was much harder than the first. It seemed she would never get over the nausea. And when she did, she felt bloated, awkward, drained. Pickett shied from her, wary, puzzled by the changes, both in her and them. They endured long silences, an exaggerated politeness born of a fear that one or the other might say or do something that would open a rupture they could not stitch back together.

Things at work grew complicated. Stressful squabbling in the business school escalated into warring factions of faculty members and ended with the dean being forced out and nobody happy, Pickett included. Cooper thought fleetingly about quitting the newspaper but clung to the job, fearful of giving up a part of herself that she considered vital and entirely her own. Instead, she gave in to the pleading of the editor and took over the education beat, which meant night meetings of the school board. Pickett encouraged her to take the new assignment and get out of the house. He would keep Allison.

And then, when the weight of it all seemed beyond what they could stand, it happened.

She arrived home one evening after a long board meeting to find a college-student babysitter there with Allison, who was screaming inconsolably with pain. Where the hell was Pickett? Gone to some kind of meeting, the girl said. When he got home after eleven, Cooper was waiting for him at the door, stupid with fatigue, boiling with anger. He was profusely apologetic and full of news, which he seemed to think made everything okay.

The incumbent state senator had been arrested the night before for drunk driving—no surprise, since she frequently appeared on the floor of the Senate smelling of a pungent combination of Listerine and Jack Daniel's. Despite previous brushes with the law, she had never faced charges. But this time, she had taken out a fire hydrant and the lighted sign in front of the Lutheran church and had been treated at the emergency room for cuts and bruises. On this night, the local party committee had summoned her to a meeting and read the riot act. She had to go, resign now, make way for a special election. As soon as she fled weeping and defeated into the night, the committee members had called in Pickett Lanier, the popular young county commissioner, and pressed him hard to run. Pickett had put them off until he could talk to Cooper, but by the time he arrived home, it was clear he had made up his mind.

They argued bitterly and loudly. They woke Allison, who hammered at her ears with her fists. It was an hour before Cooper could get her calmed and back to sleep. By then, she was long past protest, much less fighting.

"You're a selfish, self-centered asshole, Pickett."

"Cooper," he pleaded, "honey, I just need to try this."

"Why now? For God's sake, why now?" She waved her arms, taking in everything weighing on her, on them.

"I might not ever get this chance again."

She stared at him a long time, feeling the earth lurching, wrenching apart, and Pickett on the far side. She turned away. "Then go," she said. "Just leave us alone and go do it."

The district covered three counties. He was gone day and night, walking the towns, driving the back roads, managing somehow to keep up with his classes at the university. He left early, arrived home late. She saw almost nothing of him, especially during the last frenetic two weeks in May, when the semester was over and he could devote every waking minute to the campaign. She did her best to ignore it, or at least to hold it at arm's length. She refused to even glance at the newspaper stories about what he was saying and doing.

He won, carrying his home county and splitting the other two with enough votes to avoid a runoff. On election night, she gave in to his pleading and went with him to his storefront campaign headquarters, where she spent the evening watching him win, meeting his supporters, hangers-on, political junkies. Six months along now, she felt huge and ungainly and unattractive and entirely out of place. But Pickett held her close, arm about her waist, making sure they all took note. She was polite. She shook hands and made enough small talk to get by. But she kept her emotional distance.

One of the people she met was Plato. He and Pickett had remained in touch since college. Now, he had quit his job and moved halfway across the state to run Pickett's Senate campaign.

She would look back on that later and recognize it for what it was—the beginning.

On Thursday, she arrived home from work to find Pickett's mother there, two suitcases standing by the front door. Pickett had made arrangements with her editor for a couple of days away.

"Where are we going?" she asked.

"Off. Together."

She slept most of the way as they drove, awoke to the smell of salt water and then, as she struggled into awareness of the early evening, the sight of dunes, sea gulls, weathered cottages. She sat in a swing suspended by rusting chains from the roof of the open porch, watching kids splash in the gentle surf at water's edge while Pickett brought in the bags and threw open the windows to the sea breeze. Then he sat beside her. She turned to look at him, examining him, framing thought.

He stretched his arm across the back of the swing, touching her neck lightly. "Could we just let it be us? None of the other? Just us?"

She nodded, then closed her eyes and leaned her head back against his hand. "Yes," she sighed. "We have to."

Through the long weekend, they made love, walked the beach, made love, cooked seafood, made love, slept the sleep of two exhausted human beings. They talked about the life growing inside her, the baby who seemed oddly calmer now that they were away. They had consciously avoided talking about names, not wanting to know if it was a boy or a girl, savoring the mystery. When he pressed her now for a guess, she said another girl, but she wasn't ready to talk about a name, and Pickett quickly veered away from what neither of them wanted to deal with at the moment (though for different reasons, she later realized): her mother. If it was a boy, Pickett wanted to know, would she consider Carter, for his father? She thought that was fine. She then found herself hoping for a boy.

By Sunday evening, as they huddled together in a blanket next to a driftwood campfire in front of the cottage, the beach darkening, waves sliding with a soft rush over sand, moon playing tag with ragged patches of clouds, she felt rested and renewed, something old and comfortable easing back into her soul. Pickett had given himself back to her, reaching to fill her need for warmth, belonging, being held and cherished. It was, at heart, all she had ever wanted.

It lasted until Monday, on the drive back home.

"How the hell did we get here?" he asked. "It all happened so fast. It's a blur to me." He looked over at her, but she was quiet, waiting. "I didn't think I had a dog's chance of winning."

When she realized he was talking not about them but about his election, she felt the air go out of her.

"Are you going to make me do all the talking?"

"It's your election, not mine," she said, making no effort to keep the edge out of her voice.

"I had to try."

His face was terribly earnest, as if he must make her understand. But she sensed something else, a holding back of some kind. *What else?*

"And then it seemed like it got bigger than me, that I was being swept up and carried along. Things, people . . ."

"Who?"

He took a deep breath, held it, let it out through grim lips. "Mickey."

She sat numb and shaken while he told her, rushing along in a torrent. Mickey had called the local party committee as soon as she heard about the incumbent senator's disaster, and had leaned hard on the members to recruit Pickett. He hadn't known anything about it until he accepted, he insisted. But once he did, Mickey called and told him what she had done and offered to help. Then she tutored him through the campaign—raising money, making connections, strategizing, lining up the advertising agency that had handled Cleve's political work.

When he finished with the telling, she sat for a long time, listening to the whine of the tires, then rolling down the passenger window to let the rush of wind sweep through and fill her mind. But there was one sound the wind couldn't muffle, a voice that said, *She is trying to steal him from me.*

"Why didn't you tell me?"

"I didn't want to upset you. I didn't want to get caught between you and your mother."

"And what about my mother coming between you and me? Have you thought about that?"

She could tell by the look on his face that he had indeed, and that it had been gnawing at him—but not enough to make him tell her what was going on. That was the worst of it, not what Mickey had done in his campaign, but that he had kept it from her. It was the *withholding*. They had, so she believed, made a compact to be open with each other. No secrets, no hidden agendas. What he had told her just now was a betrayal of that.

"Cooper," he tried, reaching across the seat to her.

"Just take me home." She began to cry, surrendering to the hurt and disappointment. She turned her face from him, into the wind.

After days of icy silence, he came to her, miserably remorseful. "Cooper, I'm sorry. I should have talked to you from the first, from the minute I found out about Mickey. What can I do?"

"It was a lie, Pickett."

"Yes," he confessed. "It was a kind of lie. I know how you feel about Mickey. I didn't want to upset you."

"Don't ever do it again," she said.

"I won't. I promise, I won't."

Still, things were altered. A sea change for both of them.

Politics on a larger stage, the winning and all that went with it, opened a new and tantalizing world to Pickett. He was young, attractive, articulate, untarnished. He could go places. He could win things, maybe even big things. But if his potential was great, there was also a price to be paid. More and more, it was about the prize. Cooper watched with a sinking heart as the part of Pickett that was original and genuine was slowly but steadily replaced by an all-too-familiar sameness, the mask politicians wear and lurk behind, part artifice, part guile. He had been, at the beginning, a free-flowing stream. But as the stakes became higher, he turned cautious, guarded, abhorrent of surprise, fearful of losing control.

He became, in short, political, in the timeworn way. Having rejected Woodrow, she had gotten . . . *Woodrow.*

Pickett's successes fed one on another until they became the central dynamic in their lives. During his two terms in the State Senate, the competing demands of his office and his teaching job left less and less time for anything else. The university made allowances for his time in the capital. Cooper was much less willing. She struggled against the current that tugged at them all, concentrating her energies, her life, on Allison and Carter while still clinging to her job at the paper. But then he got elected lieutenant governor, and that changed everything again. Pickett would have to be in the capital almost constantly. She was first inclined to simply let him go. But the more she thought about it, about all the loss she and the children had already endured, she decided she would fight to keep what of him, of them, she could. She and Allison and Carter might have to give up the comfortable ordinariness of their lives in an easygoing college town and adapt in ways she knew from her own girlhood, but by God, they would all sit around the dinner table together.

It came to her starkly, how profound the change, on a day when she was packing for their move to the capital. Tucked away in the back of Pickett's closet, behind the suits and wing-tip shoes, she found the motorcycle helmet and his guitar case. The motorcycle was long gone, sold in the days they were trying to cobble together enough money to buy the house and were determined to do it on their own without help from parents, especially (and she was fierce about this) Mickey. He hadn't played the guitar in years. She pulled the case from its hiding place, laid it on the bed, flipped the latches, and opened it. It gleamed up at her, the wood rich and deep except for the place where he had strummed away the varnish. She brushed her fingers across the strings, and it came back to her in a rush, the picture she saw from the window of her upstairs apartment that long-ago evening, Pickett slouching against the seat of the motorcycle, long legs splayed across the sidewalk, jeans and T-shirt and black boots with buckles on the sides, fingers drumming the guitar case, swaying to some tune in his head. *He sang, he wrote songs, he was crazy about me.*

That was the moment she realized she could not have what she wanted, to be loved irrevocably, and that she might never again be able to love unreservedly in return. There were things about him she still cherished, and she knew there were things about her he still valued and honored. But it was not the same. Large, important parts of him—and the ways they fit together—were gone. If she made do, as she intended, it would have to be with far less than she longed for.

She had a good cry. Then she calmed herself and finished packing.

⌒

Pickett was spectacularly good at what he did. He had a special ability to entice people to believe him and believe *in* him, to want to work for him. He gathered an inner circle, led by Plato, that was fiercely loyal and protective. His people were, he said candidly, his Teflon coating.

But he also had an incredible, almost unbroken run of luck. The economy was bustling. The old fights over things like civil rights were mostly over. He didn't have a great deal of need for Teflon. Inevitably, his inner circle became more and more like a family, demanding his time and attention. Inevitably, it bore him away.

Things grew even more complicated when Pickett became governor. He was gone a great deal, and that left a void that was much more than an empty seat at the dinner table. The children reacted differently. Allison became withdrawn and sullen. Carter loved the electricity of it. For Cooper, there were more demands, more responsibilities. She was a conduit to power, and people pressed in from all sides. She knew they would, if given the chance, pull and tug and maneuver and use, serving their own interests. She craved genuineness in people and knew there were many out there who, like her college friends, were good and true. But it was increasingly hard to find them. Eventually, surrounded as she was by the pullers and tuggers and users, it became virtually impossible. In time, she realized she had no close friends.

She put up defenses—tripwires, listening posts. She became less trusting of everything and everyone, and that became even more evidence of what was missing and unfinished in loving Pickett.

She saw how it happened in other marriages: love undercut by mistrust, mistrust leavened by love. A delicate balancing act that somehow kept men and women together despite betrayals, infidelities, wounds, neglect. Hearing a woman say of her humiliation, "I should have killed him," she would think, *Then why didn't you?* But she knew why. It was a sort of loving *in spite of*, but at a great price.

She thought it might have been easier, the giving up, if Pickett were, like so many political men, a philanderer—power and testosterone in league, one kind of conquest fueling the other. Winning political office seemed to give many the illusion of being able to live on the edge. Pickett, on the other hand, was one of those who, having won a prize, was fearful it might be taken away, and that made her reasonably confident he wouldn't run the risk of screwing around.

Instead, in his hunger for control, he created the self-illusion that he truly could bring order to things, minimize uncertainty and surprise. He couldn't, of course, and when things seemed to get out of hand, he railed against chance and circumstance.

She watched, aching over the changes in him. She helped him when she could without letting it take over their lives completely. She cared for Allison and Carter and waited for the day, however distant, when it might all be over. Then they would see what leftovers they could find from their beginning. She would see if anything was left of the man with the guitar.

So this life they had now started back with the State Senate, and that had started with Mickey. It was near the top of her litany of grievances against her mother. Mickey hadn't created him—Pickett was the one who made the choices—but her hands had been all over it all along. And whatever chance for peace they might have once had, well, that was long gone. Cooper kept Mickey at a distance. That was barren, wretched territory she vowed not to visit again. Ever.

NINETEEN

Then there was the League of Women Voters—a small, close-knit, vociferously activist group that Pickett referred to as "amateur do-gooders." But that didn't stop him from cozying up to them when it suited his purposes. The state chapter had been in business since shortly after the national organization was founded in 1920. Over the years, it had advocated for things like civil and voter rights, clean water and air, and public education. When the members had thrown their weight behind Cleve Spainhour's free textbook effort, they contributed toward pushing it through the legislature. It helped that some of the league's members were married to legislators and lobbyists. As Cooper had heard Mickey say, "Lots of politics gets done in bedrooms."

The state chapter invited Cooper to speak at its annual convention in the capital. She would normally have run the invitation by Pickett, but he was in Japan on an industry recruiting trip. She accepted, and after he returned, she never brought it up.

It was a fairly bland, safe, familiar speech, mostly about the growing involvement of women in government. The ladies of the league listened politely and gave her a nice round of applause at the end. And then the president asked if she would take a few questions. She could have begged off, pleading another appointment, but she really didn't need to be anywhere else at the moment, so she said yes.

"I'll start things off," the president said. "What do you think about what the legislature is doing to our public education system?"

That was a hot topic across the state. The legislature, in a frenzy of budget cutting to offset cuts in the state income tax, was siphoning off money from the public schools to fund thinly disguised pork-barrel projects it had slipped into the budget bill. Pickett supported the tax cuts—"Who doesn't like a tax cut?"—and was taking a wait-and-see attitude toward the spending side.

The question hung in the air. Cooper's heart went to her throat. *I shouldn't have done this.* But then she thought, *What the hell.*

"I feel the members of the legislature should be ashamed of themselves, stealing from our kids and teachers so they can pay for things like a new agricultural exhibit hall in Vincent County and a donation to the Elks Lodge in Canesboro. Do they really think those kinds of things are more important than giving kids a decent chance to make something of themselves? I hope not."

Dead silence prevailed for a moment, but then came a burst of enthusiastic applause.

"So," the president said, "what do you think we"—she placed a hand on Cooper's elbow—"should do about it?"

"Raise hell," Cooper said. "Tell it like it is."

Then she thought, *I believe I just kicked over a shit can.*

More questions rapid-fire on everything from the environment to dental hygiene programs. Cooper parried as best she could, trying to stay away from anything else controversial. It went on for ten minutes, and then she cut a glance at the president, who stepped forward and said, "All right, time for just one more."

A big, horse-faced woman with a loudspeaker voice at the back of the room (who reminded Cooper somewhat of Mickey): "Why don't you run for governor?"

Cooper laughed. "I think one politician in the family is quite enough."

"Put your money where your mouth is," the woman shot back. "You come here talking about how more women need to get involved in politics and government. Well, walk the walk, honey."

A ripple of nervous laughter passed through the room, and then the president put an end to the questions. Cooper escaped to the hallway and the security man waiting outside—waiting with Wheeler Kincaid.

"Oh, my God," Cooper said softly.

"A helluva speech," Kincaid said, and that was when he took her aside and told her about the naked parties at the lake house.

Before they parted, Cooper pointed in the general direction of the meeting room. "Are you . . . ?"

"I'm a reporter," Kincaid said, and left.

She went to the Capitol to tell Pickett about the young personal assistant, but she didn't say a word about the League of Women Voters. Pickett found out when he opened the *Dispatch* the next morning at the dining-room table and read Kincaid's story. His cry of rage brought Mrs. Dinkins and several of the house staff running, but before they could ask what was wrong, he was taking the stairs two at a time toward their bedroom.

Cooper was pulling on her slip when he thundered, "What in the holy name of shit are you trying to do to me?"

She hesitated a moment, hiding behind the silk, then pulled it down to see him standing in the doorway bug-eyed, face flaming, waving the paper so wildly that pieces of it were beginning to shred and fly off.

She tried to play it lightly. "Kincaid must have been wearing an invisibility cloak. Maybe he knows Harry Potter."

Pickett was having none of it. He threw the paper aside and took a step into the room. "How could you do something like that? And why?"

"I didn't mention your name, Pickett. I just said what I thought. I might not have said it if I'd known Wheeler Kincaid was lurking in a corner." She paused, feeling her spine tighten. "Then again, I might have."

"Well," he yelled, "you can't do that!"

"The hell I can't!"

"Do you for a nanosecond realize what you've done? Do you know who stuck that thing in the budget about the cow barn in Vincent County? Figgy Watson. The goddamn speaker of the House. Do you know why he put it in there? Because his cousin Eddie is chairman of the county commission, and when Cousin Eddie's construction company gets the contract to build the cow barn, he'll stick some money in Figgy's pocket. And the Elks Lodge? That's the work of the goddamn chairman of the Senate Finance Committee. Look, dammit, I am trying to squeeze a budget through the legislature, pay for some things *I* want to do, and here you come cutting the legs out from under me."

"Pickett," she said, struck suddenly by the gravity of it, "I didn't know what—"

"No, you didn't. You don't know. So stay the hell out of my business, Cooper. Now, I'm going to the Capitol and see what, if anything, I can salvage from this bomb you've set off." He threw up his hands—"Shit!"—and bolted off down the hall.

At midmorning, when Cooper was still shaken, the strangest thing happened. Mickey called. "Attagirl," she said, and hung up.

As it turned out, things weren't quite as bad as either of them feared. Pickett wheeled and dealed and kissed fanny and smoothed feathers and spread *mea culpa*s and money on the aggrieved legislators. At the same time, the League of Women Voters was, as Cooper had advised, raising hell. The members descended en masse on the Capitol, buttonholed legislators, made ferocious pronouncements, and sparked a public outcry. Legislators felt heat from back home, and with the league's members stalking the halls, there was no place to hide. They, and Pickett, quietly went about restoring most of the education money. Figgy got his cow barn and some money for an unneeded building at his local trade school. Cousin Eddie would be busy for a couple of years. The chairman of the Finance Committee was able to double the Elks Lodge appropriation for what was vaguely referred to as a "pilot educational project." Just about everybody got a little something.

The legislative session was supposed to end at midnight, but the two chambers stopped the clock and wrangled some more. At three in the morning, the budget passed. Pickett monitored things from his office, conjuring up last-minute deals to grease the skids, then stayed on until dawn, drinking scotch with Figgy and his crowd. He stumbled in just before first light, a bit drunk, totally exhausted. When he climbed into bed, they both lay there a long time, listening, waiting.

Finally, she said, "I'm sorry I made things hard for you."

"Oh, what the hell. Working with that bunch of idiots is hard even when they're not pissed off." He fell silent for a moment. "Cooper, this is like that condom thing when you were student newspaper editor. If Mickey hadn't put a leash on you, Cleve would never have gotten the free textbook business passed."

"You knew about that? About mother?"

"Everybody knew."

"What did you think about it, at the time?"

"I admired your spunk. You were always willing to swim upstream. I was disappointed you backed down. But that was then. This is now."

She was careful. She spoke up when she thought something was important—prenatal care, backlogs in an underfunded court system, a controversy at the university over a student fee increase to expand the football stadium. But she didn't blindside Pickett. She was careful to let him know when she was ready to say something, and if he convinced her it would cause problems for him, she usually backed off. There were a few times when she didn't, and a few times when Pickett sent Plato to argue with her.

"All right," she finally told Pickett. "I have things I care about. Some of them, I hope you care about. So don't tell me what I can't say, tell me what I *can* say that will help you."

To his credit, he did, and to her credit, she chose her audiences and her words carefully. It all seemed to come to an accommodation of sorts. But the whole business left a growing wariness on both their parts, and for Cooper, more of that creeping sense of loss, disappointment, loneliness. Again, politics as thief.

It was the third winter of Pickett's second term.

They drove to the upstate on a Sunday afternoon, just the two of them, Pickett joking about how rusty he was behind the wheel. An unmarked state trooper car behind them bore a couple of men from the security detail, keeping an unobtrusive distance. Pickett had surprised her that morning as they dressed for church. Some farmland he wanted her to look at, a place for a getaway. The thought of it—the echoes of the rambling little log house in the woods where they had started—lifted her spirits.

The hundred acres they trudged—Pickett with a plat map, both of them in jeans and parkas and hiking boots—touched that deep place in her that yearned for refuge. The tract was part woods—tall, thick-chested hardwoods, bare now in January, and a copse of pines covering a rise on which they could build a house, log and stone, where they could have a comforting fire on a day like this, and a screened porch with an overhead fan, and wicker furniture for June days when they could sit for hours with books, surrounded by the smell of earth and blessed quiet, underscored by the gentle whoosh of the fan and whatever nature had in mind. And best of all, the bold little creek coursing through the property, skirting the rise of pines, could be dammed and made into a pond. A place to lose herself, or better, to rediscover herself.

Pickett sat on the creek bank, watching as she walked its edge. Then, stepping carefully, bare stone by stone, she stood in midstream, listening to the rush and burble of the water.

"So?" Pickett called, breaking the silence.

"Buy it," she said.

"All or part?"

"The whole thing. If you don't buy it right now, I'll leave you and take up with whoever owns it."

"He's the local probate judge. Family made a lot of money in the fifties running juke joints. He's broke. Drank up all the profits. He wouldn't be a good investment."

"I'll go to work and support him."

"Doing what?"

"I might open a juke joint."

He pretended to think about it. "All right, you win."

So they stopped at the sagging white frame house where the probate judge lived with his shopworn wife and a pack of hunting dogs that seemed to have the run of the place. The judge served some fairly decent scotch while Pickett wrote a check for five thousand dollars to put a hold on the land and promised the rest by wire transfer the next day. The judge held the check, studied it, licked his lips. Then he placed it in the insistent outstretched hand of his wife. They all finished their scotch, and Pickett and Cooper took their leave.

"I'm putting the deed in your name," he said as he started the car. "It seems to be your kind of place." He leaned across the seat and kissed her. "Happy Valentine's Day. Or whatever. I love you."

They stopped at a Burger King, and one of the security men brought them hamburgers and milk shakes. They ate in the car, unnoticed, and then she settled in her seat as Pickett drove toward home.

Home? she thought just before drifting off to sleep. No, the place where they lived now, the white-columned mansion on the tree-lined street across town from the Capitol, was not home. Just a residence, and one she would happily escape before long. But on this chill afternoon, perched on a rock in the middle of a bold stream, she had found what she imagined might become home.

She awoke when the tires crunched on gravel, and she knew instantly and exactly where they were. She turned with a jerk to him, eyes wide. "Pickett, dammit!"

He shrugged. "I just thought . . . We're in the area. She's been feeling poorly. Virus, I think the doctor said."

"Shit."

"Cooper, come on. She's your mother. Just for a minute."

And then they pulled up in front of the house, the security car swinging in behind. Pickett gave a tap on the horn, and Mickey's housekeeper was at the front door, beckoning them in.

Mickey was propped queenlike in the vast sea of the four-poster bed against a mound of pillows, a clutter of orange plastic prescription bottles and a box of tissues on the bedside table, the lamp turned low to make the light flattering. A cigarette was in her hand, from which she took a long drag before stubbing it in an ashtray and peering at Cooper through the curling smoke.

Pickett held back, taking up a post by the door while Cooper stood at the foot of the bed, waving away the smoke while she and Mickey stared at each other.

" 'Hello' would be all right for starters," Mickey said in her dry, feathery voice.

"Pickett says you've been sick."

A flutter of Mickey's hand. "Well, I'm not ready to check out yet." She plucked a tissue from the box and dabbed her nose. "I'm feeling better already, just knowing you're here."

"Bullshit," Cooper said.

"Now, now," Mickey clucked, "let's not have any tacky language, Cooper. It's unbecoming."

"I learned at the feet of the master," Cooper said.

Mickey shrugged, then turned a smile on Pickett. "Pickett, honey . . ."

She motioned him forward, and he crossed to the bed, gave her a gentle hug and a peck on the cheek. He stood for a moment holding her hands before he let go of one of them and turned to Cooper.

"I, ah . . . There's something we need to talk about."

They all just looked at each other.

Finally, Mickey said, "I don't know what the hell this is, but it's beginning to smell a little grim. For God's sake, either sit down or crawl into bed with me. And take off your friggin' coats."

They sat, waited for Pickett, who was fumbling in his jacket pocket. *Buying time*, Cooper thought. It was an old trick. Whenever he wasn't quite ready to say whatever he was going to say, he fumbled.

Finally, he tossed the jacket aside and looked at the two of them, back and forth.

"All right, Pickett," Mickey said, "get on with it. What's on your agenda?"

"I'm thinking about running for president."

Silence, broken eventually by Mickey. "Bully for you, Pickett. You might even win." More silence. She looked at Cooper. "So, how long have the two of you been cooking this up?"

Cooper turned a withering glance on Pickett. "I never heard a god-damn word about it until just now."

Mickey's eyebrows went up, but she didn't say anything.

"Pickett," Cooper said, anger building, "did you have a revelation just now when we were tramping in the woods? Did God whisper in your ear, 'Go forth, Pickett Lanier, and lead my people'?"

Pickett scrunched up his face. "Well, I've been thinking."

"For how long?"

He shrugged. "Awhile. Actually, a pretty good while."

Mickey plucked a tissue from the box and blew her nose loudly. Then: "Okay, Pickett. If you've been cogitating over this, you've obviously given some thought to the messy details. Mostly, that you'll have to raise a helluva lot of money. Have you figured out how you'll do that?"

"Jake says—"

"You mean," Cooper broke in, "that you've been talking with Jake Harbin, and I'm just now hearing about this?"

"Honey, I just thought, before I went very far with it—"

"Pickett," she said, "you aren't *thinking* about running for president, you're *running*. So just go ahead and cut to the chase and admit it. Am I right?"

"Yes."

"Well, shit."

She stood, turned away from them, looked out the window toward where the pond was, there in the darkness. Cleve's pond. Only he'd never known it, never stopped long enough to get it built and sit in a boat with cane pole in hand and let the day become what it would. There was, for Cleve and Pickett, for their breed, always the next thing and the next thing. So all of today's hiking and buying land and talking about a getaway was a farce. *Hell, he wants to get away to the fucking White House.*

And then it was like she wasn't even there. She stared through the window while Pickett and Mickey talked. His strategy: announce soon, start working the early primary states. The primaries were a good way off, but a couple of senators were in the race already, people with national exposure, and more coming. He would start from way back but would work his ass off. An early primary win, or a close finish, and things would begin to fall into place.

Mickey eventually came back to the money. "The instant you announce, you're a lame duck, Pickett. You've got to get the early money here at home, and who the hell is going to shell out for somebody who can't do 'em any good anymore? And after that, you've got Woodrow. He'll be the next governor, and you know what that means. He'll kick your ass every chance he gets."

"I haven't figured that part out," Pickett admitted.

Cooper turned from the window. "Well, while the two of you plan for the inaugural, I'm going home." She started for the door.

"Give me just a few minutes," Pickett said.

"Take all the time you want," Cooper tossed over her shoulder.

She took her time getting downstairs, thinking, *This is the very last time I'll be in this goddamn place.* She got in the dark blue Ford and drove away, leaving Pickett to ride home with the security detail.

⌒

They mostly avoided each other for several days. Allison and Carter, antennas always out, felt the chill.

"Mom, what's going on?" Allison asked.

"Have you talked to your father?"

"Oh, yeah, something's going on, all right. When you start calling him 'your father,' you're pissed. So what are you pissed about?"

"*Dad* is running for president."

Allison shrugged. "So what? He's always running for something. I'm going to school in Atlanta, and all I want is to get the hell out of here and live my own life for a change. I'm damn sure not gonna stand on some platform with a shit-eating grin on my face while Dad campaigns."

"So he hasn't said anything to you about it?"

"We don't talk much."

"No," Cooper said, "you don't."

"How long have you and he been plotting this?"

"For Dad, apparently several months. I heard about it Sunday."

Allison wrinkled her nose. "So that's why you're pissed. Well, get over it, Mom. Dad's always done what he wanted. The rest of us, we're bit players, always have been. But I'm not gonna be anymore. You can make up your own mind."

Carter bustled in from college just after Allison left.

"I saw Allison downstairs," he said. "She told me what's going on." He sat beside her on the loveseat in her office, took her hand. "Dad should've told you. A long time ago. He does that a lot. Keeps things close to his vest. But he shouldn't ever do that to you."

She touched his cheek. "Honey, I'm okay. I'll get over it. It was a shock, but it'll pass. I'll go along, like I always do."

"Maybe you shouldn't."

"Aren't you excited? A presidential campaign? You love politics. I'm sure he'll want to involve you."

He leaned over and kissed her on the cheek. "Right now, that's the last thing on my mind." He stood. "I've got to go."

"Where?"

"To raise hell with Dad."

⌒

She was in the den having a glass of wine, watching the early-evening local news. Pickett was away, the National Governors' Conference. He was the chairman. He would be home tomorrow, and next week he would make his announcement. Plato would leak a hint with Pickett's blessing. Big crowd, some national press people. And then it would start for real.

On the newscast, videotape of a press conference, the commissioner of agriculture. Something about milk prices. There on the front row was Wheeler Kincaid, glowering under unruly eyebrows, asking an impertinent question. She didn't pay any attention to Kincaid's question, or the commissioner's flustered answer. She didn't care. But the sight of Kincaid startled her. She didn't know why until she realized the scene was taking her back to that day at the League of Women Voters meeting, the brassy, braying woman at the back of the room.

She thought about it, wrestled with it, long into the night.

The next evening, she met Pickett at the door. "We've got to talk."

When she had him to herself, he said, head down, "Honey, I'm truly sorry about . . ." He waved his hand in the general direction of the presidency. "I really screwed up. I didn't want to worry you with it until I thought it through, but that's no excuse. We should have thought it through together." He paused. "We haven't done enough of that lately." He reached for her hand. "I am really, really sorry. It won't happen again. From now on, you're in on everything."

She made him wait for a noncommittal minute before she said, "Would you like to make it up to me?"

"Tell me how."

"I want to run for governor."

Before he could catch himself, he laughed. Then he sobered. He took a long time before he answered. "Cooper, honey, that's about the most . . . unlikely thing I've ever heard come out of your mouth. There's not even the remotest chance you'll run for governor. I can't imagine why you'd even want to."

"Don't you want to know why I want to?"

"Okay, why?"

"I want to help you, Pickett. You talk about holding your home base. Who else could you trust? For damn sure, not Woodrow."

"Cooper, it's not possible. You can't win. So let's put the idea aside and get on with reality."

So that was that. Until two weeks later. He took her out to dinner, a private room in a small Italian restaurant, a favorite place from the time Pickett had gone to the State Senate years ago. Candlelight, expensive wine. They stayed away from politics, talked about the kids—Allison, finished with college and going on to art school, Carter at the university, custom-tailored double major in political and computer sciences. Where had all the time gone? They held hands across the table. With the wine glowing in her, Cooper felt herself let go, reaching back.

And then Pickett said, "Woodrow's not gonna run."

It took a minute to bring herself back from the glow, to focus on what he had said. "I don't believe it. You talked to him?"

"Yes. His wife is sick, he's distracted, his campaign operation is floundering. He wants to run for another term as lieutenant governor. Cheaper, less work. He'll win it without breaking a sweat."

She stared at him hard. Pulled her hand away. "What have you done, Pickett?"

"We had a talk. We came to an accommodation. My folks will raise the money he needs and provide the muscle. He might not even have to leave home."

"You bought him off."

"No," he said emphatically. "I gave him a way to do what he really wants to do."

She pondered it, knowing he had more. "What's the rest?"

"I want you to run."

She was speechless, her brain hitting a wall.

"We've done some polling. You've got good name recognition—your father, me, all that. And God help me, you've hit enough hot buttons over the past few years that you have a solid approval rating. You'll face a couple of other fairly substantial candidates, but they can't raise the money. We've got a lot of it tied up, and we've got the machinery. Cooper, with Woodrow out of the way, you can win. And this is the clincher: Woodrow will endorse you."

"What about the risk, Pickett? If we fail . . ."

"What about the reward? If we pull it off, imagine the effect. Nationally."

"So this is about your presidential thing?"

He shook his head. "This is about us, Cooper. It's something we can do together. We haven't had anything like that in way too long."

She sat back in her chair, folded her napkin, placed it beside her plate. "This is too much."

"You said you wanted to run. Okay, you can run. You can win. I can help. We can do it."

"I need to go home. I've got to think."

"Sure," he said. "I know this is a lot. Give it a couple of days. But we've got to start the ball rolling. I announce the end of next week. You announce—if you decide to go through with it—a week after that. So we've got to have an answer in the next couple of days."

He reached for her hand again, but she stood, backing away.

"All right. But until then, don't mention it to me again. I mean it."

He held up his hands in mock surrender. "The ball's in your court."

~

She awoke thinking of Jesse. She dreamed sometimes about him, but never about what happened in Vietnam. She could not bear the thought of him in agony, scared, alone, dying. She supposed that part was locked away so far back in her mind that it wasn't accessible even to dreams. No, she thought of his slow, sad smile; the way he read to her, eyes rolling when he happened upon a word especially delicious; his quiet, stubborn insistence on being himself; the way he gave himself to her in times and places and ways when she really needed him.

She had tried to understand how it must have been for him at the Big House. He had lost his mother in early boyhood, and then in precious ways had lost his father to Mickey just at the cusp of adolescence, when surely he needed Cleve most. The clash of wills with Mickey must have been inevitable, no matter the added flash point of Cleve's burgeoning political career and Mickey's hand in it. As she thought about their relationship, she came to the notion that Jesse might have needed her as much as she needed him. She adored and idolized him, thought him the most special person in her life, and he had needed that. It was something she held on to fiercely, something she also needed.

She thought about that incredible ride in Cleve's car in the fullness of July, heard the crackle of the bag of sunflower seeds, felt the hot breath of wind at the window, smelled his joint, heard the horns of the other cars honking as they led the parade down the two-lane, Jesse softly humming Fats Domino. She dwelt on that, not on what came after the ride. Another person—Mickey?—might say that Jesse used her that day. But that wasn't it at all. They were allies, compatriots in crime. It was a spectacularly audacious thing they did, something no one could ever take from either. If only they could have ridden forever.

Then she thought about Miami, all those McGovern kids in the park, hopelessly giddy with themselves and their ideas. Jesse's people, her people. She had been a part of him that day. And there were other times since then when she had taken heart from Jesse. Defied people and convention. Insisted on her own-ness. She had not done it enough in these later years, but she still knew how.

She lay there for a long time in bed thinking about him. Pickett had risen early, slipped out of the room, fled the house for his world. She summoned Jesse in the quiet and held on to him.

And then she thought, *I have never really shared him with anybody. But there is someone . . .*

She waited for Carter on the steps of the classroom building. It was chilly, a brisk wind tingling her face. She had on jeans and a parka, the same as when she and Pickett had tramped the woods.

He was almost down the steps before he saw her, and then his face lit in grinning surprise. "Mom!" He grabbed her in a hug, pulling her tight against him. "What are you doing here?"

"I was in the neighborhood, just thought I'd say hello. Are you free for lunch?"

"Sure!" He fished out his cell phone. "Let me make a call."

She waited while he finished, hung up, stuffed the phone back in his jacket pocket with a sheepish grin.

"Girl," she said.

At lunch in an off-campus diner, he told her. A basketball player. He was getting a ribbing about that from friends, dating a jock. Nothing real serious, he said, but she was nice. Not too tall—a guard, not a center.

"Just be sure you always treat her like a lady," Cooper said.

"I know how to do that. I've had a good example."

He went on about classes, social life, an internship he was doing in the Dean's Office. He was taking some marketing courses, studying why people made the choices they did, how to get them to make the choices you wanted. Like Pickett. She watched, smiled, listened. He was animated, gregarious, open. She always knew exactly what was on Carter's mind.

Finally, he said, "I'm sorry. I'm yakking on about me. What about you?"

She hesitated. "I'm okay. I came today because I wanted to see you, see how you're doing. You haven't been home in several weeks. But I also wanted to tell you about somebody."

His eyes went wide.

"Oh, no." She laughed, realizing how it sounded. "I'm not fooling around."

"Oh," he said. "Good."

She sobered. "I need to tell you about your uncle Jesse."

"He was killed in Vietnam."

"Yes."

"I don't know much about him."

"You should." She smiled. "You look a great deal like him. And you would have liked him."

She talked for a half-hour, telling him all she knew and remembered. He listened attentively, nodding occasionally. She tried to bring Jesse to life for him, knowing she could never do it justice but needing Carter to understand as much as possible. Needing, herself, to share this.

"Why now, Mom?" he asked when she finished.

"I'm not exactly sure," she said. "But it seems to have something to do with a decision I've got to make."

He gave her a puzzled look.

"Have you talked to Dad about his plans?"

"Briefly. We talked about me maybe working in the campaign."

"Don't get ahead of yourself. You've got school."

"Just for a semester, a bit longer if he catches on. Then back to school." He held up his hands with a smile. "I mean it." Then he leaned toward her. "But what's this decision you've got to make?"

She told him.

He listened wide-eyed. Then, softly: "Good gosh. Are you gonna do it?"

"I don't know. It was my idea a couple of weeks ago, and Dad dismissed it. But now, with Woodrow out, he's asking *me*."

He picked up his iced tea glass, twirled it in his hands, ran his finger up and down against the beads of moisture. "Have you talked to Allison?"

"You first. If either of you says I shouldn't, I won't."

He set the glass down and looked hard at her, then smiled his lovely smile again. "It's crazy," he said softly, "but if you did it, Uncle Jesse would bust a gut."

She returned the smile. "Maybe that's why I've been thinking about him so much the last couple of days. But Jesse . . . That alone isn't enough of a reason."

"No," he said, shaking his head. "Uncle Jesse's not here anymore. But if you do it for yourself—not Dad or anybody else, just yourself—that will be."

~

With Allison, it was quick. She sat stoically while Cooper told her. Cooper didn't mention Jesse. *It wouldn't register*, she thought. So she came to the point, gave the essentials.

"Is that all?" Allison said.

"I guess that pretty much is."

"Have you talked to Carter?"

"Yes."

"And knowing Carter, he agrees."

"I told Carter that if either of you doesn't think I should, I won't. I mean it."

"Well," Allison said, "don't let me stop you. It's another good reason for me to get the hell out of here."

She left Cooper sitting there with the sad disappointment that had been at the heart of their relationship for so long. What could she do?

And then the thought occurred to her: *Me and Mickey. There came a point when we just couldn't connect anymore. Too much damage done. I won't let it come to that with Allison. But right now, I don't know how. So I'll get on with things. She didn't say no.*

It was almost nine. She was at the dining-room table, finishing her dinner alone, when Pickett came in. He had eaten with his legislative leaders, he said. He sat with her, chair edged back a ways, legs crossed, waiting.

"All right," she said. "How?"

When he had finished telling her, she said, "I have one absolutely nonnegotiable condition: My mother stays out of it. Completely, no excuses, no exceptions."

It took a moment, but then he said without reservation, "Done."

At first, they faced a barrage of criticism. It came from all angles—political rivals, pundits, civic groups, newspapers. Especially newspapers, and most especially the *Dispatch*. Felicia Withers foamed at the mouth on her editorial page, calling it "the most blatant, inexcusable, craven power grab in the state's history. Cleve Spainhour would be ashamed of his daughter and the man she was unfortunate enough to marry."

That truly stung. Cleve would have blessed her, no doubt. He would have said, "Be your own person." He would not have been ashamed.

"Pay no attention," Pickett said.

"Easy for you to say."

"At least consider the source. Felicia is so mean, her urine could etch glass. She hates me, and therefore she hates you. And she can't stand the thought of another woman with real clout in the capital. So forget about Felicia and the other whiners. Concentrate on what matters."

What mattered first, she came to realize, was that the odds were in her favor. Pickett had seen to that. Woodrow had been the prohibitive favorite for so long that he had effectively kept several other prospects out of the race, and now, with him suddenly dropping out and Pickett's machine sewing up money and endorsements, it was very late in a game that demanded months, even years of preparation. An influential state senator would be on the ballot, along with the mayor of the state's largest city, but the rest of the primary field was a motley collection of minor figures. Pickett's polls showed that Cooper was being cautiously appraised by voters who were keeping an open mind, who remembered Cleve Spainhour with admiration and affection. What Cooper had to do was get out there among them and convince them she was legitimate.

So she did. Pickett's people gave her a crash course on issues, the back-room machinations of the political process, the hot buttons. She absorbed it, drawing on her days as a journalist, when she had to size up a situation, make sense of it, ask tough questions, be persistent. The more she learned, the more she began to stake out her own positions.

"I don't agree with you on some things," she told Pickett, "and I'm not going to parrot the party line."

"My God," he said, "have I created a monster?"

"Maybe."

"That's okay. In fact, it's good. You have to convince people you'll be your own person, not just keep the chair warm. Just go easy on me, okay?"

"Then don't cross me."

She had her own ideas about how to campaign, too. For the past few elections, Pickett's focus had been mostly on civic clubs, photo opportunities, TV and radio interviews, advertising.

"It's not enough," she said, her instincts taking over. "I'm going to do it Daddy's way."

Cleve's way had been to hire a band and a truck with a flatbed trailer and travel to every town and crossroads in the state. Set up the trailer on a town square or empty lot, then the band, thirty minutes of music to help draw the crowd, then Cleve. A speech, not too long, then into the crowd, shaking every hand, listening to everybody who had something to say, while the trailer and the band went on to the next stop. Pickett's Posse thought it was corny, amateurish, useless. They balked. She went to Pickett, who listened and then said, "Try it your way. See if it works." And he set his people to making it happen.

They talked more than at any time in years. She felt glimmers of their old life returning, back when each thought the other was so special. It was warm and comfortable. She felt truly needed.

She was ready, on a brisk day in early March, to go do it.

She had chosen the early stops on the tour herself. She asked for county-by-county voting results from Cleve's campaigns. He was solid in the upstate, his home country, less so at the other end. She remembered Cleve's quoting a wise political consultant years ago: "'If you want to pick cherries, go where the cherries is. Find your people, ask 'em to help, get 'em to the polls, and hope all the other folks forget there's an election.'"

So she began in the town a few miles from the Big House, in the parking lot of the courthouse where she had driven with Jesse those eons ago.

The band, a soft-rock group—Cleve had favored hillbillies, but that was then—was finishing a number when her car pulled up at the back of the trailer. She climbed nimbly up the steps, took the microphone from the lead singer, and stepped to the front. No podium, just Cooper and the people. Polite applause. A good crowd— not big, but good. She saw some familiar faces. The old sheriff, Joe Banks, long retired, feeble in a wheelchair. She waved. He gave her a wobbly thumbs-up. No sign of Mickey.

"Thank you for welcoming me home," she said, the loudspeakers at either end of the trailer booming her voice across the lot. "I grew up here among plain-spoken folks, and I want to be plain-spoken right off the bat. I am not a stand-in. I am my own person, and that's the kind of governor I intend to be. I don't owe anything to anybody except my daddy, who taught me what it is to be a governor who cares. And here are some of the things I care about. . . ."

When she finished ten minutes later—after plain-spoken words about education, jobs, clean air and water, clean politics, honesty, accessibility—the applause was more spirited. She climbed down from the platform and waded into the crowd, talking and hugging and listening until the last person had been attended to. In the car as she started for the next town—an hour late but flushed with adrenaline—she thought suddenly of Woodrow. The faculty picnic, Woodrow politicking everybody he could get his hands on, so earnest about making everyone feel special for a moment. He was, even back then, a master at it.

Maybe she had learned something from him.

She campaigned without Pickett. The governor's race was just hers, and she had to convince people of that. Besides, he was already diving into his own campaign—and taking criticism for spending so much time out of state. She made reference to that, gigging him a little. "I will be a full-time governor," she told the crowds. They liked it. Pickett bitched, but she didn't back down, and he dropped it.

She was good at campaigning, and got better. She listened and learned. Pickett's people grudgingly admitted she was on to something—the give and take, the time-honored laying on of hands—and she sensed that people were finding something both ambitious and genuine in her. The crowds grew in size and warmth. She didn't need

Pickett's polls to tell her she was gaining ground. She felt it, felt the momentum, the growing acceptance, the way she was sure Cleve had years ago. There was more to the pedigree than she ever imagined. Her opponents' radio and television ads were slick and artful, full of the language of attack. They weren't talking about themselves, they were talking about her. Fine. Her own TV ads were full of images of her out among the folks—brief sound bites not of her speeches but from the questions she got from people, the way she answered.

By the middle of May, two weeks from the primary, Pickett brought polls that showed her a hair below fifty percent and climbing. Toward the end, she got the grudging endorsement of most of the state's major newspapers. Not the *Dispatch*, of course, but that was fine, too. Felicia was beginning to sound hysterical. Let her.

She won without a runoff.

⌒

Then there was Micah Gladstone.

He was a dumpy, bug-eyed, young minister with thinning hair and no chin, pastor of a mega-church in the southern part of the state, idolized by a huge congregation captivated by his ringing nasal voice and strident fundamentalism—a Bible-thumping Ross Perot, as one columnist put it. He had enjoyed a meteoric rise among the religious right. Now, he crisscrossed the state holding revivals that attracted thousands. His Sunday sermons were televised live.

What brought him to political prominence was Highway 69, a brand-new, four-lane, limited-access ribbon of concrete connecting the state's two interstates. Pickett pushed the funding through the legislature and had it unofficially named the "Progress Parkway."

Just after the primary was finished, so was the road, millions of dollars over budget and mired in controversy after a big contractor and a minor functionary in the Highway Department were indicted by a grand jury on bribery charges. In June, a ribbon-cutting ceremony was to be held at the north end of the road. It was one of the few times during the election that Cooper and Pickett appeared together.

It was a beautiful day—eighty-five degrees, cloudless sky, large, festive crowd. And Gladstone. He drove up in an aging, rust-encrusted sedan thirty minutes before the ceremony, took a large placard out of the trunk, and placed himself squarely in front of the platform. The placard read, "PICKETT LANIER STOLE THIS ROAD."

Two uniformed state troopers politely invited the Reverend Gladstone to remove himself. He politely agreed, then planted himself again a few yards away, followed by the troopers, who now not-so-politely told him to get his ass back in his car and go home. He not-so-politely called them "Pickett's Gestapo" and moved to the rear of the crowd, where he was surrounded by reporters and cameras.

"This road is paved with evil," Gladstone said. "Decent folks' land was summarily taken from them by the state, the project has been a boondoggle for greedy contractors and corrupt officials of the Lanier administration, and"—he took a deep breath and arched his eyebrows—"the name is a vile abomination."

The reporters looked at each other. *What?*

"Highway 69. It's a perversion."

The reporters began to snicker. "You want to explain that, Reverend?" one of them asked.

"People know what I'm talking about. A perversion that Governor Pickett Lanier and his wife are throwing in the faces of the good people of this state, to go along with all the waste and fraud and invasion of property rights."

"Is that your *position?*" another reporter asked, to the laughter of several others.

Gladstone's icy gaze swept the crowd. People stopped laughing.

"Ladies and gentlemen, I am not some illiterate, holy-roller kook.

I speak for thousands of godly folks in this state. You can laugh if you want, but just put what I said in your newspapers and on your newscasts, and see what kind of response you get."

Then he stowed his placard in the trunk, climbed in his old sedan, and left.

The news people did what Gladstone asked. The reaction to the Highway 69 business among viewers and readers ranged from guffaws to clucking, depending on what Pickett called "the prude scale." But then the viewers and readers got past that and began to talk about the road and all its baggage. Gladstone organized a caravan along the highway, ending in a rally in front of the Capitol steps attended by several thousand people, who listened and muttered to themselves and each other as he blistered Pickett and his administration with accusations of cronyism, waste, arrogance, fraud, and godlessness.

A series of unfortunate events followed. A state trooper was arrested for running a prostitution ring out of his patrol car. A member of Pickett's cabinet was slapped with a divorce suit by his wife, who said in her complaint that he was addicted to pornography, and produced disks copied from his home computer to prove it. And finally, the news of falling revenue from the oil and gas fields along the coast, which had pumped billions into the treasury and fueled Pickett's health, education, and economic development projects. The wells were beginning to play out. One piece of bad news piled on top of another.

There was enough fodder to feed Gladstone's charges that Pickett's administration was a disaster, the state was in moral decline, and the evil of tax increases was lurking just around the corner. Fueled by the reverend's incessant carping and the staggering number of times he carped, from pulpits to street corners up and down the state, the mud began to stick. Sure, people said, Pickett Lanier had seemed to be a good governor. But behind the scenes, something stunk. Did the state need four more years of this?

Pickett's inclination was to ignore him, which he mostly did until

Gladstone announced he was running for governor as an independent. The state's legion of fundamentalist ministers piled on his bandwagon. The ministers were a powerful force, and Pickett had felt their wrath before, in what had turned out to be the only major blunder of his first term. In his run for office, backed by opinion polls, he had championed a state lottery to raise money for education. Once in office, he quickly pushed a lottery referendum through the legislature. It appeared certain for statewide approval—until the preachers went to work. They railed against the lottery from their pulpits and raised money for radio and television advertising. Evil trying to pass itself off as good, they said, a program that preyed on the poor and marked the state as a haven for gambling and all manner of associated sin. Almost overnight, the tide swung and the lottery was crushed. Pickett was chastened. For the rest of that term and all of the next, he made nice with the preachers. But they had never forgotten.

And now, with the Reverend Micah Gladstone carrying their banner, they became a howling horde, crying for Pickett Lanier's political hide—and by implication, his wife's as well. Gladstone handily gathered the petition signatures required to get on the ballot and prepared to skewer the Lanier bunch in the November general election.

In public, Pickett maintained an air of equilibrium. At home, he was nearly hysterical, no more so than on the evening he barreled in, color high, eyes wild, holding new poll figures that showed Gladstone only ten points behind Cooper and closing. The other party's nominee was third.

"The sonofabitch!"

"Isn't that a little strong to describe a preacher?"

"He's not a preacher, he's a demagogue."

"A sonofabitch demagogue. If his congregation only knew."

"Cooper, goddammit, this idiot could screw up the whole thing!"

"Yes," she said, "he sure could. But Pickett, that's politics."

But Micah Gladstone had a past, and Pickett's Posse found it.

As a teenager named Haskell Feaster in his native Oklahoma, he had served time in a juvenile facility on drug and weapons charges. He had fathered a child and been briefly married to the mother. Not long after abandoning wife and child, he had some sort of come-to-Jesus experience at a tent revival. He legally changed his name, served a hitch in the army that gave cover to his new identify, and, once discharged, began a life as a self-proclaimed evangelist. He said he was an orphan but in truth still had a large, nasty family in Oklahoma with a sizable collective criminal record.

A cousin, long ago ratted out by Haskell/Micah for an armed robbery that landed the cousin in prison, tipped off Pickett's people. They sat quietly on the information until October, then discreetly told Wheeler Kincaid at the *Dispatch*. The story broke in the Sunday paper. By sundown Monday, it was on nationwide television and virtually every political blog on the Internet. The preachers who had been Gladstone's core of support fell all over themselves in a righteously indignant stampede to denounce him. Gladstone called an emergency meeting of his mega-congregation. As live TV cameras beamed the spectacle, he sobbed confession, pleaded for forgiveness, and collapsed in a wretched heap at the altar. It was all over. Whatever taint had clung to Pickett Lanier was buried with the corpse of Micah Gladstone's political ambitions.

There was no need for Cooper to say a word. The campaign scaled back her appearances in the days before the election. Nothing to do but let the debacle unfold while the state and nation watched with morbid fascination.

When the votes were counted the first Tuesday in November, Cooper had a handful over fifty percent. Gladstone's name was still on the ballot, and he got almost two percent statewide. Through two recounts, her vote held up. Micah Gladstone, it turned out, had helped her win.

Her campaign headquarters hosted a big celebration when the last recount was done and the state elections board certified the outcome. Champagne, some stronger stuff in the back. Cooper and Pickett stayed until the last inebriated volunteer stumbled out the door.

Pickett sat on the floor, his back to a desk, champagne bottle in hand. She sat beside him. They nestled against each other. For a long time, neither said anything.

He took a swig. "We did it." He passed the bottle to her.

She took the last swallow and set the bottle aside. "Yes," she said with a smile, "I sure did."

He kissed her. Then: "Yes, you sure did."

PART FIVE

TWENTY

From the airport, she went straight to Mickey, who sat stone-faced while Cooper told her about Pickett and Woodrow.

When she finished, Mickey said, "It never sounded right to me, what Woodrow said about backing out. Did you suspect anything?"

"No," Cooper said, "I didn't. Maybe I didn't want to."

"I can understand that. And I'm sorry."

"Me, too. If I'd known at the beginning, I'd never have run."

"I don't mean I'm sorry about the political thing. I'm talking about you and Pickett, the personal."

Cooper bowed her head. *Yes, that most of all.*

"Cleve and I, we didn't always agree. And when we disagreed, it sometimes stopped just short of trading blows. Two bull-headed people. But we thrashed it out, and when we were done, we said, 'Okay, this is how we'll do it.' And we did it. Never once did we lie to each other."

Cooper was close to tears, her voice strangled. "It wasn't so much that Pickett lied . . ."

"There's all kinds of lies, honey. There's the kind when you misuse someone's trust, not so much about the obvious things, but about the big picture—what you both had back there at the beginning. Over the years, you've cut Pickett enough slack to stretch the length of the state. You went along."

"And I've seen what it's done, to both of us. I share the blame."

"Yes, you do."

Cooper raised her head now, choked back the tears. "You started it."

"The State Senate thing?"

"Yes."

"Guilty."

"I thought back then you were trying to steal him from me."

Mickey blanched, fell silent. "I saw Pickett as a young man with a helluva lot of potential, and I thought the two of you would make a great team—not so much the way your father and I did, but in your own way."

"We were never a team."

"I know. You fought it for a while, and then you just gave in. But you're right, I started it, and both of us left you out. No wonder things turned out the way they have. And I am profoundly sorry, Cooper." Tears were now in Mickey's eyes. "That's why I want so terribly to help you, to help clean up the mess I've made." Mickey's face collapsed.

Cooper, without giving a thought to what she was doing, went to Mickey's wheelchair, knelt beside it, took Mickey's hands. No words were necessary.

"So now," Mickey asked after they both got control of themselves, "what are you going to do?"

"I told Pickett I won't quit, no matter what. But on the way here from the airport, I thought, *It's too much. I can't do this. Let Woodrow have it.*"

"That," Mickey snapped, the old bite back in her voice, "is goddamn well what you will *not* do. I won't let you, for your sake and mine. There's not much piss and vinegar left in me, daughter, but there's enough to help you kick some butt."

⌒

Wheeler, like Mickey, didn't seem a bit surprised. "What Pickett owned up to, do you think that's all of it?"

"What else?"

"I've been around a lot of devious, ambitious politicians. Pickett will cut your nuts out and hang 'em in a tree for suet. Or rather, get Plato to do it. Am I speaking out of school here?"

"Under the circumstances," she said, "no."

"So you're gonna stick it out. You're firm on that."

"Yes."

"What about Woodrow?"

"I'd love nothing more than to haul him in here and tell him."

"To what end?"

"Instant gratification. But I won't. Pickett's right—it would wreck the legislative session, and I won't do that. I've got things I want to accomplish. So I will keep my own counsel. I can always change my mind. That depends partly on Pickett."

Wheeler's brow furrowed, his bushy eyebrows danced. "You know that this makes things more complicated. When the legislature gets here, with Woodrow believing the deal is firm, he'll do everything he can to throttle you. No sense in you getting credit for something if you're gonna be out in a year."

"You make it sound damn near hopeless, Wheeler."

"It's not. You're the governor, and there's power in that alone. There's a helluva lot you can do, or refuse to do. But the best thing you've got going is *you*."

"What do you mean?"

Wheeler smiled. "You've got the best of Cleve and Mickey. And I think you're beginning to realize that. So fine-tune your bullshit detector, keep your head up and your ass down. I'll do my best to help." Then he looked up at the portrait of Pickett on the wall behind her desk. She turned to follow his gaze. "What are you going to replace that with?" he asked.

"My father."

"What do you think he'd do next?"

"What I'm going to do. Get Pickett's cabinet in here."

By the time they gathered at three o'clock, Colonel Doster's tersely worded letter of resignation was on her desk, along with a copy of a news release from Pickett's headquarters announcing that Doster had been appointed director of campaign security and special advisor on matters of law and order.

Two of the cabinet members had left weeks ago to join Pickett's campaign, and now that Doster was gone, nineteen were left at the massive table that had been the meeting place of governors' closest advisors for more than a hundred years.

Cooper stood at the end of the table, Wheeler at her left, Grace at her right, notepad in hand.

"I apologize for taking so long to get us together," Cooper said. "It's been a busy few days, and I didn't want to take you from your jobs with so much going on. Thank you for all you and your departments have been doing to help us deal with the snow. We have a lot of work ahead, but we're past the crisis stage. Right now, I want to dispense with a formality. When a new chief executive takes office, it's customary for the appointees from the past administration to tender their resignations.

And then it's up to the incoming governor to decide on the makeup of the new administration. I'd like to have your letters—undated—on my desk by the close of business today. If anyone wants their resignation accepted immediately, let me know. Otherwise, I'll meet with each of you individually over the next week to talk about where we go from here. Any questions?"

They all stared, dumbfounded.

"Thank you for coming, and for your service to the state. General Burgaw, please join me in my office."

Her office had a seating arrangement in a corner—a comfortable loveseat facing a high-backed chair, a coffee table with a leather-bound Bible and a pictorial history of the state, low light, gilt-framed portraits of venerated Confederate generals on the walls behind.

General Burgaw sat on the loveseat, deep-etched fatigue lines on his already-weathered face, but holding himself resolutely erect. He had put on a dress uniform for the cabinet meeting. They sipped coffee.

"General, do you know the background of this little corner?"

"I don't."

"Pickett arranged it when he took office. He called it his 'wrestling ring.' He thought if he could get a fellow in this corner, get him to feel the weight of all these symbols of state legacy, and use the right combination of arm-twisting, horse-trading, and gentle persuasion, he could bring him around to wherever he wanted."

Burgaw set his cup down. "I've never had occasion to be in the ring. So where do you want *this* fellow to be?"

"Across the street. I'd like for you to be director of the Department of Public Safety."

He fixed her with his steel-gray eyes. "Why me?"

"I've watched you work the past few days. You pull people together. You lead. You cut through the nonsense and get to the meat of things. You know what you're doing."

"I don't have any experience in law enforcement."

"I consider that an advantage. The people with law-enforcement experience who've been running things over there are a disaster."

"Yes, ma'am, they are."

"I'm told we have plenty of good people in the department throughout the state, but they've come to accept the way things are. They are uninspired and demoralized."

"That's my impression," he said.

"What they need, and what I need, is somebody who can knock heads, clean things up, build confidence and morale, and get the place running like it should. I need you, and I will back you with every power of this office."

He bent forward, clasped his hands, stared at them. When he didn't answer for a long while, she thought, *He's looking for a gracious way to say no.*

Then he looked up and straightened his shoulders. "I've had my military retirement papers drawn up for several weeks. It's not like me to dither, but something kept telling me to wait. I guess this is why. So, yes, it's an honor, and I'm pleased to accept."

She let her breath out with a whoosh. "Thank you, Lord. I hope all of my wrestling matches are that easy. When can you start?"

"I can resign as adjutant general this minute. Then I'll just be a retiring military reservist with a new job."

They rose together, and she stuck out her hand. His firm grip enveloped hers.

"I accept your resignation, and you are hereby appointed. Now, if you have another few minutes, I'd like to walk with you over to Public Safety, gather the troops, issue a call to arms, and turn them over to you."

He picked up his cap from the coffee table and stuck it under his arm. He had a glint in his eye. "I guarantee you, I will take care of business."

⁓

She found Mickey propped up in bed, telephone in one hand, cigarette in the other.

"You are the worst patient I've ever seen. I've never known anyone so dead set on doing everything she's not supposed to."

"I love you too, Cooper," Mickey said. Her hand shook as she slowly hung up the phone. "Now, I ask you sweetly, will you give it a rest for a few minutes?"

Cooper settled into a chair. "Whose ears were you bending?"

"This one and that one. You've been marching through the Capitol like Sherman through Georgia, and I had to get all my news on the telephone."

"My abject apologies. I should have brought my entire staff over here and given you a detailed briefing."

"The one who *wouldn't* talk was Wheeler. He stonewalled me."

"He works for me," Cooper said, and didn't try to keep the irritation at bay.

Mickey smiled. "That's the way it should be, but damn, it pisses me off. We've been trading secrets for years."

"All right, all right." Cooper waved her hands. "I'll tell Wheeler he can tell you anything he knows. Does that make you happy?"

"Supremely. Hell, it'll all be buried with me before long."

"Okay, so you know what's going on. Advice?"

Mickey pulled the bedcovers up to her chin and thought for a moment. "Cooper, your fanny is so far out on a limb, there ain't much but air beneath you."

"I know that."

Mickey looked at her appraisingly. "But what you did today, that's staking out territory. Keep doing it. Like Cleve and the Highway Department."

"I don't remember that," Cooper said. "I was more worried about braces on my teeth than what was going on downtown."

"When he took office," Mickey said, "the Highway Department was in about the same shape as Public Safety is now—maybe worse, because the opportunity for corruption was incredible. Bid rigging, kickbacks, people in and out of government—including some of the ones who helped Cleve get elected—making money off road contracts. People, me included, told him, 'Go slow. Don't stir up a fuss at Highway. Ease into things.' But he did anyway. It was one of our colossal arguments, and he won hands down. Buckets of blood were shed, including his. The money people and their people in the legislature blocked him at every turn. But then the feds got wind of what he was up to and started investigating. A grand jury, indictments, trials, people going to prison. There were times during those first two years he thought of himself as a failure. But he wasn't."

"You think that may happen to me?"

"Possibly. But when you believe in something, be like your father, not me."

"Anything I should have done today that I didn't?"

"Yeah, you shoulda pushed Pickett out of that helicopter at about two thousand feet." Mickey closed her eyes and lay back against the pillows. "Now, go away. I'm pooped. Call Estelle to get this bed cranked down."

"I can do it," Cooper said.

She found the control, lowered the bed, then stood there for a minute while Mickey's labored breathing slowed, her face relaxed, and she slept. She took Mickey's hand—brittle bones barely covered by thin, mottled skin, veins snaking cordlike just under the surface. It occurred to her that she had never really, truly looked at her mother's hands. She had no recollection at all of Mickey's hands in her childhood. Surely, she had been picked up, hugged, fussed over. Surely, they had been kind hands at times. She could not recall Mickey's hands ever being used against her in anger. She could not recall ever being jerked, slapped, spanked, even shooed away. Of course, there was that terrible moment at the sheriff's with Jesse. She recalled with absolute clarity the whack of Mickey's purse against Jesse's head. But it was the purse she remembered, not the hand that wielded it.

She thought now of the insistent feeling that had been with her the past couple of days—the yearning, the empty place where she had so often wanted Mickey to be. She felt her heart and soul opening to it now, each of them opening to the other.

And at the edge of all that was the memory of Cleve in his last hours: "We are the sum of our regrets."

No. Not here.

TWENTY-ONE

She got a briefing from Burgaw. The weather was warming—highs in the fifties over the next several days—and that, along with the massive effort, was beginning to bring about a sense of normalcy.

She scheduled a news conference in the afternoon. She would face questions about the snow, but more than that about what had happened with Doster and Burgaw. The *Dispatch* was full of speculation, much of it wildly off base. Felicia Withers's column in the morning paper had given grudging approval of the change but questioned Burgaw's credentials. Cooper had to address that. Along with all the other.

The intercom buzzed. Grace sounded frantic. "We've got a problem with Wheeler."

"What do you mean?"

"They called from the Finance Department. He's over there creating a fuss. Going through files. Yelling at people."

"My God. Tell him to get over here. Right now."

He came ten minutes later, waving a thick file folder, his color high. "I knew it!"

"What are you talking about?"

He dropped the folder on her desk. "The state bought fifty tractors from Jake Harbin on a no-bid contract. They called it an emergency and paid a premium price. I've been sniffing around this piece of crap for months, but everybody was afraid to talk. Now, I've got 'em."

She realized she was sitting on the edge of her chair. She took a breath and settled herself. "Wheeler, sit down."

It took a moment, but he finally sat. His unruly eyebrows twitched.

"Is this your idea of what being a chief of staff is about?"

Wheeler pointed at the folder. "The sonofabitch is stealing."

"The way it was done, was it legal?"

"Technically, yes. The Finance Department can declare an emergency under certain circumstances."

"When did the state buy the tractors?"

"Last year."

"Who was governor last year?"

"Doesn't matter," he said stubbornly. "It's still wrong. Don't you want to do something about it?"

"Not right now, I don't." Cooper picked up the folder. "Wheeler, we can't undo everything that's been done before. We can try to keep it from happening on our watch. I'm going to make you a promise: I'm not going to do anything illegal, and I'll try my best not to do anything underhanded."

He ran his hand through his hair. "All right. That's fair enough."

"But keep digging. Quietly. What you find, it may be something we'll need later." She handed him the folder.

"This isn't an isolated case," Wheeler said. "Pickett and Jake Harbin are joined at the hip. Fifty tractors? That's peanuts."

Home for lunch, she heard the sound of canned laughter from the downstairs den. Mickey was in her wheelchair, Nolan Cutter and Nurse Dubose sitting on either side.

"What in God's name are you people doing?"

Estelle said, "This channel's running *Seinfeld* back to back all day."

"Hush, Estelle," Mickey commanded. "I can't hear with you yammering. Cooper, go get some lunch."

Nolan followed her to the dining room, where Mrs. Dinkins was setting a plate at her place—the head of the table now.

"Want some?" she asked Nolan.

"Mrs. Dinkins already fed me. Mrs. Dinkins, will you go home with me and do that every day? Marriage would not be out of the question."

"Ha!" Mrs. Dinkins said, and prissed off.

He sat with Cooper while she ate.

"Nolan, you don't have time to make house calls."

"I was on the way home, taking the afternoon off. Just thought I'd stop by."

"So, how is she?"

"If a cat has nine lives, she's on her tenth. Fragile, but holding on. She's got a purpose, and that's better than any medicine I know. She says you're her last political hurrah."

Cooper laughed, then sobered. "She tells me things it would take me months to figure out, if ever. And then there's . . ."

He waited, then finished for her: "The heart-and-soul thing."

"Mother and I have been at odds a great long while."

"What's propping her up now is more about that than politics. Unfinished business. She has to deal with things now. I've been honest with her. It's the only way I know how to be. She's clinging by her fingernails, defying gravity. But she can't do that much longer. With congestive heart failure, you just keep losing ground until there's no more to lose. It could happen anytime."

Cooper pushed her plate aside. "We're trying. We both have something to give." She folded her napkin and stood. "One other thing: How the hell did she get downstairs?"

"I carried her. She weighs almost nothing."

"I have people on the staff who can do that kind of thing, Nolan."

"Look, there's not much I can really do for her now. But I can do that. So bug off."

They stopped outside the den. Mickey was asleep in her chair, Estelle still watching TV.

"All the other stuff," he said, "is it going okay?"

She had an impulse to unburden—Pickett, Woodrow, the rest—but she stopped herself, seeing the fatigue lines on his face, how depleted he looked. An afternoon off—he needed that. He had enough on his mind without the weight of her business.

"I'm making it."

"If you need to talk, to somebody who has nothing to offer but listening . . ."

She gave him a kiss on the cheek. "I know that. If I call crying—"

"I'll be here with a shoulder and a handkerchief."

She walked with him to the door, then went back to the den.

"Estelle," she said, "don't you want to go home and get some rest?"

"I'd rather stay, if you don't mind."

"Of course I don't mind. You're wonderful."

Cooper sat back in a chair. A new episode was starting: *Seinfeld buys a cigar-store Indian to impress Winona, who is offended because she's Native American. Kramer wants to write a coffee-table book about coffee tables.*

Her eyes popped open when the closing theme song came on. She felt guilty for a moment, but then thought, *To hell with it.*

⌒

"Tell me about Wheeler," she said to Mickey. "I really don't know much about him beyond the *Dispatch*."

"Almost nobody does."

"But you do. He had a wife, I know that."

"Sara. It was a horror show," Mickey said. "They married young, in the heat of the moment, and it wasn't long after that he figured out she was the worst kind of violent, suicidal manic-depressive. She made Wheeler's life a nightmare. But he stuck with her, kept her at home until he just couldn't do it anymore. She tried a couple of times to kill him. He finally got commitment papers. She went to a state mental hospital, and last year she managed to commit suicide. Despite all reason, Wheeler blames himself."

"He's a driven man."

"He escaped into his work. I met him when I started clerking in the legislature. I was fascinated with what he did, and how well he did it, and how much he knew about politics and politicians. We became friends. When I picked up some scuttlebutt about one thing or another, I'd sometimes pass it along. When Cleve and I married and I moved upstate, Wheeler and I stayed in touch. Neither of us ever tried to take advantage of what the other one knew. He's always had a great interest in you, especially after you decided to go into the news business. You should appreciate who and what he is."

"Believe me, I do."

⌒

She was on the way to the Capitol when Carter called. He had an edge to his voice that bordered on fright. "Mom, what's going on with Plato?"

"What do you mean?"

"He's gone. Just walked out, disappeared."

"Maybe Dad sent him on an assignment."

"No, I think Dad fired him. It's really weird around here. There are all these new people. Everybody's clammed up, including Dad. I asked him, but he said it's nothing for me to be concerned about. He was pretty short with me. I thought maybe you'd know."

"I'm as surprised as you are. Plato and Dad have been together from the beginning."

"Would you ask Dad?"

She thought about it. "No," she said. "I'm trying to keep Dad's business at arm's length. I've got plenty on my own plate."

His voice was shaky. "I'd just like to know what's up."

"Are you okay? Do you need to come home, honey?"

"Not yet."

"Okay. Call me if we need to talk, tonight for sure."

"I will." A moment, then he said, "I miss you."

Purvis Redmond was waiting when she got to the office, a stack of documents in hand. He placed it on the desk in front of her and stood there fidgeting.

"What is all this?" she asked.

"Just routine stuff," he said. "Appointments to boards and commissions, proclamations, executive orders, so forth."

She picked up the top sheet and read it. "We're appointing . . . who? Pearl Reddock to the Cosmetology Board? Who is Pearl Reddock, and why am I appointing her?"

"Pickett—"

"Purvis, when I appoint somebody to something, don't you think I ought to know who he or she is, and why I'm doing it?"

"It's all been checked out," he said, his voice going up an octave. "Thoroughly vetted. This is just leftover stuff."

She went through the pile. At the bottom was a thick bound document that at a glance seemed to have something to do with real estate.

Cooper sat back in her chair. "All right, Purvis. I'm sure you've done your job, and I appreciate that."

He looked relieved. He straightened, pulled a pen from his jacket pocket, and thrust it toward her.

"But," she said, "it's going to be my signature on these things, and that makes me responsible. Give me a one-paragraph description of each, what I'm doing and why."

His face fell. "The big one there," he said stiffly, "I'd appreciate your going ahead and signing that now."

"Why?"

"It's a land swap. A lot of negotiations have gone into putting it together."

"What kind of swap?"

"The state is getting some prime land on the coast for a park, in return for a tract upstate that some folks want to turn into a resort development. It's a straight exchange, no money involved. The governor signs off, then it goes to the legislature for approval."

"As I said, I'll look it over."

"But—"

"Thank you, Purvis."

He stood a moment longer, hands twitching. Then he put the pen back in his pocket. "Well, all right," he said finally. "If you say so."

"I do."

When he was gone, she called Wheeler. "I'm sending you a thing about a real-estate transaction. Look it over, see what you think."

Purvis Redmond was back the next morning with a couple of sheets of paper summarizing the proclamations and appointments he had handed her the day before. She read while he waited.

"They look fine, Purvis. Grace will get them back to you."

"If, ah, you could go ahead and sign the real-estate thing . . ."

She glanced again through the briefing sheets. Nothing about the land swap. "You don't have anything here about that."

Purvis shifted his weight from foot to foot. "It's like I told you, land on the coast for land in the upstate. It's a good deal for everybody." He paused, opened his mouth to form a word, then quickly closed it. She saw that he had almost spoken Pickett's name. "We wouldn't want the parties to get the idea there's a problem."

"The parties?"

"It's all right there," he said.

"All right," she said after a moment, "I'll get to it. Thank you, Purvis."

She called Wheeler. "Have you had a chance to look over that business about the land deal?"

"Not yet."

"Can you take a few minutes?"

"Is something wrong?"

"Purvis Redmond seems anxious about my signing off on it. Maybe he's just being Purvis."

"Do I hear the hum of a built-in bullshit detector?"

"Maybe."

TWENTY-TWO

Mickey was settled in her wheelchair, swathed in a garish purple robe Nolan had brought, smelling of lilac water from the bath Estelle had given her, hair clean and tied back with a ribbon. She was reading a newspaper, turning the pages noisily, making an occasional mumbling comment.

"How are you?" Cooper asked.

Mickey grunted, put the paper aside. "I'm trying real hard to make it to March. Six weeks to go on a ticker that's running on two cylinders. March, I can handle. Not February. It might snow again, and that would cut down on the funeral crowd."

"But with a good band and an open bar, they might brave the elements."

"You'll see to that?"

"I reckon."

"I mean a really good band. Maybe the Eagles."

"I thought you'd say Guy Lombardo."

"Ha! He's dead. But that would be a hoot, a dead guy playing at my funeral."

"What on earth do you know about the Eagles?"

"You'd be surprised what I know," Mickey said.

"No, at this point, I probably wouldn't. What do you know about Plato?"

"Personally?"

"Yes."

"Everybody has secrets," Mickey said. "Why?"

She told Mickey about Carter's call.

Mickey pondered it. "Maybe, all of a sudden, there's more than speculation. But so what? The homosexual thing isn't the issue it used to be."

"It might be for Pickett," Cooper said.

"Yes, knowing the stakes now, it might be. I do know this: Pickett wouldn't be where he is without Plato Underwood. If there's been a rift of some kind after all these years, it's cataclysmic. I know some people who might know."

"Don't wear yourself out with the telephone."

Mickey smiled. "In my next life, I'm going to have one implanted in my head. All I'll have to do is think of somebody I want to talk to and, bingo, I'm connected."

Cooper's cell phone rang. Wheeler.

"I looked it over," he said.

"And?"

"On the surface, it seems straightforward. But it's a pretty big deal, and it's apparently been in the works awhile, and I haven't heard a whisper about it. Did I miss it, or has it been kept completely under wraps for some reason? It has an odd smell about it."

"I'm getting some pressure to sign it," Cooper said.

"That says something. I need a few days to do some digging, see if I can figure out what's what."

"Buried bodies?"

"Maybe. I've got my shovel out. This is what I do."

"I know," she said. "That's why I keep you around."

After disconnecting, she told Mickey about the land swap.

"Follow the money," Mickey said.

"But no money is involved," Cooper said.

"Don't be so sure. Money, real money, is quiet. So quiet you have to listen hard to hear it. The noise in politics, it's mostly about what people call 'issues.' Folks at opposite ends of the spectrum yelling at each other. The gun nuts and Bible thumpers over here"—she stretched out one arm—"and the bleeding hearts and tree-huggers over here"—she plucked the air with the other. "Smoke and fire, thunder and lightning. But back in the shadows, being quiet, are the people with the big money, people who stand to make a lot *more* money, depending on who holds office. And they don't really care which bunch it is, gun nuts or tree-huggers. They can do business with either, or anything in between, or both at the same time. Whatever works. They are happy letting the circus go on, the nastier and noisier the better, because that's what gets attention."

"That's incredibly cynical."

"Don't get me wrong, money people have ideas and opinions, but they rarely let them get in the way of their money. So always, always, follow the money. Wheeler knows that better than anybody. If there's a body, he'll find it."

She awoke with a start. A commotion outside in the hall, a scurrying of footsteps, light filtering under the door. Estelle's voice. She sat up, trying to get her bearings. Pitch black at the edge of the window shade. The clock: just after five-thirty.

She threw back the covers, pulled on a robe, and padded down the hall, slippered feet making tiny squeaking sounds on the carpet. The door to Mickey's room was open. Estelle was hovering over the hospital bed, cranked up so Mickey was in a near-sitting position. Mickey gasped wretchedly for breath, body rigid, face ashen, eyes wide.

"Cough, Miz Mickey," Estelle ordered. "Cough and get that junk out of there."

Mickey made a feeble attempt that degenerated into a desperate, rattling wheeze. She spotted Cooper in the doorway. "Don't," she rasped, "don't let them!" She looked terrified.

"Can I help?" Cooper managed.

"No," Estelle snapped.

Cooper closed the door, backed away, stood motionless listening to the agonized sounds from the other side. She paced the hallway with a gathering sense of dread. *Just when we . . .*

She didn't know how long it took, but the door finally opened, and Estelle poked her head out. "It's all right, Miz Lanier. She just had a bad spell. Hard time breathing. I'm getting her settled down. Can you fix you and me some coffee?"

She was back in fifteen minutes with two cups. They sat together in the hall and drank.

"She's resting," Estelle said.

"Is she . . . ?"

"It's getting worse. Fluid and congestion building up around her heart. It squeezes everything—breathing, blood flow. She's losing ground, but as sick as she is, she's got a fierce will." Estelle sipped her coffee. "She talks about nothing but you. To me, to everybody she gets on the telephone. I think you're the one keeping her here."

"Does she need to be in the hospital?"

"She doesn't want to go."

"That's not what I asked."

"And that's not for me to say. Ask Dr. Cutter."

Wheeler called while she was getting dressed. "I've got to make a trip out of state."

"Where?"

"The people making the swap with the state, they're incorporated in Virginia. I don't know anything about them, and the Secretary of State's Office ain't gonna give me information on the phone. So I'm going up there."

"Is that really necessary?"

"The more I sniff around, the stronger the smell gets."

"All right," she said. "Mother had a bad time early this morning. She's slipping. Get back as quickly as you can."

Mickey was sleeping, mouth open, face slack. Gaunt, wasted flesh against the stark white of the pillow. Tortured breathing. Machines beeped and gurgled. Cooper went first to the window, pulled back the edge of the curtain. Almost six-thirty now, gathering light beyond the trees to the east. In the light from the security lamps across the front of the mansion, a cover of lingering snow. Everything quiet and still. Waiting.

She sat, leaned back in the chair, one arm resting on the side of the bed, and closed her eyes, letting all the air out, breathing so shallowly that time and her mind seemed to pause, turn inward. Then she felt a mere hint of a touch, fingers on her arm. She opened her eyes, looked at Mickey's hand, studied it, took it in her own. Mickey's breathing seemed to ease. She gave Cooper's hand a weak squeeze.

Cooper looked at Mickey's fingernails—gnarled, yellowed, much too long. Then she laid Mickey's hand aside, rose, went to the door, called down the hall for Estelle: "I need some fingernail clippers."

"Do her toenails while you're at it," Estelle replied. "They need it, too."

Nolan was there an hour later. He spent awhile with Mickey and then joined Cooper downstairs for breakfast.

"The hospital?" she asked.

"It would make things easier, but it's not a necessity. She's adamant about not going. She can stay here, if that's what she wants and you're okay with it. We'll make her as comfortable as possible, try to keep her off the telephone, make her rest."

"Can you give her something to knock her out?"

"I offered, but she told me she's got to have her wits about her if she's gonna keep you straight." He smiled. "Whatever else is slipping, her sense of humor is intact."

⁓

The resignation letters from Pickett's cabinet members were on her desk. Seven were leaving immediately. Twelve remained, and most of those, she thought, would have to be replaced. She needed her own Posse. All that to do, a budget to put together, a legislative session coming up. And Wheeler gone. She was spinning her wheels, losing momentum. She felt helpless.

Pickett called. "I've talked to Woodrow."

"And?"

He didn't say anything at first, then: "All the ruckus you're causing—the cabinet, Burgaw—he's pissed."

"What did you tell him?"

"I told him everything's okay. I'm handling it, you're totally on board. The cabinet business, I reminded him he'll want his own people anyway. I got him settled down."

"Whatever you and Woodrow have between you means nothing to me."

"You're wrong there," Pickett said. "It means a helluva lot to you. So when you and Woodrow cross paths, don't screw it up, Cooper."

"Don't screw it up for *you*. You couldn't care less what happens to me, as long as it doesn't step on your toes. But I'm stuck with a lieutenant governor who has his own agenda, who thinks he's going to waltz in and take over my office—*my* office—without earning it, and in the meantime doesn't have any reason to help me get anything done."

"Dammit, Cooper, I'm trying to help you!"

"And damn you, Pickett! You have become a lying, underhanded, self-obsessed asshole. And with all of those qualities, you'll probably make a good president."

Mickey looked better—weak, shaky, diminished, but some of her color had returned, and her voice was stronger.

"Thank you for not carting me off to the hospital."

"Nolan says you're okay here. For now."

"I don't want to die in a room with fluorescent lights."

"Mother . . ."

Mickey raised a hand. "We've got to talk about it, Cooper. The string is just about played out." She paused. "Do you want to know how I feel about that?"

"Yes."

"I'm a little spooked—not about passing on, but what comes after, being called to account. It's probably too late to do anything about the ruckuses I've caused. I've never put much stock in the notion of death-bed salvation. I suspect the Lord might stop me at the gates and say, 'Whoa, not so fast, there.' I guess me and the Lord will have to work all that out. Get the sin report, take my medicine. Maybe a few eons on kitchen duty."

"That would be a switch," Cooper said. "I can't remember ever seeing you in a kitchen."

"I wouldn't know a dishwasher from a doily."

A knock at the door. Mrs. Dinkins poked her head in. "Lunch is ready."

"How long has she been here?" Mickey asked when she was gone.

"Eight years," Cooper said. "First day of Pickett's first term."

"When we were here, there was a steady stream of help." Mickey paused, wrinkled her nose. "They said I was a bitch to work for." Cooper didn't respond. Mickey tilted her head, gave a sideways look. "Sometimes, a little bitchiness is helpful. It's an art form. But I have a habit of taking it too far. Like with you."

"I never thought of you as being *bitchy* with me, Mother. I just didn't think you were paying attention. You weren't there, and I missed you."

"You blame politics."

"In part."

"Well, don't. Blame me."

"Maybe you didn't have a good example. You've never talked about your own parents."

"I'm not going to use that as an excuse, but no, I didn't learn much there. Or maybe I learned the wrong things."

Cooper waited as Mickey gathered her breath.

"I may not have much luck getting my transgressions past the Lord, but I'm trying to clean up some of the mess before I leave. And I'd like to do it at home."

"Home?"

"The Big House."

"Good Lord. Mother, there's no way—"

"I've talked to Dr. Cutter, and he's talked to Fate Wilmer. It can be done."

Cooper shook her head vigorously. "You're all nuts."

"And I want you to go, too. I need you there. I need *us* there."

Cooper slumped in the chair and closed her eyes. *Things keep piling up.*

Mickey waited a long while before she said, "If you can't manage it, I understand. But don't think about it right now. Go tend to your business. Save the world, or at least try not to screw it up."

⌣

She called Nolan. "Did you tell Mother she could go home?"

"I didn't tell her she could *do* anything. She asked me if it was possible, and I said yes. There's nothing we can do for her here that we can't do there—around-the-clock nursing, Internet monitoring, so forth. We can keep her comfortable and make the end as easy as possible."

"You know she wants me to move up there, too."

"She didn't tell me that."

"Well, she does."

"Look," he said gently, "I doctor people, not institutions, so I'm way out of my league here. But I'll throw in my two cents anyway. You're the boss. You can do anything you want, and let the rest of the bunch get used to it. But whatever you decide, it's Cooper the woman who will have to live with it, not Cooper the governor. So listen to your heart."

⌣

She sat quietly, alone, trying to listen, sort things out. She thought about the Big House with its towering columns and sheltering oaks, the stretch of its land, the pond waiting, both peaceful in its stillness and alive with possibility, back beyond the pasture. And the ghosts—Cleve, Jesse, her childhood. Even now, as always, they had a powerful hold on her soul, on who she had become.

She was still, listening, and what she began to hear was so faint she didn't recognize it at first. Then it became clear: the crunch of gravel under tires, Jesse, the car, the ride. She smiled at the memory of it, giving no thought to what came after the ride. Jesse would have been past sixty now, no doubt much changed from the teenager who went off to war, no doubt changed by war itself—middle-aged with a career and family, growing soft around the edges. She liked to think they would have been great good friends. But in some ways, he had always been with her, a calm, thoughtful, benevolent ghost, a good haunting. So it was with Cleve. She pictured him now at the rear of the fishing boat, the easy slap of water against the sides, nature's sounds, a look of intense pleasure as he sat watching the red float bobbing on the surface of Fate Wilmer's pond, turning every so often to look at her, smiling. A gracious ghost—but pain there, too, at the thought of things unfinished for both of them.

Jesse and Cleve were ghosts she had dealt with for a long time. And now, soon, there would be another. She could push that one away, face the music later. But if she wrestled with it now, she might make peace with it, and in doing so help settle affairs with the others. Mickey, she realized, was the key to so much more.

She listened to her heart a moment longer, and then she decided.

She waited until morning. Mickey was still sleeping. Estelle was dozing in a chair, but her eyes popped open when the door opened. "I'll be right outside if you need me," she said.

Cooper reached for Mickey's hand, held it lightly, massaged the fingers, watched the uneven, labored rise and fall of her breath, studied the ravages of time on her face, the shadows of who she had been, what she had seen and done. After a while, she turned to leave, but Mickey whispered, "Don't go."

"I've got some arrangements to make. We're taking a trip."

"When?"

"As soon as I can get the show on the road. A few details to take care of, then we'll be off."

"Limousine service?"

"The best," Cooper said.

"I always did like to ride in style," Mickey whispered.

⌒

Pickett called. "I heard," he said.

"She wants to go home. I'm taking her, for both our sakes."

"I understand. It's the right thing. Not long?"

"No."

"I'm sorry," he said, and she could tell he genuinely meant it. "I owe her a great deal. Is there anything I can do?"

"No." She started to end the call but then remembered. "Pickett, what's going on with Plato?"

Silence. Then: "He resigned."

"Why, for goodness' sake?"

More silence. "I think he can't handle the grind. It's brutal at this level. Plato's had some health problems. He needs to take care of himself."

That might be true, she thought. Heart bypass surgery a few years before, the stress of working for Pickett.

"What are you going to do without him?"

"I have new people. They handle things."

"The new people . . . Anybody to help you keep your head straight?"

"I hope so."

"Me, too."

"Are you okay?"

"Yes," she said, "I'm fine. Doing what needs to be done."

"Call me. Let me know."

"I will."

"One other thing. That real-estate deal. I know you're busy, but—"

"I'm taking care of it," she said.

Mickey had never been close to her grandchildren, had never spent much time with them. That was partly Cooper's doing—another way of keeping Mickey out of her life—but it had something to do with Mickey, too. In the infrequent times she was around Allison and Carter, she was both awkward and intimidating. She had no feel for being a grandmother. No surprise there. And so it had been easy to keep distance. But now, they needed to know.

She tried Allison. Voice mail. She left a message: "Call me. I need to talk to you about Grandmother."

She reached Carter. "Where are you?"

"South Carolina."

"I'm taking Mother to the Big House. She doesn't have much time."

"I'm coming home," he said.

"Carter, honey, there's nothing you can do here."

"I can be with you."

"I'm okay. Stay there, do your job. We'll talk every day."

"Have you talked to Allison?"

"No." She sighed. "I tried, but she won't answer."

"I'll call her."

⌒

She called Wheeler. "We're going," she said.

"Good."

"Where are you?"

She heard the caution in his voice when he said, "Still on that trip we talked about."

"When will you be back?"

"Tonight. But I need a couple more days. Things are coming together."

"Like what?"

He hesitated. "Not over the phone."

"All right. I understand."

"Just take care of Mickey. And yourself."

"That's exactly what I'm doing."

TWENTY-THREE

A motorcade to the upstate: trooper escort front and rear, ambulance for Mickey and Estelle, Ezra driving Cooper's car with Grace and Rick on board, two SUVs with the security detail and their assorted weaponry and gear, media people in cars and TV vans stringing along.

A trooper cruiser was waiting at the edge of the two-lane when the motorcade turned into the driveway. Two troopers got out and took off their broad-brimmed hats.

Long shadows from the brittle late-afternoon sun, bare-limbed oaks lining the driveway. Crunch of gravel. Home.

The ambulance backed up to the front steps, where Fate Wilmer waited.

Cooper climbed the steps and gave him a hug. "This is above and beyond the call," she said.

"Nonsense. This is what friends do. Thanks for bringing Mickey home."

The rear doors of the ambulance swung open, and the attendants

301

rolled the stretcher out, lifted it, started up the steps with Estelle snap-
ping out directions.

Mickey's eyes darted about from the blankets. She spotted Fate
Wilmer. "What the hell are you doing here? Somebody sick?"

"Looking for somebody to swap lies with," he said, taking her hand
and climbing the steps beside the stretcher.

Mickey gave a long sigh. "I've got a few left in me. But let me tell you
this, Fate Wilmer. If you expect me to swap lies without the benefit of
whiskey and cigarettes, you can forget it."

"I will prescribe both," he said, "and personally see to it that they are
administered on a regular basis."

"This is Estelle Dubose," Mickey said with a wave of her hand.
"She's incredibly bossy and has no respect for her elders. Other than
that, she'll do. She is taking tolerable care of me."

"I bow to superior wisdom," Wilmer said, shaking Estelle's hand.

"Then we'll get along just fine," Estelle said.

The house was alive with activity: cleaning crew dusting, vacuum-
ing, mopping, washing away months of neglect, people from the telephone company installing extra lines. Grace took over, transforming the
big living room into an office.

A van pulled up in front and, to Cooper's surprise, disgorged Mrs.
Dinkins and her staff. "I had 'em transferred," Grace said. "They'll be
housed at the prison facility down the road for as long as they're needed
here."

The crew trooped in.

"Mrs. Dinkins is on duty," Mrs. Dinkins said primly. She looked
startled when Cooper hugged her.

They all worked through the shank of the afternoon, settling into
the house while Mickey slept. Mrs. Dinkins served dinner under the
blazing chandelier at the long table in the dining room. Conversation
was desultory. They were all weary.

Fate Wilmer checked again on Mickey, then met Cooper in the

front hallway. "Dr. Cutter has me up to speed. We'll make sure she has everything she needs." He hesitated, then: "Don't look at this as a vigil, Cooper."

"I won't," she said. "It's just where we need to be right now. That's why we came."

◡◠

Mickey was propped in the big bed among a cloud of pillows. Her color was a bit better, her voice measured but serviceable, despite the trip from the capital. She had a softening about her now, Cooper noticed, a sense of waiting.

"Thank you," Mickey said.

Cooper settled into a chair next to the bed. "You're welcome. Can I get you anything? Newspaper, book, magazine, TV?"

Mickey closed her eyes. "I'm through with the howl of the world. I don't want to hear about wars and rumors of wars, weepings and wailings, presidential campaigns, none of it."

"All right." Cooper smiled. "But aren't you going to be bored without all of that?"

"Hell, I've got eternity to be bored. Let me take a little nap, then fetch me a cigarette and about an inch of whiskey in the bottom of a glass, one cube of ice, then leave me to wallow in my vices."

◡◠

Sometime in the early-morning hours, she woke with a start as headlights splashed across the wall next to her bed. Then voices downstairs.

Allison was in the entrance hall, duffel in hand, talking to a state trooper. "They didn't want to let me in," she said.

"Sorry, Governor," the trooper said. "We didn't recognize her at first."

"It's okay," Cooper said, crossing the hall to Allison, taking the duffel from her, setting it down, giving her a hug. "It's all right now. I'll take it from here."

The trooper backed out, and they stood looking at each other.

"I've been worried sick about you," Cooper said. "You don't answer your phone. Is that the case with everybody who tries to call you, or just me?"

"Mother," Allison said, "don't fuss at me at two o'clock in the morning. I'm here. I want to go to bed."

It was near noon before Allison appeared in sweatpants and hoodie—hair disheveled, eyes puffy from sleep. Cooper took her to the kitchen, where Mrs. Dinkins and her crew fussed over her, fixing eggs and French toast. Then they went up to see Mickey. Cooper was astonished to find her up and perched in a chair by the window, dressed in a lime-green pantsuit that hung loosely from her gauntness. Allison stared, shocked by Mickey's withered appearance, then gave her a mute hug.

"What a lovely surprise," Mickey said softly. "I'm glad you're here."

"Me, too," Allison said, her voice breaking.

"Now, sit down, the two of you. I've got something to say. Allison, I don't want you and your mother to make the mistake she and I did." Mickey waited.

Allison shifted uncomfortably and finally asked, "What mistake?"

"Wasting a lifetime being at odds." She fixed Cooper with a stare. "We both did that, didn't we." It was a statement, not a question.

"Yes," Cooper said. "We both did."

Mickey turned again to Allison. "I suspect the hardest relationship in the world is mother-daughter. I know it was in my case. My mother was a mousy little thing who let people—especially my father—run all over her. I hated that, and there were times I hated *her* because of it. I never made an honest effort to understand why she was that way, and by the time I began to suspect I should, it was too late."

After a long silence, Mickey spoke again. "Your mother and I are trying to correct our mistake. Someday, if she wants, she can talk to you about what's gone on between us over the years. But I hope what's important—to you and her—is what's going on between us now. And even more important is what goes on between the two of you. Don't—either of you—waste your lives being pissed off. Whatever hurts or disappointments or resentments you're carrying, let 'em go."

Late in the afternoon, the light beginning to fade, she and Allison went for a walk—across the broad pasture behind the house, over the knoll, and down to the pond and Cleve's grave. They stood beside it, looking out over the water, gray beneath the overcast, surface rippled by a brisk wind. The temperature had dropped as the day waned. They were bundled in parkas, boots, thick gloves, and toboggans. Scatterings of snow were still under the thickest trees, but the snowstorm seemed light years past. So much had happened, so much loomed.

There was a small bench a few feet from the grave marker. Cooper sat, pulling the parka close around her.

"I wish you had known him," she said. "He was as good a man as you'd ever find."

"We've never talked much about him."

"He was away a great deal, working. When he was here, we went fishing. I wish we had more of those times. But he did the best he could, I think. He tried to protect me from politics, from people prying, taking advantage."

"It's a fishbowl," Allison said.

"If you let them, people will make you think you don't belong to yourself. People who pull and tug, people who want things, need things, have their hands out and their arms around your shoulders."

Allison stamped her feet and moved a few steps from the water's edge. She knelt, picked up a pebble, tossed it with a *plunk* into the pond.

"Daddy used to say he'd rather be a farmer," Cooper said. "After his second term, he came back here, said he wanted to build his fishpond, ride his tractor, drink whiskey with Dr. Wilmer. But then he decided to run for the Senate."

"Why?"

"I blamed Mother. She was the power behind the throne, everyone said. But it wasn't true. It was Daddy's decision, and he let me know that."

"But he didn't run after all."

"He did, but he died before the election. And just before he died, he said to me, 'We are the sum of our regrets.' And I thought, *How incredibly sad.*"

Allison moved to the bench and sat. Cooper shifted to make room.

"How do you keep from ending like that?" Allison asked.

"Make sure there are things that outweigh your regrets."

They were quiet for a while, snuggling against each other for warmth.

Allison said, "I've been thinking about what Grandmother said, about us being pissed off."

Cooper smiled. "She does have an earthy way of putting things."

"I'm not pissed off. I'm just . . . disappointed. Scared, too. I've thought about how we've lived, the fishbowl. I think you were trying to protect me like your daddy did for you." Allison laughed. "I remember how you went ballistic when that woman broke Ginger."

It had happened not long after Pickett's first term began. A busload of legislative wives touring the mansion. She spotted a woman heading back to the bus holding Ginger, her ancient porcelain-headed doll, passed along to Allison, obviously snatched from Allison's upstairs bedroom. Cooper yelled, the woman dropped Ginger, her head broke.

Allison was inconsolable. Cooper, despite Pickett's howls of protest, banned tourists from any but the most public downstairs rooms, and allowed them there only one day a week. She mended Ginger as best she could, but the incident left something irreparable in Allison.

Cooper said, "I'm afraid I didn't do a good-enough job."

"What else could you have done?"

"Put my foot down more. Said, 'No, we won't live like this, in a fishbowl.'"

"But Dad . . ."

"I always went along. Too much, too often."

Allison pulled away from her. "Until now."

Cooper gave her a close look.

"Carter said Dad never meant for you to really do the job."

"Honey, it's not anything you should concern yourself—"

"Don't patronize me, Mother."

"I'm not. I'm just trying to sort through things with Dad, with you and me."

"What he did was dishonest."

"And what about what I did, telling you that when Dad's term was up, it would all be over, and we'd be normal for a change? At the time, I meant it."

"But things changed," Allison said.

"Do you think I went back on my word?"

"Yes. And I resent the hell out of that. But I've had time to think about it, and Carter's helped. When we were growing up, you got us through it in different ways. Carter loves the fishbowl. I don't. But now, we're both grown, and we have to deal with ourselves and everything else the way it is, and let you be you. Like you and Grandmother are doing."

"We've worked on it. We've reached out, both of us. We've been honest."

"And you and I, *we* have to be honest," Allison said.

"Yes."

"Carter and I agree on something else."

"What's that?"

"Don't give up, Mom. Don't you dare give up."

Cooper pulled her close, and they sat there as the day waned.

She felt her jaw tighten. "I will not. I can guarantee that."

It was late when she trudged upstairs to bed, saw the sliver of light beneath the door to Mickey's room, heard Allison's voice.

Mickey was burrowed deep in the bed, sheet and blanket pulled up to her chin, eyes closed. Allison sat on one side, Estelle on the other. Allison was reading aloud. She stopped, looked up.

"What?" Cooper asked.

Mickey opened her eyes. "Devotionals," she said.

"You're kidding."

"Don't you think it's about time?" She pointed at the ceiling. "When I get up there, I at least want to be able to talk the lingo."

Just before she turned out the light, Wheeler called. "I've got it."

"Tell me."

"I'll be there by midmorning."

"Where are you?"

"I'm there. Well, nearby. Me and another fellow. We've found some . . . stuff."

"How far is it from me?"

"About sixty miles, close to the place that school bus went off the road in the storm."

"I'm coming."

"Don't do that," he said firmly. "It's too risky. There's still a lot of snow, and it's rugged country."

"Whatever you've found, I want to see for myself. Tell Ezra where to go."

Long silence on the other end.

"Call it my old journalistic instincts, Wheeler. You should understand that better than anybody."

"I might call it bullheadedness."

"Maybe. I got some of that from journalism, too, but mostly from my mother."

~

She sneaked away well before dawn, crouching on the floorboard of Ezra's car.

They stayed on two-lane roads, passing in the darkness through small towns where nothing moved in the frigid quiet. Traffic was almost nonexistent. The faintest hint of first light arrived as they climbed out of the foothills and into the low mountains. Ezra drove slowly, carefully. The road twisted and curved back on itself. Icy patches were still on the pavement and a lingering crust of snow on the roadsides.

They had been under way for more than an hour when Ezra slowed, eyes peeled, then came to a stop. "This looks like it," he said. He reached for a battery-powered searchlight and shone it through the window. She saw what had once been a small house set back from the road, crumbling in on itself, only the narrow chimney still erect. A narrow, rutted road, barely visible as a depression in the thin snow blanket, snaked alongside the house and disappeared behind it.

"What now?" she asked.

"We wait." He eased the car to a stop behind the ruins. "They'll come get us," he said, glancing at his watch. "It won't be long."

They sat for several minutes, early light beginning to make pale grays of the landscape. She could make out the dim lines of trees a little way behind the house, and the rutted road disappearing into the woods. Deep vehicle tracks were on the road.

"What did Wheeler tell you about this?" she asked.

"Just what I needed to know to get you here," he said. "And that if I come to know more, it stays with me."

She reached across the seat and put a hand on his arm. "Ezra, I am profoundly grateful for you."

Ezra's cheeks reddened. He touched her hand. "Thank you," he said quietly. Then he turned in the seat and looked out the back window. "Here they come."

Headlights illuminated the car. She heard a throbbing diesel rumble that grew to a powerful growl as she turned to see the lights—high off the ground—swing in behind them. The car vibrated from the noise. They climbed out and stood ankle-deep in the snow, blinded by the blaze of light. Doors slammed, figures moved toward them, and then Wheeler emerged from the glare, followed by two other men—one bearded, young, the other much older, tall and stooped.

"Morning, Governor," Wheeler said. "I'm gonna try one more time. Would you please get back in the car and go home?"

"Hell no. What's going on here?"

He made a face, then shrugged and took a firm grip on her arm. "All right. Come on."

The truck was a monster, riding high off the ground on huge tires. Ezra and Wheeler helped her climb into the warm cab, and then the rest of them clambered in, the younger of the two men behind the wheel, Wheeler beside him, the others in the back.

Wheeler indicated a man in the back with Ezra. "That's Dr. Eskar Coble, geology professor at the university."

Cooper shook his gloved hand.

"Governor, pleased to meet you," he said. "I knew your father."

"And our driver," Wheeler said. "You've met him before. Carl Bumgarner."

The younger man turned from the wheel and took her hand, grinning through his thick beard.

"Where have we met, Mr. Bumgarner?"

"On the phone," he said. "During the snow."

Then it dawned on her. "Carl? The school bus, your wife."

"Yes, ma'am."

"How is . . . Stacy, isn't it? And the kids."

"Everybody's fine." He cleared his throat. "You saved their lives."

"Not me," she said. "In fact, I played the tiniest role of all."

"Well, you sure helped me get through it."

Wheeler said, "I tracked Carl down and asked him to help us. He put us up for the night and has been chauffeuring us."

"Where are we going?"

"Up."

Carl started along the road. The light was stronger, and she saw that the road was little more than twin ruts—trees close, branches scraping the roof and sides. The truck plowed on, lurching from side to side, the grinding of the engine in low gear deafening.

They crested a rise and started down, boring into the trees, the road becoming even rougher. Several more minutes of wild bouncing, tossing her about, straining her lap belt. And then the truck burst through the trees and into a clearing, rumbled another several yards, and stopped.

Cooper took a moment to catch her breath. "Wheeler, what are we doing?"

"The question is, what is *that* doing?" He pointed.

At the far end of the clearing, she saw a truck much larger than this one, massive and muscular, a huge piece of machinery on its long bed behind the cab.

"This is as far as we can go in the truck," Carl said. "The ground's soft from the snow melt, and we don't want to get stuck up here like that thing did."

They climbed down from the cab and stood for a moment. Underneath the thin crust of snow, the ground felt spongy. They were in a gap, the low mountain they had crossed behind them, another in front. They were still quite high, and through the gaunt-limbed trees at the edge of the clearing, she could see a long way over a landscape of more mountains and valleys. The wind was biting. In the minute it took them to cross the clearing on foot, she felt the grip of the cold.

The truck was mired to its axles, the ground around the wheels gouged and tossed from the attempt to free it.

"What is it?" she asked.

"An exploration rig," Dr. Coble said. "It takes core samples."

"Of what?"

"Rock. To find out what's underneath."

"Minerals?"

"This area isn't known for mineral deposits—not in significant amounts, anyway. The more likely guess would be natural gas."

"How accurately can you tell what's down there?"

"Well," Coble said, "core samples aren't the only evidence. I'm sure there's been other equipment here, taking seismic readings. You know from the cores what kind of rock you're dealing with, and then the seismic data tells you about the strata, and you put it all together."

"But if there's gas, didn't you already know that?"

"There's gas in lots of places," he said. "Deep pockets of it, mostly unrecoverable, at least until recently."

Wheeler said, "Let's get back to the truck."

It took a couple of minutes for her to warm up enough that her numb face and lips could shape words. "How long has that rig been here?" she finally managed.

"No way of knowing," Coble said. "My guess is, some work was done as winter set in. Then this rig came back to take more samples, the snowstorm hit, and whoever it belongs to got stuck when they tried to get it out."

"Carl," she asked, "if equipment has been in and out, wouldn't somebody have noticed?"

"Probably not," he said. "This area is really rough. Just a few houses scattered around the lower valleys. That's where Stacy and me live. Nothing up here but rock. And people here don't mind other folks' business."

"It's state-owned land, and posted," Wheeler added. "Nobody comes up here much."

"Some hikers now and then," Carl said, "but not in the winter."

She turned to Coble. "What about recovering gas?"

"What's down below is shale, and shale can hold huge deposits. To get at it, there's the new technique. Hydraulic fracturing."

"Fracking," Cooper said.

"You drill down into the shale and then pump in several million gallons of water and chemicals under high pressure. It fractures the rock and releases the gas. It creates environmental concerns—contaminated water supplies, gas being released into the air, even earthquakes. In states where it's being done—like Pennsylvania and New York—there's a lot of debate. Some places have imposed moratoriums or even banned it outright. We're still working out the pros and cons."

"How much gas is here?" Cooper asked.

"We don't know," Wheeler said. "But I'll bet the people who own that rig do."

"It could be sizable," Coble said.

"And if it is," Wheeler added, "whoever owns the land and mineral rights gets rich."

She was hardly aware of the ride back down, her mind spinning. *Pickett.*

Then they were at the bottom, and she was saying goodbye to Carl and Coble. Ezra started the car and let it warm up. She and Wheeler stood for a moment away from the others.

"What else do you know about this?" she asked.

"Everything I need to. I'll get Dr. Coble back to the university, and then I'll be at your place by evening." He paused. "This is ugly."

They were at the Big House by midmorning. She checked on Mickey, found her still asleep.

She and Allison, bundled in sweaters, took coffee to the Adirondack chairs in the backyard. A warming trend was muscling aside what was left of the bitterest cold. A brave sun filtered through the bare limbs of the pecan trees.

They sat quietly, Cooper absorbed with what she had seen, trying to piece together the parts of the little she knew.

"You're preoccupied," Allison said. "What with?"

"I don't know yet. Hopefully before long. Sorry."

Allison had slept late. She looked rested, the pinched look gone from her face.

"Do you need to go back?" Cooper asked.

"It's okay," Allison said. "They know the situation at school. I brought some classwork with me. I can work on my laptop and email it. So I'll stay awhile, if it's all right."

"Of course it's all right." She took Allison's hand.

"Have you talked to Dad?"

"Not for a couple of days. Have you?"

"I don't want to right now. But I have talked to Grandmother." Allison smiled. "She wants to go fishing."

Lawn chairs on a dock at the edge of Fate Wilmer's pond. Mickey had wanted to go out in a boat, but Cooper put her foot down on that. Mickey looked like a mummy, swathed in blankets, wrapped so firmly and packed so tightly into the chair that she had little room for movement. Her scrunched-up face peered out, and her mittened hands held the cane pole, which Cooper had baited with a cricket, along with her own.

It had turned into a stunningly beautiful day, the temperature in the low sixties, the air calm, the surface of the water lightly rippled. Where the shallow creek emptied into the pond, a heron fished stilt-legged, ignoring them. The quiet was broken only by the sounds of birds and squirrels.

Fate Wilmer's pond, Mickey had insisted, not the one beyond the pasture behind the house, the one where Cleve's bones rested.

"Did you and Daddy fish here?" Cooper asked.

"This was your place, yours and his. I was never much for fishing. He took me out on a big boat in the Gulf one time. I thought I was going to die."

The plastic corks bobbed listlessly.

"Can you catch fish in January?" Mickey asked.

"I've never tried before."

"You think I'm nuts."

"Uh-huh."

She heard the distant crackle of a radio. The entourage—ambulance, security detail, Fate's car with Estelle and Allison—was a hundred yards away, down the gravel road that led from Fate's house to the pond's edge.

They sat quietly, letting the afternoon settle around them, watching the floats.

"I grieved for him, too," Mickey said. Her voice seemed firm, determined, insistent.

Cooper knew instantly what she meant. She waited.

"Of all my regrets, and there are many, Jesse is the greatest. All that followed—for Cleve, for me, for you and me—grew out of that one unspeakable, unforgiveable decision."

Cooper didn't say anything for a long while. And then she said, "Mother, few things in this world are truly unforgiveable. But yes, for me, for a long time now, it has been unspeakable." She swallowed hard, trying to keep her voice under control. "I loved Jesse. I have missed him all my life."

"I know you have."

"How do you know?"

"Because I can see it in you, and in the way you and I haven't been able to . . ."

"Forgive."

"Yes. For that and all that came after."

Cooper shifted in her chair, turning toward Mickey. "It may be that's all we really have, the right to forgive."

"The right?"

"It's a choice, isn't it?"

"Yes." Another long silence. And then: "I never knew how to ask. Pride, stubbornness, meanness. And you?"

"Anger, hurt, loss. People taken away from me—Jesse, Daddy, Pickett. And you. You took yourself away."

"I didn't know how to be what you needed. When I tried, I got it wrong. So I stopped trying. We have caused each other great harm. Mostly my doing."

"But not all."

"No, not all."

"But here at the end, we haven't left it unspoken. We've been honest about the damage. Beyond that"—Cooper took a deep breath—"we can forgive."

Mickey hadn't looked at her until now. "I love you, Cooper. I'm incredibly proud of you, not for what you've won, but for the woman you've become."

"I love you, too," Cooper said, and marveled at how it sounded, how right, after all this time.

Cooper took the cane pole from Mickey, laid it and her own on the weathered boards of the dock between their chairs. Then she took Mickey's hand in her own.

"Now," she said, "I have something I need to share with you."

She told the story of the land deal, her trip, what she had seen and learned. She took her time, spinning it out. Mickey listened, and the silence hung for a time in the afternoon air after Cooper finished.

Finally, Cooper said, "Well?"

"Who else besides Pickett?"

"I don't know. I think Wheeler does."

"Sweet Jesus," Mickey said with a thin smile and a touch of awe in her voice. "That's about the juiciest thing I've ever heard."

"Any advice?"

Mickey grimaced. "Whatever you do, don't let the bastards get away with it."

As the ambulance took them back to the house, Mickey lapsed into a sleep from which she could not be roused. Paramedics took her upstairs, and Estelle put her to bed.

Fate spent a few minutes in the room, then sat with Cooper and Allison. "We're getting near the end," he said. "Things are shutting down. How long, I don't know. She's in something resembling a coma, and I imagine she'll remain there. I can stay if you like."

"No," Cooper said. "We'll keep watch. Can you have those machines taken out of there?"

"Of course."

They stayed through the afternoon. Once, Mickey's shallow breathing became ragged, and she muttered something they couldn't understand. But then she subsided again into profound sleep.

Early evening. They took turns at dinner, Allison first. Then Cooper went downstairs and sat alone in the dining room. Mrs. Dinkins came with a plate of food, set it in front of her, hesitated, then pulled out a chair and sat next to her. "Mrs. Dinkins just wants you to know a lot of people have you in our hearts right now."

Tears sprang to her eyes. She tried to speak but couldn't.

Mrs. Dinkins patted her shoulder. "I know."

Wheeler came after seven. He had bags under his eyes, the skin of his face sagged, and he was wobbly. He toted a battered briefcase. He opened it and took out the land-swap document, smudged and dog-eared from much handling. He flipped it open to an inner page and handed it to her. "See here." He pointed. "The corporation listed as the owner of the coastal property that's being traded."

"Lucretia," she read.

"Do you know who Lucretia is?"

She shook her head.

"Lucretia Harbin. Jake Harbin's grandmother."

Jake. Of course, it had to be Jake.

"Lucretia was the source of Jake's money, at least at the beginning. He took what she left him and built it into what he has now, which is a great deal."

"I know."

"Much of what makes up Jake's empire is a hall of mirrors—corporate entities, mingled trusts, so forth. Most of them, if you looked at the names, you'd never know they were connected to him. But one has the original name: the Lucretia Corporation. It hasn't been involved in any kind of business dealings for years. Until now." He reached into the briefcase for another document. "You can look through this later. It's an old report from the Secretary of State's Office on the assets of the Lucretia Corporation. There's just one—a certain piece of property on the coast, just sitting there all these years since the old lady passed away."

"Prime land?"

"A gold mine, and that's what Jake, in his generosity, is proposing to give to the state for development into a park."

She went back to the land-swap document. "In return for . . ."

"What at first glance seems like a worthless piece of upstate rock. Except it's not."

She sat there with the document in her hands, Mickey's voice echoing in her head: "Always, always, follow the money."

She focused on the paper again. Something didn't make sense, and then she saw it. The coastal land, property of the Lucretia Corporation, was being deeded to the state, but the mountain land was going to a different entity. She pointed to the name.

"PWP Incorporated," Wheeler said, nodding. "Prince William Partners. Incorporated in Prince William County, Virginia."

"I don't get it."

"You're not supposed to. That's the point. And that's why I went to Virginia. The principal is a man named Sol Vincente. A land developer. Small potatoes—strip shopping centers, a couple of mid-priced residential subdivisions. Nothing in his résumé to indicate he has the moxie or money to turn that pile of rock into a resort development."

"So, where is this going?"

"The Secretary of State's Office in Virginia has just received a document reincorporating PWP. Sol Vincente becomes a minority stockholder, nothing more than a frontman. The majority of stock is now held by"—he paused for effect—"the Lucretia Corporation."

Her mind whirled, trying to keep it straight.

"A hall of mirrors," he went on. "So we know who stands to gain. But there's a good deal more, and for that, I have a source."

"Who?"

"I can't say. I promised. But he filled in the blanks, stuff it would have taken me a long time to find on my own. Here's what happens. After you sign off on the deal and it gets through the legislature, PWP will take on three minor, silent partners: Woodrow Bannister, Figgy Watson, and Colonel—now former colonel—Floyd Doster. Anybody with even a tiny stake stands to make a great deal of money."

It came together in a rush. Between Figgy and Woodrow, they could guarantee passage of just about any piece of legislation. They'd stick the deal somewhere inside a budget bill that nobody would bother to read in detail. So neat. "You and Pickett, you owe me," Woodrow had said. Now, she knew just how much he meant. And Doster? Money would shut him up. But the biggest winner of all was Jake Harbin. Jake and Pickett, joined at the hip in so many things. Pickett flying around the country in Jake's plane, financing his campaign with money Jake was raising. Jake calling in the IOU.

"Your source, whoever he is . . ."

"Somebody I've known for a long time. I believe him. It all fits. He's given me an affidavit, signed and notarized. It's in a safe place, not to be used unless it's absolutely necessary." He pulled a manila envelope from the briefcase. "I've written everything down. This is the story."

She opened the envelope, took out the pages, glanced over them, then shook her head. "Nobody could have done this but you."

"Probably not."

"Something like this could win you a Pulitzer Prize."

"But I'm not at the paper, and I'm not gonna be. So the question is what to do with it."

"People could go to jail," she said.

"I'm not a lawyer, but I suspect no laws have been broken. Not yet. And you're going to stop that from happening. No harm, no foul. But if for some reason word does get out, the people who cooked this up will be in a world of hurt. Investigations, grand juries. And then maybe people *would* go to jail."

"Don't I have an obligation to expose it?"

"That's one way of looking at it."

"And what's another?"

"Possibly the greater good. If these people know you know, that's like having a nuclear weapon in your arsenal. Pickett, Woodrow, Figgy—none of them can afford a scandal."

"My God," she said softly. "I've got to have time to think."

"The clock is ticking. This is too big. People are going to start applying pressure in ways you might never imagine. You'll have to decide, one way or the other."

When they were done, she took him upstairs to Mickey and left them alone.

As he came back down, his eyes were red and puffy, but he seemed at peace with himself. "Thank you," he said.

She put a hand on his arm. "You were good friends. I'm so glad."

She walked with him to his car.

"You know," she said as he climbed in and reached for the door, "in there awhile ago when you talked about options, you sounded very un-Wheeler. Like a politician."

"Yeah," he said. "Who'd have thought?"

Carter arrived shortly after Wheeler left, surprising her. He looked thin and drawn, and an unmistakable sense of disappointment covered him like a cloak.

"I had to leave," he said. His voice broke. "Dad . . . I love him, but I don't know him anymore."

She took him in her arms. "I'm so sorry."

They waited at Mickey's bedside—Cooper, Allison and Carter, Fate and Estelle. Mickey seemed at ease, gaunt lines and angles of her face smooth now. She seemed almost young.

At mid-evening, Mickey's eyes suddenly opened. They were wide, staring upward. Cooper reached and took her mother's hand in both of hers.

"Did we catch any?" Mickey said clearly.

"Yes," Cooper said, "we sure did."

Then Mickey closed her eyes, gave a long sigh, and slipped away.

TWENTY-FOUR

Pickett flew home early on the day of Mickey's funeral. He was big news—poll numbers climbing, more media attention and political buzz. Money was coming in, new staff—clever, hard-nosed people, veterans of presidential wars.

The local stations televised his arrival. Cooper watched from the Executive Mansion. He said nice things about Mickey. He was full of himself—handsome, assured, riding the wave.

His entourage arrived at the house before he did. There were a lot of them now. They took over the downstairs. The few old hands still left spoke to her, but the rest seemed urgently busy with their papers and cell phones.

Cooper was in her small upstairs office when Pickett came. He kissed her, held her for a moment. He sat, but barely, staying on the edge of the chair, looking as if he might lift off at any moment.

"I'm glad you took time to come," she said.

"It was the only thing to do. We canceled some stuff, nothing we can't pick up later. Tallahassee tonight." He waved an arm. "I hope you don't mind that bunch downstairs. Wherever they go, they just take over like they own the place."

"Have they taken you over?" she asked.

He shrugged. "I guess they have. Things are running smoother. We have a message and stay on it."

"Sounds like you're being programmed."

He gave her a wry smile. "Sometimes, it feels that way. But if I don't stay focused, I just thrash around in the underbrush."

"Plato never tried to program you."

He showed a flash of pain. "I hate that happened."

She met his eyes, unblinking. "Did he really resign like you said, or did you run him off because he's gay?"

"I didn't run anybody off," he said, voice rising. "We had an understanding."

"You look fit," she said after a moment, and he did—color high, eyes quick and lively.

"I get a little exercise when I can—yoga, nothing too strenuous. Short naps."

"And adrenaline."

"Oh, yeah."

"Congratulations on the new poll."

"I could feel it in the past few days," he said. "Gotta keep the momentum. Long way to go."

It sounded like something he'd say at a news conference. Part of the programming.

His cell phone warbled. He pulled it out of a coat pocket, glanced at the display, answered. "I'm on my way. Keep 'em happy until I get there." He put it back in his pocket. "I've got a quick thing this morning. Some local people, money. God, it's always about raising money. I spend three-fourths of my time begging, kissing ass, massaging egos. I'll be back before it's time to go to the Capitol."

Mickey's body would lie in state from ten until noon in the same spot where she and Cooper had held watch over Cleve years before. The prominent and notorious would file by and murmur a few words. Mickey had known them all, had especially relished the notorious. Then a procession to First Presbyterian for the service. Tomorrow, they would take her back upstate to the place by the pond. But before that, the afternoon she'd wanted—good band, open bar.

Pickett stood and bent to kiss her again, but she turned away, opened a desk drawer, and drew out the manila envelope.

"You need to look at this."

He gave the envelope a quick glance. "Later."

"Now," she said, and her voice stopped him. He gave her an odd look. "Before you take another step, you need to know what's in here. About that land deal you're so interested in."

The color drained from his face. He took the envelope, sat back down, opened it.

Wheeler had been concise, the details boiled down into two remorseless, single-spaced pages. She waited while he read, scanning it quickly, then going through it again slowly, a flush spreading around his collar. His eyes never left the pages until he finished. When he finally looked up, it was not at her, but at some place on the wall behind her.

"That sonofabitch," he said.

"Which one?"

"Wheeler Kincaid. This is his doing, isn't it?"

"No, it's mine."

And then he looked at her. "Why?"

"Why did I start asking questions, or why did I care?"

"Both."

"Because," she said, "it's rotten and it's wrong. And I won't let it happen."

He took a long breath. "You have to. I owe Jake Harbin. I owe him big-time. You have no idea."

"Jake's your problem, Pickett, and you'll have to deal with him. And then the others. There are seven copies of that report. Jake, Woodrow, Figgy, and Doster are getting theirs about now. Plus yours and mine, and another one locked away."

"What are you going to do with it?"

"That depends. If I see the need, I can give it to Felicia Withers."

"God, you wouldn't."

She didn't have to say a word.

He took a long time reading through Wheeler's report again. Then he folded the pages and slipped them into an inside pocket of his jacket.

"All right," he said. "If you're gonna hold it over everybody's head, then nobody can afford to raise a stink, including you, because if you sit on it now and then let it out later, it looks like a cover-up."

He's not feeling, he's calculating. The political ones and zeroes. When she saw that, she realized how desperately she had been clinging to one last hope there might still be a strand of something left. But there wasn't. And now that she finally saw, she felt nothing but hollowness where the biggest part of her heart had been.

"I'm willing to take the risk. You and the others aren't."

After that, neither of them spoke for a long while. Neither glanced at the other. He walked to the window and stood there, hands clasped behind his back, looking out. When he finally turned back to her, his face was a mask of pain.

"Cooper, I'm sorry."

She looked closely at him, saw the nakedness, the sadness, the guile stripped away. For the first time in a great, long while, he was genuine.

"I'm truly sorry. For everything."

"I'm sorry, too. I'm sorry for the part that's my fault. I didn't fight when I should have. I never said, 'We're in trouble here. We're losing each other.' I just went along. I grieve over it, Pickett, and that regret will follow me as long as I live."

"I love you," he said. "It may sound preposterous, but I do."

"I believe you, but you love yourself more. And there's not room for both of us."

"Can't we—"

"I don't see how."

His shoulders slumped in resignation. A moment, then: "Will you keep up appearances?"

"Yes."

He turned to go. "The land thing, I can get through it."

"You'll find a way, like you always do."

"I'm going to be president, Cooper. I'm paying a helluva price for it, but I'm going to win."

"Maybe so. God help the country."

People said Cooper did it backwards—the wake after the funeral. But she thought it made sense, getting the ritual niceties out of the way—the lying in state, the procession to the church. Pickett smiled and hand-shook his way through the preliminaries, then sat with her at the service. The others with her on the front row were the people she cared the most about now, the ones who filled her empty spaces—Carter, Allison, Wheeler, Estelle, Nolan, Ezra, Grace. On the row behind were Fate Wilmer and the other pallbearers—people from home, old friends of Cleve and Mickey's, not a politician among them.

Cooper took the pulpit, gazing out across Mickey Spainhour's history.

"I have wondered in the past if my mother kept a little black book in which she wrote down all her political secrets. If she did, she took it with her," she said to a ripple of nervous laughter. "What she did leave was a legacy. In the days since her passing, I have heard from many of you about her impact on our state. I've heard so many say how quietly generous she was to young people who came to her for advice about starting careers in politics and public service." She looked straight at Woodrow, seated stone-faced with Figgy and a crowd of other elected officials. "Some of you benefited greatly from her advice, her knowledge, her wisdom. But the two people who benefited most were my father and me. She was proud of the way he served, and in the special time we had together at the end of her days, she shared those principles of public service with me: vigor, compassion, integrity, a sense that the people—not those of us elected to represent them, or those who try to buy us off—own state government. I will try to live up to those principles. I will have Cleve and Mickey Spainhour looking over my shoulder, and I owe it to them to try and make them proud."

Then, while the hearse took Mickey's body to the funeral home to await the trip home the next morning, nearly everybody trooped to the State Fairgrounds, where a bluegrass band made the air of the Agricultural Exhibit Hall dance with their fiddle and guitars and banjo. *Four* open bars. By then, Pickett had jetted off to Florida. Woodrow and Figgy disappeared. Doster never showed his face.

Cooper kept the security detail outside and told the press people to go home. She wanted to mingle freely with the powerful, once-powerful, wishful, and nostalgic, all of whom came to drink and trade stories about the woman who, in their telling, became even more mythic. Mickey would have loved it.

She kept Carter and Allison close at her side, enjoyed their enthrallment as people talked about Mickey. They had no idea, they kept saying. And she thought more than once, *I wish they had truly known her.*

She was visiting with Nolan when Wheeler appeared at her elbow.

"Can you take a break? Somebody needs a word with you."

He led her to an office in a far corner of the building, opened the door for her, then went away.

Plato looked wretched, the skin of his unshaven face sagging, a haunted, defeated look in his eyes.

"There's something you need to know," he said. "I'm Wheeler's source."

She took an instant to collect herself. "I had no idea."

"Call it part spite, part grief. Pickett got rid of me because of what I am."

"Surely, he knew that."

"Of course he did. But now, all of a sudden, it matters. He starts looking legitimate. The big boys show up. They've been down the road before. They tell Pickett he can't afford to have somebody so close to him with my kind of baggage. Maybe some sordid little relationship all these years? Somebody plants a rumor, and it goes viral. It could destroy him. So I'm a liability. That's the word he used. Me, the one he always called indispensable, a liability." Eyes watering, he turned away.

"That was a terrible thing to do," she said.

"You should know, I put together the land deal for Jake and the others. And the understanding with Woodrow. That and all the times before—all the messy details, the dirty work—I was always the guy."

"How did you know Wheeler was digging into the land deal?"

"The guy in Virginia, Vincente, he called me. The Secretary of State's Office told him somebody was snooping around. He had a description. Wheeler Kincaid." He stared at the floor. "Cooper, I'm a sonofabitch, and I pretended I wasn't, because that's what it took. But now, I don't have the luxury of pretense. I thought back over the years, all the things I did for him. Pickett used me, and I gladly let him." His voice went soft. "I loved Pickett. I gave up myself for him because I loved him. But the price of loving him made me rotten, and when I finally saw that, it made me sick of myself. When he told me I had to go, he offered to cut me in on the land deal, but I couldn't do it. Then, when I figured out Kincaid was on to it, I called him."

"He said you gave him an affidavit."

"Yes. If you ever have to use it . . ."

"Probably not. I don't think I will," she said. "What are you going to do now?"

"Be quiet, be as invisible as possible, somewhere else. Wheeler knows how to contact me. And if anything should happen to me . . ."

"Are you in danger?"

"I've got somewhere to go, out of state. With a friend."

She understood how it must have been for him all these years. *A friend out of state.* Maybe that helped, but it wasn't nearly enough.

He seemed very small now, and much older. A castoff. She started to say she was sorry for what was happening to him, but there was too much history, too much of taking Pickett away from her and helping him become something she no longer recognized.

Instead, she said, "Thank you for helping Wheeler."

"Good luck," Plato said.

"I imagine I'll need it."

"Even with the hand you're holding, it won't be easy."

"I understand that. I don't fool myself, not anymore."

He nodded, and was gone.

⁓

Toward the shank of the day, as the crowd was thinning, Carter pulled her aside. "I talked to the Registrar's Office. Classes have started, but they'll let me in, and I can work hard and catch up. They've got my schedule worked out."

"I'm sorry for you. About what's happened."

He shrugged. "It's not what I thought it was. It'll break your heart."

"It doesn't have to be that way. Give it some time."

Allison's car was packed and waiting at the Executive Mansion. She would head back to Atlanta in the evening. Cooper understood they had a lot of baggage and hoped they would find a way to deal with it together, but there were no guarantees.

She thought about the journey she and Carter and Allison were facing, the wrenching changes, their need to cherish each other, to survive by clinging to each other for dear life. She had a long, difficult road ahead of her in the capital, but that was a job, not a reason for being. They were.

Finally, it was over, and they went out into the waning day. Clouds had moved in—thickening, lowering. The temperature had dropped. The air bit their cheeks. It was January, after all. *She got her wish. She didn't die in February.*

Ezra was waiting by the car. Carter and Allison climbed in, but Cooper stood for a moment outside, looking toward the dome of the Capitol in the distance. And then she thought of the house in the up-state, the quiet pond beyond the pasture. She had told Fate Wilmer she planned to keep it. It would be the place where she might, when she needed it most, rest her soul. It would be home.

She smiled at Ezra and ducked into the backseat.

"It may snow again," Carter said.

"It may," Cooper said. "I can handle that."